Reality Bites

Reality Bites

A Novel

Amy Mass

HARPER PERENNIAL

NEW YORK • LONDON • TORONTO • SYDNEY • NEW DELHI • AUCKLAND

HARPER ● PERENNIAL

hc.com

FIRST EDITION

Designed by Jamie Lynn Kerner

Library of Congress Cataloging-in-Publication Data has been applied for.

ISBN 978-0-06-347565-6 (pbk.)

Printed in the United States of America.

26 27 28 29 30 LBC 5 4 3 2 1

To all my LA friends—thanks for keeping it real

Chapter One

I s it too conceited to say we're the greatest scientific minds of the twenty-first century?" Alec asks as he sifts through our findings spread out on the conference room table.

Cassie rolls her eyes. "I think Jane Goodall or Stephen Hawking would've had something to say about that."

Alex scoffs but Eliza, who is supposed to be logging DNA samples, chimes in: "You couldn't have even beaten them in a fistfight."

Cassie immediately sides with Eliza. "Oh yeah. Peak Jane Goodall, living in the jungle, fighting off chimp attacks—she would've destroyed you." She turns to me. "Grace, who would you put money on?"

Even though I'd definitely bet on Jane, it's my job to keep them on task. Which usually involves bribes. "If I bring you guys that fancy coffee from Caffe Luxxe tomorrow, will you stop trying to hypothetically fight my departed heroes?"

This shuts them up and they get back to work. I look around our lab and smile, because Alec has every right to feel cocky. We just made a major scientific breakthrough that will save thousands of lives.

Of frogs.

When people picture a nature center, they're usually thinking of a cross between a zoo and a natural history museum. And sure, half of the Southern California Wildlife Center has interactive stations with pelts you can touch and rehabilitation enclosures with injured animals. But the other half, the part that's closed to the public, is where my amphibian lab is located and where the real conservation work is done.

And we just figured out a way to save a species of frog that was on its way to extinction. So we're feeling pretty damn good about ourselves.

As the lab director and lead biologist, I handpicked my dream team. Cassie, my closest friend since grad school, is my bleeding-heart veterinarian. Eliza's a biologist like me, but she's also an unstoppable machine who does it all—research, grant writing, and fieldwork. She famously left her sister's wedding to save a hundred tadpoles from a forest fire and made it back in time for cake. And then there's Alec, our ecologist. Although I'd never admit it to him, his job is probably the hardest because of all the environmental factors he has to contend with: contaminated lakes and streams, wildfires, non-native fish species that eat too many endangered frogs, and his greatest internal conflict—cannabis farms. He loves weed more than anyone I know, but he loves protecting animals and their habitats more.

I knew Alec was too excited to stay focused for long. He turns to me and whines, "Can we at least go out for drinks to celebrate?" Cassie and Eliza look at the clock and perk up when they see it's almost five.

"You guys should," I say sincerely. "I'd love to join, but I have my monthly self-inflicted torture night." Also known as Lambert Family Dinner. Eliza winces. She's met my family—she gets it.

Cassie plays with her curly red hair and pretends to be nonchalant when she asks, "Is Matt going to be there?"

I roll my eyes. Cassie has a not-so-secret crush on my middle brother. If she weren't so good at her job, I'd test her for a brain injury.

It's not that my brother or the rest of my family are bad people. I just have absolutely nothing in common with them. I'm the only Lambert who finished college, has a job in STEM, and is not a mega internet influencer. As if it weren't bad enough to grow up in LA, I also happened to be born into a family where everyone else has an intrinsic understanding of how to go viral on the internet.

Alec grins. "I think what she means is, 'Are Matt's abs going to be there?'" Apparently Cassie's not the only one with a crush on my brother.

Eliza takes in my long dark hair, olive complexion, and hazel eyes before announcing, "If you didn't have your mom's coloring and your dad's eyes, I would think you were adopted."

"Well, you're not a geneticist, so there's still hope," I say as I start packing up for the day. "Great work, you guys, seriously. Here, first round is on me." I hand them a couple twenties as my phone starts ringing with a call from an unknown number.

Motivated by free booze, they quickly gather their belongings as I step into the hallway to answer the call. "This is Grace."

"Hi, Grace, it's Kristina from *Love Shack*. I have great news. One of our contestants didn't pass the STI test, so we have an opening. You're on the show!"

"Sorry, you have the wrong number."

But before I can hang up, the fast-talking woman laughs. "Your mom said you were funny. I'm such a fan of hers, by the way. Your brother too. What a hottie. Maybe we'll get him for next season. Anyway, we loved your pics. A little buttoned-up, but we'll make you look sexy on camera, I promise—"

"Hang on. You know my mom? Did she put you up to this?" My mom must be trying to get back at me for running out right after family dinner last month and not staying to learn a TikTok dance with her.

"She didn't tell you?" the voice on the other end asks, sounding skeptical. "Probably didn't want to get your hopes up. We almost never recruit contestants as old as you—"

"I'm twenty-nine—"

The woman ignores me and keeps talking. "And you have no

social media presence, which is usually a deal-breaker, but the rest of your family has so many followers, and honestly, we're a little desperate. Look, I have to run, but my assistant will send you the rest of the details and our legal team has a few things to go over with you. So set up your socials—oh, and please tell me you don't have herpes."

"Uh, no, I don't, but—"

"Great," she says, relieved. "Chlamydia and gonorrhea are fine, we'll have you right as rain with some antibiotics, but I swear to God if I lose another contestant—"

"I don't have an STI, but I'm also not really sure—"

"Great. Stay on the line for Legal. We're so excited to have you. See you soon."

I stare at my phone as Cassie comes over and whispers, "Who is it? You look shell-shocked."

"I don't really know. It's either my gynecologist's office or someone who's a fan of my mom's?"

Just then a deep voice gets on the phone and says, "Hello, is this Grace Lambert?"

"Yes?" I say tentatively, because at this point I'm not sure of anything.

"Hi, Grace, nice to meet you. I'm Andrew Benson, the studio lawyer. I just need to confirm your email so I can send over the liability forms and NDA before we start shooting next week."

"Shooting what?"

"The third season of *Love Shack*," he answers slowly, like this is something I should know.

I cover the phone and ask Cassie, "Do you know what *Love Shack* is?"

"The B-52s' song or the reality dating show?" she answers.

"What?! A *dating* show?" I shout before I start spewing swear words.

"Yeah, it was huge in the UK," Cassie explains, slowly starting to look excited. "It's been on for a couple seasons here. It's pretty dumb, but really sexy. Is that—"

Then I hear the lawyer's deep voice. "Grace? I can hear you muttering 'what the fuck' under your breath."

"Yeah, that tends to happen when someone is blindsided," I snap.

He pauses. "What do you mean 'blindsided'?"

"It means to be caught off guard in a negative context," I say haughtily. Even though I don't know this guy, he somehow seems to be part of the problem.

"I'm well aware of what 'blindsided' means—"

"Great, because I don't have time for linguistics, I have to go murder someone." Before I realize what I'm doing, I hang up on the lawyer. When I turn, I find Cassie, Eliza, and Alec watching me, their faces showing a combination of amusement and horror. "My mom signed me up for a reality dating show. I am going to kill her."

Alec and Eliza burst out laughing until Alec is finally able to speak: "You've never even seen a reality show!"

Eliza is still cackling. "Yeah, you hate TV. And people."

"Especially the kind of people who are on TV," I agree, looking to Cassie for confirmation, but she's suspiciously quiet.

Alec wipes the tears off his face from laughing so hard. "And let's not forget it's a *dating show.*" This just makes Eliza start laughing again.

I don't mind them laughing. I'm grateful they know me well enough to find this as ridiculous as I do. Because I don't date. Mostly because I have no interest in it, but also because the LA dating pool is the most depressing pool I've ever seen. And I've studied tidal basins disrupted by toxic waste.

"Have you ever even gone on a second date?" Eliza asks.

I think about it and nod, turning to Cassie. "Remember that guy who lives downtown and works at a bank? He took me to the Cheesecake Factory?"

Cassie shakes her head. "That doesn't count. It was only a second date because you forgot you had gone on a first date with him three years earlier. What was his name again?"

"Hell if I know. I couldn't even remember his face. He had a pug named Pickles, though." I pick up my messenger bag, which I must've dropped when I realized what the lady on the phone was talking about. "Anyway, Pickles isn't the point. The point is, I may need you for alibis when I commit matricide."

They all nod in solidarity, trying to hold it together before they dissolve into laughter again about the improbability of me on a reality dating show. I give them a quick wave as I storm out of the lab to go confront my mother.

Chapter Two

Usually, the hour it takes to get from my lab on the west side to my parents' house in Pasadena is long enough to sufficiently numb me to deal with the Lamberts. But not even my favorite episode of *The Life Scientific* podcast can calm me today. What was my mother thinking? Me? On a reality dating show?

I drive past the "iconic" palm trees that aren't even native to Los Angeles County until I turn down my parents' street with the million-dollar Craftsman-style bungalows. They're a far cry from the small Culver City townhome we lived in when I was a kid, but as my parents' social media influencing took off, so did their zip code.

It started with my dad. He created an exercise craze in the '90s by figuring out how to monetize appropriating yoga through making it more *manly* and selling it to bodybuilders and professional athletes. "Howie's Power Yoga" became a franchise that still has over twenty locations in the Southwest. But the most embarrassing part of Career Day every year in elementary school wasn't the power yoga; it was when he introduced himself as a fitness guru and handed out his aggro-motivational workout shirts. As if a bunch of ten-year-olds want T-shirts that say, "Don't count the pain, make the pain count." And yet he has eight hundred thousand devoted followers on Twitter, or whatever it's called now.

Not to be outdone, my mother, Rebecca, has well over nine hundred thousand Instagram followers, as she likes to remind me. She's always been into interior design, and her home decor blog with over-the-top holiday decorating ideas made her famous for it. My brother says she's like Joanna Gaines—if Joanna Gaines had bigger hair and were "extra."

Then there's Matt, ever the attention-seeking middle child despite being twenty-six years old. He's a former competitive skier, which means my parents spent a fortune so he could go down mountains fast. He quit skiing when he realized he'd be less likely to fracture his wrist for the fifth time if he were a TikTok model. Now he spends his days working out, buying shirts that are too small for him, and taking videos of himself. He also makes more money than I do, and I went to college for eight years.

And finally, the baby in the family, my brother Jesse, who has more followers than all of them put together for what I would consider the most absurd reason. From what I understand, Jesse has a YouTube channel where he comments on other people playing video games. He himself does not play the video games; he just offers commentary. Yeah, I don't get it either. He also has a podcast, a show on something called Twitch, and he's sponsored by brands I've never heard of. Last Christmas he gave everyone in the family an e-bike that said "G Fuel" all over it, which I promptly donated to charity. I appreciated the gesture, but I prefer a bike that requires pedaling. Or at the very least pedaling something other than G Fuel.

I pull into my parents' circular driveway, past my brother's gas-guzzling Range Rover, throw my Prius into park, and storm up the steps. I fling the front door open and shout, "What. Have. You. Done?"

"Hi, sweetheart!" my mom says as she unpacks takeout in the high-end chef's kitchen that rarely gets used for actual food prep. "I got you that vegan curry dish you liked last time."

I ignore her thoughtfulness, storm into the room, and hiss, "Don't you 'sweetheart' me! You signed me up for a reality show without asking me first?!"

She gasps. "Ohmigosh, you got on the show?" She drops the Indian food and rushes toward me.

"What about *me* made you think I would ever go on a *reality dating show?*"

She ignores my disdain and pulls me into a hug. "This is such a huge opportunity, Gracie! I can't believe you're actually going to be on *Love Shack.*"

"I'm definitely *not* going to be on *Love Shack,*" I say loudly. Okay, maybe I'm technically yelling. Either way, it's loud enough that Matt comes to see what all the commotion is about.

I try to extricate myself from my mother's surprisingly strong arms, but she's like a Lilly Pulitzer–clad sea urchin. I tell Matt, still stuck in her hug, "Mom signed me up for a dating show."

He doesn't even laugh, he just turns to her and asks, "Which one?"

But my mom is too focused on trying to convince me that she doesn't answer him. She finally lets me out of the hug, only to look me deep in the eyes and say, "Honey, this is exactly what you need. They pick the cream of the crop of guys, and there are multiple contestants to choose from. You yourself said you wanted to meet a higher caliber of men. So here they are!"

"I only said that to get you to stop setting me up on blind dates. I've never even watched a reality show!"

"Then how do you know you won't like it?" Matt teases. Then he demands again, "Seriously, which one?"

I ignore him and try to make my mom see reason. "I have to work, Mom! I have responsibilities! I'm a scientist, not a former child actor or washed-up one-hit wonder!"

She listens to my rebuttal as she takes out fancy gold-rimmed plates, then casually says, "First prize wins $250,000. That's way more than you make at the nature center."

My jaw drops. "A quarter-million dollars!? For what? How do you even win a dating show? Go on the most dates? You know what,

I don't want to know, because it doesn't matter. There's no way in hell I'm going on *Love Shack*."

"Ooh, *Love Shack*," Matt says, perking up. "I love that show. You should definitely do it. I can help you set up your socials."

"Great idea, Matthew!" my mom says, excitedly.

Feeling a headache coming on, I stand there massaging my temples. My mom doesn't seem to notice because she just hands us each a plate and an orange cloth napkin tucked inside the bejeweled napkin rings she uses whenever we order Indian food. I take a deep breath and try to compose myself.

Normally the fact that my mother has to make everything, even takeout food, Pinterest-worthy doesn't annoy me this much, but I'm not very happy with her right now. The only thing stopping me from throwing the napkin rings across the room and running out the front door screaming, "You can't make me!" is the fact that I'm starving and she did order my favorite curry.

I'm still taking deep, centering breaths when my dad bounces in, wearing too much spandex, and kisses me on the cheek. "Hey, Peanut. How's Kermit?"

Although it seems like his go-to greeting is a way of asking about my work saving endangered frogs, his eyes immediately glaze over whenever I actually talk about it for longer than thirty seconds. I usually say, "Still hopping," but I'm excited about today's breakthrough and welcome the change of subject, so I tell him, "Actually, it was a big day at the lab. We had some promising results with our vaccine, and we're ready to reintroduce fifty frogs back into their habitat."

"That's great, honey," my mom says absent-mindedly as she dishes out the food.

"So I guess Kermit is still hopping," my dad jokes, sitting down at the table next to Matt.

"Well, actually, it's a little more—" But before I can emphasize the severity of the fungus that has been killing southern mountain yellow-legged frogs by the thousands and how important it is to be able to inoculate against it, Jesse walks in. My youngest brother greets everyone with a "Yo," totally oblivious to the fact that I was midsentence. My dad gives him a stern look, and he begrudgingly takes out his earbuds before sitting down next to me.

I'm about to get back to my scientific discovery that might literally save an entire species and be a case study for future generations when my mom says, "Dig in!"

And I realize that the window for me to share with my family has closed. So, as usual, I swallow my disappointment with a bite of tofu and tune them out as they begin discussing the latest celebrities commenting on their social media.

One time in high school I overheard Matt tell his friends that I'm antisocial. But it wasn't that I was against making friends. It just seemed easier to keep to myself than try to get other people to like me. I guess when you can't easily connect with your own family, it's hard to believe strangers will be falling all over themselves to hang out with you.

I continue to eat my aloo gobi in silence until my mother's fidgeting gets distracting. When I look at her, I can tell she's dying to tell my dad and Jesse about the reality show.

Three . . . two . . . one . . .

"Grace got picked to be on *Love Shack*!" she blurts out. *And there it is.*

Jesse nods in my general direction. "This Grace?" I don't miss the side glance he shoots at Matt, who shrugs as if stranger things have happened.

"That's great, kiddo," my dad says with a big smile. "I heard one of those couples just got married." My mom claps her hands excitedly, as if the prospect of me finding a husband is the best thing that's ever happened to her.

I smile politely and say through gritted teeth, "Well, as I already explained to Mom and Matt, I'm not doing the show. And I sincerely doubt that I would find my future spouse on a television program. I'm probably less compatible with whoever signs up for these things than the horrible dates Mom has set me up on."

"They were not all horrible!" she protests.

I sigh and start ticking off first-date disasters on my fingers. "Okay, let's see, there was the surfer who called me 'dude' all night. Oh, and the professional skateboarder who I seriously thought was the same person. Neither had heard of a haircut or grammar. Then there was the celebrity blogger who spent the entire dinner looking around the restaurant to see if he could spot anyone famous."

"Which restaurant was it?" Matt asks, suddenly engaged in the conversation.

I roll my eyes at him and turn back to my mom. "You've never introduced me to anyone serious, Mom. And I highly doubt I'd find someone like that on a reality show."

My mom scoffs. "What do you mean by 'serious'?"

"I mean like normal, interesting people."

"She means lame," chimes in Jesse.

"No, I mean someone I can hold a conversation with about something other than superhero movies." Then I look pointedly at Jesse. "Or *Grand Theft Auto.*"

"So . . . *lame*?" he replies.

"Oh wait, I thought of someone serious you turned down!" my mom says excitedly, like she's winning a contest. "Remember that marketing guy I set you up with? He had season tickets to the Pantages!"

"Yeah, and when I told him I was a conservationist, he proceeded to mansplain global warming to me. I have two PhDs, and he was a midlevel ad exec who liked *The Book of Mormon.*" They all look at me as if I'm being difficult.

"What about my buddy Ryan?" says Matt, who is now apparently interested in playing the depressing game of Grace's dating prospects.

"Ryan? I don't remember a Ryan."

"The actor?" he prods.

"Ah yes, the guy who talked about himself all night and didn't ask me a single question."

"That's probably a good thing," Jesse says under his breath, and they all exchange looks.

"What? What's that look for?" I practically shout.

"Sweetie," my mom begins. "It's just . . . when you talk about your work, you tend to—"

"Drone on and on about your boring threatened toads," Matt interrupts with a mouth full of samosa.

"They're frogs! And they're not just threatened, they're critically endangered! They've disappeared from ninety percent of their historic localities. Which is a pretty big deal since they're a keystone species and other species depend on them, and if they die off, it would drastically change their entire ecosystem. Not to mention, if a frog population starts to decline, it indicates other shit's going down, like pollution, climate change, or other man-made problems that could possibly destroy entire environments!"

They all stare at me like I've just proved their point.

I take a deep breath and massage my temples again. "Why do I constantly have to defend my life choices like I'm in a sex cult and not a freakin' scientist, for crying out loud?" I push my plate away, done with eating and this conversation.

"At least a cult would be interesting," Jesse whispers to Matt.

I shoot them both a dirty look before turning to my mom. "Thank you for your concern that I will die alone. But I am not going on the show, and I would appreciate it if you'd respect my boundaries."

My mom pouts. "Well, just think about it."

My dad shrugs. "No harm in sleeping on it."

Matt nods. "What else do you have to do?"

"Save an entire species!" I yell as I get up to clear my dishes. The sooner I get out of here, the sooner I can forget this ever happened.

Chapter Three

The next morning, fueled by the fancy coffees I promised, Cassie, Alec, Eliza, and I get to work planning what is certain to be one of the crowning moments of my career: Next weekend we're releasing our first test group of southern mountain yellow-legged frogs back into the wild. Last month we introduced a milder form of the fatal chytrid fungus to the tadpoles in our lab. Then Cassie gave them the anti-fungal medicine to cure them, but only after they had developed the immune response that will protect them in the wild. Now they're vaccinated and ready to go live their best froggy lives in their native ponds and streams.

"This is basically our Super Bowl," Alec says as we sit around the conference room table.

Playing with her septum piercing, Eliza nods. "Finally, a sporting event I care about."

"I'll make vegan nachos," I offer.

Cassie grins. "Think we could get Beyoncé to play at halftime?"

I smile. After last night's dinner, it's nice to be surrounded by people who get me and are excited about the same things I am. We continue cracking jokes while we plan the release, and by the time we finish I'm buzzing with pride in our accomplishments and too much overpriced, sustainably harvested coffee.

And that's when our boss, Gregory, comes striding through the front door.

Gregory's not one of those evil bosses you see in movies. He's perfectly fine. I just wouldn't call him necessary. He doesn't even have an advanced degree. And I think he was in a fraternity. He's only my superior because he comes from a shit-ton of family money and one day he decided he was going to open a nonprofit for endangered species. Partly because he needed another tax write-off and partly because his ex-wife loved animals. (Now she loves her personal trainer.)

The thing is, Gregory is famously hands-off—because he doesn't know anything about science or animals. So when he shows up in his khakis and golf shirt, it's usually bad news. Alec spots Gregory coming down the hall and stops cleaning his glasses to shoot me a worried look.

"Hello, everyone!" Gregory booms cheerfully. I don't trust it.

We all gather around him, tentatively. "Hi, Gregory," I say. "What's wrong?"

"I can't just stop by to see my favorite scientists?" he answers merrily, like he's auditioning to be a mall Santa.

"So this is a friendly visit? There's no bad news?" Alec asks.

"All my visits are friendly visits!" Gregory declares, and I see Cassie's and Eliza's shoulders sink with relief.

Gregory's smile falters slightly. "But there is bad news too, I'm afraid." Their shoulders snap back into position.

"I knew it," mutters Alec.

The involuntary twitching of Gregory's jaw is his tell. This will be a doozy. "Well, there's no easy way to say this . . . We didn't get the grant."

"What?!" This hits me like a metric ton of bricks. "We need this grant to keep our program alive. We're all depending on this funding."

Gregory keeps prattling on about knowing how hard we've worked and how passionate we are, but I'm not really paying attention because my stomach has turned to lead.

"What happened?" I cut Gregory off. "We were a shoo-in, especially now that the vaccine is showing promising results. I don't understand."

He grimaces. "They gave it to the leatherbacks."

"The sea turtles!?" Eliza is livid. "But they're in NorCal! This money was earmarked for a Southern California species."

"You know sea turtles are a 'charismatic species,'" Gregory sighs. "They're the poster child for conservation."

"So, because the sea turtles were in a friggin' *Nemo* movie and sell more plushies, they get our funding?" Alec demands as I slump into my chair.

You'd think I'd be used to this particular blow by now, as I've encountered it my entire career. Everyone's worried about adorable animals like sea turtles and leopards, and don't even get me started on the fucking pandas, but no one seems to care about amphibians. Half my job is convincing people with money that Kermit and his buddies are important, and the other half is watching all the funding go to "cuter animals."

Which is why it takes all of my self-control to remain professional in this moment. "Look, Gregory," I say, clenching my teeth. "We get it. No one is putting frogs or salamanders on a glossy eighteen-by-twenty-four, and sure, leatherbacks help the dunes and the reefs and that's great for them, but we need the money more. We're high priority! Isn't there anything we can do? Appeal it?"

"There's no appeals process. The only thing we can do is a big push for donations."

Eliza shakes her head. "It won't be enough. We need at least three hundred thousand dollars by January to keep the lab running. The entire nature center barely made twenty thousand in donations last year. And that was only because Mrs. Roth kicked the bucket and left us ten grand in her will."

I'm momentarily impressed by how Eliza keeps all these facts and figures in her head, but then I'm immediately panicked by the direness of this situation. Ninety percent of the yellow-legged frog population has already died off. We need the money, and we need it now. I kick the closest trash can. "Fucking sea turtles!"

"If only we had a rich founder . . ." Alec looks at Gregory with puppy dog eyes.

He shakes his head. "Sorry, gang. You know I have a board to answer to. But maybe we can think of a big publicity idea to raise funds?"

I sigh because he's right. If we don't think of a big idea, we're screwed.

"I could dance around in a frog costume asking for money," Alec says, shrugging. "It wouldn't be the first time." We all give him a confused look as he grabs a dry-erase marker and writes "Publicity Ideas" on the whiteboard.

"What if we sell calendars with a different yellow-legged frog for every month?" Cassie suggests.

Alec starts writing that down until Eliza says, "We can barely tell them apart and we work with them every day. How will the public differentiate twelve nearly identical frogs?"

Alec crosses out "frog calendar" on the whiteboard, then suddenly brightens up. "I know it's not technically related, but everyone loves a good firemen calendar." He raises his eyebrows suggestively.

"Is that a real idea, or are you just letting us know what you want for your birthday?" Eliza asks as she continues shooting dirty looks at Gregory. She would definitely shoot the messenger if she could.

"We need something splashier," I say, trying to push through the nuclear fallout that Gregory's sea turtle bomb has had on my spirit. "Like maybe a gala or silent auction or . . ." I trail off when I realize those things require up-front money to organize and we don't have any.

Cassie suddenly turns to our boss and asks, "What if there's an out-of-the-box solution?"

Gregory shrugs. "What's the idea?"

Then Cassie approaches me slowly with her hands raised as if I'm a rabid raccoon. "Before you get mad, hear me out . . ." I don't like the way she's looking at me; it's making me wish I *were* a rabid raccoon. "I know you hate social media and reality TV, but *Love Shack* has *millions* of viewers—"

Gregory cuts her off. "My daughter and all her friends love that show!" I roll my eyes. Of course they do.

But then I realize where Cassie's going with this and start muttering, "No, no, no, no . . ."

She ignores my discomfort and tells Gregory, "Grace was chosen to be a contestant, and if she goes on the show, she'll get a ton of free publicity that we can use to drive people to our website and hopefully convert to donations."

"Oh my God, yes!" Alec says, dropping the dry-erase marker. "And if she wins, she'll get $250,000, which she could donate to the center and we'd almost be at our goal!"

I throw my hands in the air and look around at them in utter disbelief. "Less than twenty-four hours ago we all agreed how ridiculous that would be. There's no world where I'd win a dating show."

Alec shrugs. "America loves an underdog."

I can't blame them for being horribly delusional traitors because I know their hearts are in the right place. "Look, guys, I'm just as desperate as you are to protect our frogs, and I know how hard we've all worked, but there's got to be another way. Like Alec dancing in a frog costume. Let's revisit that!"

Cassie looks deep into my soul and says, "You've always said you would do anything you could to save endangered species."

I break eye contact with her and desperately grasp at anything that might save me. "I don't think we gave the fireman calendar enough consideration . . ."

"Are you really going to let an entire species go extinct just because you don't think you're good at dating?" Cassie asks.

"Why does it have to be me? One of you guys would be way better at getting strangers to like you."

Eliza shrugs. "Yeah, and if I looked like you, I would trade places with you without a second thought."

"What is that supposed to mean?" I look down at my slacks and sensible shoes.

"You're a babe, Grace," Alec says, like it's obvious. "If I were straight, I would totally try to date you on national TV."

I'm about to question whether Alec is high right now when Gregory claps his hands. "I like this idea! We could definitely use the publicity. And the board loves any sort of Hollywood connection."

My head is spinning, looking for any excuse. "But . . . but . . . I'd have to miss work."

"We can cover for you," Cassie immediately offers. "I don't mind staying late and working weekends."

"Me too," agrees Eliza. When Alec doesn't respond, she elbows him.

"Oh yeah, me too, I guess," Alec mutters. "Unless I have a date."

"I'm fine with you taking time off, Grace. You've never even taken a sick day. Plus, you're technically kind of working, trying to raise money and all," Gregory says with a shrug.

I sigh as I consider what they're saying. Am I being selfish? What kind of leader would I be if I didn't put my personal comfort aside to save our program? I feel my resolve melting faster than Greenland as I say, "I've never seen *The Bachelorette* or any of those dating shows. What do you have to do? Go on a couple dates? Make small talk?"

Cassie, Alec, and Eliza exchange a look that I can't decipher before Cassie quickly says, "Yeah, totally. Just a couple boring dates, that's all!"

"I thought there were challenges—" Gregory starts, but Alec cuts him off.

"The challenge will be playing nice with others," Alec quips.

"But Cassie said it was 'really sexy.' What's that about?" I ask warily.

"Oh, you know me, I'm boy crazy. I think everyone is sexy," Cassie responds in a way that sounds oddly like a cover-up.

"I should probably watch a few episodes and do some research first," I suggest.

Eliza waves me off. "It's reality TV. How hard could it be?"

"Yeah," Alec adds. "You're one of the leading biologists in a field dominated by straight, white men. You're a badass, Grace. You can do anything."

Even with their weirdness and my reservations, I can't help but notice that everyone is staring at me like I'm their only hope. I look around the lab I've poured my heart and soul into for the past three years, and my chest clenches at the thought of having to shut it down. Especially when we're on the brink of a breakthrough that could have a game-changing impact on conservation for decades to come. I exhale deeply, and before I can change my mind I say, "Okay. I'll do it."

Gregory immediately claps his hands and says, "Wow, won't it be fun to be working with a famous person? Maybe now my daughter will start coming over for Christmas again."

"I'm published in nine journals, and this is what impresses him?" I whisper to Cassie.

"We have to make you an Instagram page. And probably TikTok," Alec says. "Does anyone know how to do TikTok?" Cassie, Eliza, and Gregory all shake their heads.

I sigh. "Unfortunately, I know just the person."

Chapter Four

I thought you'd never ask. Like literally never," Matt says with an annoying grin as he stands in front of his Hermosa Beach bachelor pad the next morning. When Cassie giggles, I realize my brother's not wearing a shirt. I'm so used to his partial nudity that I don't even register his abs anymore, but apparently Cassie isn't as immune.

"Can you put on a shirt? You're distracting Cassie," I say as I push into his apartment, which could double as a showroom for frat-house chic.

"Hey, Cassie," Matt says flirtatiously as he runs his hand through his wavy brown hair. I almost throw up in my mouth.

"Hi, Matt," Cassie says with a shy wave as she follows me inside.

"Don't be gross," I whisper to her.

"I thought reality shows 'weren't for serious people'?" he asks, trying to provoke me. "And I believe you once told me that social media was all 'egomaniacs, stalkers, and conspiracy theorists.'"

I take a deep breath. This is already harder than I thought it'd be. And not just because his apartment smells like Axe body wash. "Are you going to make me grovel? Because I'm so desperate that I will."

Matt shrugs. "It wouldn't hurt."

Oh, but it would. I force a smile. "Fine." I clasp my hands and beg, "Darling brother, whose social media prowess knows no bounds, please gift me with your knowledge of how to get people on the internet to like you."

"I would love to," he says, far too smugly for my liking. But then, just like that, he gets to work. He opens the notes app on his phone and says, "Okay, what do you want your brand to be?"

I sink into his black leather couch and say, "My brand? Like Ann Taylor Loft or something?"

Matt laughs and pats my head as if I were a child. "No. How do you want to present yourself to the world? So far, it's been 'nerdy and uptight,' but I think it's time for a rebrand."

I am about to respond with an awesome retort, but Cassie senses it coming and plops down next to me, squeezing my arm. "I think a rebrand is a great idea, Matt," she says. "It's important to Grace that her passion for animals is front and center."

"Okay, I can work with that," Matt says as he paces his living room, taking notes on his phone. "I'm thinking classic *Tiger Beat* content. Like One Direction posing with puppies."

"The only word I understood was 'puppies.'" I scowl at him. "Unless 'puppies' is a euphemism."

He sighs as if *I'm* the aggravating one. "I mean, you can pose holding your turtles or whatever."

"They're frogs," Cassie and I say at the same time.

"Sure," Matt says, indifferent to the vast distinctions between reptiles and amphibians. "I also think some pics wearing your lab coat and goggles would be good too."

Now I'm the one laughing. "I don't wear a lab coat and goggles. I'm not a chemist."

"Whatever, regular people don't know the difference." When he sees I'm not budging, he sighs. "Fine, we'll get you a pair of fake glasses so you look smart."

"I am smart! I've been published in more scientific journals than any other biologist my age!"

Matt turns to Cassie. "See? Nerdy and uptight." Then he scratches his chin and says, "How would you feel about doing a few TikTok dances?"

"I would feel like you've obviously hit your head too many times skiing if you think I'll ever dance for strangers."

"You have to get over your insecurities if you're going to be on TV."

"I'm not being insecure. It's about having standards. Something you clearly don't understand."

"I'm telling you what gets followers. Do you want my help or not?"

"*Not.* This was obviously a mistake."

"Obviously."

"Fine."

"Fine."

"Children!" Cassie shouts over our bickering and claps her hands loudly in such a departure from her normal soft-spoken demeanor that I'm jarred into silence. "Let's take it down a notch. We aren't going to do any TikTok dances, but she'll wear the glasses in a few pics and pose with animals. Cool?" She looks at both of us. I shrug and Matt gives a semi-committal grunt.

As Matt starts doing something on his phone, I whisper to Cassie, "Are you only agreeing with him because you think he's hot?"

"We need him, Grace. We don't have much time." Then she considers it. "I'd say it's twenty-eight percent abs and seventy-two percent desperation."

I sigh, knowing she's right. But I'm also very concerned about her taste in men.

Just then my phone dings with an incoming email to my personal address from someone named Andrew whose email I don't recognize. When I click on it, I quickly realize it's the reality TV lawyer I hung up on.

Dear Ms. Lambert,

    Kristina told me you're confirmed for season three. I assume this means you resolved your "blindsided" issue. I've attached the liability paperwork and NDA for your signature. I didn't have a chance to go over it with you because you hung up on me, so if you have any questions, let me know. I also noticed your affinity for swearing. Please note that profanity will not be allowed on camera.

Respectfully,
Andrew Benson, Attorney at Law

"Seriously?" I scoff, and Cassie turns to see why. "I just got an email from the *Love Shack* lawyer, and he's scolding me for swearing. The show hasn't even started yet, and I'm already in trouble. Well, I'll just have to *respectfully* write back."

"Grace . . ." Cassie warns, but I'm too busy scanning the attached paperwork with a scowl.

"Jesus. I signed fewer liability forms when I worked with radioactive isotopes." I shake my head and email the uptight lawyer.

Dear Mr. Benson,

    My apologies for swearing and hanging up on you; I didn't realize lawyers are so easily offended. And yes, I do have some questions about the attached paperwork. I see that there are numerous clauses to protect the show but no language to protect the contestants. What if I get blinded by someone's bleached teeth? Or contract a communicable disease in the hot tub?

Respectfully,
Grace Lambert, PhD

I smile smugly as I hit send. A second later, Matt nonchalantly holds up his phone and says, "Okay, you're all set up on Insta, TikTok, X, and Snapchat."

"What? Already?" I say, trying to hide that I'm impressed.

"Yep. Your password is MattsBitch, all one word, capital M, capital B." He grins.

"Classy."

"I'm going live in thirty minutes, but I can do a photo shoot and make some reels for you later."

"It's okay, you've already done enough."

Matt stares at me. "I'm sorry, if you just wanted a Facebook page for Grandma's friends to comment on, you could've done that yourself. I thought you wanted an online *presence*."

I exhale, refusing to admit he may be right. "Cassie can take some pictures."

Matt turns to Cassie. "How many pixels does your phone have?"

Cassie shrugs. "Five?" Even I know that can't be right.

Matt shakes his head and asks her, "What filter is best in outdoor lighting?" Cassie looks like a deer in headlights. Then he turns to me. "Which side is your good side?"

"Um, my left?"

Matt laughs. "Good thing I'm free today. You'll also need to get some new clothes before then. Something cooler and less 'Midwestern working mom' vibe."

My hand involuntarily goes to pinch him, but Cassie swats it away and gives me a warning look. I take a deep breath and say, "Cassie and I will go shopping, I guess."

"Great." Then he gives Cassie and me a once-over and winces at our conservative clothing.

I glare back at him. "We came from work."

"I know the perfect person to help you," Matt says, already texting someone.

I immediately reach for his phone. "You better not be inviting one of your vapid girlfriends!"

He pulls away from my reach. "I don't have a girlfriend," he says, raising his eyebrows suggestively at Cassie.

"Don't hit on my friend!"

"I seem to remember it working out for me in high school."

Before we can dissolve back into our sibling antics, Cassie pulls me toward the door. "I think it's time to go. See you later, Matt."

"Bye, Cassie. Can't wait to see you soon," Matt says in what he must think is his sexy voice. I scowl at him as Cassie blushes then shoves me outside.

"Forty-six percent abs, fifty-four percent desperation," Cassie admits as we walk to my car.

Chapter Five

An hour later, Cassie and I stand by the fountain at the Grove, the mall where we're supposed to meet Matt's mystery shopper. While we wait, Cassie plays a logic puzzle game on her phone and I check my email. There's already a response from the lawyer.

> Dear Ms. Lambert,
>   Your last email concerns me. Partially because of your hypothetical scenarios, but also because I'm now thinking I may need to be concerned about trouble on set; you are the first contestant to ever take issue with our process. We have rules and regulations in place for a reason.
>
>   Respectfully,
>   Andrew Benson, Attorney at Law

I snort and start to write:

> Dear Mr. Benson,
>   New phone, who dis?

Cassie looks up from her game. "What is it?"

"Mr. Benson is being a pain in my ass, so I'm going to mess with him a little."

"Who's Mr. Benson?"

"The studio lawyer."

"Grace," Cassie chastises, "you have to play nice on the show."

"I *am* nice," I say, mock-offended.

"You are. Unless it's an authority figure. Or a guy in a tank top driving a Hummer."

I look at her like, *Well, what do you expect?*, but she doesn't cave. "Okay, fine, I'll play nice. I just don't like that this corporate guy is already telling me what to do."

"Better get used to it," Cassie mutters under her breath.

"What?"

"Nothing."

I sigh and erase my earlier draft. Then quickly type out:

Dear Mr. Benson,

    I wouldn't dream of causing trouble.

    I also wouldn't dream of lying to a lawyer.

                    Respectfully,

                    Grace Lambert, PhD

"There. Happy? I emailed the stodgy old lawyer without referencing the stick he has up his ass," I say to Cassie.

She nods. "Thank you." Then she adds, "Are you picturing Matlock or Perry Mason?"

"I'm picturing my cousin's father-in-law. He's the most boring person I've ever met, and that's coming from someone who reads scientific articles for fun."

She laughs, and I check the time before my eyes sweep over the throngs of people shopping at the Grove. I'm already getting hives. I hate malls, even fancy outdoor ones. It probably goes back to some repressed middle school memory of not being invited to Bethany Gill's boy-girl hang at the Westside Pavilion food court. Or something. I don't know, it's repressed.

"I've been dreaming of this day my whole life!" a familiar voice shrieks, waking me out of the terrors of middle school only to run smack dab into a whole new nightmare.

"Matt invited your mom?!" Cassie gasps, as she sees my mother striding toward us.

"I'm going to fucking kill him. Or worse, I'll switch out his protein shakes with something that will make his abs flabby."

"Don't you dare," Cassie says. Then she greets my mom. "Hi, Mrs. Lambert!"

She hugs us both too tightly. "Hi, Cassie! Gracie Doll! Isn't this so much fun? A girls' shopping day! When your brother told me you wanted my fashion expertise, I was beyond flattered. And *so so sooo* happy you changed your mind and saw I was right about the show."

Cassie grabs my hand, a silent warning to stay calm. LAPD should give this girl a medal. She's prevented at least two homicides today.

"Hello, Mother." My jaw is clenched so tight I'm at risk of chipping a tooth.

She hooks an arm around each of us and pulls us along. "We better get going. We have a *lot* of work to do." Then she power-walks past Talbots and Banana Republic and all the usual places I'd consider shopping, and instead we head toward the boutiques with bright colors and small pieces of clothing.

"I thought these stores were only for teenagers or Eastern European tourists," I say as I wince at the loud house music playing in the first shop we walk into.

My mom laughs as if I'm joking and greets the supermodel behind the counter by their first name, Abel. As they start pulling outfits, I text my brother.

ME: Well played. But I will be seeking revenge.

MATT: what? she has good style way better than urs

ME: You better sleep with one eye open.

MATT: lol have fun

"We're ready for you in the dressing room," the supermodel says.

I turn to Cassie. "I will give you any organ you want if you sneak me out of here."

Cassie laughs. "Come on. It's kind of fun."

I roll my eyes at her and enter the dressing room, only to find my mom and Abel in there waiting. My mom hands me a small spandex-y piece of red fabric. "You expect me to wear a shirt this tight?"

"It's a dress," my mom says as Cassie tries to hide her laughter.

I shake my head as I take the inappropriately small dress from her. "I'm getting creepy pageant mom vibes from you right now." Then I wait for her and the *sales model* to leave the stall, but they don't seem to be budging. "Uh, can I get some privacy here?"

"Oh. Sure," my mom says, sounding hurt because I don't want to get naked with her and some random beautiful stranger with a cool name.

I pull a hamstring trying to squeeze the tight piece of fabric over my body. When I stumble out of the dressing room with a charley horse, my mom gasps with delight, causing me to turn and look in the mirror.

"Oh hell no." This dress is shorter than the boy shorts I wear to bed, and it leaves nothing to the imagination. I mean *nothing*. Not only are the tops of my breasts exposed, but they're extremely high up. As I consider the physics of how this feat of cleavage is even possible, my mom claps.

"Honey, you look great!" she says, oblivious to the fact that I'm trying to stretch the *very* red dress to cover my *very* exposed body.

I look at Cassie for help, but she just looks back at me in shock. "Whoa. You look hot."

I give her a *not helping* glare before Abel chimes in with a seemingly intentional Valley Girl affectation. "For real. I can't believe you were hiding those legs under pants."

I turn to my mom. "I can't wear this in public."

"This is the kind of stuff all the contestants will be wearing. You want to catch the men's eye and make a good first impression."

"It won't be a good impression if I fall on my face because it's too tight to walk in and then my boobs pop out. And secondly, I don't want to catch a guy's eye because of how much skin I'm showing."

My mom gives Abel a look that says, *See what I'm working with?*, then turns to me. "You need to get out of your comfort zone, Grace. Clearly what you've been doing hasn't been working, honey." She obviously tagged the "honey" on there to try to cushion the blow, as if I care I'm single.

"Have you ever thought that *I'm* not the problem? That it's the guys who are? If it's not an atrocious blind date you've set me up on, then I'm getting asked out at a work event by some *fratologist* who automatically assumes that because I'm a woman, I must be the research assistant and not his peer."

I see Cassie texting. I'm sure she's letting Alec and Eliza know they're missing one of my classic straight men diatribes, but I'm too wound up to stop. "Don't you want me to find someone who's interested in me because of my brain, not because of a tiny piece of spandex? And if I'm out of my comfort zone, by definition, I'll be *uncomfortable*. How sexy do you think I'll be awkwardly pulling down my dress all night?"

My mom considers all this and nods. "Good point." My eyes widen in shock that she's finally agreeing with me. "Confidence is sexy. What about something like this?" She holds up a navy blue wrap dress and I groan.

Cassie tries to salvage the situation. She takes the dress from my mom and turns to me. "Sure, it's a little lower cut and more form-fitting than what you'd usually wear, but it's not in the neon family and it'll go below your upper thigh, so it's not wildly inappropriate."

I exhale. She's not wrong. For the millionth time today, I think about what's at stake and why I agreed to go on this stupid show.

And so I take the dress from Cassie and retreat into the dressing room. For the frogs.

As I get changed, I overhear my mom whispering to Abel. "She went through a bit of an ugly duckling phase when she was younger. I don't think she realizes what a beautiful swan she's become."

I pause, mid-undress. I don't know if I should be offended or complimented. I mean, she's not lying. If you saw any of my school photos where I'm tall and gangly with braces, acne, and unruly hair, "ugly duckling" would be the nicest thing you could say. It wasn't until college that I grew into my limbs and started washing my face with something other than Dove soap. And then my sophomore-year roommate showed me how to use product to tame my thick hair and convinced me to cut bangs. I ended up looking like the "after" photo of myself. So much so that the former water polo heartthrob of my high school didn't recognize me at a bar one night and asked me out. It would've been the ultimate redemption moment if he hadn't been so drunk he puked on my shoe.

So, yeah, I may not be the ugly duckling that I once was, but I also wouldn't go so far as to say I'm a "beautiful swan." My mom is genetically biased. But it doesn't matter; I'm a scientist, not Miss America. So I throw on the wrap dress, put up my "I don't give a fuck" force field, and walk out of the dressing room.

I'm immediately met by three smiling faces.

"Gorgeous!" Cassie beams.

"Classy," agrees Abel.

"You need a better bra," my mom says. "But yes, I think we can make sophisticated sexy work."

Chapter Six

After what may have been two hours or thirty-seven days, Cassie and I head back to work. My trunk is full of shopping bags containing more dresses than I have ever owned and some sort of torture device called Spanx, which I have *never* owned.

Cassie offers to drive so I can catch up on the emails I've missed playing dress-up. I reply to a request to be a guest lecturer at a conservation seminar before I see an email from Mr. Benson.

> Dear Ms. Lambert,
>
> To be clear, you <u>cannot</u> be on the show without signing the <u>MANDATORY</u> paperwork.
>
> Respectfully,
> Andrew Benson, Attorney at Law

I sigh heavily and open my electronic signature app. I'll sign the paperwork, but I don't have to be happy about it. When I'm done, I attach the documents to an email back to him.

> Dear Mr. Benson,
>
> Please see the <u>SIGNED</u> paperwork. I now have a cramp in my hand.
>
> As a lawyer, could you please advise whether I can sue for <u>pain</u> and <u>suffering</u>.
>
> Respectfully,
> Grace Lambert, PhD

Cassie must notice my self-satisfied grin. "Are you messing with the lawyer again?"

"No," I say quickly. Cassie raises her eyebrows. "Okay. Just a little. He's just so easy to rile up. It's kind of entertaining."

Cassie shakes her head but I turn to her and say sincerely, "Hey, thanks for coming with me today. I don't know what I would've done without you there reeling my mom in. To express my gratitude, I shall gift you all these small scraps of clothing when I'm done."

Cassie smiles. "You don't need to thank me, Grace. We all appreciate what you're doing. I know being on *Love Shack* goes against everything you believe in—"

"That's an understatement."

"But you really did look great in those new outfits," Cassie says sincerely. "I wish you could see yourself like we all do."

I shrug off the sentiment. I hate it when Cassie gets mushy. "They weren't all horrible," I finally concede as we pull into the nature center.

It's after five but Alec and Eliza are still there, picking up the slack for Cassie and me. I immediately dive into work and at least an hour passes before I hear giggling. I shudder because I know what that sound means.

I walk out to the lobby to see Matt flirting with the Fox Girls. That's what we call the biologists who work with the San Joaquin kit foxes. They're tiny and super-cute, with big ears. The foxes, not the girls. We have an unspoken rivalry with the Fox Girls since we're constantly vying for funding with them, but I will *always* support other women in science. So it's my duty to warn them off my brother.

"The inflated-ego clinical trials are down the block," I say to him as I approach. The Fox Girls look up at me in confusion. "This is my dumb brother. Dumb brother, these are the Fox Girls."

"Yeah, they are," Matt says as he openly checks them out.

"Great, we have to go," I say as I pull him toward my corner of the lab.

"Buzzkill. How was shopping with Mom?" He gives me an innocent smile.

"How many layers of hell are there?"

Matt laughs, then pulls out his phone. "I thought these three dresses were the best," he says as he scrolls through his photo gallery.

"She sent you pictures?"

"And video. It helps me get an idea of how to shoot you."

Yes please, someone shoot *me.*

"Also, I made this hilarious gif of you trying to walk in heels," he says as he shows me his phone.

I push it back at him. "Let's just get this over with."

"Let me consult my shot list," he says as he looks at his notes app. "Okay, we'll start with the navy wrap dress, hair up, holding a frog. Let me just check the light in here." Matt taps his phone a few times, turns me so the sunlight streaming in through the window hits me in a different way, and snaps a pic. Then he swipes on it and says, "Adding a filter to soften it a bit and enhance the color." He shows me the final product. And *wow*, it's not bad. My normally hazel eyes look really green. Huh, maybe he *is* good at this.

Cassie walks over and takes a look. "Oh my gosh! That's already the best picture I've ever seen of Grace."

"Don't encourage him. If his ego gets any bigger, it'll need its own Instagram account."

Matt taps away at his phone and a second later shrugs. "'Matts_Ego' is available."

Twenty minutes later, I'm dressed in one of my new outfits and standing in my lab, holding one of my amphibian babies, as Matt snaps pictures.

"Now kiss the frog," he orders.

"Not happening," I say, shaking my head. Then I look over to the bullpen where Cassie, Alec, and Eliza have been watching the photo shoot and lobbing comments like they're watching a fashion show. Cassie gives me an encouraging look as Alec mouths, *Do it.* Eliza is eating popcorn.

I sigh, discreetly flip them off, and pretend to kiss the frog.

"Okay, now give me more pout, less grimace," Matt says, as he photographs me from different angles. "Better. Okay, now one where you look coy."

"Like this?"

Matt snorts. "I said coy, not constipated. Just put on the fake glasses and we can fix it in post," Matt says with an impatient hand motion.

"Are we done yet?" I whine.

Matt scoffs. "You think we're only doing one outfit? Also, can we get some cuter animals in here? You got a wolf or sea turtle or something?"

I take off one of my heels and am about to puncture his aorta when Cassie, Alec, and Eliza jump into action. Eliza grabs my shoe-weapon as Alec valiantly steps in front of Matt. Cassie calmly whispers to me, "I know we like to hate on the charismatic animals, but there's a reason why they get all the attention. And we need attention right now."

Another twenty minutes later, I'm in a new dress and fake glasses holding a tiny kit fox. And goddammit, it *is* cute and cuddly, and I totally want it on a poster. Matt takes a million pictures as the Fox Girls *ooh* and *aww* at either the kits or my brother. Then someone from the raptor department comes walking over with a Swainson's hawk.

"Oh good, the hawk is here," Matt says, as if he were hosting a dinner party. "Can you put it on her shoulder?"

"It's a bird of prey, it has talons," I say, shaking my head.

"Ooh, I love that," Matt says, and I roll my eyes. I give the little kit fox back to the Fox Girls before the hawk gets any ideas and put on the leather raptor gloves.

"Well, aren't you beautiful," I say to the hawk as she climbs onto my gloved arm. She just gives me a look that says, *I know, bitch.* Respect.

Matt starts taking pictures. "Look fierce, Grace. You're a bird of prey."

"No, I'm really not."

"Whoa. This is actually working," Eliza calls from her prime viewing location. She shows Cassie my phone.

"Holy cow, how do you already have over five thousand followers!?" Cassie asks.

"I made a reel of the photo shoot and posted it to all my accounts," Matt says. When is he doing these things? He's like a multitasking social media ninja.

Cassie reads the caption Matt posted: "I may be the brawn, but my sister is the brains."

"Aww," Alec says with cartoon hearts in his eyes. Cassie has the same look. Eliza is still eating popcorn.

"Five thousand is weak sauce. You can't even get a start-up makeup brand sponsorship with five thousand followers. And a quarter of those are probably bots," Matt says, bringing us back down to earth.

"What's a bot?" I ask, and I swear the hawk rolls her eyes at me. Everyone else ignores me.

"How many followers do you have?" asks Eliza.

"Seven hundred forty-five thousand, three hundred and eleven," Matt rattles off the top of his head.

"Wow, your abs must be really nice," Eliza says.

"They are," Cassie, Alec, and Matt say at the same time.

I give the hawk back to its handler and look at the Instagram account Matt set up on my phone. He's already posted a bunch of pics from our photo shoot. And they're surprisingly classy. Like an educational wildlife brochure meets a women's magazine. And there are already a ton of people commenting on the picture of me kissing one of my frogs. Angela516 even wrote, Aww, these little guys are sooo cute!

I immediately have two thoughts: *Suck it, sea turtles.*

And: *Holy shit. This might actually work.*

Chapter Seven

There's nothing like waking up to annoying emails," I tell Cassie. She came by my condo this morning to help me pack. Because she's a good friend . . . and she wants to make sure I actually go through with it. I read her Mr. Benson's latest correspondence:

> Dear Ms. Lambert,
> No, you cannot sue for pain and suffering because you signed the liability paperwork, waiving the production's liability for any potential harm, injury, or negative consequences. May I suggest that the next time you sign a legal document, you read it more thoroughly.
>
> Respectfully,
> Andrew Benson, Attorney at Law

Cassie laughs. "Well, he's got you there."

I shake my head. "I can't wait to meet this guy in person. I have some select words for him."

"Go easy on poor old Mr. Benson. He already has his work cut out for him. You wouldn't believe the number of alcohol-induced injuries on these shows," Cassie says as she folds my new dresses.

"So he's an overpaid babysitter who makes sure people don't drink too much and get into fistfights?"

Cassie nods. "Or do anything else too inappropriate."

"Isn't that their goal, though?" I reply as I hustle around my small but tidy bedroom, looking for anything I forgot to pack. "Ply people with alcohol and hope they do inappropriate stuff?"

"There's a fine line between good TV and lawsuits."

I shrug, not worried because I've never been a big drinker. I like a buttery chardonnay as much as the next girl, but I never drink enough to impair my judgment. "There's got to be more to do on set than get drunk and act like an idiot."

Cassie's voice is very high-pitched when she says, "Yeeeah, totally, of course."

"Your shrill squeaking isn't instilling confidence."

Cassie doesn't meet my eye. "You're the one who said, *'It's reality TV. How hard could it be?'*"

"It was Eliza who said that."

"We could try to watch an episode if you want, but you probably don't have time if you need to be there in an hour," Cassie says evasively.

I narrow my eyes at her, and she shrugs, giving me an apologetic smile. "Just remember you're doing this for the frogs. And your research. And your friends." She hugs me. "Try to keep an open mind, okay?"

"You sound like my mom."

"Harsh," she says. "But maybe Rebecca's onto something. It wouldn't be the worst thing in the world if you meet someone."

"Why does everyone keep assuming I'm looking to meet someone? I'm not. Especially not some Neanderthal who willingly goes on a reality show. I'm happy with my life the way it is—I mean, as long as I can keep our lab running. I'm only doing the bare minimum to get publicity and hopefully not make a fool of myself on national TV."

She hands me a razor. "Well, shave your legs just in case."

I scrutinize Cassie. She didn't shave her armpits all of senior year. Why is she suddenly interested in my self-grooming? "It's not like you'll be able to see my hairy legs on TV. And I'm certainly not planning on getting up close and personal with anyone." When she looks away, I shriek, "Cassandra Lynn Shapiro, what aren't you telling me?!"

"Nothing! Just hurry up and pack. We have a mansion to get to!"

Cassie drives twenty-five minutes north on PCH, until we pull up to an enormous European-inspired chateau. It's like they dropped some duke's ancestral home on top of a mountain in Malibu. It's castle chic with a stone exterior and oversized wooden doors. It also manages to have a sprawling green lawn despite California's perpetual drought. The juxtaposition of all this with the 180-degree view of the Pacific Ocean is both breathtaking and intimidating.

Cassie whistles. "This is even bigger than it looks on TV."

"I feel a sudden herpes outbreak coming on. We better tell that crazy producer lady. I should probably cancel."

"You have to be in proximity to another human body to get a sexually transmitted infection," Cassie says as she follows a bright yellow sign that reads Talent.

"Stop fact-checking my excuses," I sigh. But I don't get out of her car when she parks. "I can't miss our Super Bowl!" I plead. When I agreed to be on this stupid show, I didn't realize it was going to overlap with the day we're releasing our immuno-boosted frogs back into the wild.

Cassie pats my hand reassuringly. "You don't have to worry, Grace. We've got everything handled. And I'll take lots of pictures."

"But . . . it's like missing your kid's first day of kindergarten. This is a milestone I will never get back."

Cassie nods. "They grow up so fast. One minute they're swimming around with their little tails, the next they're taking their first hop." I look at her hopefully. "But you're still doing the show."

I groan dramatically, and Cassie pushes me out of her car as an attractive woman with a chic blond bob comes striding toward us, wearing a headset and carrying a clipboard. As soon as her frenetic, no-nonsense speech begins, I recognize her voice. "You must be Grace. Welcome to *Love Shack*. I'm Kristina, one of the EPs, we spoke on the phone. Did you have a chance to read through everything?" She surveys me critically. "I guess you didn't see the part that asked you to arrive ready for intros with hair and makeup done."

"Um. Hello. And yes, I did my hair and makeup."

She raises her eyebrows. "Oh. I see. Okay, well, maybe we can get Shantae's team to touch you up."

"Shantae's the host," Cassie whispers to me.

"Yeah, and she demands that her glam squad be on call at all times," Kristina says, walking away and expecting us to follow. "She came in fifth on *America's Next Top Model*, like a billion years ago, but still acts like a total diva. Apparently she didn't get the memo that there's only one Tyra, you know?"

"No, I do not," I respond, my head swimming.

"Is this your assistant?" Kristina says, gesturing to Cassie.

"This is my best friend, Cassie."

"Hi," Cassie says meekly, holding out her hand, as we try to catch up to the force of nature that is Kristina.

Kristina just gives her a quick nod, then snaps her fingers. A second later, someone who must be a lowly production assistant rushes over and collects my suitcase. "Where's the rest of your luggage?" Kristina asks.

"This is it."

"What?"

"This is all I brought," I say, confused. There's got to be a washing machine in a mansion this big.

"*One* bag?" Kristina says, standing still for what might be the first time in her life. "That's a new record. We've never had a contestant, man or woman, with only one suitcase before. Last season one chick brought twenty-two. We had to store half of them in a broom closet."

"Cool?" I say, because what do you say to that? As Kristina keeps walking and Cassie and I jog to keep up, I whisper to Cassie, "Who owns more than two pieces of luggage?"

She shrugs and whispers back, "Who has enough clothes to fill twenty-two bags?"

Kristina calls back to us, "They'll put your *one bag* in your room for you while I give you a quick tour." She glances at the time and somehow walks even faster. "We try to keep you away from the other contestants until you're on camera. We want your genuine initial re-action. Then we'll get pickup shots where you re-create your genuine initial reaction for different camera angles."

I'm barely listening as I take in this amazing house. I guess if I'm stuck in reality TV purgatory, this place makes it palatable. We walk through a kitchen with a giant marble island and rustic wooden beams on the ceiling, then past a living room with brown leather club chairs and a fireplace I could stand in. Finally, we follow Kristina out to a back patio and gardens that belong on the cover of a magazine. Not only do they overlook a massive infinity pool but also the ocean in the distance. *Damn.*

I whisper to Cassie, "Whoever owns this beach castle isn't a biologist working at a nonprofit, that's for sure."

Kristina gestures to the outdoor patio with lounge furniture and cabanas. "This is where you'll spend most of your day. There's a full-time bartender at both the tiki bar on the beach and the pool-side bar. There's a part-time chef in that outdoor kitchen over there, but the PAs can get you whatever you need. In fact . . . Blue!" she shouts. "I'm going to have one of our PAs finish the tour and get you in hair and makeup. I've got a million things to do." Kristina has a quick exchange with a guy with blue hair who I'd guess is probably in his forties, and I swear I hear her say, "Show the Sexy Scientist around." Then she yells, "Glad you're here," over her shoulder at me and hustles off.

Cassie shakes her head. "Talking to that producer lady felt like whiplash." I nod as the PA with blue hair and a faded band T-shirt walks over to us.

"Hi, I'm Blue. Welcome to *Love Shack*."

"Thanks. Though not sure this constitutes a shack," I say, pointing at the mansion, trying to sound playful instead of entirely overwhelmed and completely out of my comfort zone.

Blue looks at me like he's trying to tell if I'm joking, then says, "The shack is on the back of the property."

I laugh. He doesn't. I look back and forth between him and Cassie, who looks guilty.

"Well, I should probably get back to the lab," Cassie blurts. "Have a great time and remember, we're all counting on you and I'm sorry." She gives me a quick squeeze and scurries off toward her car.

"Sorry? Why are you sorry?!" I yell after her. Then I turn to the guy with blue hair who I've known for ten seconds. "Why is she sorry?"

Chapter Eight

When Cassie is out of sight, Blue fidgets with his headset as he asks, "Have you ever seen the show?"

"Oh, God, no. I hate reality TV."

"Why are you here then?" he asks.

"It's a long story, but I'm starting to think I've been misled."

"Yeaaaah, that's probably why she's sorry," he says with a wince. "Let me give you a tour and you'll see why."

I follow Blue back inside, and he leads me up a staircase that can only be described as grand and down a long hallway with a posh runner. "This is where you'll be sleeping for the first night." He opens the door to a gorgeous bedroom with a four-poster king bed and French doors that open to a charming balcony with bougainvillea winding around the railing.

"Whoa. This is nicer than the hotel I stayed in for the International Conservation Convention. I don't mind staying here the whole time."

"Yeah, about that . . ." Blue plays with his headset again before shoving his hands into the pockets of his jean shorts. He gives me a real smile. "I really wish I didn't have to be the one who breaks it to you, but only the top points leaders get to sleep in the mansion. Everyone else sleeps in the shack."

"Wait, what? There's an actual shack?"

"Well, technically, I think it was a tool shed or where they kept their lawn mowers or something. Have you ever seen *Big Brother*? It's like the 'have-not' room."

"I *have not* seen Big Brother and I *have not* a clue what you're talking about."

He rubs the back of his neck, another nervous tic, and says, "Wow, you really weren't kidding. Come on, I'll show you."

We walk past the infinity pool, a putting green I hadn't noticed earlier, and the beautifully landscaped gardens with a view of the ocean . . . until we get to a dilapidated shack at the bottom of the hill. It's about the size of a small garage, and the door creaks when Blue opens it. There aren't any windows, but the sun streams in through the cracks in the boards, allowing in just enough light to take in the empty room. There are no furnishings, just six bedrolls stacked in a corner, and it somehow manages to be both musty *and* dusty. This is where every horror movie takes place.

"Were a bunch of Girl Scouts murdered here?" I ask, pointing at the bedrolls.

He laughs. "Good one. But no, that's where you sleep," he says apologetically. Then he quickly adds, "There's an outhouse, cold showers, and no electricity. Phew, it feels good to get that off my chest. I hate being the bearer of bad news."

"What?! I didn't sign up for this!"

"Didn't you read about all of this when you applied to be on the show?"

I shake my head in response as my fists clench involuntarily. "I'm going to kill my mom. And Cassie. And Eliza and Alec. And I think I'd enjoy killing Kristina too."

Blue smiles. "I like you. And don't worry, you only have to sleep here if you're at the bottom of the leaderboard." We start walking back up the hill.

"How do I get points? Please say trivia. Or logic puzzles. Or even regular puzzles. Anything but physical challenges."

He looks like he's choosing his words carefully but also biting back a laugh. "Well, they're physical challenges in a way. You know what, I'm going to let someone else explain the rest of the rules to you. I don't want to be added to your hit list."

Blue leads me around the pool toward the back patio, which reminds me of the restaurant in Miami where my cousin had her rehearsal dinner. All the lounge furniture, chaises, and umbrellas seem overly curated for "coolness."

When we pass the bar, we almost bump into someone coming from the opposite direction. I look up and see a guy I definitely haven't met yet. Unlike the crew members I've seen hustling around in cargo shorts and carrying heavy-looking cameras, this guy is wearing what is undoubtedly a custom-made navy suit. He's several inches taller than my five-foot-eight frame, with short dark hair and a five o'clock shadow that is too perfect to be accidental. He says hi to Blue and apologizes for almost running us over, but his confidence and presence make me want to apologize to *him*.

He turns to me, and his smile catches me completely off guard. He might be the most handsome man I've ever seen. Which makes me realize he's probably one of the contestants I'm not supposed to be meeting yet. I look to Blue to make sure it's okay that I'm interacting with another contestant before the camera captures my "genuine reaction." He doesn't seem concerned.

The handsome suit guy puts out his hand to introduce himself but before I can shake it, he pulls back when recognition hits. "Grace Lambert?"

I nod and start to ask him his name, but Blue cuts in, saying, "She also goes by 'Sexy Scientist.'" Blue gives me a devilish smile.

I groan. "That can't seriously be a thing."

The guy in the suit nods. "I've already heard it on set. It's definitely a thing."

I gesture at him, waving a hand at his overall handsomeness. "And I guess this is your thing?"

He looks down at himself, then back up at me. "You don't like my suit?"

I really do. But since I still don't understand how the show works and he may end up being my competition or something, I decide to stay neutral. So I shrug and say, "It looks expensive."

He raises an eyebrow. "It is." Then he turns to Blue, as if he's done with our conversation. "You went more turquoise this season. I like it."

"Thanks." Blue runs his fingers through his hair as a flattered blush creeps up his face. "It was more of a robin's egg last season," he explains to me.

The handsome suit guy was a contestant on last season too? I didn't realize they could do that. What if that gives him an unfair advantage? "They brought you back for this season?" I ask him, trying to contain the injustice in my voice.

He nods. "Is that a problem?"

Well, his rudeness is probably why he didn't win, but I decide to take the high road. "Well, good for you, trying again, I guess." He gives me a confused look, so I tack on, "Good luck this season."

He just stares at me. "I think I'm going to need it."

Ahh. So he *is* my competition. That explains his attitude. I level him with my fakest smile. "Oh, you definitely are."

He opens his mouth, but before he can respond Blue interrupts, pressing a finger to his earpiece. "Crap. That's Kristina. She wants you in hair and makeup. Now." Blue hooks his arm in mine and leads me away. It seems like he's stifling a laugh.

I give a parting salute to Overpriced Suit. There's no way I'm letting that guy win the $250,000 over me.

Blue hustles me toward the hair and makeup trailer and yells back, "Bye, Andrew," without turning around.

I feel a drop in my stomach. "Andrew?"

"Yeah, Andrew Benson. He's the on-set lawyer."

"That's Mr. Benson?! I thought he was a contestant!"

Blue starts laughing. "I know."

"Why didn't you correct me?"

"Because it was hilarious. The look on his face . . . I've never seen him look so ready to fight with someone before the show's even started filming."

I shake my head in disbelief. "That's the stodgy old lawyer I hung up on and have been emailing?"

"I don't know if you hung up on him or not. But I wouldn't say he's stodgy. Or old."

"Well, that makes sense why he was so obnoxious. That seems to be his baseline." I turn to go after him. "I have some issues I've been waiting to bring up with him—"

But Blue cuts me off, puts his arm around me, and keeps leading me in the direction we were headed. "You can yell at him later. I'm sure he'll love that. But I need to get you to the glam squad before Kristina has my head."

I walk with him for a moment before blurting out, "I can't believe that's Old Man Benson." Then I shake my head. "I didn't know lawyers could be that attractive in real life."

Blue laughs, then puts on a fake posh accent. "This is TV, darling. Everyone is attractive." He keeps hurrying me along. "Which is why we need to get you to hair and makeup."

Forty minutes later, I have so much shellac on my face I can barely scowl. I'm sitting in a tall hairdresser's chair in a trailer that's been converted into a beauty salon, and two very nice women have done "a quick touch-up" to my hair and makeup. Except it wasn't quick and the fake lashes they glued on feel like tarantulas crawling on my eyes. Not the cute *Poecilotheria* genus native to Sri Lanka either.

I sit there pondering whether women on reality TV shows are

obligated to put on this much makeup every day when a beautiful Indian American woman struts into the trailer, immediately commanding everyone's attention.

"I'm getting shiny," she whines, and immediately the sweet makeup artists who were buzzing around me rush over to her with all sorts of powders and lotions.

"Hi, I'm Grace. You must be Shantae." I extend my hand. She doesn't take it. *Okaaay.*

"Aw, yes. The Sexy Scientist."

"I really wish everyone would stop saying that." One, because it's degrading, and two, because it reminds me of my interaction with Andrew Benson, Attorney at Law. Cassie may be right. I may have a tiny little issue with authority figures. Especially men who try to tell me what I can and can't do without hearing what I have to say. It's an unfortunate by-product of being a woman in STEM.

Shantae doesn't seem to care what I think about the nickname because she shrugs and says, "After a few seasons, all the contestants start to blur together. I need a way to keep everyone straight so I'll call you by the right names on camera," she says in a way that makes it seem like the mental equivalent of passing the LSAT. "Last year, I had Sob Story, Unapologetic Asshole, and Racist—so be glad you're just the Sexy Scientist."

"Thanks, I guess?" I watch as Shantae pouts her lips, and a makeup artist immediately reapplies a glossy red lipstick. "Hey, maybe you can answer something for me," I say to her. "How does one win points so she doesn't have to stay in the creepy murder shack?"

Shantae laughs. "I didn't believe Kristina when she told me."

"Told you what? That I don't want to sleep on the floor of a condemned garage?"

"That you really haven't seen the show before. The writers are going to have a field day with you," Shantae says smugly.

"I thought this was a *reality* show."

"There are still writers. They hire a comedian to write the snarky commentary I say," she says as she kisses a tissue to remove excess gloss. "And the producers storyboard the rest of the show. They love a 'fish out of water' plotline."

I shake my head. "I really should've insisted on doing research before I came. I'm starting to suspect my friends blindsided me on purpose."

Shantae must take pity on me because she turns and says, "You get points by doing sexy challenges, being in a couple, and of course, the more you hook up, the longer you stay."

I cough on the stale coffee Blue brought me. "Hook up?"

Shantae raises a perfectly manicured eyebrow. "Wait till you hear what this season's challenges are. They're even sexier than last year's. All right, I'm done here." She begins to saunter out of the hair and makeup trailer, then turns back to me. "Good luck," she says sarcastically, as if even luck won't help me now.

I sit there in shock until Blue comes to collect me. He raises his electric blue eyebrows at me. "By the look on your face, I'm guessing you've met Shantae. Did she make it onto your hit list?" I try to respond, but my head is still stuck on the *hookup* bombshell. "Don't worry about her. She's just bitter that her modeling career never panned out the way she wanted it to." Blue puts an arm around me and ushers me out of the trailer.

"She told me how you win points," I mumble as we walk back up toward the pool area.

"Ahh, I see," Blue starts. "Well, the good news is—" but before Blue can tell me anything remotely redeeming about this situation, he listens to his earpiece. "Kristina is yelling for the Sexy Scientist."

Blue must notice my grimace at the unwelcome moniker, or maybe he just senses my imminent panic attack about being woefully unprepared for whatever the hell I've gotten myself into. He stops walking, puts his hands on my shoulders, and turns me to face him. Then, in a gentle voice, he says, "Don't worry, Grace. You can do this."

I take a deep breath, already feeling better with his support. Until he says the thing no woman wants to hear.

"Now let's get you in a bathing suit and introduce you to the world!"

Chapter Nine

I look down at my bathing suit and the microphone that hangs around my neck, designed to look like a necklace, and question my life choices. What would my professors at Stanford think if they saw me like this? Oh shit—what if my professors at Stanford watch the show and *actually* see me like this? Before I decide to move to Siberia and surgically remove my fingerprints, I take a calming breath, visualize poor endangered frogs, then walk out to the pool area.

The first thing I notice is the guy with the camera pointed at me. Kristina said not to look at the camera, but that only makes me want to look at it more. It's like when there's a solar eclipse and you know you shouldn't stare directly into the sun but you just have to sneak a peek. I try to snap out of it and force myself to awkwardly look above the camera. It requires all my concentration, which means I'm not looking where I'm going and immediately stub my toe on a chaise lounge.

"Fuck me!"

"Language," the cameraman softly warns from behind the camera. Yep, that's right. "No swearing" was one of Andrew Benson's annoying decrees. Damn, I haven't even been introduced yet and I've already broken two rules and a toe.

I take a moment to regroup while my phalanges continue throbbing. And that's when I notice the bar area and the group of scantily clad beautiful people drinking heavily in the morning. It looks like they're filming a high-end tequila commercial or attending a celebrity beach wedding. Different ethnicities are represented, but everyone has the same polished look. I wonder if they all use the same plastic surgeon. Suddenly my old self-consciousness comes flooding back. Maybe I haven't mentally molted my ugly duckling plumage after all.

But even if you weren't teased for your looks for two-thirds of your life, I still think it'd be hard not to be intimidated by these Adonises. Three very muscular, shirtless men and two beautiful women in bikinis are all waiting for me to walk over and introduce myself. This is like that recurring nightmare where I have to relive high school all over again . . . except now on national TV.

I debate turning around and limping back to the mansion when I hear a male voice yell, "What the hell is that?" I turn to see the tall guy who Blue told me is the executive producer, Brett. I've come to learn that he's technically a level higher than Kristina, but he doesn't seem to do any of the work. He and Kristina are marching in my direction.

"What are you wearing?" Kristina asks by way of greeting.

"Is that some sort of religious garment?" Brett asks.

"Uh, it's a one-piece bathing suit," I say, looking down at my black Speedo. "I never get this sort of reaction when I swim laps at the Y."

Brett smacks his forehead, taking this personally. "Can someone get Michael Phelps here a bikini?"

"We don't have any extras," Kristina says, pinching the bridge of her nose. "Please tell me you have another bathing suit in your *one* suitcase, Grace."

"One? One suitcase?!" Brett throws his arms in the air and storms off, leaving Kristina to deal with me.

"This is the only one I brought," I say quietly. Normally, I'm not a shrinking violet, but I'm also not used to being berated, especially while only partially clothed.

Kristina talks into her earpiece. "I need wardrobe down here ASAP. And bring the glasses."

I look back at the bar to find the other contestants staring at me. A woman with brown wavy hair whispers to a guy with a shiny muscular chest wearing a cowboy hat and they both laugh. You know you've hit rock bottom when a cowboy who rubs oil on his pecs is mocking you.

Then a beautiful blond contestant smiles and gives me a sympathy wave. It's a kind gesture, but I doubt that this beach goddess could possibly know what I'm feeling. This woman probably has boats named after her. I give her an awkward wave back as the wardrobe assistant rushes over and hands Kristina a pair of glasses.

Kristina puts the faux glasses on my face and waves in my general direction saying, "Make this better." Before I know it, the wardrobe assistant is taking scissors to my bathing suit and cutting holes in it.

"What the hell—"

"Don't move. Unless you want to lose a nipple," Kristina says, and then points to another spot on my lower back. "Can you make it dip really low here? I want to see ass cleavage."

I'm already a little afraid of Kristina, particularly when she's controlling someone with a sharp instrument, so I don't say anything. After several excruciating moments of watching giant swaths of Lycra fall to the ground, Kristina steps back and nods. "If you don't look too close, it's kind of a sexy peek-a-boo suit now. And the glasses make you look smart."

Before I can scowl and recite my GRE scores, the wardrobe assistant snaps a picture on her phone and shows me. My former bathing suit is now small strips of fabric that are barely hanging onto my body. The sides are completely missing, the straps are thinner, there's a deep V in the front and in the back. This is clearly something I would never wear, but I have to admit, she did a good job of making me look like someone you'd see in Ibiza. Well, in a library in Ibiza. "Um, thanks?" I say, as I push up the glasses and the woman rushes off.

Brett, the EP, who never actually introduced himself to me, walks back over. "That's better. More geek chic, less Mormon Olympian. Let's take it from the top."

Kristina ushers me to my mark, the place where I walked out from a few minutes earlier, while Blue hovers off camera and mouths, *You can do this*. It takes all my stubborn resolve to not cover myself up with a towel and cry. Instead, I picture my mom calling me a beautiful swan and try to mentally siphon some of my brother's confidence as I take a steadying breath. I'm starting to understand why they need to ply people with so much alcohol on these shows.

Then Brett yells, "Action!"

I walk back out and head over to the bar as instructed. This time I somehow manage not to look directly into the camera, swear like a line cook, or break any bones. The blond swimsuit model who had waved at me bounces over, all smiley, and says, "*Ohmigod*, I love your bathing suit! Is it custom-made?" She gives me a conspiratorial wink the camera can't see.

"Yes, I guess it is."

"I'm Madison." She holds out a hand.

I shake it. "Grace. Nice to meet you."

Madison puts her arm around me and guides me over to the rest of the contestants. "Everyone, this is Grace! Doesn't she look awesome?" I can't help giving her a curious glance, but she doesn't seem to notice.

I must be the last one to be introduced because they're all already acting like old friends. But maybe that's just how beautiful people interact, like they're cosmically connected by their DNA or something.

A handsome Asian American guy comes over next and says,

"Hey, Grace, I'm TC. Great to meet you." He has warm brown eyes that sparkle, and I wonder if it's a natural twinkle or some sort of enchanting new contacts. Then he gives me a kind smile and goes for a hug as I awkwardly offer him a handshake. I want to tell him, *I'm not a member of your beautiful people club. We're not on hugging terms yet.*

But before I can establish my boundaries, an energetic guy with shoulder-length, curly brown hair comes over, scoops me up, and spins me around. "Grace!"

"Who are you?" I manage to squeak out from the air.

"Javier, your future boyfriend." He sets me down and gives me a once-over. "I love your glasses."

"They're fake."

"All the better to see me with," he says with so much cheesy machismo, I can't help but laugh. He gives me two thumbs-ups, and somehow, because he's so confident and seemingly not afraid to come off as a little goofy, it works for him. I laugh again, surprising myself. I can't remember the last time a guy made me laugh.

Then, one by one, all the shampoo commercial models come over and introduce themselves. Their collective beauty is overwhelming, and I now understand why Shantae needs mnemonic devices. Name tags would be helpful, but I can't imagine they'd stick to oiled-up bodies.

I learn that the brunette with the wavy hair who was whispering about me is Beth Anne, and that if you call her Beth she'll correct you and say, "it's Beth *Anne*." She has a Southern accent, which confuses me, because it seems like she should be sweet and hospitable but instead she's a total nightmare. She's said, "Bless your heart," three times already, and everyone who's ever visited Georgia knows that really means "Fuck you."

The shiny cowboy who was laughing with her is Bill, and he's from Texas. He tells me how much he can bench-press, so needless to say, I have zero interest in ever speaking to him again.

And it turns out that the smiley blond swimsuit model, Madison, is an actual swimsuit model. The overly touchy but charming Javier is in hospitality, which he self-deprecatingly explains means starving actor who waits tables. And TC, the handsome guy with twinkling eyes, is a musician, and he's offered to give me free piano lessons.

I use my own memorization trick that helped me in grad school, but instead of classifying by species and genus, I make a mental chart of what they look like and what they do for a living:

> Madison: Smiley Blonde—literally a swimsuit model
> Beth Anne: Bitchy Brunette—in marketing or PR (is there a difference?)
> TC: Kind Eyes—musician and wedding DJ by night
> Javier: Curly Hair—wants to be an actor, currently a very flirty waiter
> Bill: Shiny Chest—cowboy who works in Big Oil, obviously

After the introductions, they all make their way back to the pool bar to order liquid lunch. I think that's the real reason why they don't let us have phones: If we can't check what time it is, it's always happy hour. But I need a break from forced small talk for a bit, so I get myself a sparkling water and sit at one of the bistro tables by the pool. When I look at everyone I've just met, I can't help but think Cassie would have a field day here. I mean, she'd be too shy to talk to anyone, but she loves her "eye candy." Her words, not mine. Obviously.

The other contestants aren't just attractive—they also all exude some sort of magnetic confidence that's making me a little light-headed. Beth Anne is flirting with Texas Bill, and even from across the patio, the sexual tension is so palpable that I almost feel indecent watching them. It reminds me of the pheromone-driven mating rituals of silk moths. Beth Anne must be secreting some strong ecto-hormones.

And then I laugh at myself, because I'm clearly the only one here comparing Beth Anne to a silk moth. As if the cut-up bathing suit isn't evidence enough, I obviously don't fit in here. Just like at a Lambert Family Dinner, I feel much more comfortable sitting off to the side, quietly observing.

As I start to spiral, certain that I'm completely unprepared and won't last a day on this show, I notice someone walk onto the patio. And it just so happens to be the perfect person to take my feelings out on.

Chapter Ten

Now that I've met the actual contestants, it makes sense that Andrew Benson isn't one. While, annoyingly, he's tall enough and handsome enough to be on the show, the dead giveaway is that he's in a suit and tie and we're all clad in toddler-sized swimwear. Which reminds me—I'm currently wearing an arts-and-crafts project. I stand and wrap a towel around myself as he strides toward me.

"I didn't get to introduce myself properly earlier," he says. "I'm Andrew Benson, the studio lawyer. Not a *contestant*." He says "contestant" like it's contagious.

"I'm glad we cleared that up. That must've been embarrassing for you." Before he can respond, I continue. "Now that I know you're the uptight lawyer from the emails and not a failed dating show contestant, I have some concerns I'd like to bring up." At this, he raises his eyebrows and looks around, as if someone is going to come rescue him from this conversation. I plow on. "Despite what you may think, I did read the contract you sent. And nowhere does it state that I'd have to 'hook up' with someone."

He's staring at me as if he's never heard anyone speak English before. "Physical intimacy isn't required. No one is *forcing* you to do anything," Andrew says, as if that should be a given.

"You mean, other than wearing a more revealing bathing suit?" *Ha. One point for me.*

His eyes flick down to my towel, but he doesn't admit that I'm right. He just crosses his arms and looks back up at me. I narrow my eyes at him. I've seen *Law and Order*—he's not going to *lawyer* me. So I keep going. "Shantae told me that you get points by doing sexy challenges where I'm assuming physical contact will be required. I was also told that if I don't get points, I'll end up in the murder shack—"

"There's zero evidence that murders have occurred in the shack."

He says it so automatically that I assume it's a company line, but his brown eyes now have a hint of mischief. Wait, is *he* messing with *me*?

"I'm glad you find unsafe living conditions so amusing." I cross my arms to match him.

He shakes his head and opens his mouth to argue, as if he would take issue with the word "unsafe," but then appears to rein himself in. He stands up a little straighter, arms still crossed. "Sadly, this is all moot seeing as how you've signed a legally binding contract. Maybe instead of sending snarky emails, you should've asked more questions."

The nerve of this guy! Before I can react emotionally and insult his perfect suit, I calmly say, "I would've thought that, as a lawyer, you'd have been clear with me about what kind of show you're representing. *Respectfully.*"

His arms drop as if I've struck a nerve, the twinkle in his eyes gone. "And I would've thought that, as a scientist, you'd have researched what kind of show this is before agreeing to be on it. *Respectfully.*"

I flush. He's got me there. Normally, I *never* would've signed up for something without researching the hell out of it first, but I wasn't really given the chance, was I?

We're staring each other down, both of us seething, when the beautiful blond swimsuit model, Madison, walks over, calling my name. When she sees us, she stops. "Oh, sorry. I hope I'm not interrupting."

Andrew says to her kindly, without taking his eyes off of me, "No, it's fine. We're done here." Then he has the audacity to give me a polite smile, which just annoys me more.

"For now," I say with an even politer smile.

Something that looks like challenge flares in his eyes. But as if he remembers he's at work, he takes a breath and composes himself. "Unfortunately, Ms. Lambert, I know you have my email address. So, if you have any further concerns, please put them in writing." Then he dismisses me, turning to Madison. "Good to see you, Madison. Have a nice day." Without looking back at me, he walks off.

I clench my fists and want to scream. How has this lawyer gotten under my skin so quickly?

"Everything okay?" Madison asks gently.

"No." I unclench my fists and sit back down at the bistro table. "I find those kind of guys insufferable. And that one is especially infuriating."

"What kind of guys?" Madison asks as she sits down across from me. "Tall, handsome lawyers?"

"Men who think they know everything and have to prove it by constantly trying to one-up you." As I say this, I look across the patio to where Andrew is standing with Kristina. "And then they're so smug about it." He glances over at me and catches me looking at him. I give him a dirty look that only seems to make him smugger. Ugh!

Madison cocks her head. "I haven't gotten that impression of him, but I've also never seen him lose his cool like that before. He seems so professional around everyone else."

"Oh great. It's just me who pisses him off." I shoot him another glare, and Madison quickly changes the subject in an attempt to prevent me from murdering Andrew with my eyes.

"I know they're fake," Madison says, "but you look great in those glasses. They look super-cute with your bangs."

"Oh. Thanks," I say, caught off guard by her sincere-sounding compliment. "I like that your bathing suit hasn't been chopped up."

"Thanks, I try." Then she gives me a dazzlingly bright smile. And it doesn't blind me. Instead, it helps some of my tension float away.

I look back at the bar area. "So this is it then? My mom made it seem like there'd be more people."

"Your mom?"

I nod, lowering my voice. "She signed me up without my knowledge. I've never even seen the show."

Madison gasps, but quickly recovers so as to not offend me. "Well, I'm glad you're here. And she's right. There will be more people soon. They randomly introduce new contestants to change up the dynamics. Once couples form connections, the producers will bring in a new contender who will tempt them the most."

"They have even hotter people waiting in the wings?"

Madison laughs. "Yep, it's pretty savage."

I picture Kristina and her cronies moving pictures of us around like pieces on a chessboard, making couples and then breaking them up for maximum drama.

"Speak of the devil . . ." I mutter as I see Kristina striding toward our group. She motions for the cameras to stop rolling.

"We've got the introductions," Kristina announces without fanfare. "We're moving on to Shantae's opening. Get yourselves settled in the cabana and make sure you cheer for her when she makes her entrance. I want to see a lot of excitement and engagement." Kristina makes eye contact with each of us in a silent threat that if we don't do what she says, there will be consequences. Damn, she really is intimidating.

Everyone else must agree, because we all hustle over to where Kristina ordered. The cameras start rolling when we sit on the white lounge furniture underneath the blue-and-white-striped cabana that I'm sure was focus-grouped to ensure maximum viewership.

When Shantae struts in, looking every bit the part of Wannabe Model Turned Reality TV Host with her glossy red lips and perfect shiny hair, I half expect her to somehow acknowledge that we already met in the hair and makeup trailer. But nope. Her eyes sweep blankly over all of us until she turns on the charm for the cameras.

"Hello, everyone, and welcome to *Love Shack*!" We all dutifully clap and cheer. "Look at all of these beautiful people!" Shantae fans herself. "Damn, you're showing more skin than a dermatologist's office."

I raise my eyebrows at Madison and whisper, "They hired a comedian for that?" She snickers but quickly covers to make it seem like she's laughing at Shantae's lame joke. I try to follow suit, but pity laughing is not a special skill on my résumé.

Next, Shantae explains the rules to the viewers—and me, I assume, because everyone else already seems to know what they signed up for. "The goal of the show is to form meaningful love connections. We'll help you along by organizing sexy challenges to get you up close and personal, as well as romantic one-on-one dates. You'll earn points for the challenges you complete and the successful matches you make on your dates. Those who are putting themselves out there the most and are on the top of the leaderboard get to stay in the luxurious mansion. But those of you who find yourself at the bottom . . . sorry, it's the Love Shack for you!"

All the other contestants groan fittingly. Oops, I missed the cue for that one. I also notice they're all sitting in sexy poses while I'm still not sure what to do with my arms. Crossed? Draped on my legs? Certainly not above my head. Was there some sort of sitting training I missed?

I look over to see Beth Anne mugging for the cameras. I'm about to roll my eyes but then remember that I might be on camera too. It's disturbing to know you're constantly being watched. What if I have food stuck in my teeth? Oh God, I hope there aren't cameras in the bathrooms.

I'm roused from my worrying when I hear Shantae say, "And don't forget, if you're not in a couple or showing adequate effort to make a love connection, you'll be voted off the show."

A wave of panic washes over me, bringing with it an even bigger worry. While I may not want to be here, I have to be. Did my coworkers know I could get voted off for not making an immediate love connection? Something I've never accomplished in my life! I feel like I'm being set up to fail. On national TV. And the stakes are my life's work. I take deep breaths to calm my anxiety-nausea and try to focus on the task at hand.

Shantae interrupts my spiraling by announcing, "And now let's break the ice a little with a round of Suck and Blow."

This must be something everyone else is familiar with because an excited tittering makes its way around the contestants. Shantae hands a playing card to TC, and he puts it to his lips. It stays there because he's sucking in. Then he leans in toward Madison, and their lips touch with the card in between them. I watch Madison inhale deeply, then turn away. The card has been transferred to her lips.

As I'm calculating the amount of aspiration needed to keep the card in place, I realize in horror that the game will eventually make its way to me. Madison passes the card to Bill, who then passes it to Beth Anne. I'm starting to sweat. I know it's not a real kiss, but I haven't been intimate with anyone in years. Plus, think about all the germs on that card—people severely underestimate how debilitating a summer cold can be!

Then Shantae's warning about getting voted off replays loudly in my head. I can't mess up the first thing out of the gate. Surely I can suck and blow, or at least "show adequate effort." Before I can overthink, Javier turns toward me with the card on his lips. I take a deep breath like I saw Madison do and lean in. But as my lips make contact with the card, it falls and Javier's lips crash into mine. It takes me a minute to realize we're kissing. When I pull back sputtering for air, the other contestants are cheering, and Madison looks at me like a proud mother hen.

"Sorry, bella! When I see an opportunity, I have to go for it," Javier says with a devilish grin. I want to be pissed at him, and if it had been Cowboy Bill who pulled that little stunt, I would've broken his nose. But Javier seems impossible to stay mad at, and despite being taken by surprise and almost asphyxiated by him, it wasn't a bad kiss. I don't have time to process anything else because Shantae is "oohing" loudly.

She addresses the camera: "Things are already heating up here on *Love Shack!*" Which I take to mean I passed the first test. Then she turns back to us. "Contestants, you have some time before your first one-on-one dates, so you can hang by the pool and get to know each other. Have fun, make connections, and I'll see you later."

The second Shantae struts off and the cameras stop rolling, Javier pulls me aside. "I'm sorry, Grace. I just got caught up in my role."

"It was certainly a surpri— Wait, what do you mean by 'role'?"

"You know, how Kristina gives us all a character to play. Before the icebreaker, she told me I had to lean into my 'Latin Lover' role more."

"What? She said that? Isn't that stereotyping?"

Javier shrugs. "Yep. But I'm an actor. I'm used to being cast because I tick a box. Especially on reality TV."

My heart breaks at the resignation in his voice. "Well, I'm not used to it, and I'm pissed on your behalf!"

Javier laughs. "I'm sure I'll never live it down with my family after it airs, but if it means getting to kiss you, I'll let Kristina objectify me any day." He gives me a playful wink.

"You're a shameless flirt," I chide half-heartedly.

"Is it working?" he asks with a roguish grin.

I smile back, because it is kind of working. But then I shake my head. "Hey, stop trying to distract me from injustice. I'm going to talk to Kristina." Javier starts to shake his head, so I quickly add, "I won't tell her you told me, and it's not just about you. Trust me, I have bigger issues with this show. If I ran my lab like this, we would've been shut down years ago!"

Javier smiles and covers his heart. "Thank you for defending my honor . . . even after I sucked your face off." I laugh and give him a gallant bow as I walk off to find Kristina. Yes, she's intimidating as hell, but I also can't stand by while she makes Javier feel marginalized.

I wait until she's done bossing around a PA. When we're alone, she addresses me as she jots down a note, "Yeah?"

She's not even looking at me when I answer, "You can't just make Javier into a token caricature for your show."

When Kristina finally glances up at me, her expression is pitying. "That's how reality TV works, Grace. Everyone has a role to play. It's not just Javier."

She consults her clipboard. "TC is our 'Sensitive Musician,' Beth Anne has the 'Bitchy Southern Belle' down pat, Bill is the 'Good Ol' Boy,' Madison is our 'Sweet Girl Next Door,' and you're the 'Nerdy Fish Out of Water,' which you're crushing by the way. It's the conflicting personalities that make it a good show. Which gives us high ratings, which attracts advertising revenue, which is how we can provide prize money at the end."

I'm shocked that she not only admits to assigning us stereotypes—like we're archetypes in a classic literature lecture and not actual human beings—but also makes me feel bad about questioning it. Damn, she's good.

She doesn't wait for me to object. She just chirps, "Great chat. Thanks for the feedback." Then she walks away. I stand there in shock. Is this how cutthroat all of Hollywood is?

I'm finally distracted by the grumbling of my stomach. I realize I haven't eaten in hours, so the only thing I'm filled with is a healthy heaping of regret and a side order of desire to disown my friends for coercing me into this nonsense.

Chapter Eleven

Since we seem to have some free time, I tie my towel around my waist and head over to the outdoor kitchen area to find the lunch buffet. There are carnitas tacos, tuna salad, and turkey sandwiches. So, nothing I can eat. As I look for some garnish to chew on, Blue comes over to check on me. "Hey, Grace. Looking for anything in particular?"

"I'm vegan," I say, gesturing to all the meat on display. "Do you have any vegetables?"

"Oh shoot! No one told me. Um, I think I saw carrot sticks. And we have some nuts. Is that vegan? Oh, and cantaloupe."

"Aww, the filler fruit." I smile at Blue playfully.

"The carnation of melons," a deep voice says to my left. I'm amused by the metaphor until I turn to see the voice belongs to Andrew Benson, Esquire. My amusement immediately turns to vexation. He may have won the upper hand in our previous exchange, but I refuse to let him ruffle my feathers. I school my expression into neutrally pleasant and give him a bland "Hello, Mr. Benson."

He raises an eyebrow at my formal tone and nods as if he too can play this game. "Hello, Ms. Lambert. Kristina tells me you've only filmed one segment and you're already stirring the pot."

"If that pot contains racial stereotyping, then yes, I'm happily stirring it. Does this mean you're complicit?" I ask as cheerily as if I were offering him a ride to the airport.

He looks exasperated, and I smile, mentally giving myself a

point for riling him up first. "Everyone knows what they signed up for here," Andrew says. "This is *reality television*."

"Not everyone," I say pointedly. "And just because it's the way things are always done, it doesn't mean it's right."

Andrew squeezes the bridge of his nose and asks, "Are you going to be a problem all season, Ms. Lambert?"

"Most likely, Mr. Benson. Especially if I'm going to be hangry all the time," I say, gesturing to the meaty buffet. Andrew furrows his brows.

"She's vegan and there's nothing for her to eat," Blue explains from behind me. I realize he's been standing there witnessing our bickering.

"Here," Andrew mutters, taking a granola bar out of his leather messenger bag.

"What a gentleman," Blue coos, elbowing me because I'm still scowling.

Andrew narrows his eyes at me and says, "I just don't want her causing me unnecessary paperwork."

I take the bar from him with a begrudging "thank you" as Andrew calls to the chef, "Hey, Marv, can you please make sure we have vegan options available at all meals?"

The chef gives him a thumbs-up, and when Andrew turns back to me, I tilt my head. Was he just being . . . nice to me? He must guess what I'm thinking because he quickly says, "I really hate paperwork."

I take a bite of the granola bar and shrug. "Free granola bar. At least I'm getting *something* out of this experience."

Andrew shakes his head at me. "There are thousands of people who wish they had gotten this opportunity."

"But what? They all had herpes?"

Before Andrew can respond, Blue gives him an imploring look. They seem to have an unspoken conversation before Andrew sighs and gives him a nod. Then Blue looks around to make sure there aren't any cameras pointed at us and covers the microphone on my necklace before whispering, "You should probably start acting like you want to be here. Otherwise, they'll say you aren't here for the *right reasons*." This is the big secret he needed Andrew's permission to reveal?

"What are the *right reasons* for someone with two PhDs to prance around in a cut-up bathing suit on national TV?" I ask earnestly, because I sure as hell don't have a clue.

"To fall in love, of course!" Blue says dramatically.

I burst out laughing. Blue and Andrew don't join me. "Oh wait, you were serious? People actually think they'll find love on a TV show?"

"Or they're here to get famous," Andrew says pointedly, and I scoff.

"I have zero interest in fame."

"That's surprising. I thought it was the family business," he says, his brown eyes boring into mine.

I have the sudden urge to punch him in his stupid chiseled jaw. "I'm nothing like my family," I grind out. But even as I say it, it feels harsh coming out of my mouth. Why should I care what this guy thinks anyway? "You know nothing about me or my family," I say.

Blue quickly steps in because he knows this is going south fast. "Grace has never seen a reality show," he explains to Andrew.

Hands on my hips, I take them both in. Blue looks concerned, like he genuinely wants to help me. But Andrew just studies me as if I'm a puzzle that he's going to crack. Blue turns to me and whispers, "You have to at least pretend to play the game, Grace, or they'll eat you alive."

"Who is 'they'?" I ask.

"The producers, the other contestants, the viewers—" Blue begins, but Andrew cuts him off.

"If you're not here to fall in love or get famous, then why *are* you here?" And surprisingly, it doesn't sound judgy this time but curious, like he actually wants to figure me out.

I'm tempted to tell him about my lost funding so he'll understand that I'm not someone who willingly goes on reality shows, but

I keep my mouth shut. If the "right reason" for being on the show is to find love, then could I get kicked off for being here for the "wrong reason"? I shrug and tell a partial truth: "My mom signed me up."

Andrew purses his dumb full lips as if he doesn't believe this is the whole story.

"Look," Blue says, tearing my attention away from Andrew's lips. "I don't know the real reason why you're on this show, and it doesn't really matter to me, but if America doesn't love you or love to hate you, you won't last long."

Shit. He's right. Now that I know I can get voted off, I need all the help I can get. So I ignore the annoying lawyer beside me, swallow my pride, and ask Blue, "How do I get America to like me?"

"Just be yourself," Blue says reassuringly.

Andrew snorts. I glare at him while Blue continues: "The audience will like that you're different. You're the Underdog."

"I thought I was the 'Nerdy Fish Out of Water.'"

"You are also that." Blue nods. "Which is why people will want to root for you. You're a long shot, and America loves a long shot."

I groan. "This is way more complicated than I thought. You've got to be an anthropologist to survive around here."

"Or a drunk influencer," Blue says with a shrug.

"But as you like to remind us," Andrew says, "you have two PhDs, so if they can do it, surely so can you."

"I know you're mocking me, but you're right. I've done much harder things than be a contestant on a reality show." And now part of me wants to win this damn thing just to prove it to him and wipe that permanent smugness off his face. So I stand up straight, roll my shoulders back, and hope the determination in my eyes outmatches the goading in his. "If you'll excuse me, I'm going to go try to *find love*." And with that I march toward the pool area.

Chapter Twelve

Even though the contestants now have "down time," the cameras are still rolling. I decide that, if I have any hope of winning over America and competing with the drunk influencers, I need to take Shantae's advice and "put myself out there." And since I'm still wearing the tattered remains of my Speedo, I'm putting quite a bit of myself out there. I discreetly tuck my boobs back in and walk over to where Javier and TC are lifting weights.

There are glistening muscles as far as the eye can see. Unfortunately, I'm incapable of appreciating them because I'm having PTSD flashbacks to high school, when I used to avoid the cool jocks in gym class. At the time it wasn't hard. I was so far off their radar that I was the teenage equivalent of a stealth fighter jet. I shake off the trauma of adolescence and remind myself that I'm a *grown-up* now, a *respected grown-up* with a team of scientists working under me.

As I get closer to the outdoor gym, I hear them discussing their favorite whey powders and protein shakes. I rack my brain for something to talk to them about. I could explain how the peptides in proteins are broken down by the hydrochloric acid and proteases in the human stomach, but even I suspect that's not a great pickup line. And the only thing I know about weights is that they seem heavy, so I don't lift them.

Maybe I'll see what the other contestants are doing and check back with these two later. I give the guys a wave and keep walking.

Madison is doing yoga by the side of the pool in a matching hot pink sports bra and yoga pants set. Her downward dog looks like it could be on the cover of *I'm Bendy and Perfect* magazine, whereas I once pulled a muscle sneezing. So probably best to move along. Which leaves me with Mean Girl Beth Anne and oily Cowboy Bill.

They're drinking at the bar, and Beth Anne is touching Bill's bicep. As I get closer, I hear Beth Anne say, "Yeah, that's why I want ass implants." I immediately try to veer off before they see me, but Beth Anne notices me and calls out, "Grace! Come here!" *Fuuuck*.

"Oh, hey, guys," I say, pretending I wasn't trying to avoid them like the plague.

"You can settle a debate for us," she says. "What do you think of Bill's calves?"

I look down at Bill's legs, not sure what I'm supposed to be looking for. "Um, there's not too much leg hair, but also not too bare, so I would say they're optimally hairy?"

Beth Anne laughs like I'm an idiot. "No. Do you think he needs implants?"

"In his calves?!" I ask in shock. "People really do that?"

"Yeah," Bill says. "A bunch of guys at my gym got it done."

"But doesn't that defeat the purpose of going to the gym?" I ask.

"I told him he has sexy calves and doesn't need it," Beth Anne says as she snuggles closer to Bill.

"Yeah, I definitely wouldn't inject anything into your legs, Bill. I don't think women care about that kind of thing."

"You'd be surprised," Bill says, and Beth Anne nods.

"What about you, Grace?" Beth Anne asks in a way that makes me picture a boa constrictor slowly circling a small mammal before squeezing it to death.

"What about me?"

"Have you considered getting filler for your crow's feet?" And there it is. I knew it was a trap, and yet I waddled into her clutches.

"Pleasure as always, *Beth*," I say, purposely trying to piss her off as I walk away.

"It's Beth *Anne*!" she calls after me.

Well, I tried socializing, and now I'm exhausted. I plop down on a chaise lounge and take the fantasy novel out of my tote bag that Blue ran back to my room to get for me. It's not my fault he assumed I was talking about medication when I said I needed my "emergency supplies."

I get less than a chapter in when I see Kristina rushing toward me. When she's not striding self-importantly, she's rushing. And to be fair, her stride is still pretty high-speed. "How'd you sneak contraband in here?"

I look around to see what she could possibly be talking about. "It's physically impossible to hide drugs or weapons in this bathing suit. I can barely hide my private parts."

Kristina points at my book. "No books, phones, electronics, or contact with the outside world. Didn't you read the paperwork?"

I sigh. "I can't go a week without reading. My brain is already atrophying in here."

"You're not here to catch up on your reading list. You're here to meet people. Go mingle."

"I tried. Beth Anne told me I needed plastic surgery."

"Oooh, I hope the cameras got that. She's such a bitch, I love it." Then Kristina grabs my book. "Go."

I angrily get up and storm off. "I can't believe you've banned books! What is this, Texas?"

"Woo! Texas!" Bill says from his spot at the bar.

I roll my eyes, then walk over to Madison and plop down next to her in the grass. "Hey, sorry for bothering you, but Kristina told me I have to mingle."

"You're not bothering me. I have an extra mat if you want to join me!" she says, looking at me upside down.

"I'm good. I'll just sit here and try to touch my toes."

Madison does some crazy contortionist move where she balances on one leg and puts her other leg over her shoulder. "Can I ask you something I've been wondering, Grace?" she casually asks, as if she weren't currently starring in Cirque du Soleil.

"Sure," I say, giving up on stretching altogether and sprawling out in the grass.

"I guess I'm just surprised you're on the show. You're so beautiful and smart and successful. It doesn't seem like you would have any trouble meeting guys."

I snort in disbelief that Malibu Barbie is asking me this. "Me?! How about you? You're so gorgeous and smiley and flexible."

She takes her leg off her shoulder and sits down next to me like we're old friends. "That is so kind of you." She sighs. "I don't know about you, but I can never seem to meet the right kind of guys. Like actual, serious ones." I give her a nod, surprised I have that in common with her.

"I'm going back to school for a master's in psychology," she continues. "So I bartend and model to help pay for it. But the guys I meet at the bar or on photo shoots . . . well, let's just say, they don't seem to be interested in *relationships*."

"You're getting a master's in psychology?"

Madison laughs. "You say that like you're surprised."

I wince, realizing I'm being rude. "I may have underestimated you because you're so pretty and wearing pink."

Madison laughs again. "You can't wear pink in grad school?"

I shrug, and before I can say anything else offensive about her clothing choices, I change the subject. "Why psychology?"

Madison's face lights up. "I started a nonprofit two years ago and realized my true passion is helping others. Now I want to make it official."

"That's really admirable. What's your nonprofit?"

"It's a mental health website for kids and teens to give them resources and community support to help with bullying and depression.

I partnered with a few teen centers around San Diego, and we run programs from there as well."

Holy shit.

She must read the expression on my face because she smiles like she's on to me. "It's okay, most people assume, because I bartend, I'm a party girl."

"I'm sorry I made assumptions before I knew you," I say sincerely.

"Are you still talking about wearing pink?" Madison teases.

"No. You're like actually nice. It's not just an act."

"Oh God, I would never. Wait, what made you think I was acting? Did I do something to upset you?" Madison asks with concern.

"No," I say quickly. "I thought you were being fake for the show. I'm sorry, it's nothing personal. I just assumed that was what everyone did on reality TV."

But the look on her face says that she might be taking it personally. Not only did I judge her unfairly, but I'm also upsetting her. *Shit.* I feel horrible. It must be guilt that drives me to do something I *never* do . . . talk about my feelings.

"It's just that, in the past, the pretty, popular girls didn't want to hang out with me," I begin awkwardly. "I was a bit of an outcast." I laugh at myself. "Pretty much straight through grad school." I take a deep breath. Damn, this is harder to talk about than I thought.

"You actually remind me of this girl from high school," I say. "You look a lot like her." I look up at Madison and continue. "I thought she was my friend. She was always nice to me in our honors classes, but the minute the bell rang she'd ignore me, like she was embarrassed to be seen with me." I can feel my cheeks warming.

But when I look back at Madison, she's not judging me. She just nods and kindly says, "Thank you for sharing that with me. It must've been hard feeling like you didn't fit in."

I feel some of the tension leave my body. Damn, she's going to be a great psychologist one day.

Then, with a sweet smile, Madison adds, "I think there's a special place in hell for mean girls." I laugh at her unexpected turn, but she shrugs and continues: "Life, especially in high school, is so difficult as it is. We should be lifting each other up, not making things worse. That's part of what I'm trying to achieve with my nonprofit. Helping people realize we're all going through shit and if we take a moment to understand our differences, we could be more supportive of each other." Then she gives me a meaningful smile and says, "I was bullied as a kid too."

"You were?" I'm simultaneously stunned and outraged.

"We didn't have a lot of money growing up. And it didn't matter how nice I was or smart I was. There were always kids who singled me out for being the poor kid. They used to pick on me for getting free lunch at school and only having one pair of sneakers, stuff like that."

"Wow. I've never wanted to kick a bunch of teenagers' asses I've never met before."

She laughs. "It's okay, I've processed it. When I could finally afford therapy." Then Madison looks around a bit, covers the mic on her necklace, and whispers, "To be honest, my nonprofit is the real reason why I'm on the show. The more publicity and followers I get, the more people I can help."

Maybe Madison and I are more alike than I thought. "Your secret is safe with me," I whisper back. Then I debate letting her in on my own secret motivation. She trusted me enough to share with me, but I'm still worried that I could get kicked off if anyone found out that I'm using the show to make up for my lost funding.

Madison covers my hand and says sincerely, "Thanks for listening, Grace." And in that moment, I decide to open up to her.

I cover my mic and tell her all about the endangered southern mountain yellow-legged frogs and why *I'm* really on the show. Madison continues to impress me by asking all sorts of follow-up questions before saying, "I want to help! I'll post your fundraiser to my socials.

I feel like we have a crossover audience—people who are caring and want to help the world."

I'm so touched by this. "I would love that. Thank you. And once I have enough followers, I'll be happy to return the favor." Then a funny thought crosses my mind. "Huh. I don't think I ever considered social media could actually have a positive effect on society."

"That's a big part of what I do. Counteract cyber-bullying with cyber-positivity." Then she looks at me with a hint of a challenge in her eyes. "If Kristina hadn't made you come talk to me, would you have come over on your own?"

I think about it for a moment. "No. Probably not."

"Why not?"

I shrug sheepishly. "Maybe because I didn't think we'd have anything in common?"

"Or maybe you still feel like you don't fit in," Madison says gently. "But you're funny and smart and easy to talk to, and anybody would be lucky to be your friend, Grace. I think you just have to be willing to put in the effort too."

Well, damn. Kristina has Madison all wrong. She's not the "girl next door," she's a freaking sage. I give her an appreciative smile. "Thank you." Then I admit, "I've been told I can be a little antisocial. But you're helping me realize that maybe it's something I should work on."

Madison is about to respond when we hear, "Hey, girls!" Kristina stride-rushes over toward us, with Brett and a camera operator trailing closely behind. "What are you whispering about over here?"

Madison says, "Boys," at the same time I say, "Books." Madison quickly covers for us by saying, "Bill looks like he belongs on the cover of a romance novel."

"Ooh, that's a good sound bite. Make sure you say that in your confessional." Kristina nods to Madison. Then she turns to Brett, who looks annoyed that he left the air-conditioned control room for this. "Let's get the pickup shot Brett wants. Grace, you walk over and ask Madison why she's on the show." I shoot Madison a panicked look, but she gives me an encouraging nod.

I nervously get up, walk a few steps away, and then come over and plop back down next to Madison's yoga mat. I've never been a good actor. Granted, I've never tried. But since this was literally the same conversation we were just having, I think I can handle it.

"Can I ask you something I've been wondering, Madison?"

"Sure, Grace."

"Why did you come on the show?"

"To find love, of course!" Madison gushes. "How about you?"

"The same. Of course," I say stiffly. Everyone pauses.

"Okay, let's take it from the top," Kristina says with annoyance. "This time, Grace, try to make it sound more natural. No one finds robots sexy." Brett shrugs in disagreement.

"Ew," Kristina says, shaking her head at him. Then she turns to me. "Let's go again. And try to nail it in one shot. We have to get you camera-ready for your first one-on-one date. You better have an outfit in your suitcase that doesn't look like something a self-conscious eighth-grader would wear in gym class."

I laugh at the specificity of her burn, but neither she nor Brett look amused. "I thought I was supposed to be the Nerdy Fish Out of Water," I say with a shrug.

"The *hot* Nerdy Fish Out of Water," Kristina says. "We don't want people changing the channel."

Before that diss can sink in, Madison comes to my rescue. "Don't worry. I'm sure Grace has the perfect dress. It might even be pink." She winks at me.

I smile back at her. And for the first time in a long time, it feels like I've made a new friend. Or at the very least, a co-conspirator.

Chapter Thirteen

After five takes of the same excruciating conversation with Madison about how desperate we are to meet the loves of our lives, Blue comes to escort me back to my room to change for our first one-on-one dates. I'm relieved to finally be able to take off my chopped-up bathing suit.

I look down at it while we walk back to the mansion. "Think I can return this to Speedo for a new one?"

Blue shrugs. "Just tell 'em it was a shark attack."

I shake my head. "I'd feel too bad."

"About lying?"

"No. About perpetuating the myth that sharks are indiscriminately aggressive."

Blue just laughs at me and says fondly, "I'll see you after you change, weirdo."

When I walk into my room, I flop down on the big canopy bed. I wish I could curl up under the covers for the rest of the week. I feel as emotionally and physically drained as I did working on my first dissertation. Between navigating unfamiliar territory, meeting all these different personalities, and trying to one-up an annoying lawyer, I'm so far out of my comfort zone that my body is telling me it's time to hibernate until it's safe. Most people have a fight-or-flight response; I have a very strong nap response.

I use all the energy that Andrew's peanut butter Clif bar afforded me to push myself off the bed and look for an outfit in my suitcase. As I rustle through my new clothes, my fingers hit some-thing hard. I pull out an old-school iPhone I've never seen before. On the back is a Post-it with a phone number. *WTF?!* Is this part of the show? I look around my room for hidden cameras but don't see any. They took my cell away when I got here, and Kristina said I'm not supposed to have a phone, so is this some sort of a test? Curiosity gets the better of me and I dial the number.

"Hello?" a familiar voice says.

"Cassie?!"

"Oh yay, you found it!" my best friend says, like this is a totally normal conversation.

"You packed me a contraband phone?"

"The paperwork you signed said no contact with the outside world, but I figured you'd need some emotional support, so I stashed a burner phone in one of your shoes. Well, it's just my old phone. I'm glad they didn't confiscate it!"

"Wow. I'm impressed. I feel like an international woman of mystery," I whisper into the phone.

Cassie laughs. "I wouldn't go that far."

"This almost makes up for you, Eliza, and Alec gaslighting me. *'It's reality TV. How hard could it be?'*" I say mockingly. "Don't get me wrong, I'm still plotting my revenge, but the phone bought you some time."

"Is it really that bad?" Cassie asks, and I can hear the guilt in her voice. "I'm so sorry, Grace! We were desperate, and I knew if I told you all the details about the show you wouldn't do it. Do you hate me?"

"No," I sigh. "I mean, yes. It is that bad. Worse than bad. But I don't hate you. I definitely would've said no if I knew what I was get-ting myself into." I sit on the edge of the bed and squeeze the burner phone, grateful for the lifeline to the real world. "Cassie, this is se-riously some sort of fucked-up psychological experiment. Kristina, that Machiavellian producer, treats us like we're all just characters in her play. She lives to stir up drama and doesn't seem to care that we're actually sentient beings. And this one contestant, Beth Anne, somehow manages to be super-bitchy while sounding super-sweet. It's very confusing. And do you know how hard it is to not look at the camera when they tell you, 'Don't look at the camera'?"

"Are there any hot guys at least?" Cassie asks hopefully.

"Yeah, they're all hot. *Everyone* here is attractive—the producers, the PAs, the lawyer, even the camera operators who will never be on TV."

"Eye candy!" she squeals.

"I knew you'd say that," I say, shaking my head. "But they're not fun to look at, they're so good looking, it's unnerving."

"Wait, did you say 'lawyer'? What happened to Old Man Benson?"

"Yeah . . . it turns out that 'Old Man Benson' is actually 'Our Age Andrew,' and he's somehow even more aggravating in person."

"But he's attractive?"

I immediately picture the way his eyes burn when we're sparring. And how his voice gets even deeper and rougher when I'm pissing him off. And how that damn suit fits him so perfectly. "He's okay."

Cassie is quiet for a moment before she asks, "What does he look like?"

"Andrew? Why?"

"Just curious."

"Well, he's the opposite of how you'd picture a guy that makes you sign that much paperwork."

"Not your cousin's father-in-law?"

"Definitely not. He has dark hair and brown eyes and the annoyingly right amount of facial hair. You know when it's a little past stubble? And when he's not reprimanding me, he has this smug grin that you want to slap off his face."

Her only response to this is, "Ooohh."

"No. Not 'ooohh,' more like 'ewww.' He's the worst. It's like he woke up one day and realized he has a soul-sucking job working for corporate overlords and is taking it out on me. Seriously, I've seen him with the other contestants. He's perfectly nice. Almost charming even. Yet he saves his spite just for me."

"Hmmm," Cassie says.

"What?" I demand.

"Nothing." She drops it. "Are any of the contestants nice?"

I let her abrupt subject change slide because frankly, I've already spent too much time thinking about Andrew Benson. I flop back on the bed and tell her about Madison. "This one girl is really sweet and not at all what I expected. She made me feel better when they cut up my bathing suit—"

"They did what?"

"They cut up my Speedo to make it more revealing!"

"But that's what you wear to swim laps at the Y!" Cassie exclaims.

"I know!"

"Ugh. I'm sorry. That sounds horrible. But at least your pic looks amazing on the show's website! #sexyscientist is already trending."

"That sentence is all my recurring nightmares in one."

Cassie laughs, but then switches into what I know is her pep talk voice. "This is going to work, Grace. You just have to hang in there and try to focus on the positives."

"You sound like a motivational poster," I groan. "I'm so far out of my comfort zone I wouldn't even be able to see it with a James Webb telescope."

"I know, but if anyone can figure out a way to power through this, it's you. Remember the time at the World Wildlife Fund gala when that guy implied you were hired for your good looks and you threatened to smash a beaker and shiv him with the borosilicate glass?" I smile fondly at the memory. "That's the kind of confidence you need right now," Cassie insists. "Except maybe less violent."

"I don't know. There's definitely a lawyer I've considered shivving."

Cassie laughs as I exhale deeply, considering her words. But before I can ask her for more inspirational platitudes, there's a knock on my door.

"Grace?" Blue calls from the hallway. "You okay? They're waiting for you."

"Yep, just getting changed. Be out in a sec!" I yell back.

"I gotta go," I whisper to Cassie. "I hate you but I love you. Bye." Then I hide my new spy phone back in a shoe in my suitcase and quickly throw on the only dress my mom didn't pick out.

The producers asked us to dress up for our first round of dates, but I don't have the emotional fortitude to survive wearing Spanx tonight. Kristina even went so far as to warn me that I couldn't wear pajamas, so instead I'm throwing on a sundress I bought a few years ago. It's long and comfy and basically a nightgown anyway. *Ha, take that, Kristina!*

When I open the door, Blue gives me a once-over. "What's with the poncho?"

"Hey, this is from Talbot's. I wore it to a baby shower once."

"Were you the one having the baby?"

I laugh. "Are you saying you wouldn't be falling all over yourself to date me on national TV?"

"You're not my type," he says unapologetically.

"Let me guess. Madison is your type? Like every other guy in the world?"

"I mean, I like blondes, but preferably with bigger penises."

I immediately think of Alec. "Ooh, I have this coworker who—"

"Are you about to try to set me up with your one gay friend?"

"Yes . . . ?"

"You straight girls are all alike."

"But I really think you'd like him. He's cute, smart, funny—do you like weed by any chance?"

"I'm a forty-year-old PA with blue hair. Of course I like weed." I burst out laughing, but before I can be the matchmaker for once, Blue hooks his arm in mine and leads me away.

As we head out of the mansion, I see Andrew talking to some of the crew by the back door. I pull Blue's arm to get him to go out the side door, so we don't have to walk past Andrew. Except he quickly catches on. "Are you trying to avoid the lawyer?"

"Yes," I hiss. "He'll just find a reason to scold me or give me another fucking oppressive rule to follow."

"Like no swearing?" Blue asks with a laugh.

"Exactly!" I sneak a furtive glance at Andrew again, and he turns to look at me at the same time. His eyes capture mine and I suddenly feel like prey. He stops talking to the crew and just takes me in. I awkwardly pull at my dress, feeling completely unnerved when he looks at me like that. "Fuck."

Blue laughs again. "Yeah, I can see how that rule is hard for you, and yep, he's walking over here."

"Why?" I groan. "There are plenty of other contestants to harass. Why am I the only one who gets his wrath?"

"Maybe you're just special," Blue teases as Andrew stalks toward us without breaking eye contact with me. Blue elbows me before whispering, "Be nice."

He stops in front of us and looks up at Blue as if he's just realized he's standing there. "Hey, Blue." Blue nods hello before looking back and forth between us, awaiting an impending showdown. Andrew turns to me and with an unreadable tone asks, "You excited for your first one-on-one date?"

"Oh boy, am I ever!" I say and then turn to Blue with a look that I hope conveys *How's that for nice?* Blue rolls his eyes at me.

But Andrew only grins. "I feel bad for whoever's on the receiving end of that tonight."

I ignore him and ask Blue, "What do we even do on these dates? Eat dinner and make small talk?"

Blue shrugs. "Sometimes. It depends on what works best with the producer's plotline for the week. Other times it's hang gliding or bungee jumping or something," he says way too nonchalantly.

My stomach sinks. "That's not funny." I look at Andrew to see if Blue is joking. But Andrew isn't laughing. Instead, he raises an eyebrow at me. I feel my heart rate going up as I explain to them, "I have acrophobia."

"You don't seem like the kind of person who'd have an irrational fear of heights," Andrew says.

I narrow my eyes at him. "It's not *irrational*. Because *rationally*, if you fall from somewhere really high up, like, oh, I don't know, *the sky*, you'll die."

Blue laughs, but then quickly covers, giving me a reassuring smile. "Sometimes you go horseback riding or snorkeling."

"Can I formally request a ground-based date then?" I ask Blue.

Andrew studies me. "We've never had any incidents, and all of our operators have been through strict safety protocols and clearances. I can assure you it's perfectly safe."

I don't like the way he's looking at me. It's like he's trying to learn me, and it feels entirely too intimate for two people who can't stand each other. So I quickly counter, "Or maybe it's not and you're trying to get rid of me. I know how much you hate paperwork."

Blue gives an awkward laugh, clearly uncomfortable with the tension between Andrew and me.

Andrew shakes his head. "Just trying to make you feel better."

This catches me off guard. We stand there in a stalemate, each of us trying to figure out what the other is playing at until Blue clears his throat.

"Okaaay . . . well, I have to bring Grace to set now . . ." Blue says awkwardly, snapping us out of our standoff.

"A delight as always, Ms. Lambert," Andrew says.

"Right back at you, Mr. Benson."

Ten minutes later, all the contestants are gathered back in the lounge area by the pool. As the hair and makeup team touches up Shantae, Madison sidles next to me on the outdoor couch and conspiratorially whispers, "Who are you hoping to go out with?"

I'm about to answer "no one" when she leans in and says, "That was a pretty steamy kiss with Javier earlier."

"You mean when he tricked me into kissing him?"

"I think he likes you, though."

I laugh because how could she possibly infer that from the five hours I've known him? But I admit, "Javier seems like a nice guy. I actually wouldn't mind going out with him. What about you?"

Madison looks around conspiratorially before answering. "TC is super-sweet and so handsome, but I don't think he's into me."

"What?" I ask, sincerely shocked. "Who wouldn't be into you? You're such a catch."

"I could say the same about you," Madison says, then laughs. "Look at us, we're actually talking about boys this time."

"Shoot me." I clean my fake glasses and put them back on my face as Blue walks over carrying three comically large envelopes and hands them to Shantae. He meets my eye, and I raise my eyebrows at the size of the cartoon envelopes. We both stifle a laugh.

Then Blue suddenly looks serious and mouths, *Good luck*, before he hustles off. Fear rips through me. That wasn't a normal "good luck"—that was a *you're about to be screwed* "good luck."

"Oh fuck," I mutter.

"What?" Madison whispers.

"They're going to try and kill me from a staggering height!"

Then I see Blue standing behind the cameras, discreetly motioning to Bill, and I gasp again. "No, worse. They're going to make me go on a date with Cowboy Bill, the Biggest Swingin' Dick in Texas."

Madison gasps and covers her mouth. "They wouldn't!" Then she thinks about it. "They totally would!"

Our prophesizing is cut short when Shantae announces, "Welcome to your first one-on-one dates!" She holds up the three clown envelopes. "In my hand, I have the pairings for tonight."

TC and Javier start drumming on their knees for added effect.

"Should I just quit now?" I whisper to Madison.

"Don't you dare!" she whispers back and squeezes my hand for moral support. "I don't want to be stuck with Beth Anne."

I laugh until Shantae proclaims, "The first couple to go on a date is . . . Javier and . . ." She pauses for dramatic effect as Javier looks over at me and blows a kiss. ". . . Beth Anne."

Beth Anne looks right at me and then cuddles up next to Javier. He gives me a sad little shrug.

"They did this on purpose because she'll try to steal him away from you!" Madison whisper-yells to me in horror.

I don't have time to tell her that Javier isn't mine to steal because I'm busy willing an envelope to match me with TC. But then I see Madison sneaking furtive glances his way. *Crap.* As much as I can't stand Bill, I also want Madison to have a real chance with TC.

"Okay, next up is . . ." Shantae opens the envelope and smiles. "Madison and TC!"

Madison gives TC a shy smile, and I swear his whole face brightens when he looks at her. I lean in to tell her about this promising development when Bill comes sauntering over like a second-string Clint Eastwood and drawls, "I guess that means I get the Sexy Scientist. You ready for our date, darlin'?"

Suddenly the thought of plunging to my death isn't so unappealing.

Chapter Fourteen

Kristina knows that Good Ol' Boy Bill and I are like oil and water. *Literally.* He works for an evil gas corporation, and I once volunteered at an oil spill to clean up the polluted water. I overheard her saying, "I can't wait to see the sparks fly with this one." Fine by me, Kristina, as long as they land on Bill's flammable cowboy boots.

The good news is that we're just having dinner. At sea level.

Blue walks me down to the beach where production has set up a romantic candlelit dinner. The view is breathtaking—the sun setting over the Pacific, its pastel hues bouncing off the waves. From this vantage point on the windswept dunes, I spot a pod of short-beaked common dolphins in the distance. But even that doesn't stop me from humming Chopin's "Funeral March."

"At least there's tofu stir-fry," Blue singsongs, trying to cheer me up.

"At least I can throw myself into the ocean," I singsong in response.

"I'm honestly not sure what would be better for ratings—you drowning yourself or bludgeoning Cowboy Bill with a candlestick."

"I see where your priorities lie."

Blue laughs. "Just eat fast and get it over with. And remember, you're on national TV and you want people to like you. Now go, my little grasshopper." Then he leaves me to walk the rest of the way to the table where Bill is already seated.

I take in Bill before he sees me. As much as I hate to admit it, he *is* objectively handsome. I already know he has a very muscular, very shiny body despite his weird obsession with his calves, but tonight he looks surprisingly polished in khakis and a sports coat. And thank the cosmos, he's not wearing that dumb Stetson. Instead, it looks like he put product in his hair as if he's actually trying. When he sees me walking over, he stands to greet me. At least the cowboy has manners.

"Well, don't you look prettier than a peach pie," he says, and I want to vomit.

I thank him for pulling my chair out for me and then can't help but add, "You don't have to lean into the whole Southern charm thing for me."

He must think I'm teasing because he just laughs. Then he pours me some wine as we settle into our seats. "I'm really glad we got picked to go on this date together, Grace."

"You are? Why?" I ask as I take a big gulp of wine.

"Because we haven't really gotten to know each other, and it seems like you don't like me. So I'm grateful for the opportunity to change your mind."

Well shit, now I feel bad. "It's not that I don't like you . . ." I ramble, lying through my teeth. "It's just . . . I don't think we have very much in common. So I, uh, didn't want to waste your time when you could be looking for an actual love match that you mesh with . . . better."

"That's sweet of you. But I wouldn't rule yourself out just yet," he says with a cheesy wink. It takes everything in my being not to audibly groan. I once went out with a guy wearing a wooden tie, hinges and all—and it was still cooler than Bill's wink.

Just then, a waiter—or maybe an actor who was hired to pretend to be a waiter—comes over with our dinners and cans of what looks like designer soda. Kristina mentioned there would be product placement on our dates, and I can't help but wonder if this is one of them.

Bill leans in close to the steak on his plate and inhales obnoxiously. I divert my eyes and dig into my tofu stir-fry. I'm starving, and hopefully, if our mouths are full, we can't talk.

I must be getting punished for something in a past life because Bill keeps on chatting. "So you're a biologist, right? How much money do you make?"

"What?" I choke, whether on a bell pepper or his audacity, I'm not sure.

"Whatever it is, I bet my company would pay you double, maybe triple."

"Your *oil* company that has built the largest pipeline in the US through countless natural habitats you mean?"

"Yeah, we hire biologists all the time."

"More like *biostitutes*. I would never sell my soul to an oil company and approve construction that could devastate entire species just to line my pockets."

"Well, when you put it like that . . ." Bill laughs good-naturedly and keeps eating.

I frantically shovel tofu into my face to get this date over with as fast as possible. I consider putting food in the pockets of my baby shower poncho when Bill chuckles. "Whoa, someone's hungry. So how long have you been vegan?" He asks this in a getting-to-know-you kind of way that makes me think he doesn't realize what a complete dumpster fire this date is.

I take another sip of wine as I consider Blue's advice to play nice until the cameras stop rolling. I try to torniquet the displeasure flowing out of me and make small talk like a normal person. "Ten years. But I've been a vegetarian since I was five. My grandparents had a farm when we were little, and they had this cow that used to follow me around like a dog. I'd look into her warm brown eyes, and I swear, I could see into her soul. Daisy was just the sweetest—"

"No way! I had a pet cow named Daisy!" Bill says, slapping the table. "See? We do have stuff in common."

"You had a cow named Daisy?" I ask suspiciously, as I stare at Bill through my fake glasses.

"Yep. And then Daisy 2, Daisy 3, Daisy Jr., Day-Z because he was a bull—"

"What happened to them all?"

"We either sold them at auction or slaughtered them," he says nonchalantly.

"Oh my God, you ate your pets?!" I put my fork down because I can't even stomach tofu anymore.

Bill shrugs as he takes a sip of wine. "I grew up on a cattle ranch."

"Of course you did. And let me guess, you hunt too?"

"Sure do."

I shake my head. "This . . . this is why we would never work out. I'm a biologist who works in animal conservation, and you gleefully kill animals for sport."

"And food. And leather," he says, lifting up one of his boots. "We use the whole buffalo. Hunters are conservationists too, you know. Just ask Teddy Roosevelt."

"Are you actually saying you consider yourself an ally to animals?"

"Sure do. Hunters buy hunting licenses and pay ammunition taxes every year. That money goes to wildlife agencies, right? Not to mention our help in population control."

My head is spinning. Yes, I know state and federal wildlife agencies need to employ hunters at times to help with invasive species. But for some reason, Big Oil Bill doesn't strike me as someone who hunts out of the goodness of his heart and for the love of animals.

I exhale loudly and pour myself a very large second glass of wine. At this rate, I'm going to become a lush like the rest of the contestants. I take a sip, trying to compose myself before I say, "I'm sorry, Bill. I just think we're too different."

"But you know what they say about opposites . . ." he counters. *Oh God, please don't mansplain polarity to me.* ". . . They attract." *Yep, there it is.*

I reach for the wine bottle to refill my glass, but it's empty. Since I need something to do with my mouth before I say choice words that definitely won't make America like me, I reach for the can of whatever new trendy brand of soda this is. *Poppy Lite?* Well, that's a ridiculous name, but I take a sip anyway.

And immediately spit it out. "Oh God, this is horrible." Bill looks up at me in surprise and tries to give me a discreet headshake, but I keep going. "Seriously, what kind of artificial sweeteners and chemicals do they put in here?"

"I think it's supposed to be a healthy alternative to regular soda. It has probiotics," Bill says, like he's a walking spokesperson.

"It's criminal to call this healthy." I read the ingredients on the back. "It has a shit-ton of aspartame in it. Aspartame can damage neurons in your brain. Not to mention it can increase insulin levels, which leads to plaque buildup, inflammation, and increased risk of heart attacks."

Just then, from out of nowhere, Andrew Benson comes running in the sand toward us. He looks like business casual David Hasselhoff. He's taken off his suit jacket and rolled up his sleeves, and I'm suddenly distracted by the sight of his forearms. Why does he have muscular forearms? Is it all the paperwork? And more importantly, why of all the forearms in the world are his appealing to me? I try to shake this thought out of my head because I'm sure once he opens his mouth, he'll ruin every part of the arm for me forever.

When Andrew gets to our table, he tells the camera operators to cut, and I notice he's not even out of breath. He must exercise regularly, which explains the forearms and possibly some of his arrogance.

I'm jarred from my hate-ogling when he says, "Grace, may I speak with you please?" His voice has dropped an octave, and his eyes are darker than usual. Yeah, he's pissed at me. I try to ignore the perverse thrill that rushes through me at that thought.

I excuse myself and follow Andrew away from the table and crew. When we're out of earshot, he spins on me and says, "You can't spout off unvalidated health claims! Poppy Lite is one of our biggest sponsors."

I scoff, "Why? Were Red Dye and High-Fructose Corn Syrup already taken?"

Andrew rubs his temples. "You've only been here for twelve hours." The gesture aggravates my temper.

"Maybe you should've gotten Advil as a sponsor."

"Then you'd just rail against Big Pharma," he responds, flicking his eyes my way in annoyance.

I stop, momentarily disarmed by how quick and accurate his response was. "Probably," I admit.

This seems to both placate and surprise him. He sighs and brushes sand off his pants as we stand there in a détente.

I try really hard not to sneak a peek at his forearms, but they seem especially muscley when he crosses them over his chest like that. He catches me looking, so I snap my eyes back up to his.

He runs his hands through his hair, mussing it out of its usual perfection, as if he doesn't know what to do with me. "Look, you don't have to drink it. Just please stop badmouthing it."

Here's where most people would agree and move on. But I see an opportunity. "I'll make a deal with you: You convince Kristina that I have a headache and have to leave this date early, which could very well be true because aspartame gives people headaches"—Andrew sighs—"and I promise I won't talk shit about Poppy Cancer for the rest of my time on the show."

Andrew looks back over at Bill. "You want out of this date that bad? It hasn't even been thirty minutes." He looks at me curiously. "Did you even give the guy a chance?"

I look at him in shock. "First of all, you are the last person I want dating advice from. And secondly, Bill and I are complete opposites! We're even less compatible than you and me!"

Andrew raises his eyebrows and then his gaze sweeps over me like he's about to argue but can't. I immediately put my hands on my hips. "Can you get me out of here or what?"

"Fine. But if I catch you slandering any of the sponsors, I'll make sure the producers send you on another date with him," he says, his eyes roving over my face. "Maybe to a gun range? Or a pig roast?"

I narrow my eyes at him. "You wouldn't."

He narrows his eyes back at me. "Try me."

I back down from our staring contest first, because the intensity in his eyes is making my stomach do weird things. "Fine. I won't talk shit about the sponsors . . . on camera."

"Fine. I'll cover for you on your date."

I put my hand out to shake his. When he grasps it, I have immediate regrets. If the way he looks at me is enough to cause my stomach to flutter, then I should've guessed the electricity of our touch would be even more overwhelming.

He must feel it too because when I try to take my hand back, he doesn't let go. He just looks at me with that same damn challenging glint in his eyes as if he's daring me.

It's completely unnerving. I've never wanted to pull someone closer and push them away at the same time. But I also refuse to let him know the effect he has on me. So instead, I smile sweetly at him.

"Pleasure doing business with you. Be sure to tell Bill it's not me, it's him." And then I pull my hand away.

"And they believed you? But you suck at acting." Cassie says in bewilderment when I call her on my burner phone twenty minutes later.

"I don't think Kristina really bought the headache thing, but Andrew talked her into letting me go to bed early anyway." I close the curtains in my designated room in the mansion because going to bed sounds perfect right about now. "It's really the least Andrew could do."

"I can't believe he's censoring your health rants," Cassie says. "That's my favorite part of the workday."

I flop down on the fancy four-poster bed as an errant thought escapes my mouth. "Have you ever thought forearms are sexy?"

"Where did that come from?" Cassie asks.

"Nowhere!" I say too quickly.

Luckily, she doesn't press for details. "Of course I have. There's a reason forearm porn is a thing." I snort in disbelief, then hear the smile in her voice when she says, "I'm constantly walking around looking at men with long sleeves and wondering what they're packing under there."

I laugh but admit, "There is something strangely alluring to hidden muscles. It's like discovering a new organelle under a microscope."

"Ohmigod yes!" Cassie agrees. Then she casually circles back. "So, there isn't anyone you're interested in?"

I sigh. "Please don't get your hopes up, Cass. You know that's not what I'm here for. Especially when I'm forced to go on dates with meat-loving, rifle-toting cowboys who consider themselves conservationists."

"Well . . ." Cassie says quietly.

"Well what?"

"It's just that hunters do play a part in conservation too. I think they realized a long time ago that if they don't protect the animals, they won't have anything left to hunt."

"Are you defending Cowboy Bill?"

"No, I'm just saying . . ." She pauses, then says gently, "You know I love you, Grace, but you tend to make a decision about someone without really giving them a chance to show you more than one side."

I consider this. Then I remember my conversation with Madison and how I made a snap decision based on her looks but she ended up blowing my expectations out of the water. "I guess, maybe, sometimes, I may be a bit judgmental. I'll add that to the growing list of things I need to work on. But I know I'm spot-on about Beth Anne. Even you wouldn't be able to find anything redeeming about her—"

But Cassie cuts me off, squealing, "Oh my gosh, I almost forgot! You have almost fifteen thousand followers now!"

"How? Why?"

"Whatever Matt is doing, I guess. Plus, Eliza and Alec set up a crowdfunding page, and Matt links it to all your posts. We've already made three thousand dollars and the show hasn't even aired yet!"

"Wow, really? That's amazing." I'm quiet for a moment. "Well, shit. I guess I really can't quit now."

Cassie laughs. "I know you don't want to be there, but we're all so appreciative of what you're doing. Gregory even told the board about it, and they ate it up, just like he thought they would."

I sigh because I know what this means—the infuriating lawyers, intimidating producers, and appalling cowboys don't matter—because our plan is actually working.

Fuck.

This means I have to try even harder to stay here.

Chapter Fifteen

I wake up early the next morning with renewed focus and determination. I need to keep those donations rolling in, which means I need to stay on this stupid show. And in order to do that I have to do something I loathe: ask for help.

I sneak down the long mansion hallway to Madison's room and knock quietly. She answers the door looking as happy and perky as ever. "Grace! Good morning!"

"Hey, hope I didn't wake you."

"Not at all, I've been up for hours. You know when you wake up and just need to ground yourself?"

Nope. "Sure?"

"I just did 108 sun salutations and some tantric meditation, and now I feel ready to conquer the day," she says breezily, as if it were the equivalent of having a cup of coffee.

"Oh. Cool. So, I was wondering if you could *help me* with something?" It even feels foreign coming out of my mouth.

"Of course! What is it?"

I take a deep breath, hating myself for what I'm about to ask . . . "Um, do you know how to do that beachy hair wave thing? I don't usually—"

"Oh my gosh, you want me to do your hair and makeup?!" she says, practically jumping with joy.

"If you don't mind. I've decided that I should actually try to stay on the show, and well, I like how your makeup looks so natural."

Madison grabs my arm and yanks me into her room. "This is going to be so much fun! What are you wearing today?"

I laugh at her enthusiasm and shrug. "Clothing, of some sort," I mutter as I look around her room. It has an identical layout to mine—same fancy king bed and large walk-in closet, but hers is decorated with more blues and whites instead of the maroons and golds in mine. I can't help but think it suits her better.

"I have the perfect dress!" she says, as she rushes to the closet where she has hung up every article of clothing she brought. I wince, thinking of all the wrinkled outfits that are still in my suitcase. "I know you usually dress pretty simply, but you also have great legs, so I think this is a happy medium," she says, holding up a short aqua-colored dress. "Try it on!"

I take it from her and shrug because I know that, even if it looks terrible, she'll put a positive spin on it. I go into the bathroom, and as I'm slipping on the dress I hear, "I know it's form fitting, but you've got a great body!" I laugh as Madison continues yelling from the bedroom. "Just pretend you're doing yoga or going swimming or something!" When I walk out, she immediately covers her mouth and squeals. "You are so gorgeous!"

We have to figure out how to send this girl into war zones. Her optimism and kindness are scary contagious. Hell, I feel like I get a better-person contact high off of her whenever she smiles.

Madison moves a chair over to the window because apparently that's where the good light is and tells me to sit. Then I make the mistake of telling her the good news about our crowdfunding campaign while she's mid–makeup application. She shrieks, jumping up and down, and almost takes my eye out with the eyeliner pencil. "Three thousand dollars already? Grace, that's amazing! You're going to save those frogs!"

I smile at her. As hard as yesterday was, it's nice knowing I have someone in my corner. Madison does my hair while she gushes about her date with TC and I find myself genuinely happy to hear how well they got along. Unlike me and the cowboy, they have a ton in common. "He even volunteers with kids, teaching them music!" she says with cartoon hearts in her eyes.

"It's like if Gandhi started dating Mother Teresa," I tease, but they really would be the sweetest couple. I smile to myself as I picture Cassie saying, *"They'll make the cutest babies."* She says this whenever she sees a cute couple, insisting that, because she studied genetics in undergrad, she's qualified to make that hypothesis.

As Madison starts twirling my hair around some wand-looking device, she asks about my one-on-one date. She cringes sympathetically when I tell her all about my dinner with Bill and the irritating interaction with Andrew.

"If Andrew didn't want me talking trash about Poppy Lite, then maybe he should've told me that ahead of time."

Madison nods. "That's frustrating. Especially because he's so handsome."

"Exactly," I say absentmindedly before realizing I walked into a trap. I shake my head, seeing her grin. "He's not that handsome," I say, flustered. "It's hard to see past his obnoxiousness to even notice what he looks like," I lie.

Madison is tactful enough to let the subject drop. "Well, I'm sorry your date was a bust." She pats my hand and looks at me with a burning sincerity. "But don't worry, Grace. There's a perfect someone out there for you. He may not be on this show, but you're going to find him!"

And maybe it's only because of her fierce positivity and bubbly conviction, but for the first time ever I kind of want to believe it.

Twenty-five minutes and endless compliments from Madison later, I'm dressed and somehow look almost as tan and beachy as she is.

Turns out, bronzer is my friend. We walk out of Madison's room and meet Blue in the hall. When he sees me, his eyes light up. "Okaaaay now. Way better than the muumuu."

"Madison is a miracle worker," I say, feeling self-conscious. I tug the dress down as we walk toward the staircase.

Then I notice Andrew talking to Kristina in the foyer below us. He's wearing another expensive-looking suit. Today's, a charcoal gray, fits him perfectly, though I curse it for hiding his forearms. When I finally wrestle my concentration away from the suit, I realize that Andrew and Kristina are in a heated exchange.

I overhear Andrew say, "Seriously. You need to tone down the challenge. It's degrading."

"Did you say *ratings*?" she responds.

"Don't make me get the studio involved," he counters, and Kristina rolls her eyes.

"Ahh, he's fighting the good fight," Blue comments. Apparently I'm not the only one eavesdropping.

"Fine. We'll cut the wet T-shirt contest, but I'm replacing it with something else," Kristina says and walks off in a huff.

"What's that all about?" I whisper to Blue from our spot up above.

"Andrew's constantly trying to make the show less trashy, but the producers always push back," he says with a shrug.

"Because the studio wants him to?" Madison asks.

"I think it's more that he's a decent dude," Blue answers.

Just then Andrew notices us at the top of the stairs, and as if there's no one else in the room, his gaze automatically finds mine. I feel an aftershock of the electricity that ran through me when we shook hands last night.

And then he breaks eye contact and lets his eyes dip to take in my whole body. It's like he wants me to know he's looking. I start to feel warm all over as he takes his time. If this is some sort of power play, he's failing, because the way he's looking at me makes me feel like the powerful one. I feel a strange flutter of satisfaction in the fact that Andrew can't seem to tear his eyes away from me.

"I knew this dress would work," Madison whispers as we start down the stairs.

"Stand up tall," Blue adds, right before Madison says, "Swish your hips." It's like they're in on some sort of secret plot.

All of Madison's kind words must've sunk in, because I strut down the stairs, boldly holding Andrew's gaze. Except by the time I get to the bottom, Blue and Madison are suddenly nowhere to be seen and I'm alone with him.

"Where the hell did they go?" I ask him, looking around.

"They left human-sized holes in the wall when they went that way." He points toward the pool. I shake my head at my new friends.

"They're probably afraid you'll make them drink bleach because it's a sponsor."

He laughs before he can stop himself. "Don't make me laugh. I'm still annoyed with you."

"Not as annoyed as I am with you," I say sweetly.

"I got you out of your date, didn't I?"

"And all it took were threats and intimidation."

He gives me an amused smile, and it takes my breath away. I haven't seen him smile since before he knew who I was. I had forgotten how disarming it is. He tilts his head, considering. "I would try calling a truce, but I don't think it'll last long."

"I'm sure I'll do something that will require a stern talking-to."

His eyes seem to darken at this. As if he'd love nothing more than giving me a stern talking-to. I cross my legs. "Definitely," he agrees. "The day has only just begun. I'm sure you have plenty of mayhem up your sleeves," he says with a smirk that isn't quite as irritating as it was yesterday.

Just then I hear someone clear her throat, and I'm startled to see that Kristina has come back into the foyer and she's scowling at us. "They're waiting for you by the pool, Grace." She hands me a pair of fake glasses. "Don't forget your signature look. They're trending online."

"Oh goodie," I say as I take the glasses. Matt would have a field day if he knew he was right about the glasses.

Andrew gives me a parting head nod. "Goodbye, Ms. Lambert. Please try to stay out of trouble."

"Well, of course, Mr. Benson. I signed all that paperwork, didn't I?"

It delights me when both Andrew and Kristina roll their eyes at this. I've aggravated two birds with one stone. I smile to myself as I put on my *signature look* and hustle outside.

I make a quick pit stop in the outdoor kitchen to grab a much-needed coffee, still thinking about Andrew. I'm not ready to unpack that moment on the stairs, but the rest of our interaction felt different. Maybe we can call a truce.

I get to the lounge area and shake off thoughts of anything that won't help me stay on the show. I'm determined to try harder to be here, but where do I start? I look around at the contestants and see that Madison and TC are already deep in conversation and they both look smitten. I can't help but smile. But then Bill sees me smiling and thinks it's for him. He gives me a big wave and a tip of his cowboy hat. *Ugh. Give up already!*

Then Javier rushes over to me. "Hey. Can we talk?" He sounds serious.

"Uh, sure," I say, with no clue what he could possibly need to talk about that isn't flirtatious.

But before Javi can pull me away to chat, Shantae struts out, looking stunning in a white jumpsuit, and motions for us all to sit down.

"Good morning, lovers!" she greets us, while also beaming into the cameras. "I hope you all enjoyed your night of luxury because for some of you, it'll be your last."

My stomach drops. I was so distracted by my makeover with

Madison and sparring with Andrew that I forgot I'm definitely at the bottom of the leaderboard. I didn't even know what Suck and Blow was, and clearly I didn't form a love connection with Bill. Might as well dust off my bedroll now.

Shantae rubs her hands excitedly. "First, let's find out how the one-on-one dates went. Who wants to go first?" Beth Anne's hand shoots up. *Shocker.* "Okay, Beth and Javier, how was your date?"

"Beth *Anne*, and it was amazing, Shantae!" Beth Anne gushes. "Javier is so funny and sexy. We really connected." Beth Anne gives me a smug look.

"I heard you two even shared a steamy kiss good-night," Shantae adds, fishing for details.

"A lady doesn't kiss and tell," Beth Anne says coyly, as Javier glances over at me guiltily.

"How does that make you feel, Grace?" Shantae asks, turning to me.

I look around. "Me?"

"Yeah, you and Javier shared a kiss earlier in the day. And it really seemed like you two were vibing."

Javier turns to me and whispers, "I'm sorry, Grace. I was trying to tell you before you found out like this." Oh. That's really mature and considerate of him.

"It's okay, Javi," I whisper back. Then I think about it for a second and answer Shantae truthfully for the cameras. "I'm enjoying getting to know Javier, but I don't blame him for exploring other options. If we're here to find a romantic connection, I don't think we should limit ourselves."

"Does that mean you're exploring other options too?" Shantae asks.

"I'm just trying to keep an open mind," I hear myself saying. And then hope I can actually follow through with that.

Shantae shrugs disappointedly as if she was hoping I'd make some sort of petty remark, or maybe throw my unfinished coffee at someone. She turns to Madison. "Madison and TC, how was your date?"

TC and Madison hold hands as they talk about their romantic dinner on the veranda overlooking the Santa Monica Mountains. At one point, they even finish each other's sentences, causing them both to blush. It's adorable.

And then it's my turn. I feel my face heating with embarrassment as Shantae turns to Bill and says, "Are you and Grace going to ride off into the sunset?"

I struggle to stay quiet when Bill tells Shantae and the seedy underbelly of America who watches reality TV that our date was *incredible*, and he loves a woman who challenges him. Luckily, before I can tell Shantae in some very colorful language what I thought of our date, she's already moving on.

She hands out markers and dry-erase boards as she says, "Now the moment of truth. Do you want to go out with your date again? Write 'yes' or 'no,' and then we'll reveal them all at the same time," Shantae says with a glint in her eye.

We all scribble down our answers, and Shantae counts to three. Because of the way we're sitting, I can't see anyone else's answer. But I can see Shantae's eyes widen as she says, "Savage! Two of you have said 'no.'"

Madison gasps as Shantae continues. "Grace, what is it about Bill that makes you not want to go out with him again?"

Bill looks at me with hurt and surprise all over his face. *Shit,* why couldn't this be anonymous?

As much as I can't stand Bill, I don't want to hurt anyone's feelings. So I turn to him and gently say, "I'm sorry, Bill. I told you last night, I just don't think we have much in common."

"What happened to keeping an open mind?" Beth Anne says snarkily.

Shantae nods at me, then moves on to the next couple. "Okay, Javier, why don't you want to go out with Beth Anne again?"

Beth Anne huffs in shock. "What?! Are you freakin' serious?"

Javier faces her. "I'm sorry, Beth, but—"

"It's Beth *Anne*!" she yells.

"I didn't feel as strong of a connection with you as I have with other contestants," he says in the kindest way possible.

"Ohmigod, I'm a ten and you're like a seven! And *you* weren't feeling *me*?" she shrieks. My mouth must be hanging open. Maybe a secret part of me is starting to understand why people watch this trash. This is getting dramatic.

"Do you have a response to that, Javier?" Shantae asks. He just shakes his head. "Well," Shantae continues, "that means that Beth Anne and Bill don't get points for the first one-on-one date—"

Beth Anne interrupts her by standing and shouting, "This is bullshit! I knew I should've applied for *The Bachelor* instead!" She takes off her microphone necklace and storms off. We all sit there in shock, watching her leave.

After an awkward pause, Shantae tries to recover by saying, "She's such a diva. I love her!"

"Are you allowed to do that?" I whisper to Madison, who shakes her head. "Do you think she's playing it up for the show or was she really upset?"

Kristina comes rushing on set as Madison shrugs and whispers back, "I don't know."

While everyone is distracted and Kristina is trying to figure out what to do, I stand up and tell Madison, "I'm going to go check on her." Madison nods and I sneak away toward the mansion, hoping none of the producers notice I'm breaking the rules again.

Chapter Sixteen

Luckily, the mansion is empty, and I quickly find Beth Anne's room. It's farther down the hall from mine and on the opposite side facing the front of the house. I stop outside her door and knock tentatively.

"Go away!" Beth Anne yells from inside.

"It's Grace," I say, before realizing that's not a selling point.

She cracks the door, and I see that she's crying. *Shit. Why didn't I send Madison instead? She's much better at feelings than I am.* "Why are you here?" Beth Anne asks through sniffles.

"I came to check on you. I wanted to make sure you were okay."

"I'm fine. If you tell anyone I was crying, I'll deny it. Now go away or you'll attract the cameras."

But even as she's saying that we hear Kristina downstairs, bossing around the camera operators. "Where did Beth Anne go? Find her!"

Beth Anne grabs me and pulls me into her room with a frustrated sigh, then shuts and locks the door behind us. I don't know what to say to comfort her. I finally settle on, "I'm sorry about the one-on-one dates."

Beth Anne is still crying, so I hand her a tissue from a nearby tissue box. "It's not even about Javi," she starts. "I mean, I thought we had a connection, and of course rejection never feels good. I'm sure you know." I ignore her dig as she keeps going. "But I'm more upset because I thought I'd be top of the leaderboard by now." She blows her nose, then says, "I need to stay on the show."

"To find love?"

Beth Anne scoffs tearfully. "To make money."

I wonder briefly if Beth Anne also has a charity and I've wildly misjudged everyone, but then she adds, "The last two seasons, the couple who make it to the end have made millions on social media."

"What? How?"

"They get enough followers because of the show that they can do paid posts, get endorsements, ads on their pages, that kind of stuff."

"Wow. That's insane. They end up making more than the prize money."

"Way more," she sniffles. "If I only wanted $250,000, I would've just stayed in my marketing job."

My mouth drops open. "You made that much in marketing?"

Beth Anne shrugs. "My dad owns the firm."

My head is swimming. "So, what do you need the social media money for then?"

"I hate working for my dad. He still treats me like a child. I want to get into modeling or have a lifestyle brand, you know?" I don't, but I nod anyway.

Just then there's a loud knock on the door. "It's Kristina. Open up!"

Beth Anne wipes the makeup under her eyes. "Ugh, I don't want them to see me like this. It'll ruin my image."

"They wouldn't film you when you're upset, would they?" Beth Anne looks at me like I'm stupid. "You're right. They totally would. Okay, I'll stall them." Then I cross to the door and yell out, "We're busy! We'll be out in a minute."

Kristina just pounds on the door again, causing me to jump back, startled. "You better open that door, Grace. You signed a contract that you'll always be on camera."

"Sorry, no can do at the moment . . . because . . . we are, uh, naked?" I look at Beth Anne and shrug pathetically. She laughs.

My victory is short-lived though as Kristina yells through the door, "What? Why? Someone get me the lawyer!" *Crap.*

Well, good thing Andrew and I didn't call a truce. It hasn't even been half an hour.

Beth Anne has stopped crying and she turns to me. "Thank you, Grace." I smile at her, and she quickly adds, "But don't think this means we're friends."

Someone knocks on the knock. "Grace, it's Andrew. Open up."

I say cheerily through the door, "Hello, Andrew, how are you?"

"I was better before I got called down here for this," he responds.

Then I hear Kristina's voice. "Tell her she's in breach of contract." I look over at Beth Anne. She's reapplying her makeup and taking a steadying breath. I hear a sharp but muffled conversation between Kristina and Andrew, as if he's walked away from the door to talk to her without us overhearing them, but then he comes back and knocks again.

He sounds pained when he says, "You're in breach of contract. Please open the door."

I open the door, squaring off with Andrew. We're only a few inches apart as we stare each other down. He looks at Beth Anne inside the room, clearly still tearstained, and then back at me, searching my eyes. He sighs like he wishes he didn't have to have this conversation.

"Do you like making my job difficult?" he asks in a low voice, so that Kristina and Beth Anne can't hear.

"Maybe if you didn't have such a corrupt job, it wouldn't feel so difficult."

He looks like I've slapped him. I start to feel guilty until he responds in his Important Lawyer voice, "You can't lock yourselves in a room without cameras. You signed a contract."

Just when I think there's a chance we don't have to be so combative, he reminds me that we're on opposite sides. If that's the way he wants it to be, fine. I grab Beth Anne's hand and push past him. "So sue me."

I hear the camera crew and PAs gasp in shock as I hold my head high and walk off, Beth Anne in tow. I'm sure they're not used to contestants pushing back like this, but I've never been good at playing by unfair rules.

As we walk away, Beth Anne appraises me, as if seeing me for the first time. She whispers, "The lawyer looks like he's wants to murder you. Or push you up against a wall and have his way with you."

I'm replaying what Beth Anne said about Andrew as we walk to the backyard where the rest of the contestants are waiting for us. If it's true, the intensity in his gaze takes on a whole new meaning. Why does this thought make my pulse race?

"That was pretty badass," Beth Anne says, jarring me out of my over-analyzing. She sounds both surprised and reluctant to give me a compliment.

"Thanks. It felt badass in the moment. Of course, now I'm regretting it and worrying that they're going to kick me off the show."

She shrugs. "It takes a lot more than that to get kicked off. Now, if you'll excuse me, I need to go save my image."

Beth Anne struts onto the patio, past Shantae—who looks annoyed that she had to wait for us—and climbs on top of Bill. Straddling his lap, she takes off his cowboy hat and starts making out with him. He doesn't seem to mind because he grabs her ass and pulls her closer. While Beth Anne's methods may be unorthodox, I appreciate her determination to stay on the show.

They're getting so hot and heavy that I look away as Beth Anne begins grinding on Bill. Shantae tries to regain control. She fans herself and shouts, "Save a horse, ride a cowboy!" Beth Anne finally takes the hint and climbs off Bill. She puts his cowboy hat back on his head, but he takes it off and covers the front of his jeans.

Beth Anne notices and laughs. "Oops." Then she sits back down and shoots Javier a dirty look.

I see Andrew and Kristina watching from behind the cameras. Kristina's all smiles now, loving the drama, so I guess that means she won't be kicking us off the show. But Andrew gives me a look that I can't quite decipher. And then Beth Anne's voice pops into my head: *"The lawyer looks like he's wants to murder you. Or push you up against a wall and have his way with you."* Shit. That's exactly what he looks like. I quickly turn my attention back to Shantae before I can picture what Andrew could do to me while holding me against a wall.

But it's too late. I'm already blushing when Shantae shifts into Polished Host mode and without missing a beat says, "Well, there's good news for Beth Anne and Bill. You'll have a chance to earn more points in the upcoming team competition. And there's a new twist this season! After each episode airs, we're letting America vote for their favorite contestant. And that person will receive ten extra points."

Madison gives an excited whoop, Beth Anne nods confidently, and I evaluate the odds of winning America's Favorite. Technically, I have a one-in-six chance. Though I can't imagine anyone falling for Bill's cowboy schtick. So that leaves me at a 20 percent chance. Which feels generous sitting next to America's Sweetheart, Madison.

"Unfortunately for you all," Shantae drawls, "you'll have more than just each other to compete with." *Shit.* "Please welcome our two new contestants."

Just like that, my odds fall to 14.29 percent. And when I see who is walking out to the pool, I know my chances have sunk even lower.

Chapter Seventeen

I'd like to introduce you to Ciara and Scott!" Shantae says with a hand flourish.

Beth Anne immediately stands and starts cheering. She suddenly seems less concerned about her odds of winning America's Favorite Contestant and more interested in the new arrivals. But my attention is immediately pulled away from her when a beautiful Black woman in a cherry red string bikini and tattoos walks out.

"Damn," Bill says at the same time as Javier whistles.

She strides over and stops next to Shantae, who announces: "Everyone, meet Ciara."

Ciara gives a sexy wave. "Hi, everyone."

"Oh my gosh, she's gorgeous," Madison says, and I nod in agreement.

"Holy hell," Beth Anne squeaks, and I think she's talking about Ciara until I see someone else coming our way.

"Holy hell is right," I whisper under my breath to Madison. The guy walking toward us is one of the most attractive men I have ever seen. He'd have to be for me to finally agree with Beth Anne.

As he steps into the pool area in European-style swim trunks, he seems to walk toward me in slow motion. He's not too muscular, not too lanky—his fat-to-muscle ratio is Michelangelo-level perfection. His bronzed skin, clean-cut face, with a strong jaw, thick eyebrows, and piercing blue eyes, looks familiar, like I've seen it in an expensive watch or luxury vehicle ad.

"I just got nervous," TC says next to me.

"You should be," I surprise everyone by saying out loud.

Shantae immediately quips, "Looks like Grace just joined the game." TC and Javier laugh at this as Madison gives my knee an excited squeeze. Beth Anne shoots me an appraising glance, and I'm too embarrassed to look at Andrew to see if he heard.

The *GQ* model stops next to Ciara, and Shantae appreciatively says, "And this is Scott." Beth Anne fans herself and looks like she might pass out. The good news is that I'll be able to remember his name without having to make a new chart because Hot Scott is the perfect mnemonic device.

Shantae turns to the new arrivals and says, "How does it feel to know you're joining the show once connections are already starting to form?"

"I'm not worried," Scott says in a sexy voice tinged with a slight New York accent.

"Me neither," Ciara agrees. "What I want, I get."

"Shit just got real," Javier says, breaking the tension, and we all laugh.

"Well, well, well. Things are finally getting interesting around here." Shantae manages to smile in a way that is both seductive and condescending. "I'll leave you to introduce yourselves." And with that, she saunters off. *Man, it must be nice only having to work fifteen minutes at a time.*

Beth Anne immediately beelines to Scott, which is fine since I don't think I'd be able to speak to him in complete sentences. Sadly, I'm starting to understand why the Fox Girls smile and touch their hair so much around my brother.

Thankfully, Madison pulls me away to go introduce ourselves to Ciara. After we mingle for a while, I learn that Ciara is a sex-positive badass and very down to earth. When I ask about her tattoos, she explains that she's a classically trained artist but after art school decided that her preferred medium was bodies. After three years of apprentice-ship, she now owns her own tattoo parlor in Las Vegas.

Unlike Madison, I can't work up the nerve to meet Hot Scott, but she reports back that he has in fact done some modeling so I might have recognized him from an advertisement. He's also an in-vestment banker and lives in Manhattan. Which means, not only is he painfully handsome, but he's also successful and has a real job. I might be in trouble.

"Hey, y'all!" Beth Anne's sugary voice cuts through the crowd, her Southern accent even thicker than usual. "I propose a toast to welcome Scott and Ciara," she says as she lifts a shot glass. Bill helps hand out amber-colored shots to everyone, and I surprise myself by accepting one. I can count on one hand how many times I've done a shot.

"Welcome to *Love Shack*," Beth Anne drawls, and you never would've known she had been crying less than an hour ago. "May you find lasting love . . ." She stops and turns to Scott. ". . . Or at least a really good time. Cheers!"

Everyone yells "Cheers!" and clinks their glasses. I look at Mad-ison and shrug. "When in Malibu . . ."

I tip back my glass and am immediately reminded why I don't do shots. *Holy Louis Pasteur!* What kind of poison is this?! I almost cough up whatever "Fireball" is until the burning finally subsides.

After the corrosive liquid undoubtedly causes permanent damage to my larynx, Hot Scott turns to look at me. His gaze is so powerful, I can't look away. "You must be Grace. I like your dress," he says, and I feel his voice rumble around my body. I look down at Madison's tight aqua dress and make a mental note to write her a long thank-you letter.

"I like your . . ."—I look at his short blue trunks, his broad chest, his handsome face—". . . everything." I slap my hands over my mouth in mortification.

But Scott just laughs. "I like a woman who's forward. It's less work for me."

And then I do something I've never done in my entire twenty-nine years. *I giggle.*

"I have a confession to make," Hot Scott says as I stare at his lips.

"What's that?"

"I looked up all the contestants before I came on the show, and I was most excited to meet you."

"Me? Why?!"

Scott smiles, amused. "I used to have a crush on my middle school librarian, so I guess I've always had a thing for smart girls in glasses."

"Oh," I say shyly, as I wonder if the general population of be-spectacled women know how many men have a glasses fetish. I can't wait to tell Cassie. Knowing her, she'll try to ruin her eyes just to get guys to notice her.

I smile at Hot Scott and am about to attempt flirting or even just talking in complete sentences when Beth Anne comes barging over in a practically nonexistent bikini. *When did she even change?* She touches Scott's arm and asks me, "Can I steal him?"

"What?" I say, confused as to why she's interrupting our conversation.

"I'm just gonna grab him for a minute," Beth Anne says with a sickeningly sweet fake smile, as if this were normal behavior. Who drags a person away when someone else is in the middle of talking to them?

But to my surprise, Scott turns to me and says, "I'll catch up with you later, Grace." And then he follows Beth Anne over to the pool.

What the hell just happened? I thought Beth Anne and I made some headway earlier. Is she trying to sabotage me or is this some sort of socially accepted reality show etiquette I'm not aware of? I leave the bar and rush over to dissect with Madison.

"I saw you talking to Scott," Madison prompts the second I sit down next to her, Ciara, TC, and Javier on the lounge furniture. "How'd it go?" Then she must see the bewilderment on my face. "What happened?"

"It was fine, but then Beth Anne just took him away in the middle of our conversation. She literally asked if she could steal him. Who does that?"

They all laugh at my expression, and Madison explains to Ciara, "Grace has never seen a reality show."

Ciara nods in understanding. "Well, don't take it personally. It's just a thing people do on reality—ahhhhh!!" All of a sudden, Ciara is screaming.

Javier looks down and yells, "Snake! Oh shit! Snake!" and he jumps up onto the couch. TC grabs Madison and pulls her halfway across the patio. Ciara is still frozen in fear as a large brown-and-tan snake slithers underneath her.

"You're okay," I say calmly to Ciara and then reach down for it.

"Don't touch it! It could be poisonous!" Javier yells as I gently pick up the snake from its midsection and it begins crawling onto my other hand.

"No! Uh-uh. No way," Ciara is muttering near me.

"It's only a gopher snake. See its markings? It's harmless. Well, unless you're a small mammal." I carry the snake over to the tall grass on the side of the yard.

I hear Kristina yell to a camera operator to follow me. When I look back, she's hiding behind Blue and Andrew for safety and everyone else on set has stopped to watch me. I shake my head. All this fuss over a snake? I gently release it into the grass. "There you go, little buddy." And I watch as it slithers away.

When I walk back to the patio, everyone is clapping for me. Blue gives me a big thumbs-up, and even Andrew looks impressed.

Ciara rushes over and gives me a big hug. "You saved my life. I guess we have to be friends now."

"You were never in danger. It's actually a beneficial species. They help control the rodent population."

Ciara pulls back from me. "Do you want to be friends or not?"

I laugh. "I do."

Then Javier crushes me with one of his bear hugs. "I promise I'll protect you if a mugger or bear attacks, but I don't fuck with snakes."

I smile at him. "It's okay, Javi. I'll defend you. Again." I wink at him, and he laughs and squeezes me even tighter.

Then they all pepper me with questions that I actually care about. Instead of inane small talk about astrological signs and weight loss injections, I get to explain to them that the only potentially dangerous snakes in Southern California are rattlesnakes. Or sidewinders if you're in the Sonoran Desert. Ciara and Javier want to know how to identify and avoid rattlers, and Madison asks if any species are vulnerable to habitat destruction. It's the first time on this show that I've actually felt in my element. And despite what my family thinks, they're all interested in hearing more.

That is, until Kristina comes over. "Okay, that's enough Bill Nye. Let's talk about stuff that won't put the audience to sleep." Andrew rolls his eyes behind her back, but when he catches my gaze he turns away. Then Kristina motions to where Beth Anne, Scott, and Bill are drinking at the pool bar. "Can't you be more like them? Go! Drink! Do something interesting!"

The other contestants make their way to the bar as Kristina tells me to meet her for my "confessional" in ten minutes, then strides off toward the mansion.

And once again, I'm left alone with Andrew. I can't help but notice he's rolled up his sleeves again as I prepare myself for a diatribe about my little stunt earlier with Beth Anne. But to my surprise, he says, "I didn't see 'snake whisperer' on your résumé. I thought you worked with amphibians."

"You've read my résumé?"

"I vet all the contestants before the show. Did you know that you have two PhDs?" he says with that mischievous twinkle in his eyes that elicits a disturbing reaction in me. It makes me want to flirt back.

"Does my saving Ciara's life mean you're dropping charges against me? I would imagine a contestant dying from a snake bite is a worse legal nightmare than a locked door."

"Except, as you pointed out, it wasn't a venomous snake. So, while we won't be litigating, you're still my biggest headache."

"I'll take that as a win."

"It's like you enjoy getting under my skin," he says, arms crossed.

I do, I think. *I really do.* I give him a nonchalant shrug. "It was fun at first, but now it's almost too easy. Maybe your skin is too thin?" And then, without thinking, I rub his forearm. He turns it over, offering me the inside, inviting me to touch him.

So I do. I trail my fingers slowly on the inside of his arm. A muscle in his jaw ticks.

My eyes shoot up to meet his. I shouldn't be touching him. And he shouldn't be letting me. He must come to his senses at the same time because he slowly takes his arm back. Then he looks around as if he's forgotten where he is before meeting my eye. He's back to that searching gaze like he's trying to figure me out.

I shrug and say, "Sorry. Fireball."

And then he does something that truly shocks me. He laughs. And it transforms his entire being. If I had met laughing Andrew instead of uptight lawyer Andrew, I'd have formed a very different opinion of him.

I'm on the verge of laughing too, until a loud cheer erupts from the bar and I turn to see the other contestants drinking more Fireball. "Should I be doing more shots before this confessional with Kristina?" I ask him.

"You may want to," Andrew says, with a hint of disdain in his voice. "She's particularly skilled at getting people to say whatever she wants them to say." Then he raises an eyebrow, glancing at my hands. "If you think you can keep your hands to yourself." He says this in a way that I can immediately feel low in my stomach. *Holy shit, I've got to stop being turned on by Andrew Benson, Esquire!*

Luckily, Blue interrupts my racing thoughts by coming to collect me for my confessional with Kristina. "You ready, Grace?" he asks, before adding, "You look nervous."

Nervous is not what I'm currently feeling. I shoot a guilty look at Andrew, who just watches me in amusement. I feel my face heating up. Does he know the effect he has on me?

"Don't worry," Blue says. "You'll do fine."

Andrew grins at me. "I'm sure you don't have any sins to confess."

I give him my sassiest stare-down. "Wouldn't you like to know."

"Yeah, I think I would," I hear him mutter under his breath as he shakes his head, turning away.

Chapter Eighteen

Blue and I collect Ciara from the bar, and he leads us to a dining room that's lit up with all sorts of intimidating, expensive-looking lights for the confessionals.

"I think I'd rather be in church," I mutter and Ciara laughs.

"You can go first," she says as she takes a step backward.

"Hey, I saved your life, remember?" I tease as Blue motions for me to sit in a chair in the middle of the room. "Is this where they interrogate captured operatives?"

"It's easy," Blue says as he makes sure my mic is on. "Just look into the camera and answer the questions."

"I was told not to look into the camera," I counter.

"This is different," Kristina says as she enters. "This is when I get to interview you." Then she drops the tough-ass producer voice for a second to tell me, "I was a broadcast journalism major. I always wanted to be the next Diane Sawyer."

"I always wanted to be the next Rachel Carlson," I say excitedly, thinking maybe producer-bot and I have finally found some common ground.

"Who?"

"The marine biologist and conservationist? She wrote *Silent Spring*, which basically led to the creation of the EPA?"

Kristina shakes her head. "Let's just get started."

"Okay . . ." I say, exhaling away some of the tension. I've

been interviewed by scientific journals. This has got to be similar.

Kristina sits behind the camera operator and tells me, "I'm going to ask you a question, and I need you to repeat the question in your answer we can use it as a sound bite. So, if I ask, 'Who is the person you're crushing on the most?' you would say, 'The person I'm crushing on the most is . . .'"

"I would never say that."

I hear Ciara laugh off camera before Kristina says, "Humor me."

I take a deep breath. They certainly don't ask about crushes in the *International Journal of Environmental Sciences*.

Kristina clears her throat and launches into her questions. "What was your first impression of Javier?"

"Energetic."

"Please repeat the question in your answer and elaborate."

"My first impression of Javier was that he had a lot of energy. He's funny and very liberal with the hugs."

"Did you find him attractive?"

"Yeah, everyone here is attractive. It's like some weird dystopian future where all the regular people have died off in a climate change apocalypse."

I hear a smothered laugh and turn to see Andrew has walked into the room, off camera. He stands next to Ciara and Blue, with his hands in his pockets as he casually leans against the wall, looking at me. As if he has nothing better to do than watch me mess up this confessional. And suddenly, I'm back to feeling nervous.

Kristina checks her list of questions, then asks, "Who do you have the most chemistry with?"

I shrug. "I think TC is really nice. He has twinkly eyes and a kind smile."

"You just described Santa Claus," Kristina says, pinching the bridge of her nose. She mutters something about unusable quotes, and it makes me happy I'm not the only one who's miserable right now. Kristina inhales deeply and continues. "Let's try this again. Which guy do you find most attractive?"

"Um . . ." My eyes involuntarily find Andrew again. Except when he sees me looking at him, he raises his eyebrows as if he's caught me. I quickly look away, only to realize I've forgotten all of the contestants' names. Until Hot Scott pops into my head. "I think the most attractive *contestant* is Hot Scott."

Kristina laughs. "Hot Scott. That's perfect, why didn't I think of that?" Then she looks back down at her "hard-hitting" questions and asks, "Okay, what was your first impression of Bill?"

"Cowboy Bill? Total douchebag," I say, ready to explain, but then I feel the energy in the room shift. Some of the PAs are exchanging glances and looking at me pityingly while Kristina scribbles furiously on her notepad. When I catch Andrew's eye, he shakes his head subtly then whispers something to Blue.

Blue claps his hands loudly, getting everyone's attention. "I'm grabbing some waters. Who wants one?"

"I do. I'm *parched*," Ciara emphasizes, shooting a quick glance at Andrew and then me.

Andrew gives me a nod like I should say yes, so I raise my hand at the same time he says, "Me too."

Kristina looks annoyed but concedes. "Fine, quick water break." Then she gets up to talk to someone behind the camera, and Andrew walks toward me. He looks like he's choosing his words carefully before he says quietly, "Be careful what you say. If you bad-mouth the other contestants, they'll make you the villain."

"Pretty sure America would agree with me about Bill."

He suppresses a grin and says seriously, "That might be true, but don't give them any fodder. They always edit it to make someone look bad. Or mean and judgmental. It's really easy to manipulate the viewership into turning on you."

"And that's legal?"

"It's not illegal. It's just . . . a part of the game."

I shake my head at his complicity and ask, "Then why are you helping me?"

Andrew shrugs as a smile plays on his lips. "Maybe you'll remember this the next time you're about to make my life difficult."

I give him a doubtful look, which makes his smile grow wider and I feel like I've won a prize. But then Andrew quickly steps away when he sees Blue rushing back with the waters.

Kristina gives Blue an impatient look as he hands them out. "Everyone ready?"

I take a sip of water, then say, "Uh, Kristina, can I answer that one again?" Ciara gives me a discreet thumbs-up. I smile at her, then try to focus on the confessional. But I'm finding it hard to shake off the fact that Andrew just quietly figured out a way to help me.

"Okay, we'll take it again," Kristina says suspiciously.

I plaster a fake smile on my face and look into the camera. "I'm not really sure what to make of Bill yet. He's obviously in great shape, but I don't know if we have much in common."

Kristina nods, satisfied with that answer. Though I get nervous when she jots another note.

"And what about the other female contestants?"

I smirk at Ciara, then answer, "Well, Ciara is a total badass, even if she is scared of snakes. And there's so much more to Madison than I originally thought. She runs a mental health nonprofit for kids and she's so passionate about helping others. It's really inspiring."

"And what about Beth Anne?"

"Beth Anne is a total—" This time Andrew, Ciara, and Blue all cough. I take their note and quickly change course. "I haven't really gotten a chance to get to know Beth Anne. But I like her accent."

"That's interesting. Because she has a definite opinion of you," Kristina says, trying to bait me. I look over at Andrew and Blue, and they both discreetly shake their heads.

So I bite my tongue and say, "Well, bless her heart."

When I'm done with my confessional, it's Ciara's turn in the hot seat. As Kristina starts asking her similar questions, I stop listening as I chat quietly off camera with Blue. He assures me that my answers weren't as awkward as they felt. I'm tempted to ask Andrew because I doubt he'd pull any punches, but he's stepped outside to take a phone call. Not that I'm paying attention to his comings and goings. I just happened to notice he's been gone for a couple minutes.

"Uh-oh," Blue says under his breath.

"What?" I whisper.

He motions back to Kristina and Ciara. "Kristina is trying to bait her."

"To talk shit about other contestants like she did with me?"

"Worse. Sometimes she tries to make people cry or yell on camera. Then they edit it so it seems like their response is to something completely benign, so they look unhinged."

"What the hell?" I look back and can tell that Ciara is getting agitated whereas Kristina looks like the cat that ate the canary.

Kristina raises her eyebrows and addresses Ciara: "Then why were there rumors that you still have a boyfriend back home?"

"I don't. Who said that?" Ciara demands angrily.

Kristina shrugs obnoxiously. "I'm not at liberty to say."

"I would never do something like that. Loyalty is the most important quality to me."

Kristina leans in. "So you're not here to two-time and cheat?"

"What? No! That's total bullshit!"

I'm about to run in there and stop the interview, but a hand grabs my shoulder. I'm pulled into someone behind me and immediately engulfed in a masculine scent . . . a familiar, intoxicating cologne.

"I'll handle it," Andrew whispers in my ear. The proximity of his lips to my ear—and the feeling that he's lingering there behind me a beat or two longer than he needs to—gives me a tingling feeling that I try to ignore, even as it floods my body. I spin around so we're face to face. His hands come to my waist to steady me.

"Kristina is trying to make Ciara look awful!" I hiss up at him.

"I know," Andrew whispers back. "I said, 'I'll handle it.'"

"What the hell is that supposed to mean?!" I whisper-yell back.

"Just trust me, okay?" Andrew says, brushing his thumb against my waist once and then walking off.

It takes me a moment to recover from his unexpected touch before I spin back to Blue, ignoring how quickly my heart is beating. "He expects me to trust him? He's the *lawyer* for the *show*! What do you think he's going to do?"

Blue looks around and makes sure Kristina and Ciara are still in a heated discussion before pulling me farther away from the crew. "I had my suspicions last year . . ." Blue begins. "Sometimes files *accidentally* got deleted. And it always seemed to be in an effort to protect the most vulnerable contestants."

"And you think Andrew's the one who did it?"

Blue nods. "He has access to the dailies and the edit bay."

I don't know what any of that means, but Blue's implication that Andrew might be working behind the scenes to protect people surprises me. Is it possible I've misjudged him too?

After Ciara storms out of the confessional, I find her in the bathroom and try to talk her down from quitting. "Kristina is doing it on purpose to get this reaction out of you," I begin. "If you quit, she wins."

"She's going to use that footage and make me look like the exact stereotype I've been trying to avoid my whole life."

I take Ciara's hand and say sincerely, "I know, and that's really shitty and you have every reason to be furious and want to quit. But I won't let her do this to you. I can't tell you specifics because I don't want to get anyone in trouble, but try to trust me—I don't think that footage is going to end up being used."

"Really?" she asks. I nod and she gives me a confused look. "Why are you helping me? We're technically competition."

I smile at her and parrot what Madison said to me yesterday. "Because a wise swimsuit model once told me, *'Life is so difficult as it is, we should be lifting each other up,'* and, *'There's a special place in hell for mean girls.'*" Ciara laughs as I continue. "But also because this show is so insane, we have to stick together if we're going to survive it."

Ciara nods in agreement, then gives me a hug. "You have my back, I have yours. Though this is now the second time you've saved me, so can you hurry up and almost die or something so I can return the favor?"

"I'll try," I tell her. "Now come on, let's go eat. I'm starving."

We eat dinner on the back patio with Javier, Madison, and TC, and it's actually fun. I'm starting to feel like a part of the group. Almost like we're all friends and not just four extremely attractive reality TV contestants and one scientist. Bill and Beth Anne are still mad about losing the first one-on-one date points, so they're eating down at the beach with Hot Scott, who I still can't talk to without blushing. But hey, four out of seven is way higher than my usual friend conversion rate, so I'll take it.

It's especially hot out today, so I decide to test out the infinity pool after we eat. Madison lets me borrow one of the twenty bathing suits she's brought. It doesn't take me long to realize that while my microphone necklace is waterproof, this bikini is definitely not meant for swimming laps at the Y. I take two strokes before I feel it falling off. I duck underwater to rearrange myself. When I resurface, I see Ciara and Madison standing above me.

"Guess what I just heard?" Madison says as she jumps into the shallow end next to me.

"How do you get your bathing suit to stay on?" I ask, impressed.

"Years of experience?" Madison shrugs. Ciara walks down the pool steps and joins us in the water as Madison says, "One of the PAs told me the girls get to pick who we take on our next one-on-one date!"

"Very Sadie Hawkins," I say as I scoop a honeybee out of the pool and set it gently outside the water. Ciara gives me and the bee a puzzled look, so I explain: "Don't get me started on the effects pesticides have had on the honeybee population."

Madison laughs and says to Ciara, "You'll get used to it. Grace is very passionate about saving animals."

Ciara nods. "That's cool. I got my cat from a shelter."

I give her an approving nod as Madison says, "Okay, okay, back to business. Which guy are you going to pick?"

I turn to look at the guys who are working out in the outside gym area and my eyes immediately find Hot Scott. It's hard not to. Then I look over at Javier, who says something to make TC laugh, and I'm reminded of how sweet and fun he is. And then I laugh at the absurdity that I, of all people, have to decide between two men.

Madison raises an eyebrow at my laughter. I compose myself. "Sorry, I've just never been in a position where I've had options before."

I decide I should make the mature, non-libido-driven decision and pick Javier when Ciara plays with her microphone necklace nervously and asks, "Grace, would you be upset if I picked Javi? I heard you guys kissed yesterday."

"Oh, uh . . ."

Madison also looks surprised by this. "I thought you were '*what I want, I get*'?" she teases Ciara.

"The producers made me say that. Apparently that's my role on the show—'the bad girl who comes in to shake things up.'" Ciara shrugs. "But I'm strictly hoes before bros all the way and would never want to step on my girls' toes. I know he's into you, Grace, but I couldn't tell if you're into him," Ciara says, waiting for my response.

I exhale as I try to make sense of what I'm feeling. Finally, I say, "I think the truth is, I want to be into Javier. He's funny and charming and sweet and I enjoy hanging out with him . . . but I don't get tongue-tied the way I do around Scott."

"I knew you had a crush on Scott!" Madison gushes. I shush her, and we all look over at him lifting weights, his sculpted chest glistening in the sun. He must sense our admiration because he looks at us and smiles.

"Yeah, that man is gorgeous," Ciara says, fanning herself.

"He's so handsome, it hurts to look at him," Madison agrees as she playfully splashes water on me to cool me off.

"He's definitely not what I would've thought was my type. He actually reminds me of all the guys who were too hot and cool to talk to me in school," I say as I adjust the bikini.

"Ooh, you need a revenge hookup!" Ciara says.

"OMG yes!" Madison claps excitedly.

"Yeah, I don't know what that is," I admit while peeking at Scott to make sure he can't hear us.

"It's like when a Jewish guy won't date you because you're not Jewish, so then you go and hook up with ten other Jewish guys to feel better about it," Ciara says matter-of-factly.

I sputter out a laugh. "Let me get this straight—so because, historically, hot cool guys wouldn't give me the time of day, I'm supposed to hook up with a hot cool guy as payback?"

"Exactly," Ciara and Madison say, nodding.

I'm not getting this. "But the hot cool guys from high school won't know about it."

"Doesn't matter," Ciara explains. "This is about flipping the script and reclaiming your pride. You're the one in control now."

Madison smiles sunnily as she adds, "Sometimes a mental 'fuck you' is just as strong as an in-person one. Probably has the same dopamine response in the brain. I'll ask my professors."

We look over at Scott, who is now toweling the sweat off his shining pecs. Ciara whistles. "That boy is a revenge fantasy if I've ever seen one."

I laugh again as I consider it. I'm still not sure about the logic behind it, but I have to admit, between their enthusiasm and Scott's pecs, it's a persuasive argument.

And then I notice Ciara sneaking furtive looks at Javier. I can't help but smile as I tell her, "I think you and Javier would be great together."

Ciara looks at me hopefully. "Does that mean I have your blessing?"

Not only would I never want to stand in the way of her potential happiness—especially when I'm not even sure if I think of Javier as more than a friend—but I'm actually rooting for them. I nod. "Poor guy won't know what hit him."

Madison squeals with delight. "I like this pairing!"

"Me too," I agree. "And now I'm really invested in you guys finding love. Ugh, this is how the producers get you."

They laugh and Ciara says, rubbing her hands together, "Well now I'm excited for the Angels and Devils party!"

I groan as I remember that tonight is our first theme party. Which, from what I understand, involves dressing up in costumes, getting drunk, and grinding on each other. It's like every school dance I've ever skipped.

Madison looks at me. "Ooh, can I do your hair and makeup again?"

"Nope, it's my turn," says Ciara. "Tonight we're pulling out all the stops," she says, grinning.

Chapter Nineteen

"Suck it, Giselle," Ciara says an hour later when she finishes my hair and makeup in Madison's bedroom. Apparently which direction your windows are facing determines the best light for makeup application and Madison's orientation has been deemed the best.

Madison comes around and gasps, "Wow, you really do look like a Victoria's Secret angel."

"Great," I deadpan. The producers provided us with two risqué devil costumes and two equally risqué angel costumes. You wouldn't think God's messengers would look like slutty doilies, but what do I know?

Obviously, Beth Anne and Ciara claimed the devil costumes. And Ciara looks amazing in her little red lingerie and flaming fire engine red lipstick. Madison looks sweet but sexy in her white lace angel teddy. And now's the moment of truth as I stand up to look in the mirror.

I do a double take. Ciara has pinned back my bangs but added volume and large curls to the rest of my hair. I'm wearing *a lot* of makeup, and for some reason I'm sparkling. I look closer—yep, there is *actual glitter* on my face and body. The only thing that may distract someone from the fact I'm a walking disco ball is that I'm wearing something that resembles a one-piece bathing suit . . . if it were appropriate to swim in white lace. The only parts that aren't see-through are around my nipples and crotch. And for some inexplicable reason, I'm wearing thigh-high white tights and garters.

Ciara walks around me, taking me in. "Damn, I'm good. You look hot."

"I'm supposed to look angelic."

Madison laughs. "Oh, don't worry. Scott will be on his knees when he sees you."

I shake my head at the ridiculousness of my life right now. "A week ago, I was asked to contribute an article to *Scientific American*, and now I'm dressed like a promiscuous cherub in hopes someone named 'Hot Scott' notices me at a theme party."

"Yeah you are," Ciara says, offering me a high-five.

I laugh and take a deep breath, pushing all thoughts of men, especially a confusing attorney, out of my mind. For some reason, I can't stop thinking about the fact that I may have misjudged Andrew. I was so sure I had him pegged as a self-assured asshole who was only looking out for the show, but now I don't know . . .

"Let's do this," Madison says as she loops her arm in mine.

"Wait, I want to be in the middle," Ciara says, playfully wedging herself between us. And so we walk outside arm in arm as a devil flanked by two angels.

"Ooh-la-la," Madison comments when we see that the back patio has been transformed into a cocktail party with the help of string lights and high-top tables. It's strangely classy for a group of people dressed like they're about to shoot some sort of Old Testament porn.

TC waves to Madison from the other side of the pool. He's also dressed like an angel . . . if angels wore white hot pants and no shirt. But he *is* wearing wings, which, I have to admit, do look strangely erotic on him. He and Madison are literally a match made in heaven.

"Go say hi," I tell her.

"No. It's girls' night."

"We're on a dating show. There's no escaping the boys. Seriously, it's fine." I give her a little shove.

"Okay, I'll be right back," Madison says before rushing over to TC.

I watch as Madison cozies up to him, laughing when their wings bump into each other. I smile at them, then tap Ciara's shoulder when I see Javier walk in. He's wearing an open white vest with wings and tight white leather pants.

"I'd wish you luck, but you don't need it," I tell her.

Ciara blows me a kiss then struts toward Javier. I've never been so happy to watch a sexy devil flirt with a muscular angel before. I laugh at them and get a warm fuzzy feeling in my chest.

But the laugh gets caught in my throat when Hot Scott walks in. And the warm fuzzy feeling gets doused with lighter fluid when I see he's shirtless and wearing the red equivalent of Javi's leather pants. He has on a crimson eye mask like you'd see at Carnival in Brazil and carries a pitchfork. This half-assed Halloween costume shouldn't do it for me, but I think I may have a bad boy fetish now. He just looks so powerful and confident as he walks straight toward me. Maybe it's the air of danger his costume evokes, or the intensity with which he's staring at me, but I'm finding it hard to breathe.

"Hey there, angel," he says as he gets closer. He greets me with a tight hug and whispers in my ear, "I'm hoping I can tempt you with my devilish ways tonight."

I find myself exhaling, "Okay," because my libido has officially taken over for my brain and I can't think of anything else to say.

He kisses my cheek innocently. Then his lips trail lower. He softly kisses his way down my neck and my whole body feels like it's on fire. I let out a surprised gasp. Scott leans back, eyes gleaming, loving the reaction he's causing in me.

"You know where to find me," he says, as he heads into the party.

I stand there, afraid to walk just yet because my body still feels tingly, until I notice Andrew is not only on set but looking straight at me. And he looks angry. Suddenly a metaphorical cold shower hits me but I can't tell why. Am I feeling embarrassed? Guilty?

Andrew walks over and I brace myself for whatever rule I've

broken this time. But instead he says quietly, "Can I talk to you for a second?"

I nod and he takes my hand to lead me away from the cameras.

When we get to the edge of the patio, he lets go of my hand but stays close to me. Distractingly close. He checks to make sure Kristina is talking to a PA before he says, "Look, I'm not supposed to talk about the contestants but . . . be careful around Scott."

"What? Why?"

"He's not a good guy."

"Says who?"

He sighs like he *really* shouldn't be telling me this. "They make me look at everyone's background checks and social media before the show starts to see if there'll be any potential issues. There are pictures of him with different girls every week and comments from some very angry women, who appear to have had legitimately bad experiences with him. I tried to warn the producers he's sleazy, but he had enough followers that they didn't seem to care."

"So this is based on social media? You don't actually know him—"

"And you do?" he throws back at me. Then he runs his fingers through his hair like he does when he gets frustrated. But then it dawns on me.

"Wait. Are you mad that I let him kiss me just now?"

"He had his hands all over you," he snaps. Then he looks away like he's embarrassed by this admission.

"So?" I ask. Does he not want Scott touching me because of the show or because he's . . . jealous?

"Look, do whatever you want. I just wanted to give you a heads-up in case . . . well, just in case."

"Okaaaay," I say because that's not really an answer.

His gaze dips briefly to take in my angel costume, and he looks like he's on the verge of saying something else. I hold my breath, desperate to know what he's thinking. That same muscle in his jaw ticks, but then he just turns and walks away.

God, this man is infuriating! I start after him to ask what the hell is going on, but Ciara intercepts me and drags me to the bar. I wonder if she can tell that I need to clear my head of Andrew.

I'm just desperate enough that I agree to do another shot with her. "But not Fireball!" I quickly add.

"You're telling the devil not to drink Fireball?" she laughs. Then she orders us two Cazadores shots.

"Salud!" Ciara calls. We say "Cheers," then tip 'em back.

I start coughing. "What was that?"

"Tequila."

"It burns almost as bad as Fireball," I say, making a face.

"Sounds like you need another one then." She motions to the bartender for another round.

Madison walks over as the bartender hands us another shot. She must see my grimace because she says, "You may want to take it easy, sweetie. You only had salad for dinner."

"She only ever eats salad for dinner. She's vegan," Ciara retorts. "She'll be fine. It's only a couple of tequila shots. Or as we say in Vegas . . . breakfast."

Madison laughs but shakes her head. "Just remember she doesn't have the tolerance you do. No one does."

I look up at them and burst out laughing. Madison is staring at me with a concerned face and a halo headband, while Ciara is handing me the shot wearing her devil horns. "You're really not seeing the irony in this situation?"

Ciara realizes what I'm talking about and starts cracking up. "I've always wanted to be the devil on someone's shoulder! Let me corrupt you, Grace! Please!" We clink glasses and down the second shot.

Madison laughs with us, then sighs. "I guess that means I'll be the one holding her hair back later."

Ciara convinces Madison to do a shot to catch up—she really is very good at peer pressure. Then she orders us all a glass of white wine.

"If you get nervous talking to Hot Scott and think you might say something stupid, take a sip of wine and compose yourself first," Ciara explains.

Not bad advice.

That is, until I'm sitting on a chaise lounge next to Hot Scott polishing off my second glass of white wine in less than twenty minutes. Every time he looks at me, I get nervous and take a sip.

But I have managed to learn that he lives on the Upper East Side, he's from Queens originally, and . . . there was something else, but I forgot. I was too busy staring at his face.

So far Scott has been the perfect gentleman. He even offered to get me another glass of wine. I don't know what Andrew was getting so worked up about.

Luckily, before I can get any tipsier, Shantae surprises us by walking out looking fierce in a full-length, skin-tight red gown. She's wearing a red cape and devil horns; I'm sure the wardrobe department was more than happy to cast her high-maintenance ass as a devil.

"Who's ready for a points update?" Shantae calls and waves us over to her. Scott takes my hand and leads me to the white outdoor couches where Shantae is waiting. When we sit down, I realize we're all coupled up. Even Beth Anne and Bill look cozy, dressed in matching devil costumes. But I can't help but notice that Beth Anne keeps sneaking glances at Scott.

"Before I reveal the current points leader and who won the first 'America's Favorite Contestant' vote, I want to announce a new twist." Shantae pauses for her signature dramatic effect as the camera operators get close-ups of our *shocked* reactions. Shantae holds up a golden key card. "This is a special award for the points leader. It's the key to the Privacy Villa!"

Beth Anne claps excitedly as I whisper to Javier and Ciara, "What's that?"

"The Privacy Villa," Shantae continues, "is the most secluded, most romantic part of the property."

"It's the guesthouse above the garage," Javier whispers to me, and I laugh.

Shantae shoots us a look that reminds me of an annoyed librarian, then says in her most important host voice, "It has a king-sized bed and a soaking tub, and most importantly, there are no cameras." As I'm thinking of how nice a relaxing bath sounds and maybe being able to sneak in a book, Shantae keeps talking. "The points winner chooses someone to spend the night with *or* they can opt to gift the villa to another couple. But that means they'll spend the night in the shack instead."

"Well, that's a no-brainer," Javier says, shaking his head.

"All these twists seem unnecessarily complicated," I say to Scott, but his stunning teal eyes are glowing when he looks back at me.

Madison whispers to me, "Oh my gosh! I hope TC wins America's Favorite Contestant. We could really use some alone time."

I raise my eyes suggestively at her until I see Blue rolling out what must be the leaderboard, covered in a sheet. "Yay, Blue! Roll it!" I catcall at him. *I may be drunk.*

Madison must also clock this because she hands me the rest of her water. "Thanks, Angel," I say as I guzzle it down.

Shantae stands in front of the board and gives us a recap. "Yesterday, Madison, TC, Grace, and Javier were all awarded five points for the first one-on-one date."

Beth Anne rolls her eyes. "We remember. When do the challenges start?"

"Tomorrow," Shantae says, trying to hide her annoyance at the interruption. "Okay, where was I?"

"Madison and TC are winning!" I remind her enthusiastically. I hold Madison's hand up in the air like a victor.

Shantae nods and seamlessly shifts back into her normal composed self. "Yes, Madison and TC are tied for first along with Javier and Grace, but don't forget, every time America votes for their favorite contestant, they're awarded ten points."

I put Madison's hand down. "Oh yeah. Bummer."

TC looks at me and then says to Madison, "What's gotten into Grace?"

"Tequila," she answers, and they share a look. It might be a look of concern, but there's currently four of them so it's hard to tell.

Shantae holds up an envelope. "God, they love envelopes on this show." Everyone laughs, and I realize I said that louder than I thought.

Shantae takes out a piece of paper and says, "America's Favorite Contestant is . . . Grace!"

"Wait, what? Like me?" I ask Shantae as Madison gives me a big hug and everyone but Beth Anne cheers.

Shantae ignores my question. "Which means, our current points leader is . . ." She whips the sheet off the scoreboard. "Grace!"

Before I realize what's happening, Madison and Ciara are jumping up and down with excitement, Beth Anne is muttering, "For fuck's sake," and Shantae has handed me the golden key card. This is all happening so fast that all I can say is, "Huh?"

Shantae looks annoyed with me when she asks, "So, Grace, who are you going to choose to stay overnight with you in the Privacy Villa?"

Oh shit. I forgot about that part.

Chapter Twenty

I turn to see Scott eyeing me and my knees go weak. While my tequila-soaked sex organs are urging me to pick Hot Scott, if I were being honest with myself, I'm a little scared of being intimate with him. I mean, he's like the *Discovery* space shuttle of sex . . . and I'm . . . space junk? Hmm . . . it's harder to come up with analogies when you're intoxicated. Plus, even though I'd never admit it to Andrew, what he told me is still swimming around in the back of my head somewhere.

I look past Scott and see Madison and TC holding hands, and I'm immediately convinced that my friends deserve this. They're forming a meaningful connection, whereas all I know about Scott is an adjective that rhymes with his name and the fact that he's from Queens. So I take a deep breath and say, "Actually, Shantae, I think I want to gift it to the people I think deserve it the most." I hand the golden key card to Madison and TC.

"Are you sure, Grace?" Madison asks. "But you'll have to stay in the shack."

Oh yeah, definitely didn't remember that little detail. But I just shrug. "It's all part of the experience, right?"

"And that must be why you're America's Favorite!" Shantae says as Beth Anne rolls her eyes.

Madison immediately launches herself at me, and TC wraps his arms around both of us. "Thank you so much, Grace!" he says. Then

Ciara and Javier are joining in on this impromptu group hug until we all start laughing.

From somewhere inside the hug, Ciara yells, "This calls for shots!"

The next thing I know I'm doing another tequila shot, despite Madison's angelic protests. And then a DJ materializes and music starts playing. The formerly classy cocktail party turns into a poolside nightclub complete with strobe lights and a dance floor.

I haven't gone out dancing much in my life, and I'm not what you would call coordinated, but I'm drunk and happy and don't care what I look like. I bounce around merrily with Madison and Ciara, and even dance with Javi for a little until Hot Scott comes over and asks to cut in. I giggle because it sounds so Victorian. But when Scott pulls me close, his hands on my hips, and we gyrate to the music, it feels anything but.

The song has a slow but pulsing, sexy beat. Because of the heels Ciara made me wear, certain parts of me line up with certain parts of Scott in a very nice way.

He's taken off his devil mask, so I see the naughty twinkle in his eyes when he leans in and says, "So you'd rather sleep in the shack than hook up with me?"

I shyly avert my gaze. "Sorry. I was trying to be a good friend."

"But you're also scared of me."

I laugh nervously, wishing I still had my social lubricant Chardonnay. But instead, I answer truthfully. "I just don't think I'm as experienced as you."

Scott slowly looks me up and down. "Trust me, Grace, there is nothing you could do that I wouldn't find sexy. And I'm happy to teach you whatever you want to learn."

He reaches around and grabs my ass, pulling me even closer. I gasp when I realize he's hard. *Like really hard.* And God, it feels good being pressed up against him as he rolls his hips to the beat of the music.

After a few minutes, Scott asks in a low voice, "Do you want to go in the hot tub with me?"

"Now?" I ask. I glance over at the far side of the pool where the hot tub is. It's dark over there and away from everyone else.

"Yeah."

I look down at what I'm wearing. I guess if I take off my tights and garters, I'm basically wearing a bathing suit. "What are you going to wear?"

"Nothing," he says, and my heart stumbles.

"Okay," my mouth answers before my prude brain can catch up.

Scott takes my hand and starts to lead me off the dance floor. But Madison steps in our way. "Sorry, Scott. I have a quick question for my girl. One sec."

Madison pulls me out of earshot and whispers, "Where are you going?"

"The hot tub. Tub. *Tuuub*. That's a funny word."

"You're drunk, Grace, and everyone knows the hot tub is code for hooking up."

"It is?"

Ciara comes over. "What's going on? Why are we whispering?"

"Grace is going in the hot tub with Scott," Madison says disapprovingly.

"Nice! Get after it!" Ciara says, giving me a high-five.

"She's extremely drunk!" Madison counters with a loud whisper.

"Do you want to hook up with Hot Scott?" Ciara asks me.

"You're the ones who told me about the revenge hookup!" I answer. Ciara looks at Madison and shrugs. Then I burst out laughing. "Angel and Devil . . . still funny."

I catch Madison giving Ciara a look, but Ciara points to the cameras surrounding us. "There are cameras everywhere, Mad. She's fine."

Madison sighs and says to me, "Just be careful, Grace. And don't do anything you're not ready for, okay?"

What could possibly happen in a hot tub other than kissing and splashing? So I shrug and say, "Okay, bye!" Then I skip over to Scott.

Scott takes my hand and pulls me toward the hot tub. It really is out of the eyeline of the rest of the party, and it suddenly feels very secluded. Scott starts to unbutton his pants, and I cover my eyes. He laughs, then a moment later says, "I'm in now, you can look."

I peek through my fingers and see him sitting in the water. I kick off my heels, then bend over and start unhooking the garters. I slowly take off my thigh-highs, and I notice Scott is watching my every move. "God, you are so fucking hot," he says.

I ride that wave of confidence over to the hot tub, walk down the steps in my lacy, white body suit, and sit down next to him.

"Come here," he says, his voice gravelly. He takes my hand and pulls me on top of him. "That's better," he groans as I straddle his lap. I can feel his erection pressing against me, all the way up to my stomach.

I look down and see that there's only a very thin piece of lace between us right now. There's something I feel like I'm supposed to remember that Madison told me, but the thought of a naked Scott underneath me is very distracting.

"Oh shoot," I say, standing up and moving away from him as I suddenly remember. "We're not supposed to be off camera." I back up and sit across from him on the other side of the hot tub.

Scott laughs and motions to a camera pointed right at us. *Well, shit.* I'm either drunker than I thought or I've gotten so used to there being so many cameras around that I don't even notice them anymore. I also now understand why they say alcohol lowers your inhibitions. I'm pretty sure sober me would never make out in a hot tub on TV, but I don't currently seem to care.

But then I realize my white angel costume is now very wet and very see-through. I quickly cover my hard nipples with my hands as Scott floats over to my side of the hot tub and kneels in front of me. He settles in between my legs and begins kissing my neck. All thoughts of cameras disappear. Scott moves my hands away from my breasts and places his hands there instead. He begins squeezing and my hips move involuntarily.

I lean into him as he pinches my nipple through the lacy fabric and suddenly I'm writhing around. "Do you like that, Grace?" he whispers into my ear. I think I nod yes, but it's hard to tell because I've lost control of my body.

His hands keep roaming as his kisses lazily make their way from my ear to my jaw and then finally, a soft, teasing kiss on my lips. But when I kiss him back, there's nothing teasing or soft about it.

Scott immediately pulls me off the hot tub seat and on top of him and kisses me back just as hard. The friction is driving me crazy and I'm already so turned on. Then one of his hands leaves my ass and finds it way between my legs. As he touches me, I feel pressure building and I squeeze his shoulders tighter.

I'm seconds from Scott taking me over the edge when I hear, "What the hell is going on over here?"

I pull away from Scott's mouth and see Andrew walking toward us. It takes me a second to register it's even him.

"Well, if it isn't the Buzzkill," Scott says, annoyed. "We're not breaking the rules, there's a camera rolling."

"What about ethics?" Andrew asks, his voice gritty with barely controlled anger. Then he turns to the camera operator and motions for him to stop filming. The second the cameraman walks away, Andrew spins on Scott. "You think it's okay to hook up with a woman who's had too much to drink?"

I stand up. "I'm not drunk." But then I undermine my point by wobbling and plopping back down in the water with an ungraceful splash. "It's just slippery."

"Trust me, she was very enthusiastically consenting," Scott says in a smug voice.

Andrew looks like he's about to lose his shit, but instead he grabs a towel and says, "It's my job to make sure nothing goes too far, particularly when there's alcohol involved. You can pick up where you left off tomorrow, when you're sober. Grace, get out of the hot tub."

I look at Andrew and then back at Scott. They're staring at each other in some sort of alpha male standoff. I grab the railing and climb out of the hot tub with Scott trailing behind me. Andrew angrily wraps a towel around me but ignores Scott.

"Why are you mad at me?" I ask him.

"Do you really think it's a good idea to get into a hot tub with him after what I told you?" Andrew asks.

"What's that supposed to mean?" Scott says, getting in Andrew's face.

But I'm already there, mad enough for the both of us, and I yank on Andrew's arm to get him to look at me. "I didn't break any rules. I didn't do anything wrong," I spit out.

Andrew's eyes travel over my soaking body, now covered partially by a towel. Scott snorts, and then Andrew shakes his head. "No, you're right. It's not your fault. It's his." And then he turns around and punches Scott in the face.

Chapter Twenty-One

My startled scream alerts the rest of the contestants and crew members, who come running to the scene and see that Scott's nose is dripping with blood. I quickly pull Andrew away before Scott can retaliate.

Kristina rushes over. "What the hell happened over here?"

"The fucking lawyer punched me," Scott says, holding his nose. Blue hands him a towel for the blood.

Kristina spins on Andrew. "You. In the production office now." Andrew shakes out his hand and storms off as Kristina calls for a medic.

Madison rushes over and puts her arm around me. "Are you okay? What happened?"

I shake my head. "I don't know. I think Andrew thought he was protecting me?"

I look back and forth between Andrew walking away and Scott standing there bleeding . . . and I go after Andrew.

I grab ice from the outside bar, wrap it in my towel, and speed-walk to the production trailer. When I get there, I find him inside, alone, writing something. I knock on the door, and he turns as I say, "I brought ice."

He puts his pen down, and I walk over to where he's sitting. He silently watches me as I step between his legs and take his bruised hand in mine. I gently wrap the towel around it, making sure the ice is on his swollen knuckles.

"Thanks," he says as he blows out the breath he had been holding.

I realize I'm standing too close, but neither of us makes an effort to move. "Want to tell me what that was all about?" I finally ask.

"I shouldn't have done that," Andrew says, shaking his head. "It's just . . . when I heard he was in the hot tub with an intoxicated contestant, I was pissed. I knew he'd pull something like that. But then I heard it was you . . . I just lost it."

"Oh," I answer quietly.

"I'm probably going to lose my job."

"Only if Scott presses charges, right? I'm sure Kristina will convince him not to. She'll find a way to make a bloody nose good for the show."

Andrew shrugs. "Either way. It's not a great look when the studio lawyer breaks the 'no violence' clause." His hand twitches where I'm holding the ice on it, but he doesn't pull it away.

"For what it's worth, no one has ever defended my honor before. I don't usually condone violence, but that was hot."

I meant it as a joke, but he quickly looks up at me, searching my eyes. And I realize that maybe I wasn't entirely joking. There was something possessive about the way Andrew came in and tore me away from Scott. I swallow hard and busy myself checking his knuckles under the ice. "The swelling is going down."

He nods. "Just in time to write myself up in an incident report." But he doesn't take his hand away, and I don't let go of it either.

I'm distracted by the nuances I'm discovering this close to him. The slight smattering of freckles on his nose and the specks of gold in his warm brown eyes. I always thought green eyes were my favorite, because of their genetic rarity, but suddenly brown is in the running.

Then he inhales deeply. "Do you have another towel?" he asks, gesturing vaguely to my body.

I realize that in my rush to bring him ice, I used the towel that was formerly covering my still see-through angel costume. "Oh. I used it for the ice."

He looks up and closes his eyes like he's asking a higher power for strength. "I'm trying really hard to be a gentleman. Which is difficult when you're wet and essentially naked." He reaches for his suit jacket from the back of a chair and hands it to me.

I use his thigh for balance as I wrap the jacket around me. "Hey, I didn't pick out the costumes," I say.

"I know. And I'm going to talk to the producers about them. They're ridiculous."

"I'm supposed to be angelic." I pout.

"There is nothing about the way you look that's angelic," he says, looking down at my hand that is still holding onto his thigh, as I continue to stand between his legs. He's clenching the fist that isn't currently being iced as if it's itching to grab onto something.

I should really move my hand, but I can't help but feel smug that I have this effect on him. It's even more fun than trying to piss him off.

He must notice the glint in my eye because he shakes his head. "You like torturing me."

"No, if I liked torturing you, I'd let this jacket slip off."

"Please don't," he grinds out, but his eyes say the opposite. We stand there in a game of chicken until he reaches out and holds onto my hip, his thumb on my bare skin, under his jacket. To keep me away or pull me in? I don't think he knows.

Then he sighs heavily and shakes his head like he's trying to shake sense back into himself. "Come on, I'll walk you to your shack while I wait for Kristina."

I exhale a breath I didn't realize I was holding and reluctantly take a step back so we're no longer touching.

Andrew grabs a flashlight, and I groan, "I forgot about the damn shack." He laughs and guides me out the door.

Despite sobering up in the aftermath of the punch, I might still be tipsy because as we head down the grassy hill toward the shack, I stumble. Andrew catches me before I face-plant, holding me by the waist and pulling me upright so I'm standing directly in front of him. His hands are still on my waist, and I like the way they feel. Too much. I also like the way his face looks in the moonlight. *He really is very handsome.*

"Thank you," Andrew says.

"Did I say that out loud?"

Andrew laughs and takes my hand. "That's two compliments tonight. I think you better stay away from tequila or I might get the impression you don't hate me as much as you pretend you do."

"In that case, I'm never drinking again," I say as he helps me down the hill.

As we get closer to the shack of doom, Andrew says, "It was really nice of you to give Madison and TC the Villa, by the way."

"What can I say? I'm a saint."

He squeezes my hand. Which I realize he's still holding even though we're now on flat ground. "Aren't you?" he says, holding up the towel of ice I brought him. "You're always looking out for everyone else." Andrew stops in front of the shack door and turns toward me. "Who looks out for you?"

I think about the granola bar he gave me, and his advice during the confessional, and his protectiveness around Scott. "Usually no one. But lately . . ." I raise our entwined hands, and the implication just hangs in the air.

We stand there, holding hands, for another charged moment. Except this time, I pull away first. The thought of him looking out for me changes things. Because this isn't just us messing with each other or trying to get a reaction out of each other. I don't know what it means, but it seems like something I should figure out when I'm sober.

I hand him his jacket back. "Good night, Andrew."

He hands me the flashlight and looks conflicted. Like there's more he wants to say or do. "Good night, Grace."

And then I watch him walk all the way back up the hill to find out his fate with Kristina.

Two things wake me up the next morning, and I can't decide which is more annoying: the light streaming directly into my eyes from the hole in the shack wall, or the fact that Cowboy Bill is curled up mere feet away, snoring at 150 decibels.

I sit up, and my back immediately reminds me that I slept on the ground last night. But luckily, my back pain is overshadowed by my splitting headache and monstrous thirst. I look around to see if there's any bottled water or even an old rusted can of rainwater when I see Beth Anne sleeping on the other side of the shack. She's wearing a silk eye mask and ear plugs with a bottle of Evian next to her. She's even set up a battery-powered noise machine and humidifier. She's created the Four Seasons of murder shacks. Good for her.

I ruffle through my suitcase in hopes that I packed some painkillers when I see that I have a text from Cassie on my burner phone.

CASSIE: You didn't call me to check in last night. How are you?

I sigh and text back.

ME: Well, I'm lying on the floor of a haunted tool shed with a massive headache and dry mouth. So, you know, I've been better.

She immediately texts me back.

CASSIE: Oh no! What happened?

And then last night comes flooding back with a vengeance. The shots, the wine, the dance floor, the hot tub, Andrew punching Scott. *Shit.* I tiptoe out of the shack and walk down to the beach in my pajamas so I can call Cassie without getting caught. She answers on the first ring.

"Why are you in the shack?" she asks without even saying hello. I cringe at her morning peppiness before explaining that I actually had the most points, but I gave the golden key card to Madison and TC.

Cassie claps loudly when I tell her I was "America's Favorite Contestant," and I move the phone away from my ear. "Please be less excited for me. I'm hungover. And the shack is the least of my problems right now," I say before I launch into the drama of yesterday, starting with, "So, I kind of hooked up with Hot Scott yesterday."

"Who's Hot Scott?" Cassie asks as I walk along the shore.

"He just got here and he's a model and really hot."

"What do you mean by 'hooked up'?" And then she whispers, "Did you have sex with him?"

"No! Wait, is that what 'hook up' means? No wonder Madison was so protective about me going in the hot tub with him."

"Hot tub?! Everyone on reality TV knows that's code for sex."

"Well, not everyone," I mutter as I seriously consider drinking the Pacific Ocean to quench my thirst. Instead, I sigh and explain, "Hot Scott and I did some dirty dancing at the Angels and Devils party, and then we made out in the hot tub with some touching until Andrew interrupted us. And then he punched Scott in the face."

"You're hungover? You made out in a hot tub? Men are fistfighting over you? Who are you and what have you done with my best friend?" Cassie demands.

Even though I know she's teasing me, I let everything sink in as I pace back and forth on the beach. "You're right. This isn't me. I don't do tequila shots or hook up with strangers. I don't know what the hell is happening, Cass. There's some serious Stockholm syndrome mind-fuckery going on around here. I bet my brain imaging would be very similar to a cult member's right now."

"I can't believe some sleazy model was trying to take advantage of you in a hot tub!"

"Yeah, that wasn't cool of Scott. But maybe he was drunk and making bad decisions too? And it's not like I was telling him no . . ." I say defensively.

"Because you were intoxicated! I don't like this guy for you," she says. And in the somewhat sober light of day, I don't either.

"What's this Scott guy like anyway?" Cassie asks.

"I dunno. Hot?"

"So, Scott was just the proxy for all the hot cool guys who never gave nerds like us a second glance growing up?"

"How does everyone know about this theory? It's insane," I say as I throw a seashell into the water.

"It makes sense. You're helping to reset the equilibrium of the universe."

I laugh, then wince. "Don't make me laugh. It hurts too much."

Then Cassie asks, "So what about Not-So-Old Man Benson?"

"Andrew? What about him?"

"He punched a guy for you! That seems very unlawyerly!"

I want to immediately deflect and say it wasn't for me, and he was just protecting the show, but then I remember what he said in the production trailer last night. *"But then when I heard it was you he was trying to take advantage of, I don't know, I just lost it."*

"I really don't know what Andrew's deal is," I answer honestly. "I thought he hated me. He was so grumpy and annoying in his emails and when we first met. And he's constantly reprimanding me. But then last night . . ."

I try to make sense of his actions, but when I force my synapses to fire, more scenes from the production trailer come flickering back. I groan loudly when I remember how flirty and inappropriate I was, and oh my God I touched his thigh and threatened to take off his jacket.

"What?" Cassie asks when I groan.

"I think I may have drunkenly hit on him." I hide my face in my hands and tell Cassie, "Don't ever let me drink again. I can't be trusted."

But Cassie just makes a "hmm" noise.

"What's with you and the 'hmms'? What does 'hmm' mean?" I demand.

"Nothing. It's just interesting." But before I can ask her to elaborate, she says, "I actually have to run, though. It's time to go release our babies."

"Oh my God. I can't believe I forgot that today is the big day!" I say, stunned. I throw myself down into the sand. No amount of tequila should make me forget the day I've been working toward for three years of vaccine research. This is an all-time low for me.

"It's okay," Cassie says, sensing my depressive state. "You've been busy navigating a whole new world, Grace."

"How could I possibly let myself get caught up in all this bullshit fake dating drama? I got distracted by douchey guys and an infuriating lawyer instead of focusing on the things that really matter! What the hell is wrong with me?"

"It's understandable that you're overwhelmed," Cassie says sincerely. "And don't worry. Seriously, we've got it covered." I appreciate her kind words, but they don't make me feel any better about losing focus.

I sigh heavily. "Thanks, Cass." As disappointed as I am in myself now, I'm equally grateful that I have her in my life. "Good luck today, and call me right after to tell me everything. Seriously, every single detail."

"I will. And I promise we won't let you down."

"I know you won't. I miss you."

"Miss you too. Oh, I packed some Advil in your toiletry bag," Cassie says.

"You're a lifesaver!" I tell her before she hangs up, and I'm suddenly overwhelmed with homesickness. Well, *work*-sickness. I should be there with them.

I sit in the sand, staring out at the ocean and feeling helpless stuck inside this reality TV prison. All I can do is say a prayer to the environmentalist ghost of John Muir that my little froggies will do well in the wild today. Then I take a deep breath, dust the sand off my pajamas, and vow to try harder. If my coworkers are picking up the slack for me outside the mansion, I need to do my part in here.

But first . . . Advil. *Hmm, maybe Advil really should have been a sponsor.*

Chapter Twenty-Two

I sneak back into the shack where Bill and Beth Anne are still sleeping. As I discreetly change into a tank top and denim cutoffs, I hear hushed voices outside.

"You go in first."

"No, you."

"I hate horror movies, and blood makes me pass out."

"If Grace has been murdered, I'll never forgive myself."

"And I'll never get the image of her dead body out of my head, so you go first."

"Rock, paper, scissors?"

I open the door to find Madison and Ciara. Madison jumps backward while Ciara screams, "Don't kill us!"

When they realize I'm not attacking them with a chainsaw and I also haven't been attacked by a chainsaw, they launch themselves at me for a hug. "Oh, thank God!" Madison says from somewhere wedged between Ciara and me.

"This shack is creepy as fuck," Ciara adds. "Glad you weren't dismembered."

I laugh. "Me too."

"Your bangs and mascara are tragic, though," she continues as she tries to flatten down my hair, which must look like the result of an electrostatic experiment.

"She looks fine. Let's go to breakfast," Madison chirps, hooking her arm in mine before I can protest.

* * *

We sit by the pool, and I guzzle coffee. For once, I don't even care if it's fair trade or organic. I just need the caffeine to constrict the blood vessels in my brain and make this headache go away.

I catch Madison and Ciara sharing furtive glances until Madison finally says, "We need to tell you something."

"Can you tell it a little more quietly please? My head is throbbing."

Ciara laughs knowingly. "My bad."

"How are you alive right now? You drank like five times what I did." And she somehow looks the opposite of how I currently feel.

She just shrugs. "Years of practice? Superhuman liver?"

Madison is about to talk when I suddenly remember the golden key card. "Oh wait, how was last night in the Privacy Villa?" I ask her.

Madison smiles shyly and says, "It was really great. Thank you again. So *so* much. But that's not what we need to talk to you about." She takes a deep breath. "Last night after you and Scott were in the hot tub and Andrew broke Scott's nose—"

"Oh shit, it's broken?" I interrupt again.

"Yeah, but don't feel too bad for him," Ciara continues. "It didn't seem to hold him back."

"After you went to bed and his nose stopped bleeding, Scott came back to the party," Madison says slowly. "And he was flirting with Beth Anne . . . and they went down to the beach for a while."

"Okay . . . ?" I say, not understanding where she's going with this.

"Well, they kinda, sorta . . ." Madison trails off.

"They banged on the beach, Grace," Ciara says bluntly.

"What?" I'm partly shocked and partly offended that I could be replaced so easily. "Well, he certainly moved on quickly . . ."

"Don't take it personally. He's clearly just here to get laid," Ciara says, and Madison elbows her.

"You think he was trying to use me for sex?" I ask.

"He's a dick. Don't let him mess with your head," Madison says as she rubs my arm.

But it doesn't help. I feel stupid. "I should've known," I say, blowing out a breath. "I'm such an idiot. Of course Scott wasn't really interested in me. He just picked me because he knew I'd be flattered that he was even talking to me. I was an easy target."

"First of all, you're not an idiot. Everyone thought he was into you. He acted like he really liked you. And maybe he did," Madison says gingerly.

"Yeah, it's not your fault Scott's a fuck boy," Ciara adds.

"What's a fuck boy?" I ask, looking back and forth at them, hoping the Advil and coffee kick in soon.

"A player. Someone who doesn't want to settle down. He just wants to sleep around," Ciara explains as Madison nods.

"And people wonder why I don't date," I say with a bitter laugh. But then an errant thought crosses my mind, and because I'm still hungover as shit I voice it. "I've always said it's because there are slim prospects in LA, but maybe I didn't date because I was trying to avoid feeling exactly what I'm feeling right now."

"Oh honey." Madison takes my hand. "Then you should be proud. You overcame your fear, put yourself out there, and took a risk. Maybe it didn't pan out this time, but it could next time. And this is the perfect place to practice!"

"Yeah, because what's getting rejected and looking stupid in front of millions of people?" I say, only half-joking.

"Trust me," Ciara says. "You'll end up looking better than he will."

"Yeah, America will side with you. They already love you!" Madison chimes in.

I shake my head. "I should've listened to Andrew when he warned me that Scott's not a good guy. He's obviously not here for the *right reasons*." I immediately wince. "Did I really just say that?"

Madison and Ciara laugh, but my stomach sinks when I consider my own motives. If, as Blue said, the right reason for being on the show is to find love, then I'm obviously not here for the right reasons either. If anyone found out, I'd lose whatever goodwill with viewers that Madison thinks I currently have.

But as I worry about my future, another more pressing concern hits me, and I'm almost afraid to ask. "Did he get fired?"

"Who? Andrew? No," Madison says. "Scott didn't press charges, so Kristina just gave him a warning."

"She also asked him if he knew anything about some missing confessional footage," Ciara says as she conspiratorially raises her eyebrows at me. "But he said he didn't have a clue."

I give a big sigh of relief, and they both look at me suspiciously. "Is something going on with you and the lawyer?" Madison asks.

"No!" I answer truthfully. Because there is nothing going on between us. Okay, maybe he flew off the handle defending my honor . . . And last night in the production trailer he kind of looked like if he couldn't touch me he might die . . . But before all that, I would've sworn he hated me. And didn't I hate him right back?

But judging from the way Madison and Ciara are looking at me, it doesn't seem like they believe me. And I'm not sure I believe myself. I take a large gulp of coffee before I do something stupid like admit I find Andrew attractive.

My attention is pulled away when Beth Anne finally emerges from her beauty sleep and struts along the other side of the pool toward the buffet. "Oh shit," I exclaim, and Madison and Ciara turn to me. "We have to warn Beth Anne! What if Scott is just using her for sex?"

"Oh, she's aware," Ciara says with pursed lips.

"What do you mean?"

"After Beth Anne heard that Andrew dragged you out of the hot tub because you were drunk, she explicitly told Kristina she was sober and able to make her own decisions," Madison explains.

"So . . . you think she was planning on having sex with him all along?" I whisper, scandalized.

"Say what you will about the girl, but she knows what she's doing. She'll go far on the show," Ciara says, picking at her fruit plate.

I sigh audibly because Ciara is right: Beth Anne is a fierce competitor, and she's much more cut out for a reality show than I am. Madison notices the change in my demeanor and quickly says, "Hey, don't worry about Beth Anne or Scott. Just keep doing what you're doing and crush it in the team challenge today."

Ciara nods in agreement. "Oh yeah, I think this is the perfect challenge to make Scott regret ever messing with you. Blue told me what it is." Ciara pauses for dramatic effect, and the gleam in her eye tells me I'm not going to like what she's about to say. "It's a sexy obstacle course!"

I groan loudly. I have a feeling there will be plenty of regret in this team challenge and none of it will be coming from Scott.

"No way in hell."

It's not even 10:00 a.m. and I'm already in the middle of a tense standoff with Blue in the mansion living room. He summoned me because Kristina sent another one of the PAs to buy me a new bathing suit and what she brought back is the tiny, crocheted bikini that Blue is currently holding. It leaves *nothing* to the imagination.

Blue turns to Madison and Ciara, who are waiting for me so we can walk down to the beach for the team challenge. "Girls! Please tell Grace she can pull off this bathing suit."

Madison's face lights up. "Of course you can, Grace!"

"It's not a question of if I can or can't, it's a matter of I won't," I answer definitively.

Ciara looks me up and down and then at the crocheted bikini. "Yeah, that's too grandma for you. I've got something better." She pulls a hot pink string bikini out of her beach bag. "Here. It's brand-new."

Blue smiles like he's won the argument. "That works."

"I want to see what your grandma looks like at the beach," Madison says to Ciara as I take the bikini between my thumb and pointer finger like it's covered in nuclear waste.

"But, but . . . it's pink," I protest.

"She has a thing against pink," Madison explains.

"What do you have against pink?" Ciara gasps as if I've insulted her.

"It's just so . . . girly."

Ciara laughs. "Being feminine isn't a weakness."

"Tell that to a room full of male scientists," I scoff under my breath.

But Ciara isn't hearing any of this. "Fuck that! And fuck them! You can be girly and still be smart, powerful, and a badass!" She pauses for emphasis. "Being comfortable in who you are and what you like is power. Now, for the love of God, go put on that bathing suit and look in a mirror."

"Okay, geez. I've never been peer-pressured to put clothes *on* before." I take the hot pink bikini and pop into the hallway bathroom. I quickly change into it, throw my cover-up on, and meet the girls outside.

Ciara and Madison insist on walking me down to the beach because there's "power in numbers." And when we walk past the shack and down the hill to the dunes, I'm glad they're by my side. Because next to the tiki beach bar, sitting all cozied up on a daybed, are Beth Anne and Scott.

Ciara tsks. "Should we ignore them completely?"

"No way. Kill them with kindness," Madison responds. Then she turns to me and says, "Show them you don't care."

But before I can kill anyone with kindness, I notice Andrew standing with the crew in the shade of a pop-up tent. I tell the girls I'll be back in a sec and hustle over to him.

"Hey, can we talk?" I blurt before he even sees me coming.

His eyes widen in surprise and then concern. "Yeah. Sure." He scans the crowd for Kristina, but she's busy talking to Brett. Apparently deeming the coast to be clear, he walks with me toward the dunes, away from everyone.

When we're out of hearing range, I say, "I just wanted to say thank you again for last night." And then I realize how that sounds and how I could also be thanking him for whatever the hell it was that transpired between us in the production trailer. "For stopping things in the hot tub," I quickly clarify.

He raises his eyebrows, as if he's curious what else I could've been thanking him for, and I silently curse my brain for thinking dirty thoughts. "You're welcome," he says, then nods to the bar area where the rest of the contestants are gathered—specifically, to where Beth Anne is now sitting on Scott's lap. "You doing okay?" he asks, and I wonder if he's heard about their romp on the beach too.

I nod. "Well, besides the hangover and the fact that I forgot that today is the most important day at my lab in years and now I have to compete in a sexy obstacle course, yeah, I'm okay. I probably should've listened to the guy who tried to warn me about Scott, though. But I figured he was just being annoying and litigious, as usual."

The grin is back. "That does sound like him."

I take a deep breath and say what I really pulled him away to say. "I'm also sorry if I was inappropriate last night and made you feel uncomfortable."

He looks at me with a gleam in his eye, like he just took back some of the power in this ongoing battle of ours. "If I seemed that way, it was only because you were drunk," he says, not breaking eye contact, as if he wants to make sure I understand.

"Oh," I say as eloquently as I can with the world's sexiest lawyer staring at my mouth.

"I wouldn't want you to do anything you'd regret," he adds.

"I wouldn't have regretted anything," I tell him.

Andrew's pupils darken, and I know we're back on even footing in this ever-changing dance of ours. I see him calculating his next move, but before he can respond, Blue comes over and says to Andrew, "I heard you didn't get fired. Congrats?"

Andrew steps back from me and laughs. "Thanks?" he says in the same questioning tone as Blue. "I did get a lengthy lecture from Kristina, though."

I wince sympathetically. "I'm familiar with those."

Andrew makes sure no one is listening before he says, "She was more upset that she couldn't use the footage since I'm not a contestant."

Blue laughs. "That sounds like her."

But my heart drops. "I'm now remembering what other footage they may have."

Andrew shoots a look at Scott before saying quietly, "I worked out a deal. Scott won't press assault charges against me, and we won't air the footage from the hot tub where he's taking advantage of an intoxicated woman. Or send it to his employer."

"You did that?" I'm tempted to throw my arms around him, but Blue is here, so instead I just say, "Thank you."

"What can I say?" Andrew says. "I'm good at my job."

"Well, besides the whole punching a contestant thing," I tease.

"Besides that." He smirks.

"It must've been weird filling out paperwork about yourself and not some infraction of mine."

"I started writing 'Grace' out of habit." We both laugh, and it's like we're in on the same scheme—the way we seamlessly transition to normal banter mode in front of Blue, instead of the weird one-upping of sexual tension we've been playing at.

But Blue doesn't seem to be fooled by our casual act. He's looking back and forth at us suspiciously, like he's trying to figure out what's going on. Finally, he asks Andrew, "How's your hand?"

"Fine. I had a good nurse." He smiles, but doesn't look at me. I can't help but smile in return.

I catch Blue rolling his eyes like he can't believe we think we're being covert. I quickly wipe the smile off my face, right before Blue turns to me. "And you." He captures me with his glare. "Are you wearing an appropriately indecent bathing suit?"

Now it's my turn to roll my eyes. "Yes, Blue."

Andrew raises his eyebrows at me. But I just shake my head. Blue puts his hands on his hips. "Okay, let's see."

"What? Now?"

"Yeah, the challenge is starting soon, and Kristina told me that if you were dressed like, I quote, 'an old-timey circus performer,' she'd key my car."

My skin starts to feel warm at the thought of Andrew looking at me in this skimpy bikini. Which doesn't make sense—I was dressed much more scantily last night. But then again, Andrew and I were alone last night . . . which somehow made it easier.

I toy with the hem of my cover-up as Madison and Ciara, already stripped down to their bikinis, walk over to tell me the team challenge is starting. When I pull it over my head, Blue says, "Thank God," as he claps appreciatively. Ciara and Madison whistle and cat-call.

"Okay, that's enough," I say, turning away from them so they won't see me blushing, but in the process I catch Andrew quickly looking away, a faint blush on his cheeks as well. When he meets my eyes, his pupils are blown and he has that same strained expression that he had last night, like he's trying so hard to be professional. My stomach flutters as I wonder what would happen if he weren't.

Blue clears his throat. "If you two are done here, we have an obstacle course to attend."

I look away from Andrew, embarrassed, only to find Ciara and Madison watching us as well. I give them a *knock it off* look, and we follow Blue to where the rest of the contestants are gathered. When I look back, Andrew is watching me walk away. He mouths to me, *Torture.* I smile but quickly try to hide it.

Ciara notices. "I thought you said *nothing* was going on?"

I shush her. "That *was* nothing."

"The hot lawyer that you find *so annoying*, huh? I knew it," Madison says.

I shush them again. "I don't want him to hear you."

Madison and Ciara raise their eyebrows at each other as we meet up with the other contestants. I know they're not going to drop it, so I might as well ask them for advice. I'm about to try to explain the complicated feelings I've been having when Blue claps his hands to get everyone's attention. Madison and Ciara look disappointed that the moment has passed, but there's no need to get distracted talking about Andrew when there's a task at hand. If I want to continue being the points leader and work my way out of that damn shack, I need to do well in this team exercise.

We all quiet down as Blue gestures to two identical, complicated-looking obstacle courses set up in the sand. I was so distracted by Andrew that I'm just now noticing them . . . and they look like something the military uses to break recruits. Despite the tranquil oceanside setting, a panic attack threatens to creep in.

I must be hyperventilating because Madison squeezes my hand and whispers, "Breathe."

"This may surprise you, but the awkward science nerd is not a natural athlete."

She shakes her head at my self-deprecation. "This isn't gym class. You'll be fine."

"I actually made a deal with my gym teacher senior year. If I cleaned the mats and weights every day so he didn't have to, he'd look the other way when I read on the bleachers during class."

Madison laughs. "Of course you did."

I can still smell the ghost of disinfectant past when Shantae walks onto the beach wearing a designer black bikini and a leopard print sarong. Seriously, what is this girl's wardrobe budget? She doesn't bother with pleasantries, she just stands on her mark and says, "Welcome to our first team challenge! We'll split into two teams and compete in the sexy obstacle course, relay race style."

When I scan the course, I notice that the producers and Andrew have moved down closer to watch. At first blush, I'm happy to see him. But then the realization that he's about to watch me attempt athletics sets in and so does a literal blush. Maybe I can offer to clean the mansion bathrooms instead.

Chapter Twenty-Three

W here's a tsunami when you need one?" I mutter to Madison.
Shantae motions for the contestants to follow her toward the obstacle course. Scott tries to get my attention, but I ignore him. I don't know if he wants to apologize for the way things went down or if he wants me to apologize for his broken nose. Either way, I have no interest in engaging.

"Let me walk you through the erotic challenges!" Shantae sing-songs and the sand beneath my feet turns into wet cement.

I groan and catch Andrew's eye. I mouth, *Erotic challenges?* and give him a look that says, *Is this for real?* He has to turn away to hide his laughter. I reluctantly catch up to the group, glad the Advil is finally kicking in.

Shantae stands at the starting line, marked off by orange cones, and points to two buckets fifty feet away. "First, you'll have to run to the buckets and dump water all over yourself—which we'll obviously play in slow motion." She faces the next section. "Then you'll go down the sand dune on the slip-and-slide and cross the balance beam."

She walks to the next part of the course, and we follow her to see that they've set up monkey bars in the sand, with a window hanging from them. "Good news, you don't have to cross the monkey bars." Blue hands her a canister of shaving cream, which she sprays all over the window. "But you do have to wipe the shaving cream off the glass with your booties!"

This is met with laughs by everyone except me. And Andrew. When I sneak a peek at him, he's scowling and writing something down on a notepad. I wonder if he's preparing a warning about the overly salacious nature of this challenge. Whereas I'm picturing the room where the writers and producers are coming up with this crap and dropping a mental hydrogen bomb on it.

"Next you'll grab a balloon and sit on it until it pops," Shantae continues. "I gotta warn you—trying to pop a balloon in the sand, while covered in shaving cream, is harder than it looks.

"And finally," Shantae announces, "you'll have to jump over the hurdles until you get to my favorite part, which I call, 'Pass the Banana.'"

I shake my head. I'm starting to think reality shows don't appreciate subtlety.

Shantae holds up a banana. "Ladies, you have to pick up the banana and put it in your cleavage. Then rush back to the next person in line who will have to accept it with their mouth."

"Oh yeah!" says Cowboy Bill. Normally, I'd think he was being immature, but now I wonder if he's just playing it up for the cameras because he felt discarded by Beth Anne.

Shantae ignores Bill and continues. "Gentlemen, same thing, but you'll have to tuck the banana into your shorts." When the camera pans away from her to catch our reactions, I see Shantae cringe. At least she has the decency to look like she's questioning her life choices. Blue told me that both her parents are doctors. I bet med school is looking pretty damn good right about now.

Shantae then divides us into two teams. And because the producers love drama, guess who's *conveniently* on my team? Javier, Bill, and . . . Beth Anne. She gives me a smug smile. But I take Madison's advice and pretend like nothing bothers me. Besides, aren't you supposed to keep your friends close and your competition closer?

"Ready?" Javier says as he loops his arm through mine and drags me over to our team's side. I shake off thoughts of Beth Anne and Scott and what they did on this very beach and instead try to mentally prepare for the shit show my lack of coordination and stamina will inevitably cause.

"I should probably go first," Beth Anne tells our team. "I'm a gymnast and a cheerleader."

I raise an eyebrow at her. "I thought you worked in marketing?"

"Yeah, now," she huffs.

"So you're a retired gymnast and an old cheerleader?" Javier says, shooting me a grin.

Beth Anne gives us a dirty look and starts stretching like she's about to compete in some sort of banana-based Olympics.

Madison lines up in front of her team, and Beth Anne struts to the front of ours.

"Are you ready?" Shantae asks them. "On your marks, get sexy, go!"

The whistle blows, and as I watch Beth Anne drenching herself seductively and gyrating her hips to clean off the shaving cream, I can't help but think back to Alec's fundraising ideas. Suddenly dressing up like a giant frog sounds a hell of a lot classier than it did back then. But I gotta hand it to Beth Anne—for an old cheerleader, she's making good time.

When Beth Anne runs up to Bill with a banana in her cleavage, he grabs it with his mouth, spits it out, and then sprints to the refilled bucket.

I look over at the other team. We seem to be neck and neck: Scott has dumped their bucket over his head, and water is cascading down his chiseled bare chest. Despite the fact that I've seen Scott's true colors and am no longer drooling over him, I have to admit that I get what the producers are going for. *No subtlety needed.*

I'm startled back to the present by Beth Anne and Bill yelling, "Go, Grace!! Go!!!"

I look up to see Bill thrusting a banana at me. It's stuffed into the front of his bathing suit and dangling out provocatively. I shake my head with disgust and shout, "I'm a scientist!" before I lean forward and grab the banana with my teeth. I quickly spit it out and jog toward the first obstacle.

"Go faster, Grace!!!" Beth Anne yells, jumping up and down.

"What about me makes you think I would be fast?" I yell back.

I dump the bucket over my head, wishing I could waterboard myself instead. I have to shake the water off my glasses before I sit down at the top of the slip-and-slide and give myself a gentle nudge forward. I'm not throwing my body down it like I've seen the others do. I bruise easily.

When I look up, I see Ciara is already way ahead of me, trying to pop the balloon. I try to hurry up and climb up onto the balance beam . . . only to immediately fall off. Yeah, there's no way I'm crossing this thing upright. So I end up slowly crawling across like the least nimble cat in history.

"Come on, Grace!! Hurry up!" Bill yells. I try to flip him off but wobble and almost tumble off again.

I finally make it to the shaving cream window. I think I'm making up time, wiping the cream off with my butt, until I see TC flinging himself down the slip-and-slide on the other team's side. *Shit, where did he come from?*

When I get to the balloon-popping obstacle, it takes me three attempts until I finally use what can only be described as a mother penguin technique. I hold the balloon between my feet and drop dramatically on top of it. It's honestly a miracle the balloon is the only thing that pops.

I'm already out of breath when I make it to the hurdles. Instead of running and leaping over them gracefully like Madison the gazelle, I scramble over them like a clumsy panda cub.

I'm putting the banana in my cleavage and praying that all the cameras run out of batteries when TC rushes past me and their team bursts into cheers. And then, just when I think things couldn't get any more humiliating, I hear a cracking sound and my ankle gives out, sending me pitching forward face first into the sand. The banana doesn't break my fall.

Ten minutes later, I'm still sitting in the same spot on the beach. Luckily it wasn't anything too serious. The on-set medics said it's only a sprain and were kind enough to point out that my "underused leg muscles" were to blame. Then Beth Anne helpfully suggested that if I weren't so out of shape I wouldn't have gotten lapped and lost it for the team.

Madison and Ciara shooed them off and now hover over me like mother hens while Blue asks, "Would the hilarious meme of it cheer you up?"

"You better be making that up."

"It seems like you want me to say 'yes' so . . . *yes*?" Blue cringes.

Ciara laughs as I bury my face in my hands. Madison cheerily says, "Hey, you haven't made it until your banana-related accident is turned into a gif."

I smile at them. "Thank you, guys, for your concern but—" I start, but suddenly they're all getting up and making awkward excuses about places they have to be. I turn and see why. Andrew is walking toward me, carrying ice.

He doesn't seem fazed by their sudden departure; he's probably used to it by now. He just plops down next to me in the sand and says, "You honestly did better than I expected." I laugh and he hands me the bag of ice. "Is this going to be our thing?"

"Ice?" I ask, and he nods with a grin that makes me forget about my injury.

Until he looks down at my ankle, currently the size of a grapefruit, and winces. "That looks like it hurts." Then he takes my leg, puts it over his lap, and carefully wraps a towel around my ankle to ice it like I did for his hand.

I shiver at his touch but quickly recover and shrug. "My ankle may be swollen, but my ego will be forever bruised."

"Did you tell the EMTs you have two PhDs, though?" he teases with that damn glint in his eyes.

I playfully nudge his shoulder. And then because he feels so sturdy, I continue leaning against him. I am injured after all. "It's not my fault I'm horrible at obstacle courses."

He raises his eyebrows. "It kind of is."

"I blame my brother for getting all the athletic DNA."

"Aren't you the oldest?" He laughs, and I'm too aware that he still has his hand on my leg and is absentmindedly rubbing it. I feel flickers of electricity everywhere his fingers graze.

I snap out of the daze of his touch and ask, "Wait, how'd you know that? Please tell me you don't follow Matt on TikTok."

"I'm not on social media," Andrew says, slipping back into serious lawyer mode. "I only go on it when I have to do background checks for the show."

Instead of being annoyed by his judgmental tone, I have to agree with him. "It's the worst. I'm not on it either," I say. Until I remember. "Oh wait. I am."

He smiles. "Don't worry, I won't hold it against you."

"You might want to. I have no idea what my idiot brother and horny best friend are posting." Andrew raises his eyebrows, so I explain. "They're running things while I'm gone, and there's a good chance he's photoshopped my head onto some supermodel's body."

"That would be unnecessary," Andrew says. And it takes me a second to realize what he means. I immediately feel warm and tingly when I catch him glancing down at the bikini that isn't covering much.

"Thanks," I say, catching his eye, but my voice sounds gravelly. I wonder if he can tell that I'm turned on by him checking me out.

Andrew changes the subject, but I notice his hand still lingers on my leg. "I have some good news."

"They're canceling the rest of the show?"

Something passes over his face suggesting he wishes that were the case, but instead he says, "I convinced Kristina you were too injured to participate in this afternoon's very special challenge."

"Oh my God, thank you!" Without thinking, I wrap my arms around his neck in a hug. His deep laugh reverberates against me in a satisfying way as he hugs me back. But once I'm pressed tight against him, the smell of his cologne combines with our several body parts that are touching to give me inappropriate thoughts. I quickly let go of him and lean back casually like I wasn't just visualizing other scenarios in which our bodies would be touching.

He raises his eyebrows. Of course he's on to me. It's like he's attuned to any change in my heart rate. But I don't meet his eye. I'm not giving him the satisfaction.

After a minute my curiosity gets the best of me, though. "Do I even want to know what the challenge is?"

He shrugs nonchalantly. "It depends. How do you feel about stripteases?"

My eyes shoot to his, and suddenly the air between us is charged, like the pressure drop before a thunderstorm. Static travels through my synapses, making every cell in my body hum.

If I thought I was turned on before, my brain has now gone completely haywire. I can't help but picture what it might feel like to give Andrew a striptease. And how easy it would be to remove this skimpy bikini.

I realize I'm biting my lower lip. And Andrew is looking at me with the same intensity he was earlier. He lifts his gaze from my lips to my eyes, and I wonder if we're picturing the same thing.

He exhales and says, "You make it hard for me to do my job."

"Because of the paperwork?"

"Because I want to kiss you."

Ciara and Madison must be rubbing off on me because I decide to be brave and confident. I lean back on my elbows, letting my arm brush against his, with his rolled-up sleeves that drive me crazy, and say, "So do it."

I hold my breath. Andrew doesn't just stare at me, he smolders. Then he leans over me, his body hovering above mine. The electricity between us is palpable. I have never wanted anyone more, and judging from the heated way he's looking at me, he feels it too.

I can't help myself. I toy with the collar of his shirt, slowly pulling him closer to me without breaking eye contact. He presses into me and his weight feels exactly right. I groan as he kisses his way from my collarbone to my shoulder. Then he bites the strap of the bikini, letting it snap, and I inhale sharply. He grins at my response and continues kissing up my neck to my jaw. I can't believe this is finally happening. After dancing around it for days. I close my eyes and feel Andrew's lips gently brush mine.

But then I hear, "Fuck."

My eyes snap open, and I see the warring emotions all over his face. He growls in frustration as he rolls off of me and lies on his back in the sand. We're both breathing heavily, and neither of us speaks. My heart is racing faster than when I was trying to climb over the hurdles.

After a minute he breaks the silence. "Employees aren't allowed to kiss contestants. I signed the nonfraternization agreement." He gives a bitter laugh. "I fucking *wrote* it." He runs his hands through his hair, frustrated.

I lean on my elbow facing him. "You could always quit your job," I tease.

He turns to face me. "I wish I could," he says, more seriously than I would have expected.

"If I had known all it took to get you to stop threatening to sue me was to wear a pink bikini . . ."

He laughs. "It was your performance in the obstacle course that really sealed the deal."

I smile at him. "You must have a thing for underdogs."

"I think I'm starting to," he says, doing nothing to help my racing pulse.

We lie in the sand looking at each other. Me in a pink bikini and Andrew in suit pants and a collared shirt. All the blood must've rushed to my swollen ankle because I absentmindedly say, "You have nice forearms."

He looks down at his rolled-up sleeves and grins. "If I had known all it took to get you to stop yelling at me . . ." We both laugh. He sits up and brushes the sand off himself. "You want to try to hobble up the beach or should I get the medic cart?"

"I'll hobble," I say, sitting up. Andrew carefully brushes sand off my arms and back. I don't think he even realizes he's doing it, whereas I am acutely aware of every place on my body he touches. He offers me his hand and pulls me to my feet.

"I could just throw you over my shoulder and carry you," he offers.

"I'm good."

He grins. "Really, I wouldn't mind."

I shake my head at him. "Madison and Ciara would have a field day. I can't give them that kind of ammo. I'll hop, thanks." He laughs and puts his arm around me, taking the brunt of my weight and carrying the ice.

"You want to get lunch or rest?" he asks as we slowly make our way up the beach.

"I think I'll hide in my shack until the meme of my banana fail stops entertaining everyone."

Andrew's eyes sparkle with mischief. "We're only filming for a couple more weeks. You'll have to come out eventually."

I smack his stomach in response and immediately regret it. I don't think I can handle abs *and* forearms.

Chapter Twenty-Four

Andrew helps me back to the shack so I can nap while the rest of the contestants get ready to strip. Something I am very glad I get to miss.

"You might want to tone down the happiness at missing the challenge or people will think you got hurt on purpose," Andrew says when we get to my dilapidated home away from home.

I smile up at him. "I wish I had thought of that days ago."

He shakes his head at me. "Here," he says, handing me one of his granola bars. I notice he has a brand-new box of them in his messenger bag.

"Ooh, thank you. I worked up an appetite passing the banana."

He grins. "You didn't even get that far."

I go to playfully punch him, but because I can't put weight on my ankle, I end up wobbling. He puts his hands on my hips to steady me. Then he shakes his head teasingly. "You're too injured for violence."

I look down at his hands on my hips and smile slowly. "I've suddenly forgotten all about my ankle." His eyes blaze and his grip on me tightens. A small gasp leaves my lips. I take a quick scan; we're all alone. No one would ever know . . . Andrew catches my eye and immediately knows what I'm thinking. There's a moment of deliberation in his eyes as the heat I felt on the beach passes between us again.

Then he says the words I've been dying to hear. "Fuck it."

His lips crash into mine, and the tension from the last few days finally explodes. I can't control myself. I press even closer to him and kiss him back with an intensity I've never felt before.

Andrew squeezes my hips tighter as I press my body into his. Heat flares at the contact, and I realize that if Andrew weren't holding on to me, I would probably collapse into a puddle of hormones at his feet. When I feel his hand brush the bare skin on my back, I pant as a shiver ripples through me. When I bite his bottom lip in response, he groans into my mouth. He kisses my neck, and I whisper "yes" into his ear. I realize that we kiss like we fight. For every sweep of his tongue, I match him. For every nibble I take, he returns the favor. It's a back-and-forth that's so well matched that there's no doubt we're both winning.

As I lose myself in him, I forget about the fact that we're not supposed to be doing this. All I can think about is that this is even hotter than I had imagined. And how I wouldn't mind doing this all day every day.

Andrew changes the angle of his mouth and I'm breathing heavily. He must be able to tell that I'm about to pull him into my shack and throw him down on my bedroll because he makes the difficult decision for the both of us. He slowly pulls back, giving me one last lingering kiss. We look at each other, dazed. His hair is messy—I must've been running my hands through it. I touch my lips, and a slow smile spreads across his face.

I absently say, "Wow, for a suit, you can really kiss."

He laughs. "You're not bad yourself, Sexy Scientist."

I give him a dirty look at the nickname and he grins. Then he remembers where he is and his professional switch flips back on. He looks around to make sure no one has seen us and rubs the back of his neck. "I should go."

He really should. Before I jump him. Reluctantly, I nod. "Thanks for walking me back," I tell him with a sly smile.

"The pleasure was all mine," he says with a smugness that has suddenly become sexy. "I'll see you later, Grace." But he lingers in the doorway. Looking at my lips. Then he mutters, "Fuck," under his breath and turns to go.

I laugh and yell after him, "Now who has an affinity for swearing?"

It takes me a solid five minutes to come down from kissing Andrew. I even debate stealing one of Beth Anne's Evians to quench my lusty thirst. When I'm finally recovered from post-kiss bliss, I hop over to my suitcase and throw on a comfy pair of joggers and one of my dad's motivational T-shirts. I debate calling Cassie on the burner phone, but I don't want to interrupt them if they're still doing the test subject release. I hope it's going well. As much as the sexy obstacle course sucked, at least it kept my mind off worrying about my frogs. And making out with a sexy lawyer was an unexpected and welcome distraction.

I use a towel I stole from the pool to add more padding to my "bed" so I can nap on the floor. We've had such long days, plus drinking in the sun, becoming hungover, and being forced to participate in athletics, that I'm beyond exhausted.

A loud banging on the door wakes me up. My first thought is, *Yay! It's Andrew and he's back for more kissing.* And then I remember I'm in the creepy-ass shack alone, so my second thought is, *What if it's a serial killer?* But surely a serial killer wouldn't knock. Right?

"Who is it?" I call.

"Kristina."

I'd prefer the serial killer. I fix my hair and make sure there are no signs of the illicit make-out session, then call, "Come in." I don't have a choice; there are no locks on the shack door.

Kristina enters, trailed by a camera operator. For a moment I'm worried that she somehow found out about Andrew and is here to kick me off the show, but she just looks at my ankle, which has already turned black and blue, and says, "Gross." She doesn't bother asking me how I'm doing. Instead, she explains that they need footage of me injured in the shack to explain why I wasn't at the striptease challenge.

"Who won the challenge?" I ask as the camera operator films me icing my ankle.

"Beth Anne, of course. I wouldn't be surprised if she has a side hustle at the Spearmint Rhino."

I'm not familiar with that particular establishment, but I have a guess as to what kind of services they offer.

After they get the footage they need, Kristina tells me that everyone is meeting by the pool for the next segment. She stares at me until I realize she's expecting me to go. "But I'm injured," I plead. "The medics said I should rest."

"You're perfectly fine to sit on the couch for a Shantae segment. I'll have Blue bring you crutches." She starts to leave but turns back around. "And clean yourself up, you look like shit." Then she thinks about it. "Actually don't. This works with my storyline."

Chapter Twenty-Five

Why do you look like that?" Blue asks when he shows up at the shack a few minutes later with crutches in hand.

Oh God, is it that obvious I kissed his coworker? But then I remember what I'm wearing and that I just woke up from a nap. "Oh. Kristina wants me looking like shit."

"Well, you nailed it," he says, and I laugh. "What does your shirt mean?"

I look down at my dad's motivational T-shirt that reads, "You will never always be driven."

"I have no idea," I admit with a shrug.

Blue ties a knot in the oversize shirt so that "at least it looks like a choice." Then he helps me adjust the crutches to my height.

As I make my way up the hill with Blue's help, he casually says, "So Andrew brought you ice . . ."

"You're not as smooth as you think you are," I tell him, but he just bats his eyes at me, waiting me out. "You're worse than Madison and Ciara," I groan. But he's still staring at me, so finally I break and tell him a partial truth. "I'm a contestant. He works for the show. It's off-limits."

"That makes it even hotter," Blue says with a wink.

Oh, don't I know. I will myself not to blush as I hobble along and replay the kiss for the hundredth time.

The sun is just starting to set as we make our way up to the pool. I've learned from one of the camera operators that this time of night is called "Magic Hour" because the light is the best for shooting. I've started calling it Magic Hour because it means my reality TV torture is almost done for the day.

Everyone else is already lounging on the patio, waiting for me. Madison, Ciara, TC, and Javier give me looks of concern when they see me on crutches. Shantae just looks impatient. Clearly, we're the ones who can be kept waiting, not the other way around.

Madison makes everyone push over so I have room to sit. "How are you feeling?" she whispers.

"Delighted I didn't have to strip on national TV," I whisper back, and she laughs.

"We kept our bathing suits on. It wasn't that bad." Then she subconsciously glances at TC, and I immediately understand why it wasn't that bad.

Shantae gives us a look and says, "You ready?" Chastened, we nod. Shantae faces the camera and turns on the charm. "Welcome back to *Love Shack*!" I watch as the camera pans around to all of the contestants. TC has his arm around Madison, Javier and Ciara sit together, and Beth Anne is pawing at Scott. Everyone is happily coupled up except me and Cowboy Bill.

Shantae puts her hand on her hip in what must be her fierce modeling pose and continues addressing the camera. "As you know, our contestants have started forming connections. Some more serious than others." I see the camera operator zoom in on Madison and TC. "And sadly, some of them have not."

I assume there's a giant close-up on me happening right now. *Awesome.* I haven't showered, my bangs are probably still sticking straight up, and I'm wearing whatever is left of last night's makeup and my dad's convoluted T-shirt. *You're welcome, America.* At least I know why Kristina wanted me to look like a disheveled hot mess. I definitely fit the role of the odd woman out.

Shantae turns to us. "As I explained on the first day, if you don't form meaningful connections, you're at risk of being sent home. And unfortunately we have to say goodbye to one of you today." Madison and Ciara immediately turn to me with concern in their eyes.

A bolt of panic shocks my system. I can't go home yet! I'm nowhere near reaching my fundraising goal. If I get kicked off the show, all this will have been in vain.

I'm racking my brain for some sort of speech to defend myself or promise to take the challenges more seriously when Shantae says, "I'm sorry, Bill, but your time on *Love Shack* is over."

"Well damn." Bill gives a resigned nod and adds, "I knew I should've brought my chaps."

Madison lets out a big sigh of relief as Ciara reaches over and squeezes my leg. Bill stands to say goodbye to everyone. Madison and Beth Anne give him a hug before he does one of those hybrid high-five/handshake things with each of the guys and then walks off set.

And just like that, Cowboy Bill is gone.

"Savage," Ciara whispers.

My heart is racing. That was a close call. Too close. But once the shock wears off, I find myself feeling bad for Bill. Meat-eating, oil-drilling *Bill*. Maybe this show *is* changing me. But at least Bill tried to get to know me, and it seemed like he wanted to form a meaningful connection with someone. I can't help but feel a little guilty that he got sent home and I didn't.

Shantae claps her hands to get our attention and smiles brightly, like she didn't just send someone packing. "Before the new arrivals come, we have the next round of one-on-one dates. This time the ladies get to choose. But to make things fair . . ." She motions to someone off camera. A moment later Blue rolls in something covered in a sheet. *Oh God, what now?*

Shantae pulls the sheet off with a flourish, revealing a colorful wheel. Each segment has one of our names.

"The Wheel of Fate!" Madison exclaims, as she claps her hands.

"I don't like the sound of that," I whisper to Ciara.

"I'm going to spin the Wheel of Fate to see who gets to pick first," Shantae announces as she gives the wheel a big spin.

It goes around and around until it finally lands on Madison, who exhales in relief, then jumps up excitedly. "I'd like to pick the guy who I've enjoyed getting to know and who I think I'm making a real connection with. TC, would you like to go on a date with me?"

TC stands up with a huge smile on his face. "I'd love to, Maddie." He gives her a big hug, lifting her off the ground.

Shantae spins again. "Next up is . . . Ciara! Ooh, the new girl. This should be interesting! Who do you pick?"

Ciara stands up. "Well, Shantae, like I said when I got here, I'm not here to make friends." I have to hide my smirk as Ciara plays the role Kristina assigned her. "When I see someone I'm interested in, I go for it." She gives me a discreet wink as she confidently turns to Javier. "Javi, will you go on a date with me?"

Javier smiles at her, obviously smitten, and says, "Let's do this!" If Cassie were here, she'd already have come up with a ridiculous celebrity couple nickname for them, like Javi-ara, and I'm so happy for them that I might not even hate it.

I look past Javi and Ciara and see Beth Anne sitting on Scott's lap. If she's chosen next, she'll obviously pick him. Oooh, does that mean I'll get to go back to my shack and go to bed now?

As I'm wondering if I can pay a PA to sneak me some books, Shantae's wheel lands on Beth Anne, who predictably picks Scott. Madison and Ciara give me concerned looks, but I shrug them off.

I stand, ready to hobble back to my shack when Shantae turns to me. "And then there's Grace. The producers want you to go on your one-on-one date. Though I guess it's more of a one-on-*none* date," Shantae says, chuckling at my misfortune.

"By myself?" I grimace, but Shantae only nods gleefully. "But I'm injured!"

"The dates aren't until tomorrow, and the medics cleared you," Shantae responds condescendingly.

I plop back down, and Ciara leans over to whisper, "You should do it. They're trying to make you look like the charity case so that, when the next arrivals come and you meet someone, America will be rooting for you. Classic dating show storyline."

The thought of a new arrival coming doesn't cheer me up. Instead, all I can think about is kissing Andrew, but I shouldn't be thinking about that either. If anything, I should be thinking about how my coworkers are doing with the release today and what I should be doing so I'm not like Cowboy Bill riding off into the sunset . . .

Madison gives me an encouraging thumbs-up, and I realize I have to do the producers' bidding. "Okay, I'll go on my one-on-none date tomorrow," I sigh, immediately knowing that's a sound bite that puppet master Kristina will be all over.

The only silver lining in this humiliating development is that because I'm playing ball with the one-on-none date, the producers are letting me skip the confessionals they're filming tonight.

I pick up the veggie-and-grain bowl that the chef has waiting for me and another bag of ice for my ankle. I say good night to the rest of the contestants and hop on the golf cart that Blue borrowed from production to drive me down the hill.

When he drops me off at the front door, I notice he sounds congested. "Are you sick?" I ask.

He shrugs. "Probably coming down with a cold. I always get sick during production."

"Are you getting enough sleep?"

He laughs at this. "My turnaround last night was eight hours. It takes me forty-five minutes to get home."

"So, between commute time, you only get six hours to yourself. How many hours did you sleep? Five?"

"If I'm lucky."

"That's not sustainable! No wonder you're sick. I'm exhausted, and you were up later than me wrapping the Angels and Devils party. Did you have to help set up the obstacle course this morning too?" He nods. "Aren't you in a union? Don't they have protections in place?"

"Yeah, for what they're aware of. The show pays a meal penalty if we work through lunch or dinner. And they're required to pay overtime when—"

"What do you mean 'for what they're aware of'?"

Blue looks like he shouldn't be saying this. "The industry has been tough lately. If you find a steady production gig, you want to keep it. Which means not ruffling any feathers."

"And Kristina has a shit-ton of feathers," I say, nodding in understanding. "Can you at least go home now and get some rest?"

He shakes his head ruefully. "I need to help with the confessionals. Then set up some stuff for the one-on-one dates tomorrow. I have at least four hours left."

I take his wrist and look at his Apple watch. It's already past 8:30 p.m.! He senses my growing anger and shrugs. "It's fine. We only have a couple weeks left."

But it's not fine for me. I can't just sit back and watch these hardworking people get taken advantage of because they're afraid they'll lose their jobs if they exercise their rights. They may be afraid to ruffle Kristina's feathers, but I'm not.

That being said, I don't want to get Blue in trouble. So, to make sure he has plausible deniability, I just tell him good night, adding that I hope he feels better soon. But the minute he leaves, I find my contraband phone in my suitcase and make a few calls. The first is to 411 to get some phone numbers. Specifically, the number for the local office of the Teamsters union, the California Labor Commissioner's Office, and the US Department of Labor, for good measure. Then I make some anonymous labor violation complaints. It turns out that the state of California has strict laws in place to protect its workers, and the Labor Commissioner's Office is very interested in hearing from me.

And finally, when I feel like I've blown enough whistles for the day, I check in on my froggies' Super Bowl. I FaceTime Cassie, and when the screen fills with the faces of Cassie, Eliza, and Alec, the sight of my friends makes me tear up. I guess an impending one-on-none date will do that to a girl.

"How did it go today?!" I ask.

But Alec ignores my question and instead says, "Why do you look like shit?"

"Why does everyone keep saying that?"

"She's hungover," Cassie explains.

"Still?" Alec scoffs.

"Since when do you drink too much?" Eliza asks.

"Since she started making out with models in hot tubs," Cassie says in rapid fire and then exhales. "Thank God. It was so hard keeping it from them."

"I only told you a few hours ago!" I shake my head.

Alec gasps. "But what about Javier? I thought you guys were a thing!"

"Says who?" I sputter.

"The TV! You kissed." Alec looks heartbroken.

"Yeah, they definitely edited it like you two were hitting it off," Cassie agrees.

"Javi is great, but he's with Ciara now," I say gently, trying to cushion the blow for Alec.

"Which one's Ciara?" Eliza asks. "Perky blonde or bitchy brunette?"

"She's the late arrival," I explain.

"Oh, we haven't met her yet," Cassie says like this is real life and not some lame show they're way too invested in. "She probably comes in episode two."

"Bummer. Javier was charming. I liked him for you," Alec whines.

"Guys, let's get back to the important stuff. No one cares who I'm making out with—"

"I do!" Cassie says.

"Me too!" Alec raises his hand.

"I'm partially intrigued," admits Eliza.

"Please just tell me how it went with the release today!" I yell as I pace the empty shack. Then realize I should probably break the forbidden phone rule more quietly.

"It was amazing!" Cassie beams.

"Well, we won't really know for a few weeks, when we check the population again," Eliza counters.

Cassie rolls her eyes at Eliza's bluntness. "Everything went perfectly. All fifty test subjects have been vaccinated and microtagged, and they're happily back in their native habitat. I'd say that's a win."

I exhale a sigh of relief commingled with joy—I've poured my heart and soul into this project. This will be huge for the species. Hell, it'll be huge for frogs and amphibians in general. "Thank you, guys," I say, feeling emotional.

And then Cassie moves the phone, and I can see from the background that they're on Cassie's roof deck. Not only did I miss the release, but now I'm missing the celebration. While I'm stuck here icing my ankle in a shack. I try to push down the self-pity and jealousy, but it's hard.

Of course Cassie notices. "Are you okay?" she asks softly.

I nod. "Yeah, it was just a long, weird day." Frankly, I can't believe this is still the same day I found out about Scott and Beth Anne, sprained my ankle, and kissed Andrew.

"Would money cheer you up?" Alec asks, and I perk up. "Because we're up to fifty thousand dollars in our fundraiser!"

"Holy shit! We raised that much since yesterday?"

"Well, the first episode dropped, and Matt coordinated a big social media push with it. It was honestly kind of incredible," Cassie explains, like she's some sort of influencer groupie now.

"That's amazing," I say to Cassie. "Still don't like that you're in such close contact with my brother, but fifty grand is nothing to sneeze at." Then I look at Alec. "Promise me you'll cockblock them if it comes to it."

"Oh wow. Grace says 'cockblock' now," Alec says, equally amused and horrified.

"I also learned what a 'fuck boy' is," I say smugly.

Eliza ignores us and shakes her head. "I can't believe this dumb plan is actually working."

"Yeah, who knew you'd come across as so likable?" Alec says.

"You did! You said America loves an underdog," I counter.

"Yeah, but I didn't really think you had a chance." Alec shrugs.

"Well, I still don't. I'm the only one not in a couple." Then I relay how Bill was kicked off the show.

"I know we don't like him, but that's pretty harsh." Cassie winces.

I nod in agreement. "Yep. And I'm going home next unless I hit it off with one of the new arrivals."

Eliza shakes her head. "This show is fucked up."

"You're just realizing that now?" I laugh, then rub my temples because I might just have this hangover headache for the rest of my life.

Cassie looks pensive. "The producers must like you if they didn't kick you off with Bill. Maybe they'll throw you a bone and send in a hot cardiothoracic surgeon or something."

I scoff in response. "Yeah, right. They barely wanted to give me crutches."

"Why did you need crutches?!" Cassie asks in alarm.

Before I can explain, Eliza bursts out laughing and holds up her phone. "Holy shit, there's a hilarious meme of you falling with a banana hanging out of your tits."

"That's why." I cringe as I hear them watching the video on a loop and curse whoever leaked the video. "Okay, well I should probably rest up for my one-on-none date." This just makes Eliza laugh harder. I shake my head at them. "Good night!"

Alec calls, "You're doing God's work!"

"Yeah, keep it up, Grace! You're killing it," Cassie says, too enthusiastically.

"Other than the banana incident," Eliza adds.

Cassie and Alec blow me kisses. Eliza just walks away from the phone.

I hang up and consider the dirty shack floor I'm lying on, my hangover headache and swollen ankle, and the depressing one-on-none date that looms ahead of me while I try to block out inappropriate thoughts of the on-set lawyer I'm definitely not supposed to be kissing. Yep, I'm totally killing it.

Chapter Twenty-Six

The next morning I miraculously only feel like shit from sleeping on the ground. My hangover has dissipated, the swelling in my ankle has gone down, and when I wear the brace the medics dropped off, it doesn't even hurt to walk. I smile, starting to feel like myself again. Maybe today will be a good day.

Madison, Ciara, and I decide to eat breakfast in the fancy dining room in the mansion since it's overcast today. The solid oak table is longer than the one in my conference room at work, so people file in to sit with us. Unsurprisingly, TC sits next to Madison. He's the only other contestant who's already awake. Blue, another production assistant, and a camera operator also take their break to eat with us. They've already been working for hours at this point; I give Blue a sympathetic smile.

When Andrew comes strolling in with a paper takeout bag, I feel my cheeks flush. This is my first time seeing him since we kissed. If I smile at him, will everyone know? Or would avoiding eye contact make me seem even more guilty? I settle for a quick head nod.

Andrew, however, must overthink things less than I do, because he smiles as he sits across the table and slides the bag in my direction. I immediately notice the logo on the front. It's from one of my favorite vegan restaurants in West Hollywood.

I peek inside. "You got me a vegan breakfast burrito?" I gasp as I tear into the bag for the tofu-y goodness.

The other people at the table turn to look, and Andrew shrugs. "It was on my way."

Blue side-eyes him. "Don't you live in Silver Lake?"

Andrew ignores him and takes a sip of his coffee.

Blue discreetly raises his eyebrows at Madison and Ciara, as if they're all in cahoots. But he's not that discreet. I shoot him a dirty look that I hope conveys, *Cut it out.* He just smiles sweetly at me and nonchalantly says, "So I'm friends with your mom now."

I choke on black bean salsa as I sputter, "What? Why?"

"She somehow got my number and was texting me questions about you."

"You sound amused, and not annoyed or scared by this," I respond slowly.

"Yeah, how'd she get your number?" Andrew asks, snapping back into lawyer mode.

Blue shrugs. "She seems like a very persuasive lady. Anyway, she wanted me to give you a message." He scrolls through his phone until he reads, *"Javier is a hottie. Go for him."*

I quickly lift my eyes to Andrew, embarrassed, then to Ciara, wincing, before turning back to Blue, shaking my head. "See? She's deranged. This is what I've had to live with my entire life! Please block her."

He gives me a guilty look. "She follows me on all my socials. We're meeting for coffee after we wrap." I groan loudly, and everyone laughs. "Oh yeah, and she texted me a message about your hot brother." Blue looks down at his phone: *"Matt wants you to know he was right about the glasses."*

I roll my eyes. "I'm starting to appreciate the no-phone rule."

The camera operator then announces to the table that he swears by my dad's Power Yoga, which kicks off a conversation about my pseudo-famous family. One of the PAs tells me that, on the first day, he wanted to talk to me about Jesse's Twitch channel, but he wasn't sure if we were actually related.

I nod at him. "I get that a lot." Then I busy myself eating because I don't have anything to say about video games. I groan in ecstasy as I devour the burrito. It's been too long since I've had good food. When I look up, Andrew is staring at me.

"Sorry," I say after I swallow.

He just smiles wickedly. "I'm glad you like it."

I try to hide my grin as I feel my cheeks heat up. God, you kiss a guy one time and now suddenly everything is sexual. I feel heat pooling low in my stomach as we sit there looking at each other.

Until Kristina eviscerates my dirty thoughts when she stampedes into the dining room and yells, "Who made a fucking labor complaint?"

Everyone glances around the room in confusion except Blue, who looks at me with wide eyes. Shit. If he suspects I did it, does Kristina? But when I look back at her, she's too busy stalking into the next room yelling about "penalty fees" and "legal nightmare."

Andrew pushes away from the table and stands up, looking directly at me. He strides off after Kristina.

Andrew's look sends ice through my veins as we all sit there in stunned silence. While I'm not afraid to admit what I did, I now realize that if the studio finds out it was me, they'll probably kick me off the show. And after talking to my coworkers at the lab last night and learning that this crazy idea is actually working, I can't risk it. As everyone around me starts gossiping about the complaint, I just keep my head down and avoid eye contact.

Brett, the EP I haven't seen do any actual work, comes in a few minutes later and tells all the contestants at the table that we have to film a Shantae segment down at the beach before our one-on-one dates. I guess since Kristina is off putting out the fires I lit, Brett actually has to do something.

"It's probably new arrivals," Ciara whispers to me. We all get up to go get ready, and I hustle off to the shack to change. Since Beth Anne won the striptease challenge, she's not at the bottom of the leaderboard anymore, and Bill got sent home, so it's just me in the shack. Which is fine. I'm worried that, if I'm around anyone right now, they'll figure out I'm the anonymous tipster.

I put on my cut-up Speedo because I have no other bathing suits, leave on my ankle brace, and throw on some makeup. I'm almost done when there's a knock on my door. *Please don't be Kristina. Please don't be Kristina*, I pray as I cross to open the door.

It's Andrew. And he doesn't look happy. "I know it was you."

I open the door for him to come in. He enters with his arms crossed. There doesn't seem to be any use denying it, and I don't want to lie to him, so I admit, "I can't just stand by and watch people be taken advantage of or bullied and manipulated."

Andrew shakes his head, "Neither can I. Which is why, if you had just come to me, I would've handled it. But instead, you went directly to the US Department of Labor. And now I'm in the middle of a serious shit storm."

"I'm sorry if I caused you more paperwork, but it wasn't about you," I say, refusing to back down. "It was about Kristina and the producers and how they think they can just treat people like pawns and not actual human beings."

"It *is* about me! This is my job. I'm the one who now has to handle this and try to avoid arbitration," he says, half shouting in frustration.

"Which is why I couldn't go to you!" I half shout back, equally frustrated.

"Because you don't trust that I would do the right thing?"

"Because as long as they sign your paychecks, you work for them. You're part of the problem!" I say, getting heated.

"Is that really how you see me?"

"You're a corporate lawyer, Andrew! You're not being paid to protect the contestants or the crew. You're being paid to protect a media conglomerate that knowingly commits labor violations and produces shows where they ply people with alcohol to do compromising things for ratings. How else am I supposed to see you?"

He stands there as my words hang in the air around us. Then he slowly nods once before turning and leaving.

I stand there frozen. Part of me wants to go after him, but what would I say? I don't regret sticking to my convictions. I was only trying to do the right thing. Why doesn't he see that?

I sink down to my bedroll. Andrew's face when he walked out is burned into my brain. While he may have started off angry and frustrated, the look on his face when he left was one of hurt and betrayal.

Maybe I was too harsh in my delivery, but wasn't everything I said true? I sigh. This is the first time I can remember when being right makes me feel so bad.

I walk to the beach where they've set up the next Shantae segment, feeling numb. I replay every moment of my fight with Andrew as I give TC, Javier, and Ciara a half-hearted wave before plopping down next to Madison on the outdoor couch.

She immediately senses my mood. "What's wrong?"

I say to her quietly, "Andrew and I got into a fight."

She gives a little gasp of sympathy, then whispers, "It was you who filed the complaint."

I nod. "And he's taking it personally," I say, then quickly add, "Don't tell anyone it was me."

"I won't. I only wish I had thought of it. It's not fair the way they treat the crew."

"It's not fair the way they treat anyone."

As if on cue, Shantae struts out. Followed by two PAs carrying the damn Wheel of Fate. I roll my eyes. What fresh torture is this?

Everyone quiets down, and I scan the crew for Blue. I don't see him anywhere. Is Kristina questioning him? What if they think it was him? Or he's forced to tell them it was me? I don't realize I'm wringing my hands until Madison grabs one, in a silent reminder to act natural. I give her an appreciative squeeze.

I'm barely paying attention as Shantae announces the arrival of two new contestants. And before I know it, a beautiful Hispanic woman and a muscular Black man walk out in their bathing suits. I don't even catch their names. I'm so busy worrying about Blue getting falsely accused for my actions, and Andrew being mad at me, and Kristina kicking me off the show, and my frogs going extinct, that Madison has to elbow me to bring me back to the present.

Just in time to hear Shantae say, "So, to welcome Eliana and Chris, we're doing body shots!" I vaguely catch Beth Anne cheering. "And to make it fun, we'll spin the wheel to see who's taking a shot off of who!"

When we all move to the tiki bar, I realize I probably won't be able to avoid drinking. I'm so worried about my place on the show that I might just have to start playing by their rules. Ugh.

Shantae spins the wheel, which I notice now includes the names of the two new contestants but Bill's name is gone. The Wheel of Fate lands on TC, and when Shantae spins again, it lands on Beth Anne.

"Interesting," Shantae says obnoxiously.

I feel Madison stiffen beside me, but TC squeezes her shoulder reassuringly before he walks up to the bar. Beth Anne has already climbed on top of it and is lying down seductively, with her wavy hair splayed everywhere. The bartender pours a shot of rum and places it on her chest, the shot glass held in place between her ample breasts, now barely covered by a neon purple string bikini. Madison grabs my hand and squeezes hard.

"It's okay," I whisper. "It's just a dumb icebreaker. You have nothing to worry about."

Then TC puts his hands behind his back and leans forward to take the shot glass out of Beth Anne's cleavage, using his mouth. He wraps his lips around the glass and throws it back, swallowing the contents. Madison might break my hand.

But before Madison causes permanent nerve damage, TC puts the shot glass on the counter, comes back over to the couch, and kisses her. Despite the ridiculousness of this situation, I melt a little at his romantic gesture. It's not Jane Austen, but who knows how she would've handled body shots.

Next, the Wheel of Fate tasks Scott with doing a shot off the new contestant, Eliana. She also climbs onto the bar, in her leopard print bikini, and lies down. The bartender pours booze into the indentation between her clavicle bones, essentially turning her neck into a makeshift shot glass. Scott leans in and sucks the alcohol out before *graciously* cleaning up all the alcohol that spilled by licking and sucking her neck as well. Eliana doesn't seem to mind.

I roll my eyes at myself for letting him have that same effect on me and make a mental note to give the new girl a heads-up when I hear Shantae call my name. She spins the wheel again and it lands on Javier's name. I'm grateful it's someone I'm friends with and not the new guy, who may be very nice but I'm not ready for bodily alcohol to be consumed by him.

Javier helps me climb up onto the bar, careful not to jostle my still swollen ankle, and I thank him for his chivalry. He smiles and says that he still owes me one. Then before I realize what's happening, the bartender is pouring vodka through the hole cut in my bathing suit and into my belly button. I gasp at the sensation. Javier smiles at me and whispers, "May I?" I nod, and he leans down and sucks the alcohol off my stomach. It's all over so quickly that I don't even have time to be scandalized, and frankly, I'm just glad I don't have to be the one drinking vodka at 11:00 a.m.

Javier helps me off the bar and hands me a napkin. He really is a gentleman.

Shantae then calls up the new guy, Chris, and both Madison and Ciara since they're the only ones left. They all must've done this before because they quickly work out the logistics. Ciara licks Madison's neck, then the bartender shakes salt there. Ciara then licks the salt off Madison before she kneels down in the sand so she's eye level with Chris's crotch, where a shot of tequila is balanced inside the waistband of his bathing suit. Ciara takes the shot glass with her mouth, tips it back, swallows the tequila, and then stands back up and takes a lime wedge from Madison's mouth. Scott, TC, and Javier all cheer like this sexy show is for them.

After the body shots, Shantae makes some lame jokes about how "tequila does a body good" and tells us that it's time to get ready for our one-on-one dates. I nod, still in my own world, numb from the events of this morning.

"Because Chris and Eliana just arrived, they'll go on their date together. Grace, you're still alone," Shantae says matter-of-factly. *She just had to remind me.*

We start walking off the beach as Blue jogs over to catch up to me. "Hey."

"Hey," I say back. "Everything okay?"

He nods discreetly but waits until we're closer to the shack and away from the others before saying, "Kristina point-blank asked me if it was you who made the complaint. To which I replied, 'How could it possibly have been Grace? She doesn't have a phone.'"

I give him a quick hug. "Thanks, Blue."

"I wouldn't thank me yet . . ." He plays with his headset nervously, like he did when I first met him. "I think she's still suspicious of you—hence your one-on-one date."

"What do you mean?" I'm immediately on high alert. "Do you know what I'm doing?"

"She said it would be *'good for her personal growth.'*" He winces.

"Blue!! What is it?!! It better not be skydiving!"

"I promise you—it's not *skydiving*," Blue says evasively.

"What is it then? Blue, you know I'm deathly afraid of heights. Which I specifically told Kristina."

"Probably shouldn't have done that."

"Oh my God! I will kill you if you don't tell me."

"Not if the producers kill you first," he mutters under his breath, and my heart stops beating. "Just get dressed please."

"You are so dead!" I scream at Blue from a large field behind the mansion a mere thirty minutes later.

"It's not my fault! I don't plan the dates!" he says, backing away from me while quickly texting someone.

"Well, then please tell Kristina and her diabolical producer minions that there's no way in hell I'm getting in that death basket," I say, pointing to a freaking hot-air balloon.

"They got you on camera saying you're scared of heights. So they want America to see you overcoming your fears. Honestly, it'll be a great moment for you," he tries to reason.

"Not if I plummet to my death." I cross my arms over the floral sundress I thought I was wearing to a fake date, not what I'd be buried in.

"*Grace,*" he chides, like I'm an unruly child.

"*Blue,*" I mimic him. "You know I have acrophobia, and yet you want me to be hundreds of feet in the air, in a small wooden, *flammable* basket directly below burning liquid propane . . . *alone.*"

"You won't be alone. There'll be a very qualified balloon operator with you. And Bruce." Blue sweeps a hand in the direction of the hot-air balloon operator and the camera operator, both of whom are playing games on their phones. It doesn't exactly instill confidence. "You're not in a couple, Grace. Which means you have to keep doing things that will make America love you and vote for you. Or feel bad and vote for you. Which means going on this date and overcoming your fear while looking like a single yet loveable sad sack." Then he lowers his voice. "Not to mention Kristina is now out to get you, so you have to play the game if you want to stay on the show."

I take deep breaths to keep my panic attack at bay. I can't believe I'm considering risking my life to appease Evil Producer Barbie and to make random strangers in the Bible Belt like me.

"Will you go with me?" I plead.

"I wish I could, sweetie. I have a million things to do before the next challenge, and Kristina will make my life miserable if I don't get them done."

I shake my head. I can't believe I woke up this morning thinking it would be a good day. Andrew is mad at me, Kristina is out to get me, and now I'm going to die.

I look up when I hear people coming; it's the rest of the contestants. Blue sees the hope in my eyes and quickly dashes it. "They can't come with you either. They're just here because Kristina wants a shot of them sending you off."

The balloon operator climbs into the basket, and with a whoosh of fire, the balloon begins to fill. I jump at the sound and frantically turn to Blue. "Please. Isn't there anything else I could do? Literally anything?"

"I'll go with you," I hear from behind me. Andrew is striding toward us.

Chapter Twenty-Seven

Y**ou texted him?!"** I whisper-shout to Blue because I don't want Andrew, the contestants, or any of the half-dozen hot-air balloon operators to hear me.

"I was just hoping he'd help me convince you to do it," he whispers back.

Andrew stops in front of us, and I look up at him in confusion. "Are you even allowed to go with me?"

"Absolutely not," he says with a shake of his head.

"But they can shoot around him, so he won't be on camera. And it'll still look like you're alone. Right?" Blue says to Bruce, the camera operator.

"Yeah, sure, whatever," Bruce replies without looking up from his phone.

This still isn't making sense to me. "But why . . . I thought you were mad at me?"

"Can we talk about this in the air?" he replies, and I can't read his expression.

"It depends. Are you going to push me out of the basket?"

He rolls his eyes like he can't help it. "Aren't you scared enough without making things worse in your head?"

All I can manage to say is, "Yes." I look over to where the crew is making everyone else stand, safely away from the balloon. Madison looks delightfully in shock over Andrew's gesture, while Ciara gives me an encouraging nod. When I turn back, my eyes lock on

Andrew's steady brown ones. I find myself calming down, grounded by his quiet confidence. "Fine, but if we crash and I'm paralyzed for life, I'm suing the show."

"You can't. You signed the liability paperwork," Andrew says, with his patented grin.

I roll my eyes and try not to let him see me smile. "Let's get this over with."

"Exactly what a guy wants to hear before a first date," he says low enough so only I can hear.

My stomach immediately gets that fluttery-queasy feeling. *Wait, is this a date?* No, of course not. I'm a contestant, he's not allowed to date me. He's not even allowed to be here right now. And why is he here after I basically called him corporate scum?

Before my nerves spontaneously combust, Blue shoves a pair of fake glasses onto my face and pushes me toward the hot-air balloon. "Have fun, kids!"

Andrew offers me his hand to climb into the basket, and even though I'm sure my palms are sweaty, I don't let go once we get in. For some reason, being in physical contact with him settles me. He doesn't say anything as I continue grasping onto him like a lunatic.

We're squeezed in toward the middle of the basket, as far away from the edges as possible. But even with some distance, I quickly learn that looking out over the rim is a bad idea. I turn to find Andrew's warm brown eyes instead and I instantly feel better.

"I'm going to stare at you instead of where I can fall off and die."

"Sounds like a good plan."

As the balloon pilot fires the burner and we slowly start to ascend, I hear a voice yell from behind us, "What the hell is going on here?"

I'm still holding Andrew's hand, but I turn my head enough to see Kristina and Brett getting out of a golf cart. Kristina yells up to us, "Andrew, get off that damn balloon!"

"Oh shit," I hear Ciara say from the sidelines. My thoughts exactly.

Andrew shakes his head. "Too late, Kristina."

"You're already on probation!" Kristina screams, looking more unhinged than I've ever seen her.

Andrew shrugs and yells back, "Do what you have to do."

I look at him in shock. "What? No! Don't get fired because of me!" Then I turn to the pilot. "Can you bring us back down please?"

"Do not bring us back down," Andrew tells him.

I hear the shocked reactions from the rest of the contestants as the pilot nods at Andrew. Suddenly, there's a loud rush as the burner shoots flames into the balloon and it rises higher. I shriek and pull Andrew's entire arm around me.

Kristina yells, "You signed the nonfraternization agreement!"

Andrew looks at me and smiles before yelling back, "So sue me."

There's a communal gasp at his audacity, but none louder than mine. And then when I see that we're now hovering at least twenty feet in the air, I gasp again. Down below us, I see Blue trying to talk Kristina down. I can tell by his hand motions that he's explaining that Bruce, the camera operator, will still get the footage she needs. But Kristina is gesturing wildly back at him and doesn't look happy. Madison is giving me a thumbs-up. Then, as the ground gets farther away, I start to get dizzy.

I feel like I might throw up. I shut my eyes and hold my breath.

"Breathe," Andrew says gently as he rubs my arm. But I'm currently too freaked out to focus on how nice and tingly the contact feels.

I open my eyes and look into his. "I think you just got fired." He nods. "But why? Why get fired for me after everything I said to you this morning?"

Andrew waits a minute, still rubbing a thumb up and down my arm reassuringly before he says, "Because you were right." I open my mouth to apologize, but he continues.

"I became a lawyer so I could make a difference and help people. Instead, I'm helping media conglomerates not get sued by drunk influencers." He sighs. "So, I didn't just get fired for you. I got fired for me too." I nod in understanding as he adds, "Also I saw you pick up a snake without hesitation and go toe to toe with Kristina. You're fearless. So when you said you were afraid of heights, I knew it had to be severe. I couldn't let Kristina send you up here alone."

I squeeze him tighter. "Thank you." Then I look up at him sincerely. "I'm sorry for how harsh I was this morning and for not coming to you first."

He grins. "You've been a headache since that first phone call. I would expect nothing less." I smile, hoping this means he'll forgive me.

I attempt to look out over the edge of the balloon but quickly shut my eyes. Not ready for that yet. Instead, I ask Andrew, "So if *Love Shack* isn't your dream job, what is?"

Andrew puts both arms around me so we're cuddled together and says, "When I first started law school, I wanted to be a children's rights advocate. I did an internship with the Department of Children and Families. But it was harder than I thought it would be. I was constantly dealing with all the offenses I wanted to protect kids from—child abuse, neglect, living in homes without adults who loved them and protected them. It was heartbreaking."

"Yeah, I imagine that would weigh on you, day in and day out."

"I wish I could've stuck it out, but I knew it would break me. When the studio offered me a job after graduation, I thought it would be temporary, but then I got trapped by the golden handcuffs."

"I'm sorry you've felt trapped," I say. It seems awful to have a job you don't feel passionate about.

"I was already questioning my life choices before you called me out on it," he says, rubbing my back. "A few months ago, I applied to volunteer with a nonprofit that helps relocate refugees in Syria.

I found out my application was accepted right before production started. But I chickened out. I went back to what was familiar—the soul-sucking corporate job that pays well."

"Hey," I say softly, forcing him to look at me. "We've all made mistakes in our careers, but I truly believe you learn something from every experience. I have no doubt you'll find a way to help people."

He nods and squeezes my hand. "You're right. I just needed the reminder," he says as he pulls me in tighter.

"The reminder could've been nicer, though," I say apologetically, squished into his chest.

After a moment, Andrew admits, "I think that's why we didn't get along in the beginning. Because I saw the old me in you. The rabble-rouser who wanted to save the world. And it annoyed me. You reminded me of what I could've been."

"Well, I'm sorry I annoyed you. Especially because there were times when I was definitely trying to."

Andrew laughs. "That checks out." He exhales, and I feel his warm breath in my hair. "Then, somewhere along the way, I stopped being annoyed by you and realized those were the traits I liked most about you. Like how you always look out for the underdog, despite being the underdog yourself."

Finally I nod and acknowledge, "It's easier to advocate for the people and animals no one else is fighting for than to advocate for myself."

Andrew hums like this makes sense to him and he's putting puzzle pieces in place. "Is that why you got into conservation?"

I nod. "I wanted to save innocent creatures that couldn't save themselves. Plus, I've always been an animal lover. I was devastated when I found out I'd never be able to see a woolly mammoth or a dodo."

"You didn't care about seeing a dinosaur?" Andrew asks playfully.

"No, I was five and seeing a giant carnivorous lizard wasn't top of my list. I'd love to see one now, though. You?"

"No way. I saw *Jurassic Park* when I was too young. Scarred for life. Don't even like Jeeps."

I laugh and we hear a throat clear. I turn to see Bruce, the camera operator, looking at us. I completely forgot he was here. And damn, I also momentarily forgot we're perilously floating in the air. It's like Andrew and I were in our own world.

Bruce says in a bored tone, "Can you let go of each other please? I need to get footage of her freaking out."

"Guess he's not beating around the bush," I whisper to Andrew.

Andrew smiles and calmly says, "Okay, I'm going to let go of you now, but only for a minute. I'll be right here. You're doing great." His voice is so kind that I manage to nod and release my death grip on him. I feel his steadying warmth move away, and I frantically grab onto the edge of the balloon without getting too close.

I take a quick peek. "Holy shit! When did we get this high up?!"

I immediately squeeze my eyes shut as I white-knuckle the rim of the basket. I sense the camera operator moving around me and I wonder which angle of me hyperventilating makes me the most likable. After what I'm pretty sure is eighty-seven hours, he finally says, "Okay, I got it." I immediately turn and reach for Andrew, grabbing him and pulling myself toward him.

My face is buried in his very hard chest, and I feel his arms go around me protectively. It feels good. And surprisingly not weird, considering that a couple days ago I really disliked him.

There's another quick burst of fire and the balloon lifts higher. I tighten my grip around his waist and he rubs my back again, saying, "I've got you. You're missing the view, though. That's the best part."

"I don't know about that," I say, inhaling his cologne and snuggling in closer, this time *not for safety.* He laughs, and I swear I feel him flex his biceps underneath me.

I hate pulling myself away from the comfort of him, but I lift my head to quickly peek over his shoulder to see what all the fuss is about. I immediately gasp from both fear and wonder. We're gently floating over rolling hills and green vineyards. The rugged Santa Monica Mountains are to my right, and the Pacific Ocean is sparkling directly in front of us. "Wow" is all I can say.

Andrew smiles. "How's this?" He gently turns me around so I'm facing out toward the rim of the basket. His arms are still strong around my waist, and my back is firmly against his front. We're at least a foot from the edge, so I can't see straight down, which is helping.

I lean back into him and place my arms on top of his. Being wrapped in him feels safe. And as my breathing starts to regulate, I realize being held tightly like this by Andrew makes me feel other things too.

"Look, there's the mansion," Andrew says, pointing to a giant estate that's now in the distance behind us. "You can barely see the shack."

"And yet I can still feel the kink in my neck from sleeping on the floor." I feel Andrew vibrate with laughter behind me. *As if I need a reminder of how close our bodies are.* "Is that Sandstone Peak?" I ask to distract myself from racy thoughts that have no business being considered at one thousand feet above sea level. I gesture toward a mountaintop with my head, because his arms are quickly becoming my new favorite belt and I refuse to let go of them.

"Yep. I go mountain biking there sometimes."

"You go mountain biking?" I say, surprised. "In suit pants?"

He laughs. "No, but I've been known to roll up my sleeves on occasion," he says seductively.

"I have a sudden interest in mountain biking," I answer flirtatiously.

I feel him smiling in response. "I also hike and camp and surf." He shrugs. "I like nature."

"Me too. Preferably from the ground." But after I look out at the ocean for a while, I have to admit, "It's actually kind of peaceful up here. You know, when you're not calculating the velocity with which you'd hit the ground."

"Or the likelihood of catching fire in the air," Andrew teases back.

"Fuck, I wasn't calculating that, but now that's literally all I'll be able to think about."

He laughs behind me. "Sorry."

"You guys know I'm a professional, right?" the hot-air balloon pilot asks.

I laugh and say, "Sorry! It's not you, it's me!" Which makes Andrew rumble with laughter again. He has a good laugh. It's deep and easy, and it warms me almost as much as his embrace.

We enjoy the view in a comfortable silence for a while. Even the abrupt fire-breathing dragon sound of the burner doesn't make me jump anymore. If I survive this, it might just be the best one-on-none date I've ever been on.

"Okay, let me get a shot of you overcoming your fear," Bruce says, as he picks up the camera again. "Can you step closer to the edge?"

"Nope."

"Whatever," he says and begins filming. Andrew gently lets me go and moves away so he's not in the frame. I go back to looking out at the mountains framing the Pacific and the rocky coastline. It's less enjoyable without Andrew's expensively masculine scent cocooning me.

But then I think about what Bruce just said; I *am* overcoming my fear, and I can't help but smile as he gets the shot of me bravely looking out into the distance.

After Bruce lowers the camera, I don't even have to scramble back to Andrew before he wraps me in his arms again. I know some people consider hot-air balloon rides romantic. Mostly people who don't have a healthy fear of death, but I'm starting to get it. I look up at Andrew, and he gives me a shy smile, which may just be the most endearing facial expression I have ever seen.

I snuggle in closer as the balloon operator points to a large open field next to a vineyard. "That's where we're touching down."

"Why?" I ask, suddenly panicked. "Is there a problem?"

The operator shakes his head. "That's where they said to take you."

As we get closer to the ground, I see a picnic blanket set up with a lavish spread. Before I can make out what kind of food there is, my brain registers that the Earth is getting closer and closer. I start to get dizzy. Andrew must see it in my eyes because he quickly turns me back in toward his chest and I close my eyes. I hold my breath until we bump the ground gently and bounce a few times before we come to a stop. *Oh, thank Darwin!*

I resist the urge to kiss the ground. Or Andrew. Instead, I turn to the balloon operator. "Thank you for not killing us."

He just says, "You have three hours to yourselves, then we head back."

And just like that my nerves go haywire again. I was so distracted with potentially dying that I hadn't thought about what would happen if we made it to land safely. But now my pulse is racing for a new reason—I'm about to be on a date with Andrew.

Chapter Twenty-Eight

Andrew helps me climb out of the hot-air balloon, and we walk over to the checkered picnic blanket set up for my one-on-none date. My legs still feel shaky from the landing, so I plop down with all the elegance of a stampeding white rhinoceros.

Despite my anxiety about being alone with Andrew, I take off my fake glasses and dig into the picnic basket, because apparently not plummeting to your death makes you very hungry. "Oh my God, there's vegan cheese!" I squeal.

Andrew holds up a bottle. "And champagne. But didn't you swear off alcohol forever?"

I hand him the champagne flutes and shrug. "I can make an exception."

He smiles and pops the cork. As he pours, I take in the vineyards surrounding us. The rows of grapes form natural runways to the rugged Santa Monica Mountains in the distance. We're sitting underneath a gorgeous old walnut tree and when I look up through its branches, I'm greeted by a bright blue sky dotted with lazy clouds.

"Damn, this is romantic. What would I have done by myself?" I ask with a laugh.

Andrew hands me my champagne. "Yeah, seems like a waste just to make you look depressed and lonely."

"We still have to get that shot," calls Bruce, who's lying under a nearby tree with his camera beside him. His baseball hat is over his face, and he looks like he's minutes from falling asleep.

Andrew and I share an amused grin, then he holds up his champagne to cheers me. "To overcoming fears," he says.

I hold up my flute and add, "And to the best one-on-none date I've ever been on." We maintain eye contact as we clink glasses.

Andrew peeks inside the picnic basket. "I picked the right date to crash!" He takes out finger sandwiches, fruits, more cheese, fancy gourmet nuts, and chocolates. "The only thing we're missing is the live band to serenade us."

I sit up in horror. "That's not going to happen, is it?"

Andrew points behind me. I turn to see two men and a woman walking toward us, carrying instruments.

"What? Why?" I say, already cringing.

"They do it all the time on reality shows."

"That doesn't make it right."

Andrew looks entertained by my discomfort as the band sets up to do an acoustic performance, a mere twenty feet away from us. I give them a small wave. "Hi." Then I turn to Andrew and whisper, "This is so awkward."

"Pretend they're not here," he whispers back.

"But they're right there," I say through clenched teeth. "I feel like I have to make nervous small talk."

He grins. "Make nervous small talk with me instead. Okay, so where were we? You're an underdog who saves other underdogs, and you were sad about dodos and mammoths but not dinosaurs. Then what?"

I smile back at him and try not to look at the musicians tuning their instruments just beyond his right shoulder. Luckily, Andrew's handsome face easily captures my attention.

I sigh and shrug. "Well, after my existential crisis about dodos, I told my kindergarten teacher that I wanted to save animals, so that's what I've been doing ever since."

"You knew exactly what you wanted to be when you grew up,

and then you made it happen. Makes me feel like a slacker that I never became a professional basketball player."

"Oh, are you good at basketball?"

"Nope." He laughs. "Turns out that's a prerequisite to going pro."

After all our bickering these past few days, it feels good to laugh with him. "Maybe there's still time for you. You shouldn't be wasting your time on hot-air balloon rides, though. You should be bouncing a ball or whatever it is basketball players do."

He stretches and leans back. "I'm good here. Tell me more."

I lean back too, feeling that familiar tingle of electricity when our arms touch. His closeness momentarily distracts me as I search my brain for more to tell.

"I think I was the only ten-year-old with pictures of Jane Goodall and Wangari Maathai on their bedroom wall. I used to ask my family to make donations to the World Wildlife Fund instead of getting me birthday or Christmas presents."

His eyes open wide, like I've impressed him. "It would've been hard for me to give up baseball cards and video games. But I did adopt a manatee when we went to Florida one year. I got a certificate and everything."

"Nice. What'd you name it?"

He smiles. "Michael Jordan."

"Ah yes, I've heard of him."

The musicians begin playing some sort of twangy country song, but it's hard to pay attention to anything other than Andrew. I want to know everything about him. Which is jarring. I'm about to ask him a barrage of questions when he says, "You know, for someone who claims to hate social media, your accounts looked pretty robust to me." He grins mischievously. "I especially liked the picture of you holding the falcon."

I groan. "That was all my brother's idea, and it's a Swainson's hawk. It's a threatened species in California. They had a huge population decline in the seventies because farmers were using DDT in Argentina where they winter and—" I stop, realizing I'm doing the thing my family warned me about. "Sorry, I tend to ramble about work. I know it's boring."

Andrew raises his eyebrows. "Who told you it was boring? I think it's fascinating," Andrew says, tilting his head. "Being passionate about what you believe in is sexy."

I feel myself blush. "I can't believe you stalked my Instagram."

"I had to—for background checks, remember? It was for purely professional purposes." *Except the glint in his eye says otherwise.* "I also saw you've recently added a fundraiser for your wildlife center. That doesn't have anything to do with why you're on the show, does it?"

My stomach bottoms out. Shit. If Andrew knows, does that mean the producers know? I nod slowly, then ask, "Does that mean I'll be kicked off the show?"

He shakes his head. "Everyone on *Love Shack* has an ulterior motive. Yours is just more altruistic than most."

"What about the *right reasons*?"

"As long as the audience thinks you're here to find love, you're fine." He smiles at me. "I knew there had to be a reason you came on the show."

"I told you it wasn't to become famous."

He nods, conceding. "That's what it usually is. Or to launch modeling and acting careers . . ." His eyes get stony. "Or get laid."

I know he's thinking of Scott, and I laugh. "You're doing it again. Being all heroic and protective."

"And jealous," he admits quietly, looking at me, as his thumb rubs the back of my hand. "I hated that he got to touch you."

"Oh." My body suddenly feels like it's being heated by the world's largest Bunsen burner. It's the same heat I felt when we kissed, but unlike when he walked me back to my shack, we're not alone. It feels scandalous to be turned on in front of the band. And Bruce. Although when I turn to look, Bruce is sleeping.

When I turn back to Andrew, he's watching me with those knowing eyes, as if he's aware of the decision I'm struggling with. He raises his eyebrows in a silent challenge. So I raise mine back and quote him. "Fuck it."

I grab him by the shirt and tug him toward me. I feel him smile as his lips touch mine, but his amusement quickly turns into desire when I remember what he likes. I bite his bottom lip, and he squeezes my hip possessively. We pick right back up where we left off outside the shack. He meets me kiss for kiss, tongue for tongue, as if we're still trying to one-up each other.

I roll onto my back and pull him on top of me. "I really liked this position when we were on the beach," I whisper to him.

He kisses my neck until his lips reach my ear, and he whispers back, "Hell yes." Then he lowers all of his weight onto me. My back arches involuntarily when I feel the press of his arousal.

Andrew is even sexier when he's making out with me—that perfect fucking stubble of his rubbing against me, tickling my neck as he sucks and licks. I don't even realize that at some point I've wrapped my legs around him. There's not even a centimeter between us, but I still can't get him close enough. I don't have time to be smug that he's just as turned on as I am because I crave the friction of him too much.

I bite his earlobe, earning a groan from Andrew, when suddenly, we're interrupted by a voice calling out, "Hey, Grace." It jars me from my Andrew trance. We turn to see Bruce walking toward us. He holds up his camera and says, "Kristina called, I need the footage of you drinking alone and looking sad." He looks at Andrew pointedly.

Andrew and I, breathing heavily, share an exasperated look. But before I can ask Bruce to give us a minute or preferably a couple hours, Andrew discreetly adjusts himself and rolls off of me. Normally I'd be embarrassed being caught getting all hot and heavy, but I'm feeling more frustrated than embarrassed at the moment.

Andrew hands me my champagne flute. "You don't look very sad," he says with a self-satisfied grin. I fake a frown, and he laughs before walking off toward the hot-air balloon. *Dammit, Bruce!*

I just barely have time to fix my hair and put my glasses back on before the camera promptly blinks on. "I guess it's showtime," I sigh. I don't know what to do other than sit awkwardly on the blanket, sip my champagne, and wish I were still kissing Andrew. I distract myself from how pathetic this one-on-none close-up must be by watching the band. The guitarist gives me a pitying look, and I'm tempted to tell him I'm a scientist in the real world.

After a couple minutes, Bruce says, "That should do it. That was depressing as shit."

"Glad I could be of service," I say, standing to stretch my legs.

Bruce walks off to go finish whatever game he's addicted to on his phone, and I hear Andrew's deep voice asking the band if they take requests. A moment later, they're playing something slow but catchy, and vaguely familiar.

"Do you want to dance?" Andrew asks, walking over to me, holding his hand out.

Normally, I'm not a dancer. I'm usually the person who sits at the singles table at weddings, avoiding the dance floor, and counting down the minutes until it's socially acceptable to leave. But when I take Andrew's hand and he pulls me in close, I get the appeal. It feels like it did when I was in his arms on the hot-air balloon. Warm and fuzzy and safe.

He puts his hands on my waist, sending tingles up my spine, and I loop mine around his neck. We slow-dance for the rest of the song and don't break apart when the band starts another one. Andrew must think my two left feet are warmed up because he twirls me.

He pulls me back in and says, "I donated to your fundraiser, by the way."

"You did?" I say, looking up at him with what I can only imagine is an idiotic grin.

"Yep. I'm looking forward to my yellow-legged frog postcard."

"Oh, there are giveaways now?" I say, impressed with Cassie's ingenuity.

"Yep. And if you donate five grand, you get to name a frog."

"Were you tempted to do that so there'd be a little Michael Jordan hopping around?"

He laughs. "You know me so well." Then his smile changes from teasing to serious. "I still can't believe you were willing to put your life on hold to go on a reality show, which I know you hate, so you could save your nature center—"

"And frogs."

"And frogs." He looks at me with that intensity of his. "You're honestly one of the most passionate, most selfless people I've ever met."

My heart skips at least twenty-seven beats, but I scoff and try to play it off. He's not having it. "You even came to Beth Anne's rescue, and she's awful. You defended Ciara, Javier, and, well, the entire crew, *and* you gave away the golden key card even though it meant sleeping in the shack."

I look away, because I feel my face turning scarlet. But that means I'm making eye contact with the fiddle player and that's weird too, so I turn back to him and admit, "It's hard for me to accept compliments."

He smiles. "I can tell."

"But thank you for saying those things. It means a lot . . . coming from you."

The "you" dances in the air between us. Because it's true. It some-how means more coming from him. The gold flecks in his eyes shine. I sigh contentedly as I take it all in. This handsome man in front of me, backlit by the setting sun and with the mountains behind him, hell, even the band is growing on me. "I feel bad for the next girl you take out. It's going to be hard to top this."

Andrew gives me a long look, though I see the hint of a smile. "I know it's hard to believe, but I don't date much."

"I do find that hard to believe," I admit.

"I don't have a lot of free time outside of work, and well, you've seen the people I meet on the show."

"Beautiful, scantily clad women? Yeah, that's rough."

He laughs. "*Love Shack* contestants aren't usually my type." The "usually" makes me lean in closer to him. He looks at me meaning-fully. "I guess it's a good thing I got fired. I'll finally have time to date. And I won't have to feel bad about doing this . . ."

He leans in and kisses me slowly, languorously, like he has all the time in the world to get to know my mouth. Unlike our first two kisses, which felt needy and frenzied, this feels dreamlike. A slow love song drifts on the breeze through the vineyard, and the combi-nation of the California sun heating my skin and Andrew's fingers trailing my arm gives me goose bumps.

I follow his lead, not rushing anything. And once again it feels like we're in on the same plan. Like we're making a pact that there will be plenty of time for everything else, so for now we're just going to lazily enjoy the moment.

When we eventually pull apart, Andrew holds me close as we dance to the rest of the song. I feel like I'm floating.

After the song ends, we thank the band and promise to download their songs. Then, over some more vegan cheese and dark chocolate, Andrew and I talk about everything from our family and friends to our college years. We debate who has cooler hobbies. Me—reading, puzzles, science podcasts, and trivia night. Andrew—playing pickup basketball, mountain biking, learning guitar, and discovering new food trucks. I'm honestly impressed that I'm able to pay attention to what he's saying because all I can think about is kissing him again.

A little while later, Bruce comes back over, looking at his watch. The time spent with Andrew—dancing, talking, laughing—has flown by, but apparently it's been hours.

"You ready to risk our lives again?" Andrew asks me.

"I'm kinda tipsy now, so sure, why not?"

But Bruce shakes his head. "We're not going back yet. It's the next part of the date." He gestures past a small barn, where I see a massage table set up. Was that always there, or did they set it up while I was distracted by the sexy lawyer?

I shrug and look at Andrew. "It's up to you. Should we get a massage?"

He doesn't even hesitate when he grabs my hand and pulls me toward the barn.

Chapter Twenty-Nine

I'm standing in a bathrobe. Outside at a vineyard, next to an extremely attractive man who is wearing only a small towel. If you think I've paid attention to anything the massage therapist has said in the past twenty minutes, you'd be delusional.

Because this wasn't supposed to be a couples massage and there's only one therapist, we've had to adjust as we go. Bruce got the footage he needed—me getting a "romantic" massage alone—and then the massage therapist offered to give us a lesson. Now it's our turn to practice the techniques she showed us.

"Who wants to go first?" she asks, and my body hums in anticipation of physical contact with Andrew.

He must know I haven't been paying attention because he chivalrously comes to my rescue. "I'll go first." I relax a little until I look at his large hands that are about to be all over my body and swallow hard.

The massage therapist turns on some light music. "Here are some massage oils to choose from," she says. "There are also hot stones and crystals you can experiment with. Feel free to use the techniques I taught you or just play. I'm going to leave you two alone now. Enjoy your quiet, romantic time."

She walks away, and I turn to Andrew. "What would I have done if I were alone? Massage myself?"

"That's still an option," Andrew says, raising his eyebrows. I playfully swat at him and then start to lose my nerve. I'm naked under this robe. At least Bruce said he'd wait for us back at the balloon and give us some privacy.

I gesture for Andrew to turn around while I disrobe and climb up onto the massage table. I pull the sheet up over me and say, "Okay."

"Are you all right with this?" Andrew asks as he turns back around.

"Yep," I squeak. Because while I am very much all right with this, I'm also alone with the world's sexiest lawyer. Naked. With massage oil. My heart is pounding, and all my nerve endings are tingling.

Andrew slowly peels the sheet off me, folding it down just below my waist, and the warm breeze tickles my bare back. I hear him open the massage oil and the sound of him rubbing it into his hands makes me inhale sharply, in anticipation of his touch.

He gently begins to trail his fingers up and down my back, and the contrast between the slick oil, his rough hands, and the tender way he caresses me is already driving me crazy. I close my eyes, trying not to freak out: Not only is Andrew touching me, but it feels even better than I imagined it would.

He starts using the technique the massage therapist must've taught us because it feels amazing. "How's this feel?" he asks, his mouth right next to my ear.

A shiver goes through me. "Perfect," I say breathlessly.

Then his hands drift lower and lower until his fingertips stroke the area that can only be described as my *low* lower back. "Is this okay?" he asks, his fingers hovering.

I nod, lust making me incapable of speech. I want him to go slower and faster at the same time.

His hands continue to travel farther south as they explore my body. "How about now?" Andrew asks.

"Yes," I say. "Please keep going."

The reaction I'm having to him seems to break his resolve. He grabs a handful of my ass and groans. I feel it reverberate straight to my core. "I've been dying to do this since I saw you in that ridiculous cut-up bathing suit."

I know what he means. Except I think I've wanted him since the second I saw him in his overpriced custom suit.

With his strong hands continuing their path south, Andrew massages the backs of my thighs. Every nerve ending in my body is at full attention. I don't know what the hell that massage lady was talking about—this is anything but relaxing. It feels like my entire body is on fire.

He squeezes up and down my legs. "God, your legs are so long." This makes me squirm as the tingly feeling builds between them.

His fingers now trail back up the sides of my body, along my rib cage, and he stops right before he reaches my breasts. My body feels jittery with need for his touch. "Yes," I plead before he can even ask.

His fingers dance along the sides of my breasts, and I roll over onto my back, so Andrew has better access. I hold my breath as he takes in my naked body. "You are so beautiful," he says reverently before he starts caressing my breasts. When he squeezes my nipples, my back arches in response.

I don't know the rules of this massage lesson, but I need to touch him. *Now.* I pull desperately at his towel, trying to bring him closer to me, but he lets it drop to the ground.

I know my mouth is hanging open and I'm staring, but I don't even care because *holy shit*! He moves to the foot of the massage table, and I slowly lift myself up onto my elbows to get a better look. He lets me ogle his chiseled body. Lawyers have no business having bodies like this, but I'm not complaining.

"You've been hiding this under suits this whole time?"

He smiles. "I like the way you look at me."

"I like the way you touch me."

He takes this as a green light to climb up my body at a tortuously slow pace, kissing his way up as he goes. He starts at my good ankle, careful not to put any body weight on the bad one. I've never realized that the inside of an ankle could be an erogenous zone, but as he licks and sucks his way up my shin, I feel like I can't breathe.

He smiles up at me when he gets to the inside of my knee. And he doesn't break eye contact as he leisurely makes his way higher and higher until his head is between my thighs and my breath catches. "And I've been dying to do *this* since you told me to sue you."

I gasp as his tongue starts slipping back and forth, and I can't tell if the slickness is from him or me. Then he reaches up with one of his hands and begins playing with my nipple again, rolling it between his fingers and pinching. Between the slight pain of the pinch and the heat pooling in my stomach, I can't stop myself from trying to grind against him.

Andrew holds me down with his other hand on my stomach. He must be able to tell that I'm getting close to the edge. But right when I'm about to come, he stops. I'm about to object when he starts rubbing me with his hand, which has me moaning and bucking again.

"More?" he asks with a grin. I nod frantically because I just need him to keep going and never ever stop.

I'm so wet that his finger slides right in. He pumps it in and out a few times before adding a second. I groan in ecstasy. His fingers continue expertly working me, rubbing exactly where I need them as his mouth picks back up on its trail up my body. He kisses my stomach, then my ribs, before taking my other nipple in his mouth. Between his fingers thrusting faster and his teeth on my nipples, I'm writhing below him.

"I'm going to come," I pant.

"Not yet," he says, "I want to taste all of you."

I groan in frustration and he laughs. "Okay, okay," he says before leaning closer to whisper into my ear. "But I want you to say my name when you come on my tongue."

I almost lose it then and there.

His hands take the place of his mouth on my breasts and he makes his way back down my body. One hand twists and pinches my nipples as his tongue immediately finds my clit. His other hand pushes even deeper inside of me. I throw my head back onto the massage table and arch my back. "Oh fuck, Andrew!"

He keeps going, his fingers pumping inside of me as he licks me harder and harder. My whole body tenses. "Oh my God," I call out as the intense tingling crests over me. And then I explode. "Yes, Andrew! Yes!"

After what feels like a never-ending wave coursing through me, I finally start to come back into my body. "Holy fuck" is all I can manage to say. I can still feel my heart beating in my ears.

Andrew laughs as he kisses his way back up my stomach. Then he shifts his position so he's half lying on me, half on the massage table. I turn to make more room. And when we're finally facing each other, he kisses me. Lazily at first, as if he's giving me a chance to catch my breath. But when I feel his tongue part my lips, I'm just as turned on as I was a moment ago.

I reach down for him, needing to touch him. I hear his intake of breath as my fingers trail up and down his length, before finally taking him in my hand. He's so hard and long and he feels so good. I deepen our kiss as I slide my fist up and down him, feeling wetness at his tip. I pick up the pace as he moans into my mouth, and he somehow gets even harder.

I lean in to kiss him again, but he seems to reluctantly pull back. "I can't believe I'm saying this, but I think we should stop before I want to do more."

"Wait, what? You get me off and then don't want me to reciprocate?"

"Trust me, I want you to reciprocate. Really badly. But once we get going, I'm not going to want to stop."

"Who said anything about stopping?"

"Grace," he moans as he gently cups my face to stop me. "You're making this really hard."

I raise my eyebrow and pump him in response.

He laughs, then with a gravelly voice says, "I'd like to take you on a date first. A real date without cameras."

Oh. I reluctantly let go of him and lie back down next to him. "Fine. We can go on a date first," I groan. But I'm secretly moved that he wants to wait and do this right. And that whatever this is between us means more to him than sex. I lay my head on his chest, still breathing heavily. "Wow. That was . . . wow," I say, incoherent in my sated state. Then I laugh. "I think you broke my brain."

He gives me a self-assured smirk. "I don't think I've ever accomplished that before."

I smile back up at him. "I don't think I've ever *wanted* to give a blow job before."

He groans and drops his head back dramatically. "You're going to be the death of me."

"Not if the hot-air balloon ride home kills you first."

He laughs and pulls me closer. Then he kisses my forehead. "You know, getting fired was totally worth it. I'd be happy to do it all over again tomorrow."

Chapter Thirty

When we get back from the hot-air balloon ride, Blue is waiting for us in the field with a golf cart. Andrew and I try our best to act natural while also stealing glances at each other like teenagers afraid of getting caught by their parents.

We hop in the back of the cart and Blue looks at us suspiciously before he turns to me. "Well, you certainly seem happier than when you were threatening to kill me."

I shrug and say, "It wasn't as bad as I thought it would be."

I can tell Andrew is trying not to smile. Unfortunately, Blue clocks this too, facing him. "You're awfully calm for a guy who just got fired. I tried talking Kristina down, but she wasn't having it. She's pissed."

That brings me back to reality. It was easy enough to forget when we were in our own little world with champagne and vegan cheese and other . . . distractions, but shit, Andrew lost his job today.

Andrew sobers up a little at Blue's words. "Thanks for trying, Blue, but it's okay."

Blue starts driving as I turn to Andrew with concern. But he immediately squeezes my hand and whispers, "I don't regret it."

I squeeze his hand back and smile at him, wondering what this means for us. Because for the first time in my life, I can see a future with a guy.

"Why are you two smiling like that?" Blue asks, looking in the rearview mirror of the golf cart.

I cover my mouth and will my face not to turn red. "We're not. I'm just happy to be alive and not splattered on a mountain somewhere."

Blue looks back and forth, still trying to figure us out as he pulls up to the employee lot where Andrew has parked.

"Well, I better go," Andrew says. "I'd rather not get into it with Kristina today. She can officially fire me tomorrow." And then, right in front of Blue, he leans over and gives me a sweet kiss goodbye. "See you soon?" he whispers.

I nod and whisper back, "Thanks for coming with me."

Then we regretfully pull apart. "Bye, Blue. See you around, Grace." Andrew gives me one last meaningful smile before he turns and walks away.

Once he's out of earshot, Blue spins to me. "What the hell was that?"

"I don't know what you're referring to," I try to say casually but end up sounding like I have a posh British accent.

"Oh my God, I knew it. I called it the first day you were fighting. I bet Madison and Ciara that it was sexual tension and you guys just needed to screw it out of your systems."

I shush him, even though no one is around. "We didn't *screw*."

Blue waits for me to elaborate, but I don't. I don't know what the implications would be for me and my standing on the show if anyone found out what happened off camera. But mostly, I'm still worried about getting Andrew in trouble. Even if he's no longer an employee, I'm sure Kristina could find a way to fuck him over.

I pretend to zip my mouth shut and Blue rolls his eyes. "Whatever, I'll get it out of you eventually." Then he turns the golf cart key and snaps back into work mode. "You're the first one back. The rest of the contestants are still on their dates, so you have some free time."

"Cool. Maybe I'll put on my bathing suit and hang by the pool,"

I say. I have no intention of sunbathing, but I need an excuse to go back to the shack and get my contraband phone so I can call Cassie.

A few minutes later, Blue pulls up next to the shack. "Anything you want to tell me before I go?" he asks.

"You're great at driving a golf cart?" I say, pretending I don't know what he's getting at.

He shakes his head at me. "Fine. Be like that. I'll catch you later, sketchball," he says affectionately and drives off toward the mansion.

The second I enter the shack, I dive into my suitcase and pull out my phone, rapidly dialing Cassie. She answers on the second ring. "Hey, Grace, how's it—"

"I kissed Andrew. A few times. And . . . other things."

"—going? Okay, I guess it's going well, then. Wait, which one is Andrew again?"

"Old Man Benson," I say without hiding my excitement. "And I can't tell anyone on the show, so I had to tell you."

"Ohmigosh, I knew you liked the lawyer! You've never hated someone so much while also waxing poetic about their facial hair before."

"I do. I actually like him."

"And you're admitting it!" she gasps. "I'm so happy for you! Wow, this is really turning out to be a great day. The donations are pouring in, which means we might not lose our jobs, and you finally figured out you like the lawyer—"

"Wait, what was that about our jobs?"

"Forget I said that! I wasn't supposed to say anything."

"No way. You better say something!"

Cassie exhales loudly. "Well . . . we weren't going to tell you because we didn't want you to worry or put even more pressure on you than we already are. But the board said if we don't raise the money, it's not just the vaccine program that's in danger. They'll have to let go of at least one of us. Maybe two."

"No!" I practically shout. "They can't let anyone go! I hand-picked this team. I'll figure out a way to pay everyone's salaries. I'll sell my condo. And my car. And my bike. I'll walk to work."

"I know you would, honey. That's why we didn't tell you. But it's okay, we'll be fine because our plan is working! You just have to stay on the show a little longer so we can keep raising money."

"I'll try," I vow. "Hopefully, Kristina's sad sack storyline will help."

"You're America's Favorite!" Cassie adds. "That's got to mean something, right?"

"I'll be fine," I promise her. Because now that I know my friends' jobs are on the line, I'll have to be.

"Matt is doing a big cross-platform push this week, whatever that means. And I've told everyone I know to vote for you. Even my weird Aunt Linda."

"The one who collects spoons? You hate talking to her!"

"I know! But you can't be the only one making sacrifices." I laugh and then Cassie says, "Oh shoot. I'm sorry, I have to run. I forgot I have to test some salamanders for parasites."

"Ugh, you get to have all the fun while I'm stuck by the pool," I groan, dead serious.

"There will be plenty of parasites for you when you get back," she says.

"There better be," I whine.

"Love you! Bye!" and with that Cassie hangs up.

Not knowing what to do with myself while I wait for everyone else to get back, and still buzzing from my incredible date with Andrew, I decide I might as well head to the pool. I don't bother changing into a bathing suit, but just plop down on a lounge chair in my sundress. Before I even have the chance to risk sun damage, Kristina finds me.

My heart drops as she sits down on the chaise next to mine and levels me with her gaze. "I know you were the one who made the labor complaint. You've consistently broken your contract, and now my lawyer quit because of you."

"You fired him."

"Semantics. Point is, the protocol is to kick you off the show."

I stop breathing. This is what I was afraid of. I mentally kick myself for getting so caught up in lusting over Andrew and standing up to Kristina's injustices that I lost sight of the prize. And then I get mad. "You can't do that! I've done everything you wanted. I wore a cut-up bathing suit and played Suck and Blow and did body shots and went on a hot-air balloon ride for you—"

Kristina holds up her hand to stop me. "Luckily for you, you and Javier are tracking really high."

"Wait, what? You're not kicking me off the show?"

"Unfortunately not. You're too good for our ratings."

"What does this have to do with Javier?"

She looks deeply aggravated that she has to explain this to me but quickly rattles off, "You and Javi got the most votes for America's Favorite Contestant, and there's an algorithm that helps us track what people are saying about the show in comments on the website, social media, reality TV blogs, et cetera. And it turns out that you're the favorite couple on the show."

"But we're not a couple."

"Well, after he kissed you in Suck and Blow, America thinks you are. You even have a celebrity couple name. #Gracier is trending. Next episode we'll show him doing the body shot off you, but we also need to reestablish your connection to take advantage of the momentum."

"We're just friends," I protest.

"Eh, that's nothing tequila and a sexy one-on-one date can't fix."

"I can't do that to Ciara! She really likes him."

"You're not here to make friends, Grace," Kristina admonishes me.

"Yeah, I didn't think so either . . . but what if I am?"

Kristina rolls her eyes. "Then I guess you have to decide what's more important—making it to the end and winning the show and the $250,000 or being pen pals with a *tattoo artist from Vegas.*"

Offended on Ciara's behalf by the way she says it, I'm about to tell her what I really think of her when my phone call with Cassie flashes through my mind. If I don't stay on the show, one of my closest friends could lose their job. As much as I like Ciara and Madison, I can't put people I've known for a week ahead of the people I've worked in the trenches with for the past three years. Cassie, Eliza, and Alec are all amazing at their jobs and have worked so tirelessly for my vision that I know I'll do whatever I have to in order to protect them.

But I still feel shitty when I steady my breathing and say, "What do I have to do?"

"Glad you came to your senses. Just pick Javier for your one-on-one date tonight and get him to like you again. A kiss would really sell it," Kristina says callously, as she stands.

My stomach churns like I'm going to be sick. It's one thing for Javi and me to pretend we like each other, but I can't, in good conscience, kiss him. Not mere hours after sharing several life-altering kisses with Andrew. For the first time ever, I have real feelings for a guy. That means something to me. I don't want to cheapen it by fake-kissing someone else. Besides, what would Andrew think if he sees me locking lips with another guy right after we had an amazing day together?

Before I can protest, Kristina calls over her shoulder, "Oh, and don't tell anyone about this conversation. We need everyone's authentic reactions. It makes for better drama. If I find out you've warned anyone, even anyone on the production or *legal* side, you'll be off the show immediately. Great chat." And with that, she leaves me shell-shocked by the pool.

Chapter Thirty-One

I sit on the edge of the pool with my feet dangling in the water for at least twenty minutes after Kristina leaves. My toes are probably prunes at this point, but I don't trust myself to stand when I feel so shaky. I know she's doing this to punish me, but I've looked at it from every angle and I don't see any other option besides agreeing to her demands.

I'm not sure if my full-body weakness is shock or low blood sugar, but I decide to finally make my way to the bar and look for something to help me find composure.

"Whatcha drinking?" the friendly-looking bartender says to me. Of course, even he is handsome and perfectly fits the role of approachable barkeep. He probably came straight from central casting.

"Hi. Do you have any smoothies?" I ask.

"We have piña coladas, strawberry daiquiris, or frozen margaritas," he answers cheerily.

"Oh. Uh, what about plain juice?"

He shakes his head. "Sorry, everything is premixed. Except Poppy Lite. We have a ton of that."

I wince. "Uh, no thanks. Do you have anything else that's non-alcoholic?"

"Light beer?" he says shrugging. "It's basically water."

"Okay, sure. Thanks." He hands me a can, and I walk back to the chaise lounge. As I sip on my beer-flavored water, I contemplate all the life choices that have led me to this shitty moment.

One side effect of feeling like an outcast growing up is that the friendships I do have are invaluable to me. Although Cassie, Alec, and Eliza are what Cassie would call my "ride-or-dies," I do feel attached to Madison and Ciara. I've never had friends like them before—people who aren't nerdy scientists or who know me only because we have a career in common. Getting to know them has changed my opinion about beautiful, put-together women. And hell, even the color pink. Madison and Ciara are nothing like what I expected. They're kind, smart, funny, and . . . *loyal*. I take a sip of my beer and start to tear up thinking about the ways they've helped me this week, the lessons they've taught me, and all the support they've shown me. I wouldn't have survived this experience without them. And while I don't doubt that our friendship was accelerated by being sequestered together for a week, I really do feel like they have my best interests at heart.

And then there's Javier. He's such a sweet guy, one who actually respects women and isn't afraid to embrace his goofy side. I sigh heavily. Hurting Javi feels like hurting a golden retriever puppy. He doesn't deserve the emotional minefield Kristina is setting up. It feels despicable using him and toying with his feelings to try to stay on the show. Especially because he and Ciara would be a great couple outside of this reality TV bubble.

And then my thoughts wander to where they've been hanging out lately: Andrew. I take a large sip of my beer and exhale. *Andrew.* I've never had this sort of connection before. It's like someone took the initial physical attraction I felt toward Scott plus the friendship and ease I feel with Javier and put them in the Large Hadron Collider. I never realized that the best of both worlds could exist in one person—one person who challenges me, makes me laugh, and shares my values about wanting to change the world. Cassie would definitely call him a "keeper."

And there's the problem. I won't be able to *keep* him if I do Kristina's bidding. Despite how understanding Andrew seems, he's also admitted to getting jealous. I can't imagine he'd be cool with me kissing Javier hours after he got fired for me. I shake my head at the cruel irony of it all. The one time I find a guy I like, someone who actually likes me back, we're destined to fail.

The bartender drops off another light beer, takes one look at me, and hustles off. I call "thank you," then go back to debating what my course of action should be. Should I flip a coin? Heads, I play Kristina's twisted games? Tails, I just give up and quit the show?

"Why are you drinking alone?"

I'm startled when I look up to see Blue standing over me with a concerned look. "And why does it look like you've been crying?"

I touch my face. It feels damp. Huh, maybe that's why the bartender ran away so quickly.

"Seriously, what's going on?" Blue asks as he sits down next to me. I shake my head. I don't trust my voice to not be shaky. "Does it have to do with your date with Andrew?" he guesses.

I shake no and mumble, "It wasn't a date."

He gives me a *yeah, right* look and says, "I saw you talking to Kristina. What'd she do now?"

"I'm not allowed to tell."

"So it *was* her! That evil puppeteering wench! Do you want me to say something to her?"

I sit up quickly. "No! If you do, I'll get kicked off the show. And she'll probably fire you too. I'll be fine. I just need to figure out what I'm going to do. Do you have a coin I can flip by any chance?"

He sighs and looks at me. "I wish I could help you, sweets." He scooches me over so we're lying side by side, barely fitting on the same lounge chair. "I've seen my fair share of contestants get upset on reality shows in my day. It's hard to stay true to yourself when you're cut off from your normal life and plied with booze. If I could give you one piece of advice, though, I'd say, keep in mind why you came on the show in the first place. Let that guide you."

As I finish my second beer, I let his words sink in. We sit there in companionable silence as I take his advice and focus on the reasons why I came on the show. I didn't go on *Love Shack* to fall for handsome lawyers or make friends. I did it because I had to. I did it to protect my life's work and save my lab. But most importantly, I did it because it's up to me to ensure the future of an entire species.

When I put it into perspective like that, the choice becomes clear. I look over at Blue and nod. "Thanks, Blue. And thanks for all your help this week. I hope we can be friends when this is over."

"Hell yes, we will! Your mom already invited me over for monthly family dinners."

I laugh and hug him. "Oh boy, you don't know what you just got yourself into. I hope you like a theme."

Well, at least if Blue hates me when this is all over, it'll be because of my crazy mom and not for what I'm about to do.

"Now dry your eyes and get your ass dressed," he chides. "Everyone is getting back from their dates soon, and we have a beach meeting in an hour."

I give him another quick hug, then head to the shack to change. If I'm going to play the villain, I should at least dress the part.

I pull the most scandalous dress I brought out of my suitcase. It's the skin-tight, fire engine red one I tried on with my mom, the one I told her I would never wear. Shocker, she didn't listen and bought it for me anyway.

I squeeze myself into the too-small spandex and do my hair and makeup like some combination of what I've seen Ciara and Madison do. It takes me half as long as it takes them, so I'm probably skipping some important steps. But when I look in my tiny compact mirror, I don't hate what I see.

When I put my makeup case back in my suitcase, I see a flash of something brown and yellow underneath one of my shoes. I lean down and pick up a small yellow-legged frog pin, smiling when I recognize it. I commissioned a local artist to make it for Cassie when I was at a conservation conference in New Mexico. I know Cassie probably put it in here for moral support, but right now it's also reminding me of what's at stake. I rub its little frog belly for luck before stashing it in my purse. Then I put on my fake glasses, say a prayer to the mother of environmentalism and my own personal hero, Rachel Carson, and head down to the beach.

Madison squeals when she sees me coming and rushes over to me. Ciara isn't far behind her.

"You look hot!" Madison exclaims as she hugs me.

"You did this yourself?" Ciara gapes.

"How were your dates?" I ask, before they can continue to compliment me and make me feel more like the filamentous algae pond scum I am for my impending betrayal.

"It was so romantic, Grace! We went on a helicopter ride up the coast!" Madison gushes.

"And Javi and I took a catamaran to this snorkeling spot," Ciara says. "We saw dolphins. It was really—" Then she suddenly seems to remember the last time she saw me. "Oh shit, I totally forgot. They made you go on a freakin' hot-air balloon ride."

Madison gasps. "We're such assholes. Thank God you're okay! How was it?"

I laugh it off, while trying to figure out what I can and can't tell them. "It's okay. I freaked out at first, but I lived to tell the tale."

"Good for you," Ciara adds, then looks around before adding, "America will love you for being real and losing your shit."

"What happened with Andrew?" Madison asks, looping her arm in mine. "Did he really get fired for going with you?"

I nod, then choose my words carefully. "I feel really bad he got in trouble. But I think he was trying to do the right thing because he knew Kristina was messing with me on purpose."

"I knew he liked you," Madison whispers as we walk toward the giant outdoor sectional where the other contestants are waiting.

And here's where my deception begins. I have an overwhelming desire to tell her and Ciara every detail about my unexpected date with Andrew and how much I like him. I'd give anything to hear Madison squeal with excitement and get their advice.

But I can't let them know I like Andrew and still go through with Kristina's evil plan. No one would ever believe I want to rekindle things with Javier. Not to mention, I'm about to betray them on national TV so I don't deserve their advice. Or their friendship.

I'm debating how to respond when I'm thankfully saved by Shantae's arrival. I give them a *what can you do?* shrug, and we quickly sit down before the cameras begin rolling. Shantae hits her mark, gives us a dazzling smile, and asks us how our one-on-ones went. The other contestants take turns talking about their dates—the helicopter ride, the catamaran—and the new arrivals, whose names I've already forgotten, seem to have had a good time on their ATV date. Not Hot Scott and Beth Anne stole candy from children or something, I don't know, I wasn't really listening to them.

It's harder to ignore Beth Anne's fake looks of pity, though, when Shantae asks about my sad one-on-none date. Kristina clearly told everyone to play along with the story that I was alone despite them seeing Andrew jump into the balloon with me because they're all looking at me sympathetically.

I'm about to answer Shantae when I catch Kristina's eye. She's lurking behind the camera operator and making a "boo-hoo" crying motion. I roll my eyes but do what I'm told.

"It was really hard being alone. Especially while doing something as scary as being on a hot-air balloon," I say as pathetically as possible.

"Oh, that's right," Shantae says with delight. "You have a crippling fear of heights."

I give my most depressing nod and continue. "It made me wish I had someone there to comfort me."

"For a biologist, you're sure having trouble finding a mate," Shantae laughs with a flick of her long, silky hair. Madison squeezes my hand as I once again question who's writing this garbage.

Shantae just shrugs and brushes past my dismal dating record. "Before we write down who would go out with their date again, I have a fun announcement." She pauses for dramatic effect. "We have another theme party tonight! And this time it's . . . a toga party!" *Shoot me.*

Everyone else cheers, and I can't help but think that, if I have to wear a sheet, I'm at least going to bring it back to use in my shack afterwards.

Shantae claps her hands to get our attention before asking all the happy couples if they'd go on another date with their partner. They all say yes and are awarded five points each. "And how about you, Grace?" Shantae asks with a grin. "Would you go out with yourself again?" Beth Anne laughs as Madison and Ciara give me worried glances. I respond with an *it's okay* look.

I wish I could say dating myself is exponentially better than dating Scott or Bill, but instead I give Kristina the sound bite she wants. "I don't know, it was pretty lonely," I lie.

"Awww," Shantae coos. "Well, we better do something about that then."

My heart slows down like a hedgehog in hibernation. Ciara gives me a hopeful eyebrow raise that only makes me feel shittier for what is about to happen.

All eyes are on Shantae when she says, "Since you didn't have an actual date today and you showed real bravery in overcoming your fear of heights, we have a surprise for you. We're sending you on a romantic date with the guy of your choice."

Even though I was expecting this, the shocked look on my face is 100 percent real.

"Like one of these guys?" Beth Anne asks, as she scooches closer to Scott. *Don't worry, honey, you can have him.*

"Yep," Shantae says, loving the drama. "So, who's it going to be, Grace?"

I look around, pretending to weigh my options, including the new guy, until I finally land on Javier. I give Ciara a look of apology, and she just shrugs like it's fine. Because she thinks we're friends. Because she believes in hoes before bros. Because loyalty is the most important quality to her. *Shit.*

"Javier, would you like to go on this date with me?" I ask quietly.

Javier looks surprised but recovers quickly. "Sure."

"Great," Shantae says, clapping her hands together. "They're waiting for you two up at the mansion. The rest of you have some downtime before the toga party."

I stand and with my back to the camera, I mouth, *I'm sorry*, to Ciara.

As I walk off the beach with Javi, I wish Malibu were built on erosive limestone and a sinkhole would swallow me up. The only silver lining is that at least Andrew went home after our balloon ride, so I won't have to run into him while I stab him in the back.

There's a limo waiting for Javier and me when we get back to the mansion and standing next to it, grinning like the Cheshire Cat, is Evil Producer Overlord Kristina.

"Have a nice time on your date, you two! It's *very romantic*," she singsongs. To the untrained ear, it sounds innocent enough, but I see the threat in her eyes: *It better be very romantic. Or else.*

I give her a small nod. Message received. Then I swallow my pride, push down my nerves, and climb into the limo.

Chapter Thirty-Two

Once we're in the back of the limo with a camera pointed at us from the other end, Javier turns to me. "You look great by the way. I like the red."

I give him a quiet thanks, which might be interpreted as shy but is solidly guilty, then sit back and look out the window as we pull away.

The longer we drive toward whatever contrived date Kristina has planned, the more I begin to relax and the less I notice the incriminating cameras. Javier must feel the same way. "I wasn't expecting you to pick me," he admits quietly. Then he whispers so the cameras can't hear, "I kinda thought something might be going on between you and the lawyer."

I laugh as if that's preposterous but don't trust my acting skills enough to actually deny it. My stomach churns as I give the canned response. "I'm excited to go out with you, Javi. I'll understand if you and Ciara are serious, but I was hoping you might give me another chance. At least for tonight, to see if there's anything between us," I say, hating myself even more than the time I accidentally ran over a common gray squirrel.

Javier looks conflicted. *Of course, he does. He's a good guy.* And he has every right to be confused by my sudden change of heart. Finally, he says, "You know I had feelings for you in the beginning, Grace. But it seemed like you only wanted to be friends. And then I got to know Ciara and started liking her." I nod, giving an internal sigh of relief, and wonder if I can get away with telling Kristina I tried and failed.

But then Javier keeps talking. "But I think you're right. We owe it to ourselves to see if there's something here before things get too far along with other people and feelings get hurt." *Fuck. He's kind and rational.*

"Okay, great," I hear myself say. If I believed in the concept of hell, I'd know that's where I'm headed, because when he puts his hand out for me to hold, I take it and smile at him like I'm smitten.

We make small talk the rest of the way to dinner, and I'm grateful that Javier is so easy to talk to and that I really do enjoy his company. It's making the lead in my stomach start to dissipate.

As we pull into a parking lot off of PCH, Javi tells me about his three sisters and how close he is with his mom. "Ahh, now I get why you're so sweet but also so good with the ladies," I tell him.

He flashes his dimples. "Who, me?" With a debonair flourish, he kisses my hand.

I laugh as we stop in front of a fancy seafood restaurant on the water. I've never been here before, but thanks to my mom, I know it's popular with the rich and famous and impossible to get a reservation.

"What about you?" Javi asks. "You mentioned a brother the other day at lunch."

"Yeah, I have two younger brothers, which is why I get annoyed so easily."

Javier chuckles. "That's fair." Then he helps me out of the limo like a true gentleman and we walk inside, arm in arm.

The moment I look around the empty restaurant, I gasp. "They closed the whole place for us?"

"Que romántico!" Javier exclaims and winks at me.

If this place wasn't romantic to begin with, it certainly is now, with lit candles on every table, soft music playing, and sweeping views of the sun setting over the Pacific. Kristina isn't messing around.

The maître d' leads us down three steps to a row of tables set against floor-to-ceiling windows. He stops at what is clearly the best table in the restaurant, with unobstructed views of the waves crashing onto the rocks below us. "Have a wonderful evening," he says, bowing deeply.

I almost don't notice Javier pulling my chair out for me because I'm so taken with the view and the restaurant's elegant decor. "Thank you," I say, sitting down. "This place is incredible. The only thing missing is a private concert."

Javier laughs. "You joke, but they really do that on reality shows."

"Oh, I know. They sent some musicians to my one-on-none date." As I say it, I think about Andrew and my heart squeezes simultaneously with affection and guilt.

"No, they didn't!" Javier exclaims. "Now that's just cruel."

I shrug as a waitress comes over and hands us menus. "They actually grew on me," I say, trying to shake off the memory of slow-dancing with Andrew. I owe it to Javier to at least stay present.

"Do you have any vegan specials?" Javier asks the waitress.

"You remembered," I say, sincerely touched that he'd be so thoughtful.

"We have a seasonal vegetable plate," the waiter answers, and I smile politely.

When she leaves, Javier whispers conspiratorially, "Have you heard that Anthony Bourdain quote about throwing some slices of vegetables onto a plate and overcharging for it?"

I laugh. "Yeah, he wasn't a fan of vegetarians."

"You come to my place sometime and I'll grill you some veggies for free," he says with boyish charm.

I smile, mentally comparing my horrible dinner with Bill to Javier offering to cook veggies for me. But my smile fades when I remember I'm not going to Javier's place when the show is over. I doubt he'll ever want to talk to me again.

I sit there staring at my menu, lost in depressing thoughts, until Javier squeezes my hand. "Thank you for inviting me. It's nice being on this side of the table."

"Tell me about the restaurant where you work," I prompt.

Javier launches into entertaining stories about waiting tables at a trendy steak house with impossible regulars and a clumsy bartender who breaks at least three glasses a shift but can't be fired because he's the owner's nephew. The conversation flows easily between us as a sommelier stops by to open a fancy-looking bottle of wine.

After the waitress takes our order, Javi peppers me with questions about my job and genuinely seems interested in my answers. He especially likes my story of the time I got bit by an endangered alligator snapping turtle but couldn't scream because I didn't want to cause it any emotional distress.

"For such a smart and beautiful woman, you sure get hurt a lot," he laughs.

"Okay, now you have to tell me an embarrassing story to make up for all the times you've seen me make a fool of myself."

He laughs and pretends to think long and hard. "I forgot my lines in the middle of an audition once."

"What? That's nothing! I'm sure that happens all the time. I once forgot the binomial name of the axolotl in the middle of a lecture. In front of five hundred people. Now that's embarrassing!"

He laughs. "Okay, you win. I will never be as embarrassing as you."

"Thank you." I bow, accepting my victory. "So, did you always want to be an actor? Or did you just wake up one day, look in a mirror, and decide you should share your good looks with the world?"

He laughs at this. "Oh, I wish it were that easy." Javier explains that his mom put him in theater when he was a hyperactive kid to give him a creative outlet and he's loved it ever since. I can tell how seriously he takes his craft when he talks about which plays he's done and which ones he'd love to do one day. But when he tells me his future goals, I get my first peek past the always-happy Javier. Although he would never complain about it, I can tell he's not happy with where he is with his career—but also that he'll never give up on his dream, which I find relatable.

"It sounds like we have a similar work ethic." I smile at him and find myself reflexively reaching out for his hand. I confide in him that I've experienced some recent setbacks in my work as well. It's nice being able to commiserate with someone in a totally different field. Maybe Javier and I do have more in common than I originally thought.

Even though there are cameras rolling somewhere and a million restaurant employees milling about, it really feels like it's just the two of us. Javier must feel the same way because his flirty machismo has completely fallen away. It's like getting a glimpse of what he's normally like around people he's comfortable with. He's sincere and funny and would honestly be an amazing boyfriend.

When I finally have to excuse myself to use the restroom, I'm intercepted near the front of the restaurant by Bruce, the camera operator who was on the hot-air balloon and one of the only people who knows I hooked up with Andrew two hours ago.

"Hey, Bruce, fancy seeing you here," I say awkwardly.

"Kristina called. She wants me to get footage of you and *Javier* kissing," he reports in what I would swear is a super-judgmental way.

My heart sinks. I knew Kristina wouldn't drop her kiss agenda, but Bruce's disapproval only adds to how shitty I feel about the whole situation. I want to tell the world's most critical cameraman that however harshly he's judging me right now is nothing compared to how I'm judging myself. Instead, I just mutter, "Okay," then scurry off to the restroom.

Where I hide for ten minutes trying to compose myself.

I stare in the mirror and don't like the person I see looking back. Javier and I are really connecting tonight, and I'm genuinely having a great time with him. But the closer we get, the crueler I feel for playing with his emotions. I glance at the small bathroom window, wondering if I can squeeze out of it and swim back to Santa Monica.

I reach into my purse for my lipstick and another excuse to procrastinate when I touch something metal. Cassie's frog pin. I pick it up and laugh at the irony of a scientist who doesn't believe in signs from the universe receiving a pretty obvious one.

Granted, Javier is way more prince than frog, but this is a solid reminder that I've got to find a way to kiss him if I want to accomplish what I came here to do. I rub the little metal frog and sigh, thinking about how hard I've worked to protect them. We're the only conservation team in the country that specializes in southern mountain yellow-legged frogs. And my coworkers have all their hopes riding on me.

I drop the pin back into my purse, give myself a determined nod in the mirror, reapply my lipstick, and walk out of the bathroom.

When I get back to the table, I force a smile.

"Everything okay?" he asks.

"Yeah," I say. "I think I just ate too fast."

"You want to go for a walk on the beach and digest a little before we head back?"

"You really know how to make a moonlit stroll sound romantic," I tease.

He smiles and takes my hand. We thank the waitress and maître d' and walk out the back door that leads to a wooden staircase. When we get down to the private beach, I take off my heels and Javier offers to carry them for me.

The sand feels cool on my bare feet, but the night is still warm. It's one of those perfect Los Angeles nights. There's even a breeze blowing away some of the smog, so we can almost make out a star or two.

Despite the determination I felt in the bathroom, I still feel a pit in my stomach as I walk alongside Javi, because I know this is the perfect setting for a first kiss. *Well, second kiss, I guess.* I don't know, does kissing someone in a game of Suck and Blow really count?

After a few minutes of walking hand in hand, I catch his eye and smile. He smiles back. "I had a—" I start to say at the same time Javi also starts talking.

I laugh. "Sorry, you first."

"No, tell me what's going through that big brain of yours."

I take a deep breath, picture what Kristina would want me to say, and remind myself for the eight hundredth time that I'm doing this for a good reason.

"I just wanted to say I had a really great time tonight, and I'm glad you agreed to give me a second chance."

He pulls me into him and says, "I'm glad I did too."

I look up at him and smile shyly. Then I lean a little closer, and Javier meets me halfway. I make a silent wish that this kiss will rock my world, and I'll become madly in love with Javier. Because maybe everything would be easier that way.

I take a deep breath and prepare to fall.

But instead, when our lips meet, it's like it was the last time we kissed. It's . . . *fine*. It's more enjoyable than when he ambushed me during the game, but it's not giving me that full-body tingly feeling. And it's not making me forget that other men exist. Particularly one who wears the hell out of a suit and shares his granola bars with me.

I think I've known since the beginning that I don't feel sparks with Javi. I have so much fondness for him as a friend, but it's impossible not to compare him to Andrew. I feel the same level of comfort and ease with them both, but even when Javier and I have had a perfect date and are mid-kiss, there's only one guy I'm wishing I were with.

After a respectable amount of time, I gently pull back. I can't help but check to make sure the cameras caught our kiss, then silently curse the reality TV gods that I'm even thinking this way. Javier gives my hand a tender squeeze, while my heart squeezes with guilt over Andrew and Ciara. And when I see the affection in Javier's eyes, I feel like the worst person in the world for leading him on.

I was right to avoid dating. Except I thought I'd prevent myself from getting hurt. I never considered that I could hurt others.

Chapter Thirty-Three

After waking up hungover, followed by a champagne buzz at lunch, a couple midafternoon light beers, wine at dinner, going on two dates, kissing two men, and an emotional roller coaster of a day, I'm exhausted. So exhausted that I briefly fall asleep in the limo on the way back to the mansion. But Javier, being the nice guy that he is, doesn't say anything about it. He just lets me rest my head on his shoulder.

When we get back, the rest of the contestants are waiting for us on the beach where we left them a couple hours ago. Except now they're all in their toga gear and the beach is lit up by tiki torches. While I'm only pretty sure the tiki torch was invented in Wisconsin and plays no role in Polynesian history, I'm positive the ancient Greeks never used them for decor. I know my brain is fixating on the historical inaccuracies of a beachy toga party because it's currently freaking out about what's going to happen next.

For starters, what's Ciara going to think when she sees Javi and me walking down the path to the beach, holding hands? Maybe she'll just assume he's helping me walk because my ankle is still sore?

Javier and I make our way to the empty seats at the far end of the lounge furniture. Which means we walk hand in hand past everyone else to get there. I feel eight sets of eyes on me. But I'm a coward and can't bear to see the anger in Ciara's expression, so I stare at my feet the whole time.

"Welcome back, lovebirds," Shantae calls out, and I try not to cringe. "How was your date?"

"Good," I say at the same time Javier says, "Great."

I still can't look at Ciara or Madison. My face burns with shame as Shantae continues her spiel. "Well, I'm glad to hear it! Because now is the time to pick dates for the toga party. And guys, it's your turn to pick! First up is TC. TC, you told us Madison is officially your girlfriend now. Lemme guess, you're going to pick her?"

TC smiles at Madison and says, "Sure am, Shantae." Madison snuggles closer to him.

"You guys are cuuuute. Okay, what about you, Scott? Who do you pick?" Shantae asks.

No Longer Hot Scott is blatantly checking out Shantae in her mini-skirt toga, but then realizes she's waiting for an answer and says, "Oh, uh, yeah, Beth Anne." I want to call him out on his lack of subtlety, but I'm too busy trying not to have a panic attack.

Beth Anne, however, is a pro now, so she doesn't let her facade slip as she possessively takes Scott's hand and like a Southern debutante says, "I thought you'd never ask."

To her credit, Shantae doesn't roll her eyes. Instead, she looks at the guy who got here earlier today and says, "Chris, you said you'd go out with Eliana again after your one-on-one date. Does this mean you'll ask her to be your date to the toga party?"

Chris gives Eliana a suave smile and says, "If she'll have me." Eliana nods and giggles delightedly.

Which means there's only one guy left. Javier. I'm not ready for this. I don't want to hurt anyone. I wish I could hide my head in the sand—unlike an ostrich, because that's a myth.

My heart is thundering as Shantae turns to Javi. "And finally Javier. Are you going to pick the girl you kissed this afternoon or the girl you kissed tonight?" I hear Beth Anne gasp.

Fuck. I'm sure my face is as red as my dress. Out of my peripheral, I see Madison looking at me, shocked. And when I finally sneak a peek at Ciara, she doesn't look pissed, she looks sad. Which is way worse.

Javier squeezes my thigh, then turns to Ciara. "Ciara, I've really enjoyed getting to know you and I feel we made a genuine connection. But when Grace asked me for a second chance, we really hit it off, and I think I'm developing feelings for her. I'm sorry." Then he turns to Shantae and says, "I'm picking Grace."

My brain registers some shocked murmurs and gasps, but I can't make out what anyone is saying because I'm currently floating above my body. And not in a good, deceased kind of way.

"Wow, that took a turn," Shantae says with a bite. Then she turns to Ciara and says, "I'm sorry, Ciara. Since you are no longer in a couple, you're being sent home. Please say your goodbyes."

This brings me plummeting back down to reality. I immediately jump up in outrage, sprained ankle be damned. "What? No! What about the new people coming in? You can't send her home!"

"Should've thought of that before you stole her man," Beth Anne says, giving me a dirty look, like I'm trying to take over her brand. But I don't have time for her drama, I'm too desperate to save Ciara. "What about this guy?" I point to the new arrival and try to remember his name. "Chris! Chris, you should pick Ciara!" Eliana crosses her arms and gives me a death look as Chris puts his arm around her reassuringly.

This can't be happening. Madison avoids my gaze as she hugs Ciara tightly. They're both crying, and it breaks my heart. How could they send her home? Unlike the rest of us, she wasn't here for some ulterior motive. She wanted to find love with a nice guy for once. She deserves to be here more than anyone.

I try one last plea. "Please, Shantae. Can't she stay until the new arrivals come?"

Shantae covers her mic and says to me in a hushed tone, "I don't write this shit. The producers make the rules, not me."

I look around frantically for Kristina so I can beg her to keep Ciara, but of course, the one time I need her, she's not hovering nearby. When I look back toward the contestants, I see the pain in Javier's eyes as he says goodbye to Ciara. Then Ciara turns to walk back up to the mansion without looking in my direction.

I run to catch up to her as I feel tears running down my cheeks. "I'm so sorry, Ciara! I didn't know you'd be sent home."

She spins around to face me. "I thought you were my friend. If you liked Javi, you should've just told me when I asked you, instead of blindsiding me like this."

"I *am* your friend," I say weakly.

"No. You're really not." And with that, Ciara walks off the beach.

I collapse into the sand. I sense someone approaching and look to see a camera operator circling me for a close-up. I cover my face and yell at her, "Go away! This isn't just some lame dating show. These are real people with real feelings!"

I don't know if she leaves or not because I bury my head in my hands. A moment later, I smell Javier's cologne, and a warm hand rubs my back. "Are you okay?"

I wipe my eyes and look at him. "I didn't want to hurt Ciara."

He puts his arm around me. "I know. I feel like shit too."

"She hates me."

He pulls me close and kisses the top of my head. "No one could hate you." And that makes me cry even harder because I know it's only a matter of time before he hates me as well.

But I can't move, and even though I don't deserve Javier's comfort, being held by him is the only thing preventing me from hyperventilating. So we stay like that, hugging in the sand, until Shantae calls our names.

After the third time she shouts, "Grace! Javi!" with growing annoyance, I reluctantly let Javier drag me back over to the rest of the contestants.

I sit there staring at Shantae but can't seem to focus on what she's saying. I'm vaguely aware that she's told Javi and me to get ready for the toga party. *Right, because I'm totally in the mood to wear a sheet and dance the night away.*

As the rest of the contestants head to the bar area, I find Madison. "Can I talk to you for a sec?"

"I'm not ready to talk yet, Grace." Her voice is calm but tinged with hurt. "I'm too emotional and don't want to say things I'll regret."

"I understand," I say softly, admiring her restraint, even while she's distancing herself from me. I watch her walk away and hope against hope that giving her space will somehow help her forgive me.

I shuffle back to Javier. We're the only ones left by the lounge area. Just a couple of *Love Shack* pariahs. I sit down next to him and sigh deeply. "I'm really not in the mood to go to a party."

"I feel you. Should we make a run for it?" he says lightly, and I know he's trying to cheer me up.

"Kristina probably microchipped us when we were sleeping." I sigh.

"Do you want me to tell them you're sick? I can go to the party and cover for you," he says with concern in his eyes. And it breaks me. He's being so kind when I just ruined his chance at an actual love connection.

I manage to hold in my sob and nod gratefully. "Yes, please. Thank you, Javi. I think I just need some sleep."

He squeezes my hand. "You better take off before Kristina gets here then." I nod and stand up to leave. "Do you want me to walk you back?" he asks.

"No, I'm okay. You go to the party and have fun. Thank you for covering for me." I hug him. "And thank you for the date." He squeezes me back.

When he lets go, I walk up the beach path, cut across the backyard, and prepare to cry myself to sleep on the floor of a murder shack.

Because if tonight was any indication, tomorrow is going to be a shit show.

Chapter Thirty-Four

What the actual fuck happened last night?" I groggily roll over to find Blue standing over me waiting for an answer. I look around and see I'm the only one sleeping in the shack.

"Where'd the new arrivals sleep? Did they take my room in the mansion? Are they *shacked up*?" Then I laugh bitterly because I'm the only one who's *literally* shacking up.

"Are you still drunk?" Blue asks as he pokes me with his foot. Then he looks horrified when he sees that the floors are so dirty that he left a footprint on my butt. I just shrug. I deserve worse than sleeping in dirt.

"Nope. You sober up pretty quickly when you self-implode." I cover my face, not ready for the harsh light of day.

"Well, you better wake your ass up if you want to triage the damage."

"The damage is done," I say from inside my bedroll of depression.

But Blue is not done battling for my soul. "You need to get off this gross-ass floor and to the production trailer ASAP. Andrew just got here to pick up his stuff, and I overheard Kristina telling him he may want to look over the footage from last night before he leaves."

"Shit!" I jump up. "He's going to see me kissing Javier!"

"Probably should've thought of that before you kissed Javier," Blue says, and I can hear the disappointment in his voice. "But we might still be able to run interference."

I don't bother changing out of my pajamas. I just start sprinting toward the trailers, ignoring the throbbing in my ankle. It's one thing for Andrew to hear about what happened but having to watch me kiss Javi just seems like a slap in the face. He doesn't deserve that. He doesn't deserve any of this.

"Why is Kristina so bent on ruining my life?" I huff as I run.

"Because you undermined her all those times you stood up for the cast and the crew?" Blue guesses. "And also, ratings."

I don't know who's more out of shape, me or Blue, because we're both panting by the time we get there.

"I don't run for just anyone," Blue puffs as we open the trailer.

I rush inside, yelling, "Andrew!," but then I stop dead in my tracks. Because there, on five different monitors, is me—kissing Javier.

"There she is! One half of America's favorite couple!" Kristina says gleefully.

Behind her, I see an editor and Brett, the executive producer. And next to them is Andrew. My heart sinks. *I'm too late.*

His face is pale, but his eyes shine with emotion. Anger? Sadness? Hatred?

Kristina continues: "I was just filling everyone in on last night's developments. How you and Javier rekindled your relationship and are officially a couple now." Even if she's just trying to get back at me for filing a complaint against her, she's evil.

Brett looks at me, impressed. "Wow, that happened fast. Didn't think you had it in you."

Andrew says quietly, looking at the monitor, "Me neither."

The kiss plays again on the monitor, and I shout, "Turn it off! Please!"

Andrew looks at me with hurt in his eyes, then grabs a bank box full of personal items. "Well, I don't work here anymore," he says, and I can't help but feel like it's an accusation. "I should go." Then he marches out of the trailer.

I don't even bother trying to be discreet as I run out after him. "Andrew! Wait!"

He stops at the bottom of the stairs and turns to me. "Did you have a thing for Javier this whole time?" he asks, his eyes searching mine. "Why didn't you tell me . . . before?"

My stomach drops, because I know he's not just questioning me, but himself and what happened between us. Like maybe he was wrong in thinking that our date was incredible and we have a real connection. It kills me to see him rewriting our story as he stands here in front of me.

I open my mouth to confess, to tell him everything—that the kiss with Javier didn't mean anything, that the producers made me do it, that I have real feelings for him. But then I see Kristina watching us from inside the trailer, her arms crossed. And my hands fall to my sides in defeat.

If I come clean now, it will have all been for nothing. She'll kick me off the show and I'll have used Javier, betrayed Ciara, upset Madison, and hurt Andrew . . . for what? A couple weeks as a reality TV show contestant? I still haven't raised enough money and publicity. I still haven't saved my lab and my friends' jobs. And even if I found a way to tell him, I'd be just like all the other fake-ass contestants he didn't feel compatible with.

As I stand there with my heart breaking, Andrew waits for my explanation. And all I can say is, "I'm sorry."

He looks at me like he's waiting for something more. There's no teasing twinkle in his eyes, no specks of gold glinting in the sun. They're just sad as he shakes his head. "I am too," he says. Then he walks away.

It takes everything I have not to cry as I watch him leave. Or maybe I'm just all cried out. I've wept more this week than I have in the past twenty-nine years combined.

I refuse to even glance in Kristina's direction before I storm off.

I don't want to be around producers or contestants or cameras. I don't want to lounge by a pool or drink at the beach. I just want to wallow in my murder shack. Alone.

But apparently Blue doesn't get the memo.

I hear him enter moments after I've collapsed onto my bedroll. I cover my head with the pool towel I stole to use as a sheet. "Go away."

"I'd be nicer to the one friend you have left."

"Go away, *please*."

He takes the towel off my head and looks at me sympathetically. "That was dramatic back there. You okay?"

I moan. "I fucked everything up, Blue."

He snorts. "I gathered that. Let me guess, you had a great date with Andrew, *like I thought*. You realized you actually like him, and then Kristina made you go after Javi for ratings and her own sadistic revenge, but told you not to tell anyone or she'd kick you off the show. And now you feel like shit because Ciara hates you, Andrew hates you, and you hate yourself for using Javi, who remains clueless."

I sit up and look at him, impressed. "Yep, that's pretty much it."

He looks me square in the eyes. "So what are you going to do about it?"

I lie back down. "Go back to bed and hope being on a reality show was all just a bad dream."

"You're not Wizard of Oz—ing your way out of this one, Toots. Plus, Kristina sent me to get you for a confessional."

"I can't. I'm sick."

"Nice try. You used that excuse last night."

"Then it'll be believable! We've established I have a weak constitution. And it's not technically a lie because I do feel sick to my stomach."

"It's the swirling combination of self-hatred and depression," he says wisely. Once again, he nailed it.

"You should be a doctor."

He shakes his head. "I enjoy recreational drugs too much."

"I can't do it, Blue. I can't face Madison. I can't put on a happy face for Javi and the cameras. I don't have it in me. Please just let me wallow."

He sighs. "Fine, I'll figure out a way to cover for you. But only because I still like you and I've never seen anything sadder in my life." And with that, he leaves me wrapped in my self-pity and a pool towel.

I don't know how much time has passed when I feel a hand gently shaking me awake. "Grace. Grace, honey." I must be dreaming because it sounds like the way my mom used to wake me up when I was a little girl. I blearily open my eyes to see a mirage.

Weird, it looks like my mom too. I reach out to touch her face.

"Careful, don't mess up my makeup!"

My eyes shoot open. "Mom? What are you doing here?"

"Blue snuck us in," my mom replies casually, as if she breaks into reality TV mansions all the time.

"Us?" I ask, looking around.

Just then my brother Matt pops his head in, looking around before he enters, hands in his pockets. "Sweet shack."

I sit up, still groggy and confused. "Why are you here?"

My mom looks at me like it should be obvious. "Blue said you needed help, so here we are."

Matt plops down next to me. "We came to rescue you, dumbass."

"And how are you going to do that?"

"We still need to figure that part out," he admits.

"Your father and Jesse are on standby ready to help too," my mom says brightly.

"They are?" I ask, still not registering what's going on.

"Yep! Just let us know what you need, honey, and we'll do it."

I stare at my mom and brother in a combination of shock and

affection. "You all want to help me?" The self-loathing that's been circulating through my veins the past twenty-four hours is making this hard to believe. "But . . . but . . . I don't deserve your help. All I ever do is judge you guys." I turn to my brother. "Or insult you to your face. Half the time I'm too embarrassed to even tell people we're related."

"Try having a sister who's a boring-ass scientist. I usually just say you're adopted," my brother teases.

My mom pats my hand. "Gracie, you weren't the only one who was judgy or has made mistakes. I'm sorry I thought I knew what was best for your love life and signed you up for the show without asking you first. From now on, I'll try really hard not to interfere." She sighs loudly like she's trying not to cry. "I just love you so much and want you to be happy."

I let that sit there. Because *wow*. My mom never apologizes. And she has never admitted that she ignores my boundaries. I don't know if it's her admission or the cumulative effect of the past few days, but when she pulls me into a hug I happily lean in. And that's when it dawns on me: Despite my mom's larger-than-life online persona, she's *only human*.

Have I been too tough on her? Because even when she was annoying the crap out of me, I always knew she thought she was helping. She just can't stop her extra-ness. That would be like asking the sun not to shine.

I make a note to research whether what I'm experiencing is radical acceptance as Matt wraps his arms around both of us. "And I'm sorry for always making fun of your job," he says with an apologetic smile. "Now that I'm learning more about what you do, it's actually pretty cool."

"What?" I say with a sputtering laugh in the middle of the group hug. "Is this really happening?" After twenty-nine years, I'm finally bonding with my family . . . in a shack in Malibu.

Until Matt ruins it by saying, "So Ciara is single now? She's hot."

I push him away from me with a newly discovered sisterly fondness. "Yeah, don't remind me. I made a mess of everything. I'm the worst," I sigh.

Matt shrugs. "I accidentally sent a dick pic to my ex last week," he says, trying to one-up me into feeling better.

"I spelled Chrissy Teigen's name wrong when I DMed her," my mom admits.

"Jesse's online girlfriend dumped him because he wanted to meet in person," Matt adds with a wince.

"Your father made a shirt that said 'Two Pump Guy' and didn't understand why it was funny," my mom says with a giggle.

I burst out laughing. "What did he think it meant?"

"Lifting weights with both hands at once."

When I stop laughing, I say sincerely, "Thanks for that. I might actually feel like a Lambert for once."

"Oh Gracie," my mom says affectionately, "you've always been a Lambert. You're just smarter than the rest of us."

"Yeah, you're the smart one, I'm the buff one, Jesse's the techie one, Mom's the stylish one, and Dad . . . well, he's just Dad."

I laugh at that. And then start laughing even harder in incredulity. Is it possible that while I've felt like an outcast my whole life, they saw me as one of their own? That we're all just Lamberts in our own way?

"Now stop being all mopey and let's get to work," Matt says.

I feel a warmth of gratitude flood my body. I can't believe how much I needed this—clearing the air with them and even the unexpected group hug. I nod at them. "Let's do this. Let's unfuck my life!"

Chapter Thirty-Five

That's the spirit!" my mom cheers. Then she starts grabbing stuff out of her giant purse like Mary Poppins in high-end loungewear. "Blue is buying us some time as the new arrivals come." She pulls out a large dry-erase board. *How did she even fit that in there?*

"What's that for?"

"Brainstorming," she says, like it's obvious. I laugh at how extra she is, but for once it doesn't annoy me. It kind of warms my soul.

Then Matt makes a FaceTime call, and my dad's face immediately fills the screen. "Hey, Peanut, who do I need to beat up?"

"Hey, Dad."

"Jesse is here too."

Jesse pops his head into the screen, wearing his headphones, and says, "What up?"

"Hi, Jesse," I say, starting to get emotional because my whole family is here, trying to help me. "Sorry to hear about your breakup."

"You too," he says sincerely. And I wonder if it's even considered a breakup if Andrew and I were never really dating, but I appreciate the sentiment. I give him a grateful nod as my mom claps her hands.

"Okay, enough of the family reunion! Let's get to work!" she says.

Matt takes his position by the shack door to keep watch, while continuing to hold up his phone so my dad and Jesse can see what's going on.

My mom writes "To-Do" at the top of the dry-erase board.

"What are some ways we can fix this mess?" she asks with her marker poised, ready to write.

I sigh. "Where do we begin? Well, I'd really like it if Ciara didn't hate me."

My mom writes "Make amends with Ciara" on the board.

"I should probably try to get her and Javier back together too."

"Or set her up with me," Matt adds.

My mom nods in agreement. "She's really pretty." She writes: "Get Ciara and Javier back together and/or set her up with Matthew." She turns back to us. "What else?"

"I wish Andrew would give me another chance," I confess.

My mom covers her mouth, trying in vain to contain her excitement. "I've been trying really hard to respect your boundaries and not pry, but Blue told us all about him." And then she can't help herself. "I told you you'd meet someone here!"

I open my mouth to question her taking credit, but my dad calls out, "Which one is he again?"

"The hot lawyer, Howie!" my mom chides.

"Oh yeah. As long as it's not that cowboy jackass," my dad says, and I can't help but laugh at the fact that my power yogi father has been watching *Love Shack*.

My mom scribbles, "Win Andrew back." Then she adds below it, in a smaller font as if I won't see, "Invite Andrew to family dinner."

"One step at a time, Mom," I groan. Some things never change.

"Why don't you just quit the show?" Matt asks from his security post. "Wouldn't that accomplish most of this?"

I sigh. "I wish I could, but I still have to save the frogs and my lab. And to do that, I need the publicity from the show to raise awareness and money."

After a moment, Jesse says, "Not necessarily." I'm surprised he's even paying attention and not listening to lo-fi hip-hop on his headphones. From Matt's phone screen, I see Jesse scratch his chin, deep in thought. "We all have a shit-ton of followers. You technically don't need the show for publicity."

My mom claps excitedly. "We can all post on our own socials! We'll help you raise awareness!"

"You should've asked us in the first place, Peanut," my dad says, sounding hurt.

Jesse nods. "I just thought you were going on the show to get Mom off your back."

"Yeah," Matt says. "Why didn't you tell us you needed to save the turtles?"

"They're frogs."

He smirks. "I know. I just like fucking with you."

I look at my family, all eager to help me, and consider why I didn't tell them what was really at stake with my lab. I think having to defend my life choices and trying to explain the importance of my work, time and time again, only to see them zone out, made me give up. But maybe I wrote them off too quickly. Like Madison suggested with the girls in school, maybe I didn't try hard enough to connect with my family either. Didn't I zone out every time Matt talked about his gym routine? And roll my eyes when Jesse rambled on about video games and his horrible taste in music?

Well, damn. It's just as much my fault as it is theirs.

As that thought sinks in, I admit, "I didn't think you guys would care about my frogs. But I didn't really give you the chance to either."

"Just because we don't understand what you're talking about half the time doesn't mean we don't love you and support you," my mom says.

From Matt's phone screen, I see my dad nodding. "We might not be as into saving the world as you are, Peanut, but we would do anything to save you."

I feel that pinch in my face that means I'm seconds away from crying. "Thank you, guys. Seriously." I sniffle and look at my dad and

Jesse on the phone screen. "I'm sorry I underestimated you." Then I turn to my mom. "And I know when you meddle it's because you care."

Now she's crying too. "I care so much!"

Finally, I turn to Matt. "And I'm sorry that even when you were helping me with the photo shoot I was still horrible to you."

He waves it off. "Does this mean I can ask out Cassie when we get home?"

"What? No!"

He laughs, and I realize that maybe messing with each other is our sibling love language. Which I can work with, because apologizing to him just felt unnatural. My mom is staring at us with a dopey grin on her face.

I take a deep breath and get back to Project Unfuck My Life. "Okay, Lamberts. Let's save my lab!"

Matt puffs up. "Now that I know this is for a good cause, I'll actually try."

I look at him in disbelief. "You got me over fifty thousand followers and you weren't even trying?"

He just shrugs as he taps away on his phone. "I'll create more content that will target our crossover audience. I know lots of chicks who like abs *and* saving animals."

"That's probably true," I concede. "But followers are just part of the equation, right? We still need to convert the awareness into donations."

At this, Jesse perks up. "What about a live stream?" Even from the phone he must be able to see my blank expression, so he explains, "One of my gamer buddies has twenty million subscribers on his YouTube channel. You should see this guy tear up *GTA* and *Call of Duty*. One time he played live for a charity fundraiser. He raised millions. I bet he would team up with me on something." Then Jesse takes off his headphones and excitedly says, "Oh shit!

You know what would be sick? Everyone loves a retro game pop-up, right?"

"I have no idea what that means," I admit.

"Remember that old-school arcade game Frogger?" Jesse asks. I nod, vaguely remembering it from an arcade I was dragged into on a family vacation, but Matt must see where Jesse is going with this because he says in an awed voice, "Oh man! That's perfect!" Matt turns to me and explains, "The whole point of the game is to get the frogs safely across the street or the river without getting hit by a car or eaten by an alligator or something."

"So you're literally saving frogs!" my mom chimes in.

"Exactly," Jesse says. "I'll ask my buddy to play Frogger, I'll do the commentary, and we'll live-stream it to raise money for your lab."

"You'll reach a whole new audience too," my dad adds.

I'm floored. Could this actually work? My wheels start turning. "Besides raising money, it could be educational too. You could tell people about the actual dangers these species encounter! Humans and reptiles are only part of the problem—"

Jesse cuts me off. "Nerd!" We all laugh, but then he adds, "Yeah, give me some talking points and I'll put it in my own words."

Suddenly I hear a series of knocks on the door. "Quick! Hide!" I say, throwing my pool towel over the dry-erase board.

My mom laughs. "Don't be silly, sweetie. It's just Blue." Matt opens the door, revealing it is in fact everyone's favorite production assistant.

"Wait, how'd you know that?"

"We have a secret knock," my mom says as she hugs Blue like they're long-lost friends.

I shake my head. "Of course you do."

"Rebecca," Blue says. "You're looking lovely." Then he looks my brother up and down. "Matthew, hot as always."

Matt winks at him. "I know."

"I guess you're all best friends now," I say, trying to catch up.

Then I hear from Matt's phone, "Hi, Blue. I'm Howie!"

Blue waves at my dad. "Hey, Howie, I'm a big fan. I used to do Power Yoga all the time!"

"Awesome! I'll send you a shirt!" my dad replies as I cringe. I don't know what Blue's fashion sense is outside of work, but I can guarantee a "Two Pump Guy" T-shirt is not it.

Then Blue gets serious. "Okay, gang, I've got half an hour before they come looking for me. What's the plan?"

"Wait, what about Grace? Is anyone looking for her?" my mom asks.

"Kristina didn't buy Grace's second bout of gastrointestinal distress, but I made a deal with the on-set doctor: He confirmed she has a stomach bug and needs to rest, in exchange for a date with me."

My mom squeals, "Ooh, a doctor! I love that for you!"

Blue waves it off. "Eh, he's a bore. You know how those serious types are."

They all turn to look at me at the same time. When they burst out laughing I join in, and damn it feels good being in on the joke. I'm not going to let myself dwell on the fact that it would've been helpful to realize this, say, *twenty years ago.*

Matt paces, looking at the dry-erase board until he finally says, "I think I have an idea on how to win Andrew back."

"Ooh, you sounded just like the best friend in a Reese Witherspoon movie," my mom praises him excitedly.

"You really did," Blue agrees.

"Thank you," Matt says sincerely, then continues. "Blue, do you think there's any B-roll of Grace and Andrew talking?"

"What's B-roll?" I ask, because I'm apparently the only person in Los Angeles County who doesn't know what that means.

"It's the footage they get in the background," Blue explains to me. "We don't usually end up using it, but sometimes the editors comb through it for an innocent conversation they can add voice-over to and make it more dramatic. Or if the camera operator is slacking and misses a big moment, they hope one of the other cameras caught something." Then he turns to Matt and says, "I'll talk to my boy in post. He owes me. I get his weed for him."

My mom nods like that's a normal business negotiation, then asks Matt, "Okay, so then what?"

"Well, if you saw my last TikTok, you'll see I've really upped my editing game." My parents and Blue nod in agreement. Apparently they're all fans. "I'm going to cut together a *Love Shack*–esque montage video of you and Andrew falling for each other."

My mom swoons. "We can play it at their wedding too!"

I shake my head at her as Jesse chimes in from FaceTime: "And Grace can do her own DIY confessional and apologize for misleading people accidentally. Or for a good cause, anyway."

"How do you know what a 'confessional' is?" I ask, slack-jawed.

"I watched your episodes. Those fake glasses make you look smart." I let that comment slide because I'm so touched that my weird gamer little brother watched *Love Shack* for me.

My dad snaps his fingers. "That's great, Jesse. She can apologize to Ciara too. Two birds with one video."

My mom puts check marks next to the items on her to-do list and says, "Blue, can you try to find some cute friendship footage of Grace and Ciara too?" Then she turns to me. "Did you two happen to share a milkshake or anything?"

I shake my head. "No, but she made me take a lot of shots with her."

"That works," my mom says and adds another check mark.

"And then there's Madison," I say solemnly. "I haven't talked to her yet. But I think she's mad at me."

"She's too sweet to be mad at anyone," Blue says. "You probably just crushed her idealistic Disney princess notion that people are good."

"That seems worse," I moan.

"I'll try to pull footage of her too," Blue says as he pats my arm.

I nod in appreciation, but I feel my nerves creeping in. "Kristina is going to kill me when this video gets out."

"She'll have to get through me first," my dad says from the phone.

"Me too," my mom says as my brothers nod in agreement.

"But seriously, won't I get in trouble for doing this? I'm pretty sure I signed something that said I wouldn't do any behind-the-scenes content."

"Since when do you care about breaking your contract?" Blue asks with a smile.

I turn to him. "And what about you? I can't let another person get fired because of me."

He shrugs. "I've worked in reality TV for a long time, Grace, and no one has ever stuck up for me before like you did. I'm willing to take this risk for you."

I hug him as I groan half-heartedly. "But everyone will know that I wasn't here for the *right reasons*." Blue and my family laugh.

I break away from Blue and he says, "You've already lit the match, Underdog. Might as well burn the whole place down." He hands me some paper. "Here, script out what you want to say."

Jesse adds, "I can send you some chill low-fi hip-hop to set it to—"

"No!" my mom and dad, Matt, and I say at the same time. Then we all burst out laughing, even Jesse.

Blue smiles at us. "You Lamberts are cute. This might just work."

Chapter Thirty-Six

After I have my apology confessional scripted out, I show it to Blue. Unable to help myself, I added some colorful commentary about how reality shows treat their contestants and crews.

"While I appreciate you fighting the good fight," Blue says, "let's keep this focused on your making amends, not stirring more pots." I open my mouth to object, and he adds, "There's plenty of time for that after the season is over. We don't want to dilute the message."

I nod reluctantly and cross out what I'm sure Andrew would call my most rabble-rousing parts. Blue takes pictures of the script so he can find matching footage, and then he leaves. My mom starts helping me do my hair and makeup while Matt goes down to the beach to location scout and find the best light. If I wasn't so grateful for their help, it would be amusing how seriously everyone is taking this.

Especially when my mom comes back from her recon mission and starts talking like a Navy SEAL. "The coast is clear. Let's move."

My mom and I sneak out of the shack and hustle down to the beach to meet up with Matt. Blue told us the crew will be shooting the new arrivals by the pool, so we should be safe at the beach for the next couple hours.

When Matt sees my long, floral dress and light makeup, he gives my mom an approving nod. "She looks good. And yet still like her. Nice work." Then he shows us his shot list. "It's better to have different backgrounds for different parts of the confessional. It helps to break up the narrative and keeps it visually interesting." He sounds so professional that I wonder if I've been underestimating him his entire life.

I smile at him. "Thank you, Matt." I look at my mom. "Both of you."

My mom beams with pride, then quickly recovers. "Don't get all emotional again. You'll ruin your makeup."

Over the next hour, I learn a lot of new things from my brother. Like what a "walk-and-talk" is. He has me walk along the shore while talking directly into his iPhone camera. It makes me feel like I'm speaking only to Javier when I explain that I really care about him as a friend and feel horrible for misrepresenting my feelings for him. It must come across as heartfelt as I meant it to because I notice my mom wiping tears out of her eyes as she watches us.

Then we shoot my apology to Ciara. Matt insists that the ocean should be behind me for this because it adds gravitas. After I speak sincerely into the camera, whatever I've done must meet Matt's standards because he shouts, "Moving on!"

We change locations to film the part of the script I wrote for Madison, with the Malibu pier behind me in the distance. No matter where we go, my mom hovers nearby, constantly fixing my hair and complaining about the wind in between takes. I just shrug because honestly, as long as I don't have to wear those damn fake glasses anymore, I'm happy.

Eventually we get what we need without hair covering my face, and we pick up a few other sound bites that Matt says he needs for voice-over. Finally, Matt directs me to sit in the sand so I can talk about my connection with Andrew.

"Actually, scooch a couple feet to your right," Matt says while looking at the camera screen. "I want the dunes in the frame. They're moody and evoke romance," he says seriously.

I have to bite my tongue not to laugh. Despite our détente, I can't help but tease him. "Did you learn all this that time you were a background extra on a Nickelodeon show?"

Matt laughs, but then admits, "I've been taking some classes."

"Really? Where?"

"UCLA extension. Kind of like a continuing ed sort of thing."

"That's great, Matty."

Matt shrugs, and it's weird seeing my cocky brother act self-conscious for once. "It's not like I'm going to film school or anything. Just a couple of production and directing classes." He pauses for a beat before adding, "I guess I just want people to take me seriously for once."

This hits me hard because I realize I'm part of the problem. "I'm sorry if I'm one of the people brushing you off as unserious. For what it's worth, I think you have a real talent for this."

"Thanks, Grace. That means a lot."

Then I shudder. "Yep, still can't get used to the whole apologizing to you thing."

He laughs. Then I look over at my mom, who is discreetly snapping pictures of us.

"Mom!!" we both shout.

"It's for my scrapbook!" she shouts back, unapologetically. "When I start scrapbooking."

Matt and I shake our heads at her. Then I take a deep breath and try to compose myself.

This last part is what I've written for Andrew, and I want it to be perfect. I close my eyes and picture his signature smirk. It gives me butterflies just thinking of it. It's crazy how strong my feelings for him are when we've known each other such a short time. Ironically, now that I've lost him, I can fully admit that I'm not ready to let him go.

Directing me, Matt says that the most important thing I can do is to be vulnerable. *Great.* That feels about as natural as a tree frog in a pond. But I want Andrew to know I've never felt this way about anyone before, so I crumple up my script. If I'm going to let down my guard, I'm going to talk from the heart. I open my eyes, take another deep breath, and try to win him back.

When we're done filming, my mom sneaks back to her car, Matt and Blue start working their magic in the editing trailer, and I go back to hiding in my shack of shame.

The next three hours are the longest of my life. I spend it texting with Cassie, pacing around the shack, and trying to remember the scientific names of all the insects I can find in the shack. The highlight of my afternoon is finding a scarlet velvet ant, *dasymutilla occidentalis*. The low point comes every time I think about Andrew. Which is often. One of the PAs delivers food for me but leaves it outside the door, refusing to get anywhere near my "stomach bug" germs. Apparently the on-set doctor told everyone I'm contagious. When Blue covers his tracks, he *really* covers them.

As I eat my cantaloupe—because of course it's cantaloupe—I start to wonder what kind of debauchery everyone is getting into up at the mansion. Blue told me that today there are new arrivals and more team competitions that involve couples' yoga and a sexy limbo contest. While I'm grateful I don't have to participate and humiliate myself on national TV again, I do miss the feeling of camaraderie with the other contestants and the pride I felt when I did something outside of my comfort zone.

Finally, under cover of darkness, Blue and Matt sneak down to my shack. "I can't believe you guys were able to put this together so quickly," I say as I pull them inside.

Matt queues up the video on his phone and says, "I wish we had more time, but for having no budget and sneaking B-roll—"

"He's being modest," Blue interrupts. "It's fucking great."

"Let's let Grace be the judge of that," Matt says as he hits play.

My face immediately fills the screen. Wow, it's weird watching yourself. That's what my voice sounds like?

But my self-consciousness fades as I watch how sincerely I address the camera.

"Hi, I'm Grace Lambert. You might know me as the Sexy Scientist, but please never call me that. I have a confession to make: I didn't come on Love Shack *for the right reasons. For starters, I didn't come here to make friends. And yet I did."*

As I talk, the video cuts back and forth from me doing my confessional on the beach earlier today to footage of me laughing with Madison and Ciara in the pool. *"I met two of the best friends a girl could ask for."* Then the video cuts to footage of us dancing together at the Angels and Devils party.

Matt edited together several close-ups of Madison for the next part as my voice-over continues: *"Madison is one of the most compassionate, enterprising, and kind people I've ever met. She has single-handedly started an amazing nonprofit that combats cyber-bullying."* Then the video cuts to cute footage of her slow-dancing with TC. *"And she deserves to win the show. Not just because she shares her big heart with everyone she meets, but because she put it on the line for love."* The montage changes to a close-up of Madison and TC cuddling. *"And it actually worked. So please vote for her!"*

Then the video switches seamlessly to footage of Ciara looking fierce in the sexy obstacle course. My voice continues to narrate: *"And then there's Ciara, who taught me so many important lessons about confidence, the color pink, finding power in who you are, and not worrying about what others think. Except I am worried about what she thinks. I'm worried I ruined our friendship and broke her trust."*

Matt's phone screen is now filled with a close-up of me in front of the ocean as I earnestly say, *"I'm so sorry I hurt you, Ciara. I never meant for it all to unravel like this, and I promise I have a good explanation. If you'll give me the chance to meet up and tell you everything,*

I'll do all the tequila shots you want." I laugh when I see that Matt has included footage of us clinking shot glasses together at the bar.

I look up at Matt and Blue, who are watching over my shoulder, clearly proud of their work. If my wet eyes are any indication, I am too. And I have to admit, the ocean did add gravitas.

The video then transitions to me walking along the beach as I tell the camera, *"I also didn't come here to make a connection with any guys. And yet I did."* It cuts to footage of Javier and me laughing by the pool as my voice-over says, *"Javier, you make me laugh, you're so incredibly kind, and you always put me at ease. You are one of my best friends on the show . . ."*

Matt now appropriately cuts back to the close-up on me as I somberly say, *"But unfortunately, that's the only way I see you. As a friend. It was unfair of me to lead you on just because I needed something else out of the show. You deserve to find the most wonderful person, someone who loves you as hard as you love everyone around you. I hope you too will give me a chance to explain this all in person."*

Fuck, this is harder to watch than I thought. I pause the video for a minute to compose myself.

"You okay?" Blue asks as he hands me a tissue from the pocket of his cargo shorts. I wipe my eyes and nod. Then I take a deep breath and hit play on Matt's phone.

The video of me sitting in the sand in front of the dunes pops up. I watch as I look straight into the camera and speak from the heart. *"And lastly, I didn't come on* Love Shack *to find love. I didn't even think that was possible on a reality show."*

When the video cuts to footage of Andrew handing me the vegan granola bar, my breath catches. It's jarring to watch this intimate moment unknowingly caught on tape. It's also heartbreaking to see once again how handsome he is.

"While you haven't been introduced to him, America, I finally met someone who I'd like to date in the real world. This is Andrew."

My voice-over continues over background footage Blue some-how found of us laughing by the pool, flirting inside the mansion, and sneaking glances at each other on the beach. *"I've never been in love, so it's hard for me to substantiate my hypothesis, but I do know I've never felt this way before. I've never met someone who makes me laugh while also challenging me and at times pissing me off. Who makes me feel safe but also flustered because he's so handsome. He's not just easy to talk to, but he's forgiving when I say things that maybe I shouldn't. And most importantly, I trust him with my vulnerable, inexperienced heart."*

When the video cuts back to me sitting in front of the dunes, both the digital me and the real-life me have tears in their eyes. *"Andrew, I'm sorry for screwing this all up. I might be worse at dating than I am at obstacle courses. But if you have feelings for me too and can find it in your heart to forgive me, I'd love to finally talk without having to dodge the cameras."*

I gasp when I see the next video clip. It's B-roll of Andrew bringing me ice. His eyes are full of concern until they meet mine and he smiles. It's not just any smile. It's a smile that lights up his whole face. I turn to Blue. "Is that really the way he looks at me?"

Blue nods, smiling at me. "Once you two stopped fighting all the time. Adorable, huh?"

I wipe a tear away as I watch the end of the montage. On-screen, I'm sitting in the sand as I look into the camera and say, *"I made a lot of mistakes on* Love Shack, *but I also learned a lot about myself. And especially about the kind of person I am and want to be. And un-fortunately, some of the decisions you saw me make on TV don't reflect this. And while, legally, I'm not supposed to comment further, I will say that while reality shows aren't real, my commitment to standing up to injustice is. Thank you for your support on the show, America, but if you really want to support me, keep rooting and fighting for the underdog."* I stand up, dust the sand off, and say, *"But now it's time for me to go back to real life . . . So, sorry,* Love Shack, *but I quit."*

Matt calls this my mic-drop moment, which he accentuates by playing the iconic part of the B-52s' song "Love Shack," when they say, *"You're what? Tin roof rusted!"* Then he ends with footage of me walking off into the sunset by myself. I gotta hand it to him—it's a strong finish.

"Sooo?" Matt prompts. He sounds nervous, as if my approval means a lot to him. Instead of answering, I launch myself at him and pull him into a hug.

"Thank you so much," I whisper. Then I grab Blue and pull him in too. "Thank you both."

"Don't thank us yet," Blue says. "We still need to sneak you out of here and make sure Shantae plays it for everyone at the theme party tonight." Blue motions to my messy suitcase, and I quickly start gathering up my things. "Seriously? You had three hours, and you didn't pack?"

Blue shakes his head at me while Matt asks, "What's tonight's theme?"

"Picture a casino . . . but sluttier," Blue says with an eye roll. But I can tell it's killing Matt that he can't go.

As I shove last night's clothes into my suitcase, I ask, "We're still doing the coordinated launch, right?" I sound like a participant in a military coup, not a repentant reality show contestant. Neither is a title I ever thought I'd hold, and I can't help but shake my head at the absurdity of the situation.

"Yep," Matt says, snapping out of his casino party reverie. "Blue will forward the video to Kristina right after Shantae shows the contestants."

"I'll make it seem like we all got it at the same time," Blue confirms. "I'll also send it to Ciara and Andrew."

Matt nods. "And once Kristina has it, Blue will text the family chain so everyone can post it on their socials, and I'll add it to all of your accounts."

"Wait, there's a family text chain? And Blue's on it but I'm not?" I scoff. Blue pats my head patronizingly.

Just then it sinks in how public this all is, and I start to have second thoughts. "Do we really have to post it on social media where everyone can see it? Why can't we just send it to the people I have to make amends with?"

Matt and Blue exchange exasperated looks. Matt turns to me. "Grace, you know how important visibility and awareness are for us right now. The more people we drive to your page, the more people we can hit up for donations. And America loves a redemption story."

I roll my eyes. I've certainly learned a lot about "what America loves" this week.

"Plus," Blue adds, "we need a grand romantic gesture to win Andrew back. Just telling him you like him isn't grand. You need to think bigger. Like public-declaration-of-affection bigger." Even his saying that makes me break out in hives. But I guess going out of my comfort zone is one way to prove how sorry I am.

I sigh and put my faith in my family and my blue-haired friend. "Okay, let's do this." And with that, Blue heads off to find Shantae and Matt sneaks me and my *one* suitcase out of the "Love Shack." As we drive away, I take one last look back at the mansion and sigh. "Well, here goes everything."

Chapter Thirty-Seven

I'm disoriented when I wake up in my own bed and not on the floor of a shack. I forgot how nice it is to start your day without a back spasm. I yawn and reach over to check the time on my phone—my real one that Blue got back for me—and sit up with a jolt. I have seventy-nine new text messages?! I don't even know seventy-nine people!

I start reading texts from numbers I don't recognize.

> **323-555-8035:** Hey girl, it's Jenna from elementary school. I saw your video!!! OMG!
> **617-123-6798:** Grace Marie, I saw you on the internet. Call me right away. Aunt Mildred.
> **424-801-5555:** yo dude ur looking hot it's brody we went on a date once

WTF?! I quickly delete them and open Instagram to look at my apology video Matt posted last night. It has over thirty thousand views, and that's only on my page! Just then a text from Cassie comes in.

> **CASSIE:** Check out the fundraiser page!!!

I quickly click on the link. *Holy shit!* We've raised over $100,000! I start to do a little victory dance before I see a text from Eliza come through.

ELIZA: We're still short $200,000.

Typical Eliza. But she's right. We're not done yet. We still have a long way to go to keep the program running for another year.

I scan through the rest of my texts, hoping there's one from an unknown number . . . an unknown lawyerly number with a 310 area code. But nope, nothing from Andrew. Maybe he hasn't seen my apology yet? Or maybe he has, but doesn't care?

That thought is enough to make me plop down on my bed and contemplate going back to sleep. But as I put down my phone, it vibrates with another text. I hold my breath and quickly check to see who it is.

It's only my brother, Jesse. But when I read his text, I feel a little spark of something that resembles hope.

JESSE: Frogger is about to go live. Let's make some money!

Maybe this day won't be miserable after all. I defy science and cross my fingers for luck, then run to my laptop and click on the link Jesse sent me. It takes me to his gamer friend's YouTube channel, and holy crap, there are already twenty thousand people logged on, waiting for the live stream. Don't these people have jobs?

The old-school 1980s graphics pop up, and I hear my brother's familiar voice welcoming everyone to the live-streaming fundraiser. He's joined by his gamer friend, whose username I wouldn't even begin to know how to pronounce. Then, without further fanfare, Jesse shouts, "Let's get retro!" and his buddy starts playing the game.

I assume he's playing well because the first frog avoids getting hit by cars and trucks rather easily and Jesse is using words like "epic" and "dope." The digital amphibian makes it across to what I assume is supposed to be a river. Then it jumps on the backs of blinking red and green turtles and hops onto floating logs until it makes its way safely to the grass. All while Jesse is animatedly describing the action. I understand only about 20 percent of what he's saying. I'm guessing he's referencing other video games and cracking jokes because I hear his gamer friend laughing and the comment section is filling up with LOLs.

Then my heart swells when I hear Jesse say, "Did you know my sister Grace is a biologist?"

The comments come in quickly.

MineCraft23438!: IS SHE SINGLE?
gamez420: ive got some biology to show her
rollin4u: She sounds ugly

I shake my head, wondering if this is what trolls are, as Jesse continues. "She works to save endangered frogs IRL."

His gamer friend laughs and says back, "No shit? Do they actually get hit by cars?"

"Well, she says humans are to blame for a lot of their problems. You know, pollution and ruining their habitats and shit. Which is why she's trying to save them."

I continue listening with pride as my little brother explains conservation to a bunch of teenage gamers—or maybe old men living in their parents' basements? I don't know who watches these things. But I do know there are way more of them than I thought. The longer I watch, the higher the viewer number gets. It's almost seventy-five thousand now!

I can't watch anymore. It's making me too anxious. Between the fate of my lab hanging on a guy whose name contains numbers and symbols and the fact that there are now hungry alligators in the virtual river these little froggies have to cross, I'm a nervous wreck.

So I stupidly decide to distract myself with something even

more nerve-racking. If Andrew isn't going to reach out to me, I'm going to go to him.

Thanks to LA traffic, it takes me an hour and *many* curse words to get to Andrew's hip Silver Lake neighborhood. I finally pull up to a historic-looking building and double-check the address Blue gave me. Of course there's nowhere to park.

As I'm circling, looking for a parking spot, my phone rings with an unknown number. I'm so nervous about seeing Andrew that I distractedly answer on my Bluetooth. "Hello?"

"Grace?" *Wait, I know that voice.*

"Andrew?" I look at the phone and then at his building as I drive past it again.

"Hi," he says tentatively.

"Hi. I'm not creepily driving past your house. I'm just looking for a parking spot," I blurt into the phone.

"What?"

"Oh, uh, nothing. What's up?"

"I wanted to see if you had any time to meet up today. For coffee or dinner?"

I laugh. "Are you free right now?"

"Yeah. Sure. Where do you want to meet?"

A spot finally opens up across from his building, and I pull in and throw my car into park. "Um, your place? I'm outside."

Andrew laughs, and moments later he walks out his front door. I meet him, standing at the bottom of his stairs with my heart thundering in my chest.

"You're here," he says, smiling like he's happy to see me.

"I am." It's all I can manage because I'm so taken with the way he looks in a pair of worn jeans and a T-shirt. "You own jeans," I finally say.

"I do." He grins and gestures for me to come in.

I recover and try to be a normal person. "I hope it's okay I'm here. I just stopped by to give you something." Not completely true, but luckily I have a decoy motive ready to go. I hand him a postcard with a picture of a yellow-legged frog on it.

A smile spreads across his face. "Are you hand-delivering these to all your donors?"

"Only the special ones." I smile back as I look around his small but tidy apartment. It's tastefully furnished and reminds me of a CB2 catalog. "I have a few things I'd like to tell you," I say, suddenly feeling nervous being alone with him in his personal space. He gestures for me to sit on the low tufted couch, so I do. "Firstly, I'm sorry you got you fired," I say softly.

He sits down next to me, skewering me with the concern in his eyes. "It's not your fault. I made the choice to go on the hot-air balloon with you. If anything, I should be thanking you. I shouldn't have taken that job in the first place." He reaches for his water bottle and seems to remember host etiquette. "Can I get you anything to drink?"

"No thanks, I'm good," I say, watching him take a sip from his reusable bottle. Even the way Andrew drinks is sexy. *And* he cares about the environment. *God, he's perfect.*

"You know *Love Shack* was never my dream job," he says and I nod. "Kristina's machinations were a posthumous nail in the coffin."

Ah, the Sumatran elephant in the room. They're the most critically endangered and therefore need to be approached with care. Much like this conversation. "So . . . you saw my video then?"

"I did," he says with an unreadable glint in his eyes.

Before he can say anything else or I chicken out, I continue with what I *really* came to do. I inhale and blurt out, "Andrew, I'm really sorry for the way everything went down and for not telling you what was really happening. But if you'd give me the chance, I'd like to get to know you better. And for you to get to know me. The real me. The one who doesn't go on reality shows or give in to producers' evil schemes." I look down at my sensible outfit. "This is the real me."

I look back at him, and something in his eyes tells me that he likes the real me just fine. "I think I was starting to get to know the real you," I continue. "And I really liked what I saw." I exhale deeply. *There.* I said it in the video, and I said it in person. There's nothing else I can do. So I just sit there waiting for him to say something. Anything. *Putting your heart on the line is fucking terrifying.*

Finally, he smiles at me and his whole face lights up. It makes my stomach feel funny, like the gravitational free fall of a roller coaster. "Our one-on-none date was the best date I've ever been on," he begins. "And it did feel like I *was* getting to know the real you." He reaches his hand toward mine, and I greedily take it. He smiles and continues. "I wanted to meet up with you today for a few reasons. First, to thank you for your montage. No one has ever 'grand-romantic-gestured' me before."

"Ah, you were talking to Blue."

He nods. "He filled me in after he sent me the video. And, you know, once it went viral on the internet."

I use my free hand to shamefully cover my face. "I hope he told you that releasing it to the general public was his idea."

Andrew laughs and nods. "It was a little embarrassing when my grandma texted me that she saw it, but it was still pretty sweet overall."

I cringe while simultaneously hoping his grandma likes me. "I guess I'm sorry about that too then."

He squeezes my hand. "I was upset when I saw you kissing Javier. It made me jealous." He shakes his head as if in disbelief. "I've never been a jealous person until I met you." I try not to smile, taking this as a secret win. "But I realize it wasn't fair of me to be jealous or to get upset. I knew that you were a contestant on the show and that we weren't supposed to be together. And it's not like we were dating or anything . . ." My heart drops at this, but then he continues. "But it made me question what I thought was happening between us. After the hot-air balloon ride and everything after that"—he looks at my lips briefly, and I feel a twinge of something deep inside—"I was hoping that we'd start seeing each other after the show ended."

I want to scream, *Yes! Yes, let's do that!* But I keep quiet and let him finish speaking.

"Now that I know why you did what you did, I get it. And if I were in your position, I hope I would've done the same thing. You chose to save an entire species over me, and I'm okay with that." He looks at me and says sincerely, "You've inspired me, Grace."

My heart swells at his words. *Is this what falling in love feels like?*

Andrew smiles and squeezes the hand he's still holding. "You're constantly standing up for others, you have a passion for something important, and you're making a positive change in the world. I want that too."

I wait for him to continue and tell me that we can save the world together. But instead, I notice him glancing at something in the corner. I look and see two suitcases.

I deflate. "Are you going somewhere?"

He nods, then takes a deep breath, steadying himself like what he's about to say next is difficult. "I took the volunteer position in Syria."

"What? You're going to *Syria*?"

"The program just started last week so I haven't missed much. I called them this morning, and they said they still have an opening. I leave tomorrow."

I don't say anything. I don't know what I would say even if I could speak. Part of me is heartbroken that the only guy I've ever wanted to date is about to fly across the globe. Another part of me is happy for him for taking the risk and following his passion. And then there's the part of me who's kicking myself for encouraging him to save the world. *What a dumbass.*

"There's something else you said in your video that resonated with me." Andrew takes my other hand. "I realized I can't be the partner I want to be until I'm the person I know I can be."

Ouch. Using my own realization against me. "So that's why you really wanted to meet today?" I ask. "To say goodbye?"

He looks sad when he responds. "I wanted to tell you in person that I'm going to figure out what I'm supposed to be doing with my life. And once I do, I'll be ready to share it with someone else. And I hope, one day, that someone is you."

With his words comes a conflicting wave of misery and bliss. It's reassuring to know that my feelings for him aren't one-sided, but I still feel the bitter sting of rejection every time I look at his luggage.

If I'm being honest, I can't say I don't understand. Hell, I wasn't ready for a relationship until a couple days ago. So I nod and say, "I respect that. I hope you find the answers you need, Andrew. Because you really do deserve all your dreams coming true."

"Thank you," he says softly.

I have a million more things I want to ask him—like, *When you say "one day," does that mean twenty years from now or a few months?* But the emotion I hear in his voice is destroying me and I need to retreat before I lose it.

I stand up. "Well, I should go. You probably have a lot to do before you leave."

He immediately reaches for me, pulling me into a hug. And as I inhale his expensive cologne for the last time, I marvel at the fact that, despite it being broken, my heart still feels safe with him. "Goodbye, Grace."

"Goodbye, Andrew." I give him one final sad wave and turn to leave before the tears begin to fall.

Welp, I think as I walk away crying, *I've still never been on a second date.*

Chapter Thirty-Eight

The next few days pass in a blur. My time is spent melodramatically thinking about Andrew, working my ass off to make up for lost time in the lab, and pricing flights to Syria. But not even Blue can get behind a romantic gesture that grand.

No matter how my scientific brain analyzes it, I can't get over the absurdity that I made such a strong connection with Andrew in such a short amount of time. Cassie says I fell hard and fast because Andrew and I have enough in common to feel connected, but enough differences to keep it interesting. Also that while he ended up being a great guy, he seemed like an arrogant asshole at first, which she said is sexy.

Considering that he's the first guy I've had sincere feelings for, combined with the heightened emotions of being cut off from the outside world and his knack for consistently coming to my rescue, it's no wonder I'm a goner. It's probably a good thing Andrew took a job in another country, since I don't think my inexperienced heart could've handled any more time falling for him.

Cassie comes by frequently with pints of vegan ice cream and makes me watch sappy rom-coms with ridiculous plotlines. A thirteen-year-old waking up as a grown woman? Asking a stranger to meet you at the top of the Empire State Building? Falling in love with a mermaid? Cassie insists that they help with heartbreak, but I've yet to find any evidence supporting her hypothesis.

I'm shocked to say this, but what does make me feel better is spending time with my family, who I've learned are freakin' geniuses. Their joint efforts—Matt's montage video, my parents posting on their social media, and Jesse's Frogger stunt—have helped raise a grand total of $309,450!

Not only did we get enough donations to cover our lost funding and save everyone's jobs, but Jesse's live stream also attracted the attention of an eccentric tech billionaire, Georg Griffin. Apparently Georg, who had a pet frog as a kid, feels moved by our cause. He's pledged to give us $50,000 a year for the next ten years. The board was so happy about having this unexpected benefactor that they approved Cassie's proposal to hire her own veterinary team, which allows us to take in even more rescue animals at the center.

And the timing for that couldn't have been more perfect. After my dad posted about my lab, he got a call from a former WWE wrestler he knows, saying he needed to give up his exotic pets. Don't even get me started on all the reasons why having an exotic pet is a bad idea and why all animal smugglers should rot in hell. Instead, I'll just be glad we were able to take in an ocelot, two blue-headed macaws, three sugar gliders, and a pygmy marmoset and give them proper medical care and a good home. All of which is to say that my family's help and support have been both a blessing and a welcome distraction.

So has being reunited with my work friends. Yesterday Cassie, Alec, Eliza, and I took a field trip to visit the immuno-boosted froggies we released back into the wild. Thanks to nano-chip technology, we were able to locate most of them and verify that they're thriving. It was surprisingly emotional to see them doing so well on their own. Cassie, of course, was bawling and acting like her kids were graduating from high school. Eliza just shrugged and hiked back to the car, while Alec took a hit from his vape pen.

We're all still riding high on the success of our chytrid fungus vaccine. The results were so promising that we've been asked to publish them in several leading scientific journals. This means that my peers will be able to use our research and techniques to protect endangered amphibians in different states and countries. What started off as trying to protect a small population of frogs in Southern California will hopefully turn into an important case study that helps save species around the globe.

But the best part of all is that we were able to accomplish everything without winning the *Love Shack* prize money. Which means it will go to someone else. Hopefully someone deserving.

We'll find out who soon enough, because tonight is the season finale. My mom insisted on throwing a live watch party, and because I'm still atypically melancholy about Andrew, I made her promise it'll only be a casual family dinner with a few special friends. But knowing her, she had her fingers crossed behind her back.

Just in case it ends up being more extra than a family barbecue, I get dressed up for the occasion. Since I donated all the dresses I wore on the show, I'm back to wearing my normal, unrevealing clothes. My tried-and-true Anthropologie maxi dress might be what Blue would consider poncho-adjacent, so I do my makeup and hair for good measure. Thanks to Madison, I finally know how to achieve a beachy wave.

When I pull into my parents' driveway in Pasadena, I burst out laughing. My mom has really outdone herself this time. The backyard has been completely transformed into a whimsical fairyland meets outdoor screening room. There's a giant pull-down screen in the middle of the patio, which is now covered with blankets, pillows, and comfy-looking poof chairs. Next to the screening area is a rustic wooden table overflowing with charcuterie and different types of popcorn. And I'm pretty sure she rented the lounge furniture that's under the weeping willow. It's way too elegant and over-the-top, but now that I know this is one of the ways my mom shows she cares, I'm not irritated by it anymore. Okay, less irritated by it, because there are at least fifty more people here than I was expecting.

My mom comes bounding over. "So what do you think?" She claps her hands together excitedly.

"It's lovely. You did a great job," I answer truthfully.

"There are even specialty cocktails at the bar!" she adds proudly. "My favorite is the Sexy Scientist. It fizzes up when you add club soda. Like a science experiment!"

I laugh in mortification that there's an actual menu with that annoyingly persistent nickname on it, while trying not to think wistfully of Andrew calling me by it.

"Wow" is all I can manage in response.

"Oh, and Blue sent over several cases of Poppy Lite. He said it's your favorite."

I shake my head in amusement as my dad walks over and greets me. "Hey, Peanut."

"Hey, Dad." I hug him and when I pull back, I notice he's wearing his "You will never always be driven" T-shirt. "Nice shirt."

"Thanks to you, it sold out the day that episode aired!" he says excitedly. "And I've gotten hundreds of orders for more!"

I smile at him. "Glad I could be of service."

He puts his arm around me, then says, "Your friends from the nature center are here." He gestures to where Cassie, Alec, and Eliza mingle with the Fox Girls. I think I see Gregory by the bar.

"Is that my boss?"

"Yep, he brought his daughter and some of her friends. Apparently they're big fans of the show."

I shake my head. "If anyone asks for an autograph, I'm leaving."

"Jesse's new girlfriend is here too," my mom gushes as she points to my little brother awkwardly standing next to a cute girl with curly hair.

"He met her online. She's a gamer," my dad explains.

"I'm a little surprised she looks so normal," I admit.

"I'm just glad she was willing to meet up in person," my mom adds, and I realize with a pang of pride that my parents would support anyone we care about as long as we're happy. They keep talking about Jesse's new girlfriend, but I'm distracted when Matt walks over with two blue cocktails and offers me one.

"What's this?"

Matt smirks. "The One-on-None. That's why it's blue—because it's sad."

I roll my eyes at his delight in my misfortune and take a sip. I immediately scowl. "Ugh, it even tastes blue."

Matt laughs at me as he plops down in the rented patio furniture. "You want to hear my big news?" I nod and sit down next to him. "I'm starting my own business," he says proudly.

"Yeah?"

"Yeah. I realized I can't coast on my good looks forever." I snort and he continues. "And I really liked making that video for you."

"You were great at it," I concede.

"So, I'm gonna start my own wedding videography business. You know, making montages of people's weddings."

"Wow. You'd be perfect at that," I say sincerely. His smile gets even bigger with my approval.

"I'm offering a ten percent family discount, but it expires in twenty years, so . . ." He smirks.

I shove him and feel a pang of sadness when my thoughts immediately return to Andrew. I wish he were here. Or that I knew what he was doing right now.

I shake off thoughts of a handsome do-gooder with an inconvenient heart of gold and turn to my brother. "I'm really happy for you, Matt. I'll even help promote your company on Instagram." I wink at him, and he laughs at the irony.

"Ahh, so you *are* going to keep your social media accounts active?"

I shrug. "It's useful in teaching the public about endangered species." I pause, then quickly add, "And it's kinda fun."

Matt smiles like he just scored a point, then gets serious. "Just be careful of all the creeps that are going to slide into your DMs."

"Ewww. Being a single woman is terrifying."

Matt must be more perceptive than I give him credit for because he says, "I'm sorry things didn't work out with the lawyer." I nod in appreciation of his sentiment. But then he adds, "I have this buddy who I think you'd like—"

"I'm good," I cut him off. My brother and I might be on better terms now, but I continue to have zero interest in dating any of his friends. "Thanks, though," I add. "I better say hi to the guests." I start to walk away but turn around and whisper-yell, "And stay away from Cassie."

He yells back loudly, "I didn't hear you!" Then he sticks his tongue out at me and goes over to my coworkers. I shake my head at him. There's still a case to be made for having only one child.

While I steel myself to start making the rounds, my mom rushes over to me. "I have a surprise for you!"

"A new specialty cocktail? Let me guess, Pass the Banana?"

"Darn it! I wish I'd thought of that! But no, it's a *surprise guest*." My mom rubs her hands together giddily and my heart skips.

Chapter Thirty-Nine

Andrew? Is he here? I look at the gate leading to the backyard, hoping to catch a glimpse of perfectly groomed facial hair. But instead, I see the next best thing.

Ciara.

I run to her and am about to throw my arms around her when I remember she may still hate me. Instead, I stop directly in front of her with my hands awkwardly in midair and say, "Hi."

She laughs. "Get over here, you dork." She steps forward and hugs me.

I happily hug her back. "I'm so sorry!"

"I know. I saw the video. Thank you for using footage where I look hot."

"Is there any other kind?" She smiles at me, and I feel happier than I have in days.

"I should've known something was up," Ciara says. "I didn't really think you'd put a guy before your friends. Animals, sure, but not a guy." I laugh, nodding. Then Ciara shakes her head. "Kristina, man. She's brutal. She makes good TV, though. I'll give her that."

I roll my eyes in agreement. "Blue thinks she'll be nominated for an Emmy."

"I read that it's the highest-rated season of the show. In any country."

"People are idiots."

Ciara laughs, then looks at me with concern in her eyes. "How are you doing? With the whole Andrew thing." Then she quickly adds, "Blue told me."

"Of course he did." Though I am grateful Blue is filling everyone in, so I don't have to relive it over and over again. I sigh. "I can't stop thinking about him. Is that normal?"

"Oh honey." Ciara hugs me. "Yeah, unfortunately, when you have feelings for someone, they don't just go away overnight." She says this sadly, like she's talking from experience.

"How long do the symptoms last? What time frame can I expect?"

Ciara laughs. "You can't science your way out of this. You know what Madison would tell you—that your first heartbreak is an important milestone and you gotta feel your feelings."

I wince dramatically. "And what would you tell me?"

"To get laid, obviously," she says, looking around with a glint in her eyes. "And then there's always tequila."

"Tequila is never the answer."

"If I remember correctly, from a certain apology video, you owe me a shot."

I groan loudly and let a laughing Ciara drag me to the bar.

After I choke down some reposado, I introduce Ciara to all my work friends. My boss's daughter comes rushing over and tells Ciara that she is "such a fan." It's hard for me to keep a straight face as she quotes Ciara . . . *to Ciara*. "And look! I wore a pink dress because you totally inspired me," she adds.

Ciara thanks her for her kind words, but I'm grateful when Matt comes over and interrupts. Until he opens his mouth to introduce himself. "Hi, Ciara, I'm Grace's handsome and single brother who helped save her lab. You've probably heard of me."

I clock the mischievous look in Ciara's eye when she says, "Oh, you must be Jesse!"

I burst out laughing. "Ohhh, burn!"

Even Matt has to laugh at this. He continues shamelessly trying to hit on Ciara for a few more minutes until my mom clinks on her wineglass and loudly announces, "The show is starting! Everyone find a seat!"

Cassie finds me and squeezes my hand supportively. We walk over to the grass that's barely visible under a layer of throw pillows and I sit between Ciara and Cassie in front of the screen. And that's when I start to feel queasy. It's the same nervousness I get when I'm about to speak in front of a large group of people. Which is ridiculous, because giving the keynote speech at a conservation convention is infinitely more important than watching myself on a temporary backyard screen. But nonetheless, I'm nauseated and mortified when the opening credits begin to roll. They introduce every contestant as a horrible pop theme song plays. And then there I am, with my fake glasses, looking like a total prude out of water.

Suddenly I'm grateful that Pasadena is sandwiched between three fault lines. Maybe I'll get lucky and the earth will open up and swallow me whole.

I reflexively cover my eyes but can't help peeking through my fingers when Shantae singsongs, *"Welcome to the* Love Shack *finale!"* This is met by loud cheers in the backyard.

Shantae looks as polished as ever as she recaps the previous episodes for the audience. *"As you know, we've seen many different pairings this season,"* she narrates over a montage of clips from the show. It starts with Beth Anne kissing Cowboy Bill while wearing his hat and cuts to footage of Ciara kissing Javier on their one-on-one date. I sneak a guilty peek at Ciara. She pats my knee reassuringly. Then I cringe when there's footage of me dancing with Scott at the Angels and Devils party. And I have to look away when it cuts to me on my dinner date with Javier.

"Woooh! There's Grace!" Alec cheers, and I shoot him a dirty look at the same time Eliza elbows him.

"Some of your favorite couples are still together. While others saw their end . . ." The recap quickly cuts to a scene from a recent coupling ceremony, and Shante explains, *"After Beth Anne chose to go out with Chris, Scott got sent home."* They show footage of Scott wheeling his three suitcases out of the mansion.

"Oh damn," I whisper to Cassie.

"Serves him right!" my dad shouts from somewhere behind me. The whole backyard erupts in laughter and cheers. I have to admit, watching Scott get rejected and kicked off the show is vindictively satisfying. Maybe I'll let my dad send him a "Two Pump Guy" shirt.

"Beth Anne and Chris are the most recent couple," Shantae continues. *"They're joined in the finale by Dominique and Braden—"*

"Who?" I whisper to Ciara as video plays of a good-looking couple on jet skis.

"They came the day you left. Haven't you been watching?"

"Hell no."

Ciara points at another supermodel couple on the screen who seem to be competing in a sexy cooking competition. "DeVonte and Janelle are new too. But they're boring and have the least points."

"Aww, are they in my shack?"

"They sure are. And they definitely got more use out of it than you did," Ciara says suggestively.

"Their poor backs."

Ciara laughs, then we both fall quiet when footage of Madison and TC slow-dancing fills the screen. My heart swells and I involuntarily clap. *"Madison and TC are still going strong,"* Shantae says into the camera.

"Heck yeah they are!" my boss's daughter shouts.

"But if you've noticed, there's one couple missing," Shantae continues.

"Javier." Ciara gasps as we watch a video of Javier on the beach, picnicking with a familiar curvy brunette.

"That's Eliana," Ciara says jealously. "She asked Javi out right after you left."

When I look back up at the screen, Javier walks over to the new arrival I met briefly, while she does yoga with Madison. Now I feel jealous. *I'm* Madison's yoga buddy.

Javier says, *"Hey, Eliana, can I talk to you for a sec?"* I can see the pain in his face. I know what's coming.

She follows him over to the pool, and they sit down, feet dangling in the water. *"¿Qué pasó?"* she asks nonchalantly, with a sweet smile. My stomach drops. This poor girl doesn't know what's about to hit her. Unfortunately, I now know that feeling all too well. But at least Javier isn't hopping on a plane to Syria.

Javier takes a deep breath. *"Thank you for choosing me for your one-on-one date. I had an amazing time on our picnic. And I loved getting to know you."*

"But?" she says, finally figuring out where this is going.

"But . . . I'm just not in the right head space to continue dating you. There's someone I made a connection with before you got here, and I never gave it the chance it deserved. I'm still thinking about her and regretting it."

I turn to look at Ciara. "It's you! He's talking about you!" She shushes me and stares at the screen.

"You still have feelings for Ciara?" Eliana asks.

Javier nods. *"I do. I don't know if she'll take me back, but I've gotta try."*

"Holy Stephen Hawking!" I shout excitedly, looking at Ciara. She has a huge smile on her face as she watches the on-screen Javier wheel his luggage out of the mansion.

"I knew it!" my mom says happily to everyone at the party. "I totally called that. Didn't I call it, Howie?"

"Is your mom trying to take credit for matchmaking a couple she doesn't know, who were already matched?" Cassie whispers to me.

"I'm not sure why that surprises you," I whisper back. Then I turn to Ciara. "Are you going to take Javi back—"

I'm immediately shushed by Gregory's daughter. "They're announcing the winner."

Annoyed but amused, I close my mouth and turn my attention back to the screen. The remaining couples now sit in the familiar white lounge furniture by the pool.

"Madison looks stunning!" Cassie gasps.

I nod in agreement as Shantae addresses the contestants. *"While the points you've earned over the season got you to the finale, tonight's winner is determined by America's vote."* Shantae turns to look into the camera and talks to the viewers at home. *"We've asked you, the audience, to consider everything from how the contestants performed in sexy challenges and putting themselves out there to personal and relationship growth, and meaningful connections. And you answered! We had more than three million votes!"*

"Idiots," I repeat, and Ciara laughs.

"And we have a clear winner. With seventy-eight percent of the total votes, the winner of season three of Love Shack *is . . ."*

I hold my breath. Ciara and Cassie each squeeze one of my hands.

"Madison!" Shantae exclaims, and confetti cannons shoot sparkly bits of paper all over Madison. TC immediately picks her up in an enthusiastic hug and kiss while everyone in my parents' backyard jumps up and screams. I look at the screen to see the other contestants cheering for Madison as well. But none louder than me.

When the screaming and hugging dies down at the mansion, Shantae interviews Madison. *"What are you going to spend your $250,000 prize money on? Maybe a wedding?"* Shantae fishes.

Madison smiles brightly and says, *"No, not yet, Shantae. This money is much better spent funding more teen centers for my nonprofit."*

Then she takes TC's hand. *"But I'd be happy if TC wants to come help me."*

I realize embarrassingly that there are tears leaking from my eyes. I'm just so happy for Madison. She doesn't have to bartend or model anymore. She can finally do what she finds fulfilling.

And then the irony hits me like an electromagnetic force field. I'm ecstatic for Madison for following her dreams, while Andrew's same decision has me subsisting on vegan rocky road and watching human-fish love stories.

Cassie must sense the shift in my mood. She squeezes my hand and whispers, "Are you okay?"

I nod. "I'm so happy for Madison." But Cassie just looks at me, patiently waiting for me to try out my newfound vulnerability. I think about it for a moment and then whisper back, "Do I wish I could've walked away from the show in a relationship like Madison and TC? Yeah, maybe. But I'm also grateful that my experience finally opened my mind to being in a relationship."

Cassie gives my hand another squeeze and says, "Me too. I'm proud of you, Grace."

I squeeze her back. "Thanks, Cass."

"And who knows, maybe we can double-date sometime," she says, almost dreamily. I may be paranoid, but I swear her eyes flick toward Matt.

Before I start plotting ways to ship Matt off to Antarctica, I quickly steer the subject back to neutral territory by pulling Ciara into our conversation. "So, C, are you going to take Javi back?"

Ciara grins. "Eventually. But I've gotta make him grovel first."

Cassie looks at Ciara in worship. "You're my hero."

I laugh. "You should see her do shots."

"Did someone say shots?" my mom calls merrily as she walks over with a tray of drinks. She holds up a small cup of pink liquid and says, "This one is called Pink Power."

Ciara laughs and immediately takes one. Next, my mom motions to a bright red shot. "This one is Right Reasons." And then she points to a shot glass with some green concoction inside. "And this one is Suck and Blow."

"Ooh, I'll try the Suck and Blow in honor of Grace!" Cassie exclaims.

I shake my head. I'll be glad when the life cycle of my mini-celebrity comes to an end. So will my liver. We all pick our poison, and my mom says, "To *Love Shack*!"

We all clink glasses and cheer, "To *Love Shack*!"

After I drink the red fruity shot, I take a moment and look around at all the people who have come together to celebrate me—my friends, coworkers, and family. Everyone here believes in me, supports me, and genuinely wants what's best for me.

I can't help but laugh that it took a lame reality show to make me appreciate my actual reality.

Suddenly I hear my mother gasp, and a hush falls over the party. When I look around to see what's causing this kind of reaction, I almost drop my shot glass.

Because there, standing at the gate, is Andrew.

He's wearing jeans like the last time I saw him. But his facial hair is no longer perfectly groomed. It's almost a proper beard, and somehow this new but same version of him is even more handsome. I stand there staring until Jesse nudges me toward him. "Don't be weird," he whispers, shaking his head.

I stumble toward Andrew, aware that an entire backyard of people are watching us.

"Hi," he says.

"You're back," I observe like the perceptive scientist I am.

"I actually never left."

"What?" I ask at the same time I hear my mom gasp again.

Andrew looks up as if he's just now noticing he's crashing a party.

"Sorry, I should've called first. I was going for a grand gesture, but I think I misfired." He turns to leave, but I quickly step forward to grab his hand.

"No, it's fine. Come with me." I lead him away from all the onlookers—some of whom are staring unabashedly while others attempt to make tactful small talk—and down the side path to my favorite tree on my parents' property. It's a gorgeous old magnolia with a wrought-iron bench beneath it where we sit down.

Andrew looks at me and exhales loudly. "You're even more beautiful than I remember."

I laugh. "It's only been three days."

He gives me a shy shrug and my heart, which has been pounding since the second I saw him, kicks it up to double time. We sit there in a charged silence. I can hear bits and pieces of conversation drifting over from the party, and I try focusing on the smell of the magnolia flowers and the feel of the evening breeze on my bare arms to keep from spiraling about why he's here right now.

Andrew takes a deep breath before he looks at me again. "I couldn't stop thinking about you after you left my apartment. And I knew, if I left, I'd miss talking to you. And fighting with you. And being inspired by your passion." He smiles at me. "I've never met anyone willing to humiliate themselves on international TV to save an endangered species before."

"To be fair, I didn't know how humiliating or international it would be."

He laughs, and the sound bubbles warmly through my bloodstream. "I meant what I said at my apartment. I want to do something that makes a difference. But I realized that there are people everywhere that need help. And that maybe I could make a difference somewhere closer to you."

My head is spinning. This seems too good to be real. "So . . . you're not moving to Syria?"

He shakes his head. "I'm not." I exhale a relieved sigh.

"I wanted to tell you in person that I accepted a new job in LA. It's for one of the country's largest immigration law firms," he continues. "They have a division that helps refugees. I'll be making sure unaccompanied minors don't get lost in the system or become victims of human trafficking."

"Oh wow. That's amazing and so admirable, Andrew," I say as I automatically reach for his hand. "I'm really happy for you."

"Thank you," he says, looking down at my hand. I'm tempted to move it, but he flips his own over so we can properly hold hands, like he did the day of the hot-air balloon. My breath hitches as my body remembers what it's like having contact with his.

"You'll never believe it, but Kristina helped me get the job."

"What? No way!"

Andrew nods. "She said she felt bad firing me because she could tell that the connection between you and me was real, but her hands were tied. Her uncle is a partner at the law firm. She sent him my résumé and told him he'd be an idiot if he didn't hire me."

"Wow, maybe I overestimated her evilness? Or underestimated her humanity?" I say, and Andrew laughs.

"She did have a message she wanted me to give you. She said she was hard on you because she knew you could handle it."

"What's that supposed to mean?"

He shrugs and says, "I think she thought you were up against some of the same discrimination she was." He must see my confused expression, so he explains: "Kristina started as a PA at the same time as Brett, but somehow he failed up and now has a better title and makes more money than her. She once told me she has to act 'twice as tough as all these old white guys to make it half as far up the ladder.' Maybe she assumed it was the same in science?"

Huh. I never stopped to think about it from Kristina's perspective. Or to wonder whether we might have experiences in common.

I nod and feel some of my iciness toward her thaw. "It's not easy trying to fit into the boys' club," I concede. "But she still could've been nicer."

Andrew smiles at me. "I agree." He's quiet for a moment as he looks down at our intertwined hands. Then finally he exhales. "I think part of me wanted to run away because I was scared of my feelings for you. How hard and fast I fell for you."

I don't respond. Probably because I've stopped breathing. I tell my brain to remind my body I need oxygen. I take a forced breath and wait for him to continue.

"Blue told me that presents help with grand romantic gestures, so I brought you something." His mischievous smirk is full-blown now as he takes something out of his pocket and hands it to me.

I laugh. "A vegan granola bar?"

He nods and there's sincerity in his voice when he says, "It's also a promise that while you're looking out for every person and animal around you, I'll be the one looking out for you. Whether you have a sprained ankle from an obstacle course gone wrong or you're hyperventilating on a hot-air balloon."

Then he smiles at me and says, "There's more. I practiced this." I laugh and he continues. "I also promise to continue working to become a person you'd be proud to be with. I'll support you in all your dreams while I chase my own, knowing we'll both be successful enough to not have to sleep on the floor of a shack. But even if that's where we end up, we'll make it fun because we'll be together."

He pauses to take a breath. "But most importantly, I promise to give us a real shot this time—with the real you and the real me—if you'll still have me."

Never in my wildest dreams could I have imagined someone saying something so heartfelt and romantic to me. But then again, I didn't dream about romantic declarations until I met Andrew.

I finally snap out of it and say, "Thank you. For the granola bar.

And for everything you just said." Then, unable to bear not kissing him for another second, I grab his T-shirt to pull him toward me.

The moment our lips meet, I'm transported back to the hot-air balloon and that strange combination of butterflies and peace. The feeling that this is both exciting and exactly right, the grounding of the present and the promise of the future. As he deepens our kiss and a tingling warmth envelops me, I know this is it for me.

Eager to make up for all the kissing we haven't done the past three days, I pull him even closer, running my fingers through his hair and practically crawling onto his lap to eliminate any unnecessary space between us. But before I'm tempted to do what I really want to do with him, we're interrupted by catcalls and applause. We pull apart to see my family and friends cheering from the pathway.

"We have an audience," he says, laughing as I bury my face in his chest.

"Just when I thought I didn't have people watching my every move anymore," I groan. Andrew laughs at this and waves to my family.

"What do you say?" I ask tentatively. "Are you prepared to meet the Lamberts?"

He gives me his biggest smile yet. "I thought you'd never ask."

I shake my head as I climb off him. "Just, whatever you do, don't wear any clothing my dad gives you."

Chapter Forty

I don't complain about monthly family dinners anymore. In fact, most months they're weekly. And this week the dinner is at my condo in Santa Monica. My mom may have agreed to let me host occasionally, but she still shows up with cloth napkins and napkin holders. Tonight she shows up with an extra set of fancy plates.

"I already have plates," I object.

"These are *chargers*. You put them under the plates you eat off of for an extra pop of color," she says as she puts the leaf in my kitchen table so it will seat eight.

Ever since my mom hired an assistant, she's had more time to pursue other passions. Which apparently includes making a "table-scapes" coffee-table book. So whenever she brings over new tablecloths or weird plates that go under plates, she has her assistant photograph them for her book. Luckily, I like her assistant, so I'm fine with him joining us for dinner.

"Here are the throw pillows you wanted for Grace's couch," Blue says, handing my mom a shopping bag.

I tried to talk some sense into Blue and even told him I'd find him a job at the nature center, but my mom offered him twice what he was making on *Love Shack*. And for some unfathomable reason, he loves working for her. He's also been helping Matt with his social media while my brother gets his videography business up and running. I guess frogs and salamanders can't compete with my mom's salary and my brother's abs.

"Why do you need pillows? Aren't you just taking a picture of the table?" I whine.

"Because your living room has a depressing lack of color," my mom chides. "It's all white walls and green plants."

"It's soothing."

"It's boring," she says, then looks at Blue to side with her.

Blue holds up a bright yellow blanket. "I think it could also use a throw." My mom claps her hands excitedly, and I know I've lost the battle.

My dad chuckles as he walks into the kitchen. "It's easier to just say yes and hide them later," he says with the wisdom of over thirty years of experience.

My dad plates the Greek food we ordered while Matt and Jesse debate some techy video editing software in the living room. Jesse's girlfriend, Ronnie, sits next to him on the couch. Although we've all hung out a few times since the finale party, I still don't know her that well. She's really shy, but she always offers to do the dishes, so she's welcome at Lambert Family Dinner at my house anytime.

The doorbell rings, and I rush to let in Alec. "Finally!" I pull him inside. "They were teaming up on me again. I need backup."

A couple months ago, I introduced Alec to Blue and they hit it off, just like I knew they would. They've been dating ever since and are frequent dinner guests. My mom's annoyed that I'm one-for-one in matchmaking and she's 0-for-293,847. So of course I remind her every chance I get.

Alec gives me a hug and hands me a bottle of wine before saying, "Reeling them in is definitely a two-person job." Then he greets the rest of the fam and gives Blue a kiss hello as I help my mom finish setting the table.

"You know this just means more dishes to wash," I say to her as I hold up one of her chargers.

"That's what Ronnie's for," my mom whispers back. Then she asks at her normal volume, which is louder than most humans and jumbo jets, "Cassie's not joining us tonight?"

At the mention of Cassie's name, Matt perks up and I shoot him a dirty look. "No, someone dropped off an injured spotted owl this afternoon," I tell her. "She's staying overnight with it to make sure it's okay."

When the table is finally set to my mom's standards and more artfully arranged pictures are taken, we all sit down to eat, and I dig into my vegan moussaka. We usually go around the table, taking turns giving work and life updates, but tonight Matt speaks up first. "I have an announcement! I got my first gig!"

"That's amazing, sweetheart!" my mom exclaims as we all offer congratulations. "Who's getting married?"

I smile because I already know.

"Madison and TC," Matt says, and the news is met by happy chatter.

My dad turns to me, "Did you know they're engaged?"

"Yep. She asked me to be a bridesmaid," I say nonchalantly, though secretly I'm excited. No one has ever asked me to be a bridesmaid before.

After Madison won the show, I was able to apologize to her in person. She told me I was already forgiven, and she and TC have been frequent guests at Lambert Family Dinners whenever they're up from San Diego. I've also gone down there a few times to check out wedding venues with her. And Ciara and I are throwing her a bachelorette party in a couple months.

"Ooh, I can help you pick out a bridesmaid dress!" my mom offers.

"No thanks."

"But she has such great taste—" Blue starts.

I look at Alec for backup, and at the same time we say, "No means no."

Everyone laughs, and thankfully my mom shrugs it off before quickly turning her attention back to the news of the happy couple. "Oooh! I'll give Madison and TC a tablescapes book! It's really the perfect engagement present."

"Hey, you could cross-promote it with all your couples," my dad says to Matt, which kicks off a whole-family marketing brainstorm.

Just then the front door opens, and I hear, "Sorry I'm late. Traffic was a nightmare." And in strolls the world's most handsome lawyer. He's in a custom suit but has been letting his facial hair grow a little longer because he knows I think it's sexy. He especially likes when I tug on it.

Andrew says hi to everyone as he puts a pie on the counter. "Here's the pie you wanted, Rebecca." Then he crosses the room and leans over to give me the kiss I've been looking forward to for the past eight hours. My mom thanks him as he takes the empty seat next to me at the table. His seat.

With the crazy hours he's been working at his new job and my team putting in overtime on saving our next endangered species, the arroyo toad, we were barely seeing each other. So it just made sense for him to move into my condo. We've been living together for a few weeks now, and there's no better way to wake up in the morning than his kiss. Well, except for the other ways he often wakes me up . . .

Andrew digs into the plate I made for him. We used to wait for him to get home to eat, but he made me promise we'd start eating without him since his commute time is so unpredictable.

In exchange, I send him my favorite science podcasts to listen to while he's stuck in traffic. I lean in and whisper, "Which one did you listen to today?"

"The one about the mating rituals of silk moths. You're right, it's fascinating."

I beam up at him. "You're such a nerd."

He smiles back at me. "You love it." *I really do.* Then he asks the table, "Did I miss the weekly updates?"

Matt gives Andrew a bro nod because they're gym buddies now. "Nah, you already know all of my updates."

"I have some good news," I tell the table. Andrew raises a teasing eyebrow because he knows what I'm going to say, and he knows that it's not *my* good news.

Technically, it's Javier's good news, but I'm even happier than if it were my own. After he saw my apology video, he agreed to meet me for coffee after *Love Shack* wrapped. We cleared the air, then spent the next three hours hanging out like old pals. I'm so thankful he forgave me because he's quickly become one of my closest friends. And to my delight, one of Andrew's too.

"Well? What is it?" Blue asks.

"Javier got the part!" I announce.

"Oh my gosh! I can't believe he's doing a movie!" my mom exclaims happily.

"Which one?" my dad asks with a mouth full of souvlaki.

"It's a rom-com that Nancy Mayor is directing," I say, trying to remember the details.

"Nancy *Meyers*?" Matt says, correcting me. "That's huge!"

"Yep," Andrew says proudly.

"Wow," Jesse says. "I guess being on *Love Shack* worked out for him."

I'd say so. His likability on the show skyrocketed his acting career. A week after the finale, he booked his first big gig on some soap opera that everyone but me has heard of. According to my mother, "His charisma oozes off the screen." I texted him to stop doing whatever he was doing to make my mother say "ooze." He texted back the meme of my obstacle course fail.

Javi and Ciara reconnected after the show. Of course, she made him suffer for a week or two before she finally forgave him, but they've been dating long-distance ever since. They're hoping they won't have to do that much longer, though, because Ciara is thinking of opening another tattoo parlor in LA.

The four of us used to go out on double dates whenever Ciara was in town, but we quickly learned that the paparazzi are even more annoying than Bruce the camera operator. So now we opt for quiet game nights at home.

Blue clears his throat. "I have an update too." We all turn to look at him, and he smiles at me before he says, "I heard from friends in the Teamsters union that the labor complaints Grace made—"

"And continues to make," Andrew adds with a smirk.

Blue nods with a small laugh. "—And continues to make, have caused such a PR nightmare that the producers are meeting with the studio and a union rep to negotiate better contracts for the cast and crew. They're hoping they can set a positive precedent for the entire reality TV industry."

"Wow, that's great, Gracie!" my mom says, looking at me proudly.

Andrew squeezes my leg affectionately. "My rabble-rouser."

I can't help but smile. While I didn't go on the show to clean up the reality TV industry, it's a pretty great unintended consequence. And I don't plan on backing down until I see those changes made. Luckily, I have access to a damn good lawyer.

We gossip a little more about the other contestants as we eat. According to Blue, Beth Anne quit her dad's marketing firm and started her lifestyle brand, "Bless Your Heart." She already has more followers than Jesse. Good for her.

No one has kept in touch with Cowboy Bill, but that won't stop

Alec and me from protesting the shit out of his company's proposed pipeline through Exceptional Value Wetlands.

And my dad tells us that he reached out to Shantae to see if she wanted to be the spokesmodel for his new inspirational clothing line for women. She politely declined.

We finish eating, and as we wait for Blue and my mom to take some perfectly curated pictures of the pie Andrew brought, I lean over and kiss him.

Andrew smiles at me. "What's that for?"

"Because I can."

And because I still can't believe I accidentally found love on a reality dating show.

Acknowledgments

I'm so grateful for getting to do what I love and have dreamt about since before I could even read. I'm especially grateful to . . .

My earliest writing mentors: To Mrs. Shea, my second-grade teacher, who nurtured my burgeoning love of reading and writing. To Mrs. Gray, who knew how to challenge a young overachiever by saying, "I expect more from you." And most importantly, to my mom, Bonnie Klement. Thank you for reading to me every night and instilling in me a love of books. Even when money was tight, you would splurge on books because they were a "necessity." It's your unwavering support and writing genes that have made this possible.

My family: To all the Klements, Wilsons, and my Mass fam (Fay, Howie, Dana, Spencer, Mason, and Skylar), thank you for all your love and encouragement. And of course, for listening to my story ideas over the years. To my dad, Thomas Klement, thank you for teaching me sports and introducing me to cool music to round out my book-nerdiness. You've always believed in me and pushed me to do my best. To my sister-friend, Kyleen Klement, thank you for decades of friendship, love, inspiration, and inside jokes. Maybe constantly competing over who's funnier helped me become a comedy writer? So thanks for that too, Sissy. To my daughter, Ellie . . . You are the best thing I have ever created. You are the light of my life. And you better not read or watch anything Mommy writes until you're older. To my husband, Jared, thank you for being my biggest fan. We've shared and championed each other's dreams for twenty years, and we'll continue doing so for at least fifty more or until the robot overlords take over. You've somehow managed to nail being both my best friend and rom-com love interest. I love you.

My friends who have championed this book: To Paige Crutcher, my dream of becoming an author wouldn't have been possible without you. (Okay, maybe it would've, but it would've been much harder, taken longer, and wouldn't have been as fun.) You are my mentor, my friend, and my sounding board. I am forever grateful for you. Read her books! She's so talented! Izzy Goreshter, thank you for being the ultimate beta reader, fellow rom-com fanatic, and my number one cheerleader. I especially love when you FaceTime me the second you finish to give me your notes, but only after gushing first. To Jessica James, thank you for your early notes, they were immensely helpful! You're so kind and talented. Read her books! To my early readers (Jill Bullock—fastest reader award—Izzy Goreshter, Paige Crutcher, Danielle Artabasy, Holly Patel, Megan Kuhlmann, Kim Tiernan, and Sandra Lou), I greatly appreciate all your kind words and cheer-leading . . . but you still have to buy the final version. To my author friends/mentors: Jordan Roter, Matt Boren, Erica Rodgers, Myra McEntire, Lauren Thoman, and Alisha Klapheke—thanks for sharing your wisdom and talent with me. I appreciate your support as much as your friendship. Read their books! Also a shout-out to Team Samantha: Let's keep writing and supporting each other! To my book club community, including my LA girls, a.k.a. the longest running book club in Los Angeles, my GA Bookies, and my H+H Romantasy crew—it's been a blast sharing a love of books (and wine) with you all.

Those who have made it possible: To my literary agent, Samantha Fabien at Root Literary, I sincerely appreciate all your hard work, patience, listening to my *many* story ideas, and teaching me the importance of a "feelings pass." 😊 To my editor, Sophia Kaufman at Harper Perennial, I can't thank you enough for all your incredible notes, holding my hand while I transition from screenwriting to publishing, and coaxing the rom out of my com. I'll dream-cast with you any day! A special thank-you to Cynthia Buck, Alicia Gencarelli, Vi-An Nguyen, Nicole Sklitsis, and Daniel Duval.

My very appreciated consultants: Bekki Offenheiser, thank you for many years of friendship, listening to me vent, and being the best reality TV consultant a gal could ask for! Meg Hedeen, you are indeed a kickass biologist! Thank you for answering my questions, teaching me about charismatic species, and lending me the term "biostitute"! (Thanks for the intro, Giff!) A big thank-you to Norma Lewis at the Bear Creek Nature Center for answering my conservation questions and showing me around the center. Check them out if you're in the area! To Laura Anderson, Courtney Brooks, and Regina Mincberg, thanks for the legal consultation and responding to my random lawyer-based texts. If I got anything wrong, don't sue me! To Monica Olsen, Sheri Salata, Rachel Winn, and Stephanie Hand, thank you for your marketing expertise and advice! I still don't want to be on social media, but here we are. To Alanna LeBlanc, thank you for being my social media guru and putting up with my ridiculousness. To Megan Bell, Josh Niesse, Sandra Lou, Patience Allan-Glick, and all the independent bookstore owners and employees everywhere, thank you for your support and for doing what you do! Support indie bookstores! To all my favorite employees at Halsa, Circa, and every coffee shop where I've overstayed my welcome while writing this book: Thank you for making me feel welcome anyway.

My emotional support squad: To all my neighbors and friends in the supportive and magical 'Be, especially my Girl Gang, Ellie's Besties, and the "Sister-wives," who provided me with encouragement, porch presents, and wine while I was writing and tried really hard not to disturb me when I had my headphones on: Thank you for your friendship, advice, game nights, theme parties, coparenting, and flash mobs. To Swim Club, Friendymooners, my LA Ladies,

Ladybugs, my fellow TV writers, and all my other friends from my sixteen years in LA, thank you for all the fun times and for being there for me during such an important and formative time of my life. To my E-town crew, Yardley peeps, and NYC and BU friends, thank you for your lasting friendship and support. See you on the book tour!

And lastly, to my readers: Thank you for spending your hard-earned money and even harder-earned time on me. I hope I gave you an entertaining break from reality.

If you felt moved by the plight of the southern mountain yellow-legged frog and want to support other endangered species, please consider donating to some of my favorite conservation organizations: the World Wildlife Fund, the Nature Conservancy, the National Audubon Society, and the Jane Goodall Institute.

About the Author

AMY MASS began her career in New York City writing those "Can you hear me now?" Verizon commercials, before moving to Los Angeles, where she wrote TV comedies for twelve years, including hit shows like *Last Man Standing* and *The Goldbergs*. During the pandemic, she moved to rural Georgia, where as a City Girl in a Small Town, she obviously had to write romance novels and rom-com movies. While she's on her third writing career, she's still in her first marriage, despite her husband's questionable sports teams allegiances. She has two rescue mutts and an eight-year-old daughter, who is the funniest one in the family by far. When not writing, Amy can be found hanging upside down in aerial yoga, dressing in team costumes for trivia night, or pressuring her family and friends into flash mobs and theme parties.